BHUPENDRA M. GANDHI

IVORY TOWER

(A COLLECTION OF SHORT STORIES)

Order this book online at www.trafford.com/07-1313
or email orders@trafford.com

Most Trafford titles are also available at major online book retailers.

© Copyright 2007 BHUPENDRA M. GANDHI.
All rights reserved. No part of this publication may be reproduced, stored in a retrieval system, or transmitted, in any form or by any means, electronic, mechanical, photocopying, recording, or otherwise, without the written prior permission of the author.

Note for Librarians: A cataloguing record for this book is available from Library and Archives Canada at www.collectionscanada.ca/amicus/index-e.html

ISBN: 978-1-4251-3425-9

We at Trafford believe that it is the responsibility of us all, as both individuals and corporations, to make choices that are environmentally and socially sound. You, in turn, are supporting this responsible conduct each time you purchase a Trafford book, or make use of our publishing services. To find out how you are helping, please visit www.trafford.com/responsiblepublishing.html

Our mission is to efficiently provide the world's finest, most comprehensive book publishing service, enabling every author to experience success. To find out how to publish your book, your way, and have it available worldwide, visit us online at www.trafford.com/10510

 www.trafford.com

North America & international
toll-free: 1 888 232 4444 (USA & Canada)
phone: 250 383 6864 ♦ fax: 250 383 6804 ♦ email: info@trafford.com

The United Kingdom & Europe
phone: +44 (0)1865 722 113 ♦ local rate: 0845 230 9601
facsimile: +44 (0)1865 722 868 ♦ email: info.uk@trafford.com

10 9 8 7 6 5 4 3 2

CONTENTS

Title	Page number
Acknowledgement	4
Ivory Tower	6
Seema	12
Flying With Apprehension	17
A Brief Encounter	21
Is There A God?	25
The Midnight Mystery	27
An Epic Journey	33
Anand	38
Time Machine	48
How To Triumph Over Adversity	54
Black Madonna Of Montserrat	58
Down Memory Lane	65
Heaven On Earth	74
Lost Horizon	81
The Last Frontier	86
A Chance Encounter	91
To Hell And Back	95
Is There A Ghost?	101
Rupa	111
Penthouse And Pavement	122
Amar-jyoti (Eternal Flame)	126
Disappearing Dreams (Chandni)	160
Kismet (Fate)	170
Casa Blanca (White House)	201
Preet Na Jana Reet(Love Knows No Constraint)	221
Radhika	234
Spring Time Is A Happy Time	272
Born To Suffer	305
Love Story(Forbidden Love)	314
Dil Eak Mandir(My Heart Is My Temple)	330
Adhura Arman(Unfulfilled Desire)	343

ACKNOWLEDGEMENT

All my stories are based on true life experiences, those of my own, my family members and friends. Many have a travelling or a holiday background, as we love travelling and go on holidays all the time, so often with our friends Raj and Mary. That is where we meet people of all ages, varied background and social standing.

Somehow people are more amiable, friendly and confide in us when relaxing in an ideal place, on the beach or by a pool-side. Perhaps unfamiliarity brings closeness, a kind of confidence and trust that we may hesitate to express to a close friend or a relative.

I always make a note, keep a diary when we go on holidays and when we come home; I try to develop such ideas, incidents into an article, a letter or a short story. It is surprising how a tiny piece of information can be turned into an interesting short story.

There are a couple of stories which I have told as they happened, without adding or dramatising them in any way. Sometimes the truth may be stranger, more unbelievable than fiction. It is impossible to add to it, to sensationalize the story to make it more interesting, more dramatic. One such story is "To Hell and Back" based on my own personal experience, a hospital mishap that nearly killed me.

I went in for a minor biopsy with a three hour stay in a day ward, but ended up staying twenty two nights, undergoing a major surgery that certainly ruined my life. This mishap had a deep impact on my already delicate health and made me practically house bound.

Every cloud has a silver lining. This mishap gave me an opportunity to take up writing seriously, as I have plenty of time on hand. When I was in Dar Es Salaam, in early sixties, I used to write short stories and poems for the local papers and magazines published from India but it was in my mother tongue Gujarati.

As our younger generation here can hardly read or write Gujarati, I thought it would be more appropriate to write in English. Moreover I can not type in Gujarati on a computer. So there was no real choice. A few stories included in this book are a straight forward translation of my stories written in Gujarati, some forty years ago. That is also one of the reasons why there is so much nostalgia, a period atmosphere in my writings.

I started with letters to editors and then proceeded on to writing articles, poems, short stories. With increasing exposure in local and national press and having written some two hundred letters and articles, I proceeded on to interviewing politicians, community leaders and prominent members of the society.

One perk of being a journalist is that every one is your friend; that is until you write some thing that they may not agree with? As I am a hobby journalist and my livelihood does not depend on my writings, I can afford not to be controversial. I do not believe in the slogan that any publicity is a good publicity.

I would like to thank all these people that include past Councillor and Mayor of Brent Ramesh Patel, Cllr. Ansuya Sodha, members of parliament Shri Barry Gardiner, Shri Tony McNulty and Miss Sarah Teather who all came to my humble home, as I can not leave my home most of the time. It is practically impossible for me to travel to the House of Commons where normally such interviews would take place.

My special thanks go to Shri C.B. Patel, editor and publisher of the most widely read ethnic newspapers, Gujarat Samachar and Asian Voice, who first gave me a break, published my writings, which include letters, articles, poems, short stories and interviews.

I would also like to thank Publisher and Editor of prestigious magazine India Link, Shri Krishan Ralleigh who has given me a regular column "From Far & Near" which has proved popular with the readers.

I also owe a debt of gratitude to my wife Kumudini who has been with me every step of the way, especially when I had a mishap in the hospital. Last but not least, my family members, as we are a close-knit family, to my brothers Yogesh and especially Vinay for proof-reading, Jyoti and Gita and readers of Asian Voice, India Link and various other papers and periodicals who continuously write, email and telephone me, urging me on if I have failed to write for a couple of weeks.

I hope I will get as much support for this book as I have received for my writings in newspapers and periodicals.

****

IVORY TOWER

It was a fine, sunny day. There was not a cloud on the horizon. The long awaited summer was almost upon us. It was a relief after the long, hard and wet winter we had to endure during the last six months. Then it is a normal life here in Britain.

The Cherry trees were in full blossom, the bright yellow and white daffodils, neatly laid in flower beds, enhanced the beauty of the vast, open lawn that surrounded the modern building. The red, pink and white petals of Cherry flowers, floating gently in the breeze, were forming a soft, luxurious carpet on the ground. Apple trees, the late arrival to the feast of spring sunshine, were in the bud, trying desperately to gatecrash the festive atmosphere, make the hay while the sun shines.

The sweet smell of spring flowers was filling the rosy atmosphere with romance, anticipation and excitement. Birds were fluttering in the gentle warm air, the young ones, without partners, were flying aimlessly in the clear blue sky, making a nuisance of themselves, while others, the affiliated and kindred lucky ones, were in search of twigs, leaves and any soft material that may be useful in building a love nest, an abode for their broodings, young offspring that would emerge before the summer is over, perhaps living in hope and expectation.

On the whole, it was a busy day. Romance was in the air. The sweet smell of success was in evidence every where. It was a perfect day for the young at heart, beaming with energy and ready to take a plunge, showing their expediency and making an exorbitant demand on nature. That is the way of life when one is young, strong and full of ambition, ready and willing to conquer the world.

The luxurious retirement home I was visiting, with a view of taking up a permanent residency, was on a river bank, in the picturesque, Constable type countryside, set in acres of traditional and landscaped garden, meticulously maintained, was a sort of beauty and the beast combination, pleasing to eyes and soothing to lonely hearts. After all, even a beast has a heart, if only for the right beauty and no one else?

The sculptured marble fountain in the middle, a kind of open bath for birds, was giving an air of authenticity with water jets, shooting up high in the air, before spreading, breaking into fine spray and cascading back to the ground, a gravitational inability to stay afloat permanently in the air but not before forming a rainbow where the sun's rays were bathing the garden at the right angle, enabling the rays of sunshine to pass through misty hays of water spray and breaking up the rays to reveal the abundance of natural beauty, the magnificent seven colours of the sunlight that lay hidden most of the time, when passing through space, through blank or very thin air.

I could not help but whisper Wordsworth's poem "Bliss was in that dawn to be alive but to be young was very heaven." I passed by the room number fifty four, the curtain was drawn but the door was open.

Glancing in the semi darkness, I saw the frame of a frail, lean and delicate man of an advanced age, perhaps in his early nineties. He was sitting in leather, reclining armchair, by a simulated log fire that was gently flickering in the dark room, perhaps finding it difficult to keep going in the warm spring sunshine that was in abundance outside. May be the warmth of the rising sun would soon remove the last vestige of the lingering dampness and make the fire redundant in any case.

He seemed unaware and unperturbed of his surrounding. The glowing flame's reflection gave his weather beaten, bronzed face, prominent with wrinkles, an air of authenticity. His thinning, grey, silvery hair was neatly combed. His rheumy and bleary almond shaped eyes stared fixedly at the open door, trying to pierce into the darkness of the lonely and deserted corridor.

He raised his thin, wrinkled corpse-like hand to put on the thick glassed, brown-rimmed spectacles on his motionless face. He was still in his night dress, comfortably wrapped up in a woollen gown, to protect his frail body from the rosy, early spring morning cold that most of us would like to enjoy and savour. A hesitant ghostly shadow of him projected itself on the opposite wall. For a second, I fixed my eyes unintentionally, on his frail figure with an intense kind of urge, curiosity and inquisitiveness, tinged with abundance of respect and a kind of sorrow, a guilty feeling that one inevitably feels from time to time, often without any reason or cause. Could it be that I was seeing myself in that chair, in that vegetative state in perhaps twenty years time?

The sad, lonely face stirred my memory which had remained deeply buried and undisturbed for a very long time, in my unstirred sub consciousness. That old and lonely gentleman was the father of my once closest friend, during our carefree, happy and unforgettable school days, back in our peaceful East Africa, where the life was heaven, a sea of tranquillity.

The close family was a deep rooted tradition and old people were a jewel in the family crown, to be enjoyed, looked after, treasured and cherished as long as the Mother Nature sees it fit to keep us all together.

How the world has changed. Today priorities and the social life are completely different. Some may call it a progress but only as long as you are not on the wrong side of the age divide. My heart bleeds when I see these old, kind and caring men and women who had devoted their lives bringing up their children, making sacrifice beyond call of duty, abandoned like an unwanted luggage, used cloths that no longer feet, in their hour of need.

The aspiration of the masses that guided East African countries to independence and our haste to sample the life of affluence in the West all but destroyed our cherished and long treasured family life that was once a cornerstone of our culture, our tradition and a trademark of our noble religion Hinduism. It has stood us in good stead for some ten thousand years. But I would be surprised if it lasts another hundred rears. Mercifully we will not be here to see this decline, this eradication of our noble and cherished values.

My friend, whom I would like to call Nitin, came to London, in the late sixties, as a young man, with all his family members, his parents, his two brothers and two sisters, a brood of seven people in all.

Even in London we were in constant touch, which is until he got married and moved to Canada, a land of milk and honey, a virgin, unexplored land of enterprise, a distant dreamland for most of us who were young, educated, energetic and ambitious.

That was some thirty five years ago. With Nitin's departure, my connection with the family, slowly but surely was severed. All his brothers and sisters got married and moved away, some to Canada, others to America and Australia. I read the sad news of his mother's passing away, some years ago.

The time and absence have left us with little more than a distant happy memory in common. The old, yellowing, black and white photographs, taken mostly on seaside picnics, on soft, white and warm sand of the Kunduchi and Bagamoyo beaches in Dar Es Salaam, are the painful reminder of what we have left behind, lost at one stroke, never to regain or to recreate any where else in the world. Buildings like Pyramids and Taj Mahal can be immortalized but not the inner most memories. They are too personal to survive after we are gone.

I wondered whether this old and lonely soul, my childhood friend Nitin's father would even remember those eventful distant days when he was the head of a vibrant family, full of joy, vigour, love and expectation.

Those unbelievably wonderful days must have faded from his lapsing memory a long time ago. The old soldier, the tireless warrior never dies, he only fades away in the distant memory, may be a fitting end to a noble and a memorable life.

I was in two minds, whether to go in or not. I knew, in his semi senile state, he would not remember me. In fact he would remember nothing, a blessing in disguise if there ever was one. But I could not resist the last chance to be near him, to hold the hand of a man who had been a father like figure in my life.

As I lost my father when I was a teenager, he treated me like a son. I was Nitin's twin brother, closer to this great man than I was with any of my family members, except my mother.

Slowly but deliberately I walked in. He must have heard my footsteps or just an instinct reaction, for he turned his head, gripped the sides of the armchair, with his weak, quivering arms, as if trying to hoist himself up but obviously without any result.

He was too weak to get out of the chair without help, without assistance. Then his whole life, every day survival, every tiny necessity depended on the goodwill of others. I dread to think that one day; we all may be in his shoes, a burden to others and perhaps only paid help to look after us, after all our needs.

I sat on a small stool, beside his armchair. His eyes lit up, a sudden spark made his wrinkled face bright; a smile covered his face, a smile that said a thousand words. For the first time he looked straight into my eyes. He did not even blink but lowered his shaking hands and cushioned them on mine, seeking in a strange way a reassurance from me. It was like a reunion of two lost souls, after decades of self-imposed separation.

I sat there, at his feet for an hour, in total silence, listening to the sounds of birds that were fluttering around, the sound of the wind that was filtering through the narrow corridor and gathering strength. It seems words were not important or even necessary.

I do not know what was going through his mind but I was totally immersed in the past, feeling the warm, silky sands of Oyster Bay beach under my feet. The murmur of frothing waves and the squabbling of the seagulls were ringing in my ears, quenching the thirst with cool, sweet coconut water that was and still is my favourite drink but not the stale one that I can buy in the Wembley market.

When I got up to leave, after sitting at his feet for more than an hour, the old man, Bapuji (father) to me, muttered a few words, which sounded like " Beta Nitin, I am so happy to see you. I know you would come to see me, for the last time. I am going to see your mother soon. Then he closed his eyes and went back to his own world.

When I left the room, I had tears in my eyes. My heart was heavy, in turmoil. I knew this was the final farewell, a goodbye. The old soul was just waiting for a final glimpse of his favourite son Nitin before departing for good, was eager to meet his makers, to reunite with his lost love.

I did not have the heart to see the rest of the home nor the desire to keep my appointment with the warden.

Although I was sad with my heart in turmoil, crying from within, I did get a strange satisfaction, a satisfaction of doing my duty, performing the last rites to Bapuji, for the final time. It was the least I could do for him, who gave me so much love and took me under his wing in my hour of need.

When I came in to inspect this wonderful place for the elderly, on a serine river bank, I was in a joyous mood, reciting Wordworth's poem "Bliss was in that dawn to be alive but to be young was the very heaven."

Now when I was leaving with heavy but contented heart, I could not help but recite a poem I read a long time ago but was still fresh in my mind. It seems some events; memories are hard to shake off"

Autumn of Life

Afraid to go out where muggers abound
The arrival of Christmas brings cheers
On old, weather beaten faces and lonely
The trees are bare and lonely
Chill and damp in the air
Streets are covered with fallen leaves
All brown, wet and slippery
Rotting in the autumn rain
Days are short, the sun is shy
Warmth and sunshine in short supply
The darkness surrounds, all around
A nocturnal paradise for departed souls
The old and weak, shy and infirm
A victim of gloomy weather, light famine hearts
A visit from the nearly forgotten family members
With grand children that brings a rare ray of sunshine
It warms the hearts, mind and soul
Children's smile fills the house
It is time to be proud and count the blessings
And for a while, every thing is fine
No more loneliness or suffering in silence
At least not until New Year's Day
But soon the young ones desert the nest
Fly off in different directions
The house is deserted, the nest is empty
Loneliness soon takes the hold
Gloom and doom is doubly strong
Snow falls in absolute silence
The land is white but the sky is grey
The ray of hope is the noisy children
Building a snowman with a carrot as a nose
Whoosh! Flies a snowball past my window
Bringing the sweet childhood memories flooding back
Those were the happy, worry free days
When fun, family, love and respect
Was order of the day, never in short supply
No one was lonely, every one had a family
Love and respect in abundance
No confinement in front of a TV
The art of talking, conversation abound
Sitting in front of a live fire, young and old

Was an enjoyment appreciated by all
The streets were safe, wisdom, grey hair respected
The weather beaten face, winkle skin
Was part of the culture and pride
Muggers were still in the nappies
Old people's homes were not yet built
It was a caring, sharing society
One for all and all for one
The old and the lonely taken care of
No one was neglected or forgotten
It was a one, big, happy family
Every cloud had a silver lining
The gloom was always followed by a new dawn
How my heart yearns for the good, old days
A word of wisdom from a forgotten soul
Preserve the old, tested and tried ways
For new is silver, the old is irrepressible gold

****

Two weeks later I heard Nitin's father had passed away, peacefully in his sleep, at the ripe old age of ninety two.

I met Nitin, perhaps for the last time, at his father's funeral but did not have the heart or the courage to tell Nitin of my last encounter with his father, my Bapuji. It will always remain our secret, to be taken to the grave.

****

SEEMA

It was the happiest day in the life of Seema. In fact her life has completed a full circle. Today she has become a grandmother, a joyful day in her life that she thought will never come. Her son Rahul has become a proud father of not so tiny a baby son, weighing nearly eight pound at birth. According to Indian standard, an eight pound baby is a rare occurrence, as most Indian girls are slim, petit and tiny compared to their Western counterparts, most of whom are tall, well built and strong, an enviable physical attribute.

Considering the problematic pregnancy her daughter in law Richa had to endure for the last four months; it was not too difficult a delivery, in fact it was an all round success story with mother and child doing so well.

Now Seema's life mission was complete. She had at last managed to atone for the terrible mistake she made when she was a headstrong, idealistic young college girl, an only daughter of a millionaire father, born with a silver spoon in her mouth and some may call her a spoilt child. In some ways they may not be too far out in their assessment of Seema.

Those were the idealistic days. Bharat had just gained independence, after nearly a thousand years of foreign rule, a foreign domination that had reduced Bharat to an insignificant nation. Our culture, religion and way of life were on the decline. The Sahib mentality had affected every one and every layer of the social structure. Any thing and every thing foreign, especially English, European were considered superior, more desirable than our own culture, although our culture, our way of life goes back to ten thousand years, to the time of Lord Rama and Lord Krishna and survived, stood the test of time during all these years, especially the Mogul conquest and the brutal rule of some five hundred years that followed.

The wounds of partition were still fresh. The loss of one million life, mainly in Punjab and Bengal and the assassination of Gandhiji, the father of the nation and then the early departure of Sardar Patel, the iron man of Bharat, who single handedly united a fragmented nation even before the dust of the revolution was settled, left the nation bewildered and rudderless. That is until Pundit Nehru took sole control and gave the country a short respite.

Pundit Nehru's sheer personality dwarfed other, more pragmatic and visionary leaders like C. Rajgopalachary, Morarji Desai, Shyam Prasad Mukerjee and K.M. Munsi, a few among many who all had made similar sacrifices but did not expect or desire similar rewards.

Seema, a young, beautiful and idealistic girl, was living in a dream world, a dream to liberate Bharat in a true sense, from the influence of Europe and make Bharat a great nation, in the true Gandhian tradition, a Ramrajya indeed. Seema was immersed in slogans that were floating effortlessly around on the university campus, like a butterfly fluttering its beautiful wings, under a warm, clear blue sky. These slogans were to remove poverty, visit villages and educate, liberate women, especially from the vicious circle of becoming a mother every year or two. Seema and most of the girls in her circle thought that only girls from cities with university education were capable of carrying these messages to millions of villages scattered throughout the length and breadth of Bharat. They believed, rightly or wrongly that they were the chosen few, the messiah who can make the difference.

After graduating, Seema willingly gave up the life of comfort, a future in her father's blooming business empire, security of marriage and joined the Sewa Ashram administered by Meerabai, an English woman and a disciple of Gandhiji. It was an idealistic but hard life.

However the training, the discipline and the indoctrination which were installed in Sevikas (female voluntary workers) served them in good stead during their time at the Ashram. Sevikas visited villages and established schools, health clinics, social centres, libraries, building and running these projects, training the local women and educating them in birth control by abstaining from sex. It may sound primitive, even absurd in our present day environment and ramming the message in the minds of women, hammering in the advantages of having a small family consisting of no more than two to three children.

Those were the early days of family planning. Birth control pills were not yet invented, at least not for Bharat. Birth control was through sheer will power and the guesswork, the knowledge of safe period to avoid the unwanted pregnancy. The ultimate weapon for birth control was sterilization through surgery which would make a woman infertile for life. But there were many young and highly educated women who were ready to take this drastic action, a perfect solution in their mind.

Seema, looking at the plight of village children, more often than not, six or more to a family, Seema was determined not to bring in this crowded world any children of her own. But then Seema had no plan to get married either. She wanted to devote her life in the service of mother Bharat.

The task ahead was immense. It would take several lifetimes to make an impact on a huge country like Bharat where women were chattels, no more than a production line, an instrument to satisfy lust, an object of desire and entertainment for men.

Seema was not alone. Two of her best friends from the college days joined her in her quest to bring some sunshine, happiness in the lives of these rural people. Together they used to spend months in villages of Maharastra, Gujarat and Rajasthan, implementing school building programme, health clinic, economic independence and general, social and political awareness in these rural people, turning their dream, their life desire into reality.

On the whole, the atmosphere was cordial but now and then clashes used to take place with the men folk, who sometimes felt that these liberated women from cities who have nothing better to do, were leading their domesticated womenfolk astray, poisoning their mind and turning them against them.

They were accustomed of being waited hand and foot and being served all their needs on a silver plate. They were too selfish to appreciate the importance of self denial or giving some leeway to their womenfolk who did all the hard work, in the house, in the fields and at night in the bed as well!

Seema had given two years of her life, working all God given hours, when she caught typhoid, while working among adivasis (tribesmen) in the foot of the Saraswati mountain range. She nearly lost her life. Luckily for Seema, a young, dedicated and idealistic doctor Nimit, fresh from the medical school, was working with her at the local clinic. His quick action in getting in touch with Seema's father and prompt transfer to a hospital for tropical disease in Delhi saved Seema's life.

At the time, tropical diseases like typhoid, cholera and tuberculosis were considered deadly and life threatening, unless detected and treated early. Even then, it was luck of a draw, as to who will survive and who will succumb to this deadly disease.

For Seema, Nimit's dedication and her father's money and influence played a major part in escaping, cheating death by a whisker. Yet it took a full year and a lot of loving, tender care to make Seema well again.

But her wandering days, living out of a suitcase were truly over. She had to settle down in a city and live a normal life. Every cloud has a silver lining and out of this tragedy Seema met Nimit, fell in love and got married. This was one mistake Seema was determined never to commit in her life. But it is not in our hands whether to fall in love or not. Love is a wonderful commodity. In right circumstances, love could move a mountain, tame a lion, change the world.

Seema's parents were over the moon. Their only daughter had at last settled down, got married and did exactly what they always wanted her to do. It may be a few years late but in the end she made a right decision and above all she chose a life partner her parents could be proud of. All's well that ends well but was this happy ending?

Seema and Nimit were well suited for each other. They were both free spirit, dedicated to serve humanity and the mother Bharat. Even now, when he had a thriving practice in Baroda, Nimit gave one day a week to the charity, working in a child clinic, in a small village some fifty miles from the city.

But it was a day trip. He would leave his comfortable bungalow in the green, leafy suburb of Baroda, early in the morning, in a comfortable, chauffer driven car, accompanied by Seema and return to their homely comfort by late evening, putting in a ten hour shift but living in a comfortable environment.

While Nimit worked in the clinic, Seema would visit the women in their own homes, trying desperately to keep the pre-independence spirit, the tiny flame of idealism and quit India movement, build over so many years by nationalistic and brilliant leaders like Lok Manya Tilak, Lala Lajpat Rai, Subashchandra Bose, Sardar Patel, Rajendra Babu and father of the nation Gandhiji alive and burning in her heart.

But in common with all newly independent, emerging countries, idealism was being eroded and slowly but surely replaced by materialism; ultimately succumb to greed, corruption and political nepotism, a Western disease imported from America but turned into a fine art, a refined industry. Mercifully the decay was in the early stage.

It was now ten years since Nimit and Seema got married. Nimit was eager to start a family, become a father. But all his efforts went unrewarded. Seema's life, although a sea of tranquillity from outside, supporting Nimit in every way, was in turmoil, an emotional wreck. She was living a life of sham, and deception.

She knew it was impossible for her to conceive, to give Nimit what he wanted most, children of their own. She had in haste and without thinking, in sheer youthful zest and romantic idealism, made herself sterile for life, while still at college. In the hind sight, idealism of not bringing any more children into this overcrowded world looked like a big mistake.

It was like trying to remove the saltiness of the vast ocean with a few drops of sweet water. On the contrary, the tiny amount of sweet water will be more useful, if kept apart from the ocean water where it would disappear and become part of the salty wilderness.

Now she realised that it would be better for an ideal couple like them to bring into this world, as many children as possible, as long as they educate them, mould them and turn them into ambassadors of peace and harmony, spreading the message that may make this world a better place to live in, in line with Ashok the Great, who sent ambassadors throughout Asia and beyond to spread the idealism, love and wisdom of Lord Buddha that once gave the continent of Asia peace, harmony and progress unknown in those troubled times.

Can there be too many jewels, pearls, Kohinoor diamonds, or too many Bapu, Sardar, Bose, Guru Nanak, Shivaji, Rama, Krishna or Rabindranath Tagore? They are always in short supply and we need them all to establish the Ram Rajya in our beloved Bharat.

This wisdom came too late in the life of Seema; only after she fell head over heal in love with Nimit. In fact Seema was so afraid of losing Nimit, who loved children, that she never confided in him. As years went by, it became more and more difficult to hide the truth from him. But fortunately for Seema, Nimit was a very trusting person.

He agreed with Seema that children are a gift from God. If it is not meant to happen, then they should accept Lord's will and not dwell on it and brood. But a tragedy in the life of Kajal, Seema's best friend, in fact a soul mate, gave them a break and changed their lives for ever.

Kajal and her husband were killed in a car accident. As usual, they had left their children, a six month old Priya and two year old Rahul with Seema and they had no difficulty in adopting these children who were already part of their family, as Seema was doing the baby sitting on a regular basis.

They brought them up as their own, showering them with all the love they could muster. Rahul and Priya, on their part, proved to be lovely children. Rahul followed in his father's foot-steps and qualified as a doctor while Priya was in her final year doing PhD, having set her mind on becoming a college professor.

With the addition of Priya and Rahul, Seema soon forgot her terrible plight, her gigantic past mistake. At last her family was complete. Her slogan, when they were preaching family planning was, "Hum Dono, Kutumb Me Char" (We are two, a family of four) a family she was longing for since she got married but was destined never to have one.

Rahul's wedding with Richa was the highlight in the history of this illustrious family. Her only sadness was that her father, whom Seema loved with all her heart, was not here to grace this occasion. But having lived to the ripe old age of 82, he had a long inning and her mother was still with them.

Today, with the birth of their grandson, Seema was over the moon. At last, the biggest mistake she ever made in her life did not ruin her marriage. The event had turned a full circle. Their happiness was complete. Her life's mission accomplished, her late father's dream fulfilled, turned into a reality.

****

FLYING WITH APPREHENSION

Our last holiday to the island of Madeira, a Portuguese word which means wood, is known as a floating island and a Garden of Eden. The holiday was as usual, immensely enjoyable but full of twist and turn. As I suffer from a rare form of chronic fatigue syndrome, relatively unknown condition, not understood even in medical profession but never the less a severely debilitating for me, we normally go on holidays in Europe, our destination within two to three hours' flying time at the most.

Even for that, I had to be on a special medication. So flying to the floating island of Madeira was an uncharted territory for me, as it is nearly four hour's flying time from our local Luton airport.

But in winter months, Madeira and Canary Islands are the nearest places with a reasonably warm climate. Flying to exotic places like Maldives, Goa, Kerala, Seychelles, Mauritius and Florida, at one time our favourite destinations, until I had a mishap in hospital, are now a distant dream, out of bound for us, along with my dream destination of Nepal, Bali and in particular China which provides the most fascinating train journey any where in the world, from Beijing (Pecking) to Lassa, the capital of Tibet, a distance of some three thousand miles, passing through some of the highest mountains in the world.

It is an unique journey. The laying of the tracks took some twenty years, passing through some three hundred tunnels and bridges, reaching an astonishing height of sixteen to eighteen thousand feet when passengers may need oxygen. China is the only country than can accomplish such an unique task that took well over five hundred lives, through frost bites, accidents and sheer exhaustion. But the end result is as spectacular as landing the man on the moon. It is the equivalent of the modern day wall of China, the only man made structure visible from the moon.

So when it was announced at the airport that our flight from London was some two hours late, due to mechanical fault, I was a bit apprehensive. But when we boarded the plane, we were pleasantly surprised. Our plane was a Boing 747, the most luxurious and comfortable plane we have ever flown in.

As we always pre-book our seats, we are allocated the best seats reserved for disable passengers. We get all the help and assistance that make it possible for people like me to go on a holiday. So this was no exception nor was I surprised when we were allocated the front seats in the first class, which recline into a comfortable bed. There were only twenty seats with enormous empty space all around us. Now I understand why business people always travel first class and do not feel jet lag.

But there was a twist in the tale. No sooner we settled down in our comfortable seats, the captain announced a delay of some two hours. He was unable to start one engine and for our luck, there were no specialist engineers at the airport who were familiar with Boing 747 engine. But they were receiving guidance on the video phone, working with the help of experts based on the nearby island of Tenerife. Luckily the problem was a minor one and we were airborne within an hour.

Those who are not familiar with Madeira may wonder what all this fuss is about. This tiny volcanic island is one of the rockiest places on earth, with some two thousand peaks and there is no flat land that would measure more than one hundred yards. Rocks, boulders and stones of all shape and size litter the entire landscape of Madeira.

The airport is unique; to put it mildly. Half the runway at the airport is carved out of the mountain side rocks while the other half is built on the sea, with massive pillars supporting the runway. It is like an elevated motorway. When a plane takes off, the runway suddenly disappears underneath and only sea is visible when the plane is hardly airborne.

There is no margin for error in either landing or take off. So it is a bit frightening, especially when the plane is a huge Jumbo 747. This airport is definitely not for the faint hearted passengers like me.

Before the 9/11 scenario, a synopsis for me, flying was an enjoyment, a part of our holiday, which will start as soon as we board the aircraft. But flying became a nightmare when we had to fly to the pretty Balearic Island of Ibiza, on 12th September 2001, the day after America was so brutally devastated by suicide bombers. It was an act of unprecedented savagery which took some three thousand innocent lives of men, women and children that changed the history of aviation for ever.

While we were waiting in the plane when the engine was being repaired, the memory of the flight we took on the day after 9/11 scenario, came flooding back, reliving the experience, as if it had occurred only a few days ago, which I thought was well out of my mind by now and long forgotten. But it seems our subconscious mind can store such memories for eternity and surface when least expected?

Like any normal people, we were nervous and tried our best to cancel our holiday to Ibiza, on the day of our departure. But unfortunately our insurance policy did not cover such an unexpected eventuality. We would have lost every penny we had paid for the holiday.

In the end, after great deliberation and soul searching, we decided to go ahead, putting our faith in All Mighty, in Lord Krishna in whom I have infinite, never-ending faith. Our reporting time was brought forward by two hours; that means reaching Luton airport four hours before our departure time.

We had to stand in a long, serpent like twisting and turning queue, for a very long time. Our luggage was x-rayed and we were individually questioned to no end. Only passport, medicine and such essential items were permitted, that also in a see through plastic bag provided at the Check-In counter.

We could feel that every one standing in the queue was nervous and apprehensive. The couple in front of us, with two little children and their grand parents, decided at the last moment, while their luggage was being weighed, that they were not sure whether they wanted to go ahead and board the plane. They held up the queue for some fifteen minutes while they deliberated.

The mother was shaking like an autumn leaf; tears running down her chalk white face; make up smeared and painted her face with a rainbow of colours. They were making every one in the queue nervous. As we were standing along side them for a long time, playing with their two lovely children, we tried to assure them as best as we could.

But as we ourselves were nervous, I am sure we could not inspire much confidence. In the end, they were taken on one side by the airlines officials with their luggage, until they could make up their mind. It is needless to say that we never saw them again.

Our plane was a Boing 767 with 360 seats. But there were hardly one hundred passengers on board. We were offered every kind of luxury on board with unlimited drinks flowing free but our two hour flight to Ibiza was one of the longest we had ever endured, not to say least enjoyable.

While on board, I approached the air stewardess, to ask her if I can lie down on the row of empty seats which were mostly located at the back. As she did not see me approach, she jumped ten feet in the air when I said, "Excuse me" to draw her attention. The four hour reporting time had taken its toll on me and I was already feeling tired.

We were both apologising to each other. But obviously she was more nervous than me, even though she flies every day!

I suppose, for once my Asian origin, appearance did not serve me right. I thought we were stared at or got funny looks. But under the circumstances, as we were ourselves so nervous, it could be just our fertile imagination. We had a near perfect landing at Ibiza with relief that we had seldom enjoyed.

I thought at the time that one good thing that may come out of this strange experience was that having flown at the worse possible time, we will never be afraid of flying again. But our thoughts and prayers were with those people who were unable to board the plane, drop out at the last moment. They may have lost not only their long planned and much cherished holidays but also a lot of money they can ill afford to lose.

I sincerely hope that the insurance companies, in tandem with the tour operators, have offered a full refund or an alternative holiday to those unfortunate people, who were too terrified to fly. Surely they were decent people who were the victims of a tragedy that has shaken the world. For them and perhaps for us as well, flying will never be the same again.

We had the above experience over three years ago. Since then we have flown many times but the fear is always there at the back of our mind, in our subconsciousness. It does surface from time to time, especially like our last flight when it was announced, after boarding the plane, that there was a mechanical fault, that they could not start one of the engines.

Well, as we have mentioned before, flying is no more a pleasant experience, a joy at the start of our holiday, especially when we are getting away from our cold, dark and gloomy winter months, in our old age when heat and sunshine is more important, in fact absolutely necessary than even food.

Now with Tsunami disaster which is a million times worse than what happened on 9th September 2001 in America, I wonder what effect this will have on Western tourists who were on beach in Sri Lanka and Thailand and just escaped with their lives. Their whole economy depends on these tourists. If they stay away, these developing countries will slip back into poverty and deprivation that will ruin millions of lives.

Let us hope and pray that this is only a temporary setback. Normally tourists are an adventurous lot. It is difficult to keep them away, as the increase in the number of passengers, air travellers since the 911 scenario proved beyond any doubt.

Once the sensors are laid on the ocean floor, they will give an immediate warning. Moreover the fact that new hotels being built to replace those destroyed by Tsunami are either built on an elevated land or away from the beach, such a scenario, death and destruction on such a vast scale is impossible to occur second time around, that is if there ever is a second time. After all the lightening never strikes twice at the same place. At least that is what we are told, made to believe.

It is needless to say that our flight back from Madera to Luton was perfect, as I slept on the comfortable seat throughout the journey.

After this experience, could I ever travel in an economy class again?

****

A BRIEF ENCOUNTER

After my routine visit to the National Hospital for Neurology and Neurosurgery in Queen Square, City of London, I was having a drink, sitting on a worn out wooden bench, in the Square that occupies a fair chunk of the open land around the hospital. It is a pleasant spot, an eye pleasing greenery in an area mostly cemented, with high density of buildings and of course the people.

Then again it is the same in all the major cities throughout the world. So why London should be an exception! If any thing London is much greener than any other major cities in the world, with hundreds of parks and open places scattered throughout the city boundary.

The enormous Hyde Park and the gardens at Buckingham Palace is the prime example. But with the population of the city increasing by leaps and bound and house prices going through the roof, due to lack of suitable accommodation, I wonder how long we will be able to keep the developers at bay?

It was a warm and a sunny summer day, the green green land of England at its best. The grass was neatly cut and the air was fresh, sweet and full of aroma, a fragrance that normally goes with a bouquet of sweet smelling flowers.

The well tendered flower beds were glowing with half open rose buds, red, white and yellow in colour. The marigold, busy Lizzie, oleander and azalea were also in abundance, giving the square an aurora of superiority, a perfect place for a picnic lunch, albeit during the short lunch hour, right in the heart of the city.

Pigeons and sparrows were having a feast, on the crumbs, the leftover sandwiches that were scattered around by the bird lover office workers that monopolise the Square during the lunch break, especially on a sunny and warm summer day like today. It is a common knowledge that a scarcity makes the commodity desirable and in England, sunshine, warmth and long days are in short supply at most times, unlike in Africa where I come from.

I was engrossed in my newspaper, taking a sip, now and then, from a can of soft drink, as if it will ease the pain of Botulinum Toxin injection which I have to take at regular interval, in my right-hand, to combat the inscrutable pain of destonia, commonly known as Writer's Cramp. This treatment is my three monthly routine which I have followed for the last ten years, as without this injection, I can not write or have much use of my hand.

Disturbing my thoughts, albeit with a soft, sweet and sophisticated voice, impairing my concentration, fell on my ears. "Can I sit down here?"

Looking up from my newspaper, I said with all the courtesy I could muster, "Of course, please do so." And to show my pleasure, I gave her a broad smile, lowering the paper I was reading.

Before I can go back to reading, the lady in an expensive executive suit, obviously holding a high post, started talking with me, as if I was her work colleague or a long standing friend.

It is surprising how sometimes stranger trust each other more than their best friends, telling them the most intimate secrets which they can not tell to any one they know, even their partners. Perhaps there is trust in anonymity and the knowledge that we may never meet again?

The lady, whom I would like to call Susan, was in her mid forties, tall, well groomed with pale silky light brown hair fluttering effortlessly in the gentle breeze; with slim figure looking very elegant in her tight fitting three piece suit that brought out her limited curves with ease and facileness, was obviously pleasing to the eyes.

"I work for a blue blooded merchant bank in the heart of the city. I have been with them for nearly twenty years. I thought I was indispensable and it was a job for life.

After all I have the biggest client portfolio among the thirty or so senior executives who are directly involved with the clients. Surely they can't do without my expertise and the personal relations I have cultivated with my clients over so many years. Can they? Surely not!" For a moment she was lost in he thoughts or perhaps her anguish was trying to take over her thoughts.

But she soon regained her composure and continued. "My make belief world fell a part this morning as I opened an envelop neatly laid out on my executive desk, a solid, very expensive hard wood mahogany piece of personalized furniture, made to order. The envelope contained, along with the notice of dispensation of my services, a cheque for a very generous amount.

Our firm was taken over by a bigger fish, a city giant and I was requested to clear my desk immediately, although they were sorry to let me go! It was apparent that they would not want me to get in touch with my clients. My portfolio was immediately taken over by a trusted employee of the new bank and perhaps my clients would have known about the takeover before I did!

This is a dirty business where dogs eat dogs and back stabbing is an art, a necessity. But then there is no place for sentiment in London's murky financial world. My consolation was the fat cheque that will keep me going for a year or two. I know it would not be difficult for me to get another job but whether I would get a similar salary and the position was all together a different proposition. After all, the entire city was turning into a playground for the young whiz kids and I was not a spring chicken any more and above all I was a woman in a man's world. Unfortunately gender discrimination was rife in the city where machoism ruled the roots and very few women made to the top. I was an exception rather than the rule, the norm.

My world fell apart, the dream suddenly turned into a nightmare. I find it difficult to believe that I was going to lose my job, made redundant, a surplus to their requirement, a fat cat scarified at the altar of efficiency and consolidation, a victim of merger mania and cost cutting so that the top brass get their fat bonuses, even when the ship is sinking.

What will I do? Surely I can't retire in my mid forties? Apart from every thing else, I can not afford it. My big house in the leafy suburb, my top of the range BMW, membership of the top social clubs and numerous other commitments may not allow me to give up my job."

I sympathetically grasped her hand without thinking and said "Look at me, look at my hands. A few years ago, I was a very successful accountant but now I can hardly hold a pen. My decision to retire was made for me, from up there. I had no say in it." I said in deep, emotional voice, looking heavenly at the open, blue, cloudless sky punctured with flying pigeons and sparrows.

After a short pause, I said, "Let me tell you a short story, my true experience. When I was young, my family was poor and to be honest, most families were in similar situation in East Africa during the Second World War. I did not have even shoes to wear and during hot summer months when the tar roads melted and the cemented footpath were boiling hot, it was not easy to do without shoes.

Once when I put my foot on the melting tar and got badly burnt, I cursed my luck and sulked for a long time; that is until I met another boy who had no legs? That taught me to count my blessings, as there are people worse than us."

We talked for more than an hour, mostly about our family. I rather listened as she did all the talking, how she let go by the opportunity of getting married, settling down in the routine of raising children, as most women do, in favour of a career in the most demanding field of merchant banking.

It would be too big a sacrifice to make, to give up such a glamorous job, a job in the men's world where few women succeed, a lion's den where a lamb may enter at her peril. Perhaps for the first time she may have regretted her decision to be a career woman, at the cost of her marriage and the family. But then, it is easy to be wise after the event. After all hindsight is easy to acquire, to understand and to appreciate.

Then glancing at her expensive Rado watch, she said, "I must deposit this cheque before the bank closes. You may never realise how important this chance meeting may turn out to be. I never imagined I could have such an inner strength and that a simple chat, a few encouraging words and looking at other people's problems will bring a new purpose in my life.

Instead of crying over my misfortune, I should count my blessings"

With a twinkle in her eyes and a sweet gentle smile she continued. "At least I have good looks, a healthy body and a sharp brain. Now I know I am going to be all right. If I have to give up the trappings of my comfortable life, so what?

Thank you for listening to my problems, my rumblings." She said it all in one breath, in her sweet but assertive voice, thanking me for providing a miraculous cure?

All I have done was to give her an hour of my time, which I had plenty and to listen to her problems, nodding here and there, now and again, uttering a few words of encouragement.

In fact I was glad of her company. Obviously she was a beautiful, sophisticated and an intelligent woman. Listening to her problems took my mind of the pain of injection that I just had.

Ironically, a couple of years ago, I would have charged her for my time and so would have she if I had gone to see her in her office.

We exchanged our phone numbers, out of politeness rather than for any other reason. We were as different as cheese and chalk. Deep down we both knew that we are unlikely to see or to talk to each other ever again.

It was like what we do when we are on holidays, always exchange our addresses and telephone numbers but forget all about it when we go back home. Surely I never received a telephone call from her nor was I expecting one. But she gave me a firm hug before departing that made my day?

This chance meeting will always remain a chance meeting. It happened a long time ago. I hope she is as happy in her retirement as I am in mine, although when I go for my routine injection and sit on the same bench, I do think about Susan sometimes. It is human nature to ponder, to reflect on life. What a chance encounter it was!

****

IS THERE A GOD?

While sitting on a hair dresser's chair, having my hair trimmed, I had an interesting conversation with my hair stylist, that is how they would like to call themselves and rightly so, whom I would like to call Tony.

As I go to his saloon on a regular basis for more than a decade, we have become good friends. He knows I am a journalist and reads my various articles in the local papers.

As such I have earned his respect and the right to talk to him on any subject. I must admit Tony is a proud man. He would not enter into conversation on delicate or intellectual subject unless he feels that you are worthy of such an honour with some or rather good knowledge of the subject you would like to discuss.

He is absolutely right. After all there is no joy talking about nuclear science with a chef or about religion with an atheist or the problems, health deficiencies that go with the old age with a young and a super fit person.

As we all know, these hair stylists are more knowledgeable and street-wise than most of us, as they talk and listen all day, six days a week, with everyone, from a peon to a Prime Minister and Tony was no exception.

In view of the Tsunami disaster which claimed hundreds of thousands of innocent lives, it was inevitable that we talked about justice, fairness and whether there is a God or a divine power, a super power who looks after us, punishes the guilty and rewards the good, honest and God fearing citizens, as God is supposed to be omnipotent, all-mighty, omniscient, wise and all-perceiving divine power.

As such, it is his duty to look after the sick, disable, old, infirm and the poor people who can not look after themselves, protect them from the rogue elements in our society.

But we all know that it is not as simple as that. After all, some of the most kind, gentle, generous, charitable and saintly people like Lord Jesus Christ, Mahatma Gandhi, Martin Luther King and many more died a violent death. While modern day saintly personality, Mr. Nelson Mandela spent twenty six years in a stinking jail on the Robin Island (Robben Island) an isolated outpost far removed from the hustle and bustle of the mainland South Africa.

These were his best years of life, while evil Satanic rulers that include Stalin, Hitler, Mao, Idi Amin and Pol Pot, to name but few, who murdered millions had a relatively easy and comfortable life.

Toni is a devoted, church going Christian, a philosophical and a practical person. He can reason on all fronts. He reasoned that Jesus and Gandhi died for our sins, to save us, save the humanity. Faith is a wonderful asset but like a dream or a miracle, it can not be explained in a scientific way.

There is always some cause, some reason, some meaning behind what happens in our topsy turvy world and far beyond. One has to dig deep, search hard, to examine our conscious to find the answer. Sometimes the answer may be just round the corner and at other times it may take us a long time to make sense of an event like Tsunami.

To keep the conversation going, I tried to counter his reasoning but it is difficult to gain upper hand with someone like Tony who had answers for all my questions. In the end, although Tony won the argument hands down, he took me outside.

A couple of minutes later, we came to a sheltered spot where a young man in dirty clothes and long, unwashed and untidy hair was playing guitar to attract the attention of the passers-by.

This was his way of earning a living. Some may call him a hippy or a beggar but he would like to call himself a street entertainer, a musician. As he was a mild and a polite man and a university graduate who had opted out of the rat race, talking to him, I felt I was in the company of an intelligent and honest person. Even Tony had respect for him, although he looked so scruffy that most would not give him the time of the day.

Tony put a five pound note in his begging bowl or rather a collection box which readily attracted his attention, as there were only coins, mostly ten and twenty pence coins. Tony asked him why he does not go to a barber to get his long and untidy hair trimmed.

He looked up and gave us a weary smile and said. "My friend, are there any barbers in this town worthy of their profession? If there are, I have yet to meet them." I got my answer. The morale of the story is that the GOD is not one way traffic. We have to make an effort to find HIM. Seek and thou shall find him but we have to be worthy of him, his attention. The faith never goes unrewarded. Sooner or later one will benefit from one's kind deeds, helpful nature and belief in ones faith or in God, if you are a religious person.

****

THE MIDNIGHT MYSTERY

Tren .... tren .... tren ...... the telephone was ringing remorselessly, forcing Amit to get up in the bed, wondering who could be ringing him at such an ungodly hour. The only way to find out was to answer the damn telephone.

He switched on the bedside lamp and looked into his wrist watch. It was exactly midnight. It must be a wrong number or could it be some bad news?

Picking up the receiver, Amit answered the phone, with as much restraint as he could muster under such provocation? After all it was not easy to control his anger. He had just managed to go to sleep after tossing and turning in his bed. It was a hot, humid and oppressive night, not meant for a sound and comfortable sleep, especially as his air conditioning was on the blink.

"Hullo .... Hullo .... Can I help you?"

The answer came in a surprisingly sweet, pleasant, sophisticated, obliging, sexy and unexpected voice, not familiar to Amit.

"Sure Amit, I am dying to hear your voice. Please don't slam the phone. Sorry to wake you up so late but I can't sleep. So I thought why should you? After all you are the cause of my sleepless nights, my broken heart, aren't you Amit?" There was a pause, a mild teasing and a deep breathing at the other end of the line. It seems some one was enjoying pulling Amit's leg?

The voice was so sweet, soft and romantic that Amit lost his sleepiness and the anger turned into a curiosity. In a polite, helpful and gentle voice, Amit enquired whether she has dialled the right number.

"Of course Amit, I have dialled the number I want. I know you very well, even though you may not remember me, at least not straight away. But I am prepared to wait for you!"

Amit was surprised to hear his name. She was talking to him as if they have known each other for a long time. Could she be a ghost from his past?

"This is not fair. It is a one way traffic. You seems to know all about me but I can't place you, remember you at all. Can you give me a hint, introduce yourself?" Amit said in an excited voice, as if arranging his first date with the girl of his dream. Then for Amit, every beautiful girl was a girl of his dream, a girl in a million!

"Why do you want to know my name? What difference a name would make. Tell me Amit, what is your favourite name for a young, beautiful, charming, exciting and a sophisticated girl like me? Consider me your dream girl because I see you all the time in my dreams!"

Amit was dumb founded. Not knowing how to respond, he maintained his silence.

"OK Amit, if you are shy, then I will rekindle your memory. As far as I can remember, your favourite name for young lass like me was Darshana, at least during your college days. Tell me if I am wrong.

Amit was dumb struck. She was absolutely right. When he was studying economics at a prestigious college, there was a young, beautiful and a very smart girl in his class. Her name was Darshana. She was completely different from the rest of the students.

She used to keep herself aloof, rarely mix with the rest of her classmates. Most of Amit's friends used to think that she was a snob. Perhaps she was sour grapes, as she was unbelievably beautiful, with a tall, slim figure and an alert brain. No doubt she was very clever and obviously from a rich and professional family.

Darshana's expensive, top of the range, black, open top Mercedes Sports car; with a personalized number plate was the envy on the university campus, even among the college professors. She never used to take part in any of the college activities, except debating and literary society.

She used to write poetry and short stories for the college magazine but under her pen name, to hide her true, real identity. Her writings had a unique style, poetry with rhythm, feelings and mostly dealing with nature, wild life, beauty spots and human fragility, good enough to be published in any national magazine.

As Amit was the editor of the Uni magazine, Darshana used to talk to him but no matter how hard Amit tried, he could not get close to her. She was polite, courteous and almost apologetic but would never answer any questions about her background, about her personal life, her ambition, her dream. It was a closed book.

Although Amit liked her and would have done anything to develop a closer relationship with Darshana, Amit respected her desire for privacy and refrained from asking her too many personal questions. Perhaps that may be the reason why Darshana trusted Amit and was reasonably friendly with him and no one else.

But Amit gathered that much, Darshana was either married or at least engaged to some one who may not be her first choice. But she did not want to rock the boat or may be fulfilling an obligation to her family who may have arranged her future a long time ago.

Perhaps all her worldly wealth, like her car and the designer and expensive dresses she used to wear with ease and elegance may have come from her fiancé's side of the family. It was difficult to judge her but it was obvious to Amit that behind her glamour, show of wealth, there was a kind of sorrow, a sadness that accompanied Darshana like a shadow.

When Amit gained his degree and left the college, all connections with Darshana were severed. She disappeared from the scene, from the horizon as if it was a dream, not a reality. In the hustle and bustle of London life, the memory of Darshana soon faded from Amit's conscious mind.

Since the college days, Amit had attended many reunion dinners where many of his college friends came from as far as USA, Canada, Australia, East Africa and India but Amit never saw Darshana again.

Today, on hearing Darshana's name, Amit remembered his college days and the memory of Darshana, which has remained dormant all these years. But now it all came flooding back. After all Darshana was a unique girl, one in a million, like of her Amit has never met, either before or since his college days. Those days, in many ways, were the happiest days of his life, carefree but full of ambition, charting the path, mapping the future, not only on career front but also on the social and domestic side.

Amit would be lying if he did not admit of including Darshana in his future plans, however absurd it may sound today. He may not be alone in dreaming a life, charting a future with such an attractive, charming and a desirable girl like Darshana. Desire was an operative word.

"Amit, do you remember Darshana, of course you do. How can you forget a girl in a million? You were madly in love with her. Tell me if I am wrong." The teasing continued unabated from the other end.

"How do you know Darshana? Even I hardly remember her." Amit said with an unconvincing voice and a touch of sadness that was too evident, too difficult to hide, in his voice.

"Amit, don't worry. I do not know Darshana or any other girl in your life, past or present. It was just a shot in the dark, hoping it would hit the target and it seems it has worked? Every young man, especially those who have been to a university and live a busy social life, has some one special in their lives. She may be Darshana, Rupa, Manisha, Anita, Krishna, Mansi, Payal, Priya, Rema, Nisha or Rekha. Don't lose any sleep over it. Your secret is safe with me."

No Rupa, may I call you Rupa? It was not a shot in the dark and you know it. Darshana is not that common a name. It seems you know me, as well as Darshana. How well I cannot tell."

"Stop it Amit, don't be sentimental or make a mountain out of a molehill. OK bye. I will ring you again." And the phone went dead, before Amit could ask her real name or her telephone number.

Amit dialled 1471 but got the normal message that the caller had withheld the number. There was nothing Amit could do but wait for Rupa's phone call, her promise to call again.

Amit could not sleep. His thoughts drifted in the past, his happy go lucky college days, trying to remember who she could be. Surely she cannot be Darshana. It was not her style. She could never talk to a stranger like me in such a bold, familiar and teasing manner. It must be some ten years since Amit last talked to Darshana. How could she get my ex-directory number? No, the whole idea was absurd.

There was no other solution but to wait for Rupa's call. Surely Amit was not disappointed nor had he to wait long. Three days later, on a Sunday night, exactly at the stroke of midnight, the phone rang. Although Amit was half a sleep, he knew straight away that Rupa was on the line.

"Hello Rupa, how are you? Why did you make me wait so long?"

"Well Amit, how did you know it's me? Don't you think Amit that there is more excitement in planning a journey than arriving at the destination? The period between engagement and marriage is the happiest period in our lives? That mountain looks so beautiful and majestic from a distance. When you go near, one inevitably discovers that they are nothing but lumps of big rocks, at least on most parts, although there is always an exception to the rule, like me. I am your oasis, a green fertile land in the ocean of sand. Then sand dunes are so majestic, mesmerising in the right place, at the right time.

Amit, if I appear in front of you, then all these excitement and curiosity will disappear for good. What beauty, excitement, desire there is in anticipation and imagination is missing in reality.

As far as you are concerned, I may be a tall, elegant, sophisticated person with long, dark brown hair and milky complexion, curves in all the right places with well developed chest, wearing expensive designer and perhaps revelling dresses and driving a top of the range Mercedes car, a girl of your dream. Am I right or am I right." There was a soft murmur, a teasing reality in her voice.

"Rupa, I am now convinced that we were at the college together. Your description fits Darshana word to word. This can not be a coincidence. But please don't make a fun of me. You know I was waiting for your call with anticipation. I still can't figure out who you really are. Are you really Darshana? If you are, then you have really changed. Please don't keep me in suspense any more." Amit pleaded with Rupa.

"Sorry Amit, I was just teasing. I didn't know you are so sentimental. No I am not Darshana but even if I give you my real name, you will not be able to place me, recognize me. Consider me as a mystery, a puzzle in your life.

So forget about my real name and call me Rupa. I am happy with your choice of name for me. It is a short and sweet name. Then you always had a vivid imagination. You were very good at writing short stories, making things up, aren't you Amit?"

"Rupa, every puzzle has a solution, every question has an answer. So please tell me how can I solve this puzzle?" Amit insisted.

"Sorry Amit, my time is up. I will ring you again soon. Bye, sleep tight and have a happy dream about me, about Darshana. And before Amit can say any thing, the phone went dead.

The friendship between Amit and Rupa grew day by day but their only contact was solely by phone. They talked to each other, two to three times a week but still Amit was no nearer to identifying her, knowing who Rupa was or who she could be. Darshana, she definitely was not, unless she had undergone a personality transplant. How could Darshana, a pretty, sophisticated, shy and gentle person suddenly talk about sex, marriage and the most personal attribute with some one like Amit, a total stranger?

Today it was Sunday. Rupa had always ringed on Sundays without fail. So Amit was expecting Rupa's call. Surely he was not disappointed.

The phone rang at the usual time, at midnight. "Hai Amit. Can I call you my darling? Sure I have earned that right by now. Don't you think so?"

"Rupa, you know how I feel about you and it seems the feelings are mutual. So please stop ringing me at midnight when half the city is asleep and let us meet in person. I would like to see you in front of me, hold your hand and squeeze you with all my strength, kiss you and cuddle you until you squeak, yelp and struggle for breath."

Amit had made up his mind to find out who Rupa really was. He was not prepared to play a mind game, wait any more. Life is too short to waste on anticipation, waiting or dreaming about the future. Reality was the name of the game and only reality counts. He had used his imagination, dreamt about Rupa and Darshana far too long. It was time for action, for truth and reality "Amit, I am not too far from you. In fact I am as near as you would like me to be. You can hold me, play with my long and silky hair, squeeze me, kiss me and not on the lips either, feel my breath, touch my bosom and make me scream with sweet pain, a desirable, loving pain that every girl want.

I can see you and can tell you that you are wearing a light blue pyjama top, with matching bottom." Rupa said in a teasing but some what serious voice. Although she was always forward, she had never talked so openly about her body, about her sexual desire. It sounded like an invitation to grab her and make love to her!

"Well Rupa, half the men in London prefer blue colour and at one o'clock at night, what do you expect me to be wearing, a suit? Let me catch you and you will know what I can do to a mischievous girl like you."

"Amit, I know you are not prepared to listen to me, to wait any longer. I can see that you are over excited. You want to solve the riddle and grab me, isn't it? Well, don't blame me for the consequences of your stubbornness." There was a long pause and a deep breathing, perhaps a tinge of sadness as well.

"Look on your dressing table. Your expensive Rado watch with inscription, to our beloved son Amit, on his 21st birthday, is near the table lamp, along with your packet of cigarettes." Rupa said in a serious and some what sad and disturbing voice. Suddenly all the mischief and teasing was gone from her voice.

"So you are keeping a watch on me. You know I wear a Rado watch. Is there any thing more you want to add?" Amit said in a cool, calm voice but looked at the window to see if any one can see him through a night Binocular, as there were high rise buildings in front of Amit's third floor flat that could be easily observed from a vantage point.

Amit put down the receiver for a second and drew the heavy velvet curtains to make it impossible for any one to see him in his bedroom.

Picking up the phone, Amit said, "Hay Rupa, are you still there?"

"Yes Amit, your velvet curtain and dim light will not stop me from watching you, being near to you, observing your every movement. You know Amit, I have an x-ray vision. We can not hide from each other. Amit, I do not want to embarrass you, otherwise I can tell you what spots, birth marks you have on your most private parts."

After a long pause, Rupa continued. "I know you want a final answer today and believe me Amit, I am going to give it to you. But I am afraid it won't be what you expect. Well, why are you looking around in your bedroom? Surely I am not under the bed."

For the first time Amit felt a cold shiver. He realised that some one was watching him, his every movement and may be from within his bedroom. Rupa was not only able to watch him but read his mind as well.

"Amit darling, look at your wallet which is near the table lamp. Count it and tell me if it is a twenty pound note and three pound and sixty pence in change on the table. Besides you have another thirty pound in notes in the wallet, along with your driving licence and two credit cards. I wonder why you haven't got any girl's photo. You also have a silver photo frame with photos of your mum and dad. Your work colleagues gave that frame as a Christmas present last year."

"When you filled your tank, you paid by credit card. The receipts, along with some old ones are still in your wallet and by the way you put twenty pound of super unleaded petrol in the tank. Am I right Amit? Not only I can see you, I can even feel you, feel your breath, your warm and desirable body"

What Rupa said was absolutely true. He had checked the change when he emptied his trouser pockets.

Oh God ………. Amit started shaking and sweating profoundly. The phone slipped from his hand. When he recovered his composure, he picked up the phone but it was already dead, cut off.

Amit dialled the operator and a sweet, obliging voice, similar to that of Rupa, answered the phone.

"Can I help you sir."

"Yes please, can you give me the telephone number of the last caller?"

"Wait a minute Sir ………….. It was 020 8999 8899."

"May I know whose number it is?"

"Sure, it is of Golders Green crematorium." And Amit heard a mischievous, sinister smile before he drop the phone, as he fell down and lost consciousness.

****

AN EPIC JOURNEY

While we were in Surat, we had a wonderful, unforgettable, once in a life time experience. One sunny day, well all days are sunny in Surat, except during a short monsoon season, we were travelling in a rickshaw, not the one driven with human muscles but by a scooter, with a flimsy cabin built around which can take two people in comfort but more often than not overflowing with extra passengers that made the roads dangerous. We were trying to visit a long lost friend.

Just off the main bazaar, near Hirawadi, a place where mostly diamond merchants live; we saw or rather caught a glance of a wonderful temple. It was Lord Shiva's temple, a small but colourful temple, with an arch in rainbow colours which caught our eyes.

Whenever we go on a holiday, no matter where, it is our aim, our hobby, may be our obsession, to stop at a church, a temple, a gurudwar, a pagoda or even a synagogue and offer our prayer, make a wish and make a small donation. Some how we have affinity towards all religion where we are welcome. So we could not just pass by this attractive temple, even though we were in a hurry to meet an old friend.

In a way this stoppage, a chance opportunity proved to be a wonderful experience, a trip to remember, in more ways than I could have imagined at the time. Although this temple was very attractive from outside, with colourful arches on all four sides, a small garden with all the tropical flowers we love, such as periwinkle (barmasi) Karan (pink rose or oleander) and champo (Indian Magnolia) but above all my favourite flower Kamal, lotus or water lilies, in red, blue and white, in a small pond, in the centre of the garden. It was unusual for such a small temple to have such a beautiful, eye pleasing garden, especially with a pond.

The interior of the temple was more functional than attractive, with images of Lord Shiva, Devi Parvati, consort of Lord Shiva and Lord Ganesh, the most popular and widely worshipped God in the Hindu religion, whose blessing is sought on each and every auspicious occasion, such as marriage.

Fortunately for us, the curtains were not drawn. So we were blessed with a darshan and in common with most of our temples, there were images of Lord Rama, Sita and Laxman, with Hanuman sitting at Lord Ram's feet on one side and Radha Krishna on the other. The centre piece was Lord Shiva's domain.

Being early afternoon, the temple was deserted; the atmosphere, the peace and pin drop silence was what we like most and can rarely be found in a temple in India. After spending some fifteen minutes, we left by the side entrance. The rickshaw driver drew our attention to a small craft shop that was selling murti (images) of every Hindu god and goddess that we could think of.

Behind the shop there was a large workshop where some fifteen people, mainly ladies were working, carving wood, chipping stones and mixing chalk with a mixture of gum, fine sand and a white powder. Images produced from this mixture were most beautiful, as well as light and easy to paint.

We have never seen such beautiful murtis, made from chalk, in our life. It was impossible to leave the shop without buying at least one. We selected one of Lord Krishna with Radha, standing under a pippal tree, playing flute and a light brown cow in the background. It cost us five hundred rupees but if we had bought a similar one in stone, it would have cost us ten times more and above all, it was very heavy and not so colourful.

This distraction cost us nearly an hour but was well worth it. I met my childhood friend Dharyakant, after some forty years. When we left Dar Es Salaam in the late sixties, Dhiru, as we used to call him, went to India with his parents while we came to London.

There was a time when three of us, Dhiru, Raju and I were inseparable. After completing Senior Cambridge, Raju went to Bombay, now Mumbai, for further studies, while Dhiru and I joined the Civil service. From Bombay Raju went to America and we lost all contact with him.

Fortunately Dhiru's elder brother is in London, so we were able to keep in touch, albeit by Dipawali and Christmas cards only. This was the first time I met Dhiru since we left Dar. Old friends and acquaintances, like mountains, look pretty from a distance.

Although I was pleased to meet him, we both realised that the old charm, the warmth and the affinity that existed between us in Dar was no longer present. After all we were living in a different world. Our interest, our hobbies and even our political thinking were poles apart.

We spend a couple of hours reminiscing the past, a nostalgic era which came to an end as soon as we left East Africa. When we parted, our hearts were heavy and there were tears in our eyes, as we both knew this was our final goodbye. Dhiru would never come to London while this was my first and most probably the last visit to Gujarat in forty years. Yes, we go to Bharat but only to Goa and Kerala. But with advancing age and infirmity, long distance travel was becoming more difficult by the day.

Two days later we left Surat for Baroda. It takes some three hours by train and as we were told this train service, which runs a couple of times a day, is never full, so we turned up at the station without a reservation.

But to our surprise, the station was overflowing with humanity, men, women and children, in colourful costumes and beautiful saris. The train, which normally terminates at Baroda, was going on to Dakor, as there was a religious festival. It seems Hindus may miss their own weddings but not a religious festival, especially if it happens to be a festival of their favourite God?

Luckily our host had some influence. So we were able to buy the tickets and managed to board the train as well. It is impossible for any one to imagine the chaos, the disorder and the confusion that reigns on such a pilgrim train, unless one has travelled on it and gained a first hand experience. This was once in a lifetime journey, once experienced never forgotten, an Indian Orient Express?

Obviously there were no empty seats for us to occupy. We were more worried about our Lord Krishna's murti, as there was hardly enough space to stand. So my wife took out the piece from the flimsy packing, which was obviously not enough to protect it.

The murti was so beautiful, with Radha's colourful costume and Lord Krishna's cute baby face, with the flute, the Chakra and the costume jewellery, not mentioning the pippal tree and the holy cow? Everyone's eyes were fixed on it. There was a Sadhu, a holy man present in the compartment, sitting in a corner seat. He saw our struggle to keep the murti safe.

The Sadhu stood up and came to us, knelt down in front of Lord Krishna and said a prayer. Suddenly there was a pin drop silence until the prayer was over. Instead of going back to his seat, he asked us to take his seat. Before we could say any thing, a couple of other people, sitting in the adjourning seats, also vacated their seats. Now we had seats not only for our selves but for Lord Krishna as well. Our hesitation made no difference. We soon realized that it was time to count our blessings and do as we were told?

Every passer-by and the people sitting, standing around, wanted to kneel before Lord Krishna. Lord Krishna's image, leaning happily on an empty seat that soon became a shrine. When people started putting down money, to our obvious embarrassment but again the Sadhu came to our aid. He spread his holy bhagwa vaster (Orange or saffron cloth) on the floor where people could put their money, their offerings.

It was a slow train, stopping at every station. People were getting on and off the train at every station. Hawkers were selling all sorts of fancy goods and mouth watering dishes but we were looking for a green coconut. I was hesitating to leave the compartment but the Sadhu and all the fellow passengers urged us to go and buy the drink and promised us that they would look after our worldly possessions and of course Lord Krishna.

For the first time, while travelling on a train, we had the courage to leave the compartment, leave our seats to the mercy of our fellow passengers. When we came back after some ten minutes, with a bottle of soft drink, as we could not find green coconuts, to our relief, we found our seats empty, our suitcases in one piece, Lord Krishna smiling at us and a pile of coins, including some notes on the orange cloth had multiplied.

Lord Krishna's image became a shrine. People were reciting prayers, bhajans. It was like a prayer meeting in a small temple and we also started singing hymns, religious songs of praise of Lord Krishna. These were all familiar bhajans, some even our favourite ones, written by Meerabai, Narsi Mehta, and Sant Kabir and sung on tape by our favourite playback singer Anoop Jalota, which we always keep with us when we travel by air.

As the train was stopping at every station on the map, the journey took a long time but with this crowd and the atmosphere, we enjoyed every minute. We were indeed sad when we arrived at our destination.

It was not easy to disembark but every one was eager to help us. We only had to carry Lord Krishna's image, the rest we left to our fellow passengers.

There were more than five hundred rupees on the orange cloth. I don't know how many people knelt down in front of our valued possession, Lord Krishna's murti, as we stopped counting when the figure reached one hundred. The Sadhu whom we called Panditji, urged us to take the money but we managed to persuade him to accept it as our gift, Lord Krishna's Prasad and to spend it at the religious festival, in our name, adding one hundred rupees of our own to the collection.

This was Bharat at its best. There were Hindus, Jains, Muslims, Sikhs and Christians in our compartment, all sons and daughters of Bharatmata, all simple human beings, enjoying our common heritage. Lord Rama and Krishna was not our God, they were the God of the whole nation. Now I know why people like to travel with Kersavak, go on a pilgrimage and perform their religious rituals.

This could only happen in Bharat and in Hindu religion, which is tolerant, peaceful and culturally so superior, so rich. It is beyond our comprehension why they do not show this unity, this brotherhood on the political and social front, in their every day life?

The arrival at Baroda station was an anticlimax. No one would believe if I say there were tears in the eyes of some of our fellow passengers who were sitting near us, near Lord Krishna, who had the opportunity to chat with us. Our hearts were heavy, filled with emotion and eyes were wet when we left them, even envying them, as they were going to a very special festival.

Normally, on such occasions, we do not tell, let any one know that we are from London but it was impossible to lie to these gentle, trusting people who gave us so much respect and their love, treated us as their vadils, their elders. They even opened their hearts to us, as if we were their long lost relatives.

It impressed them even more that we the Londoners are as humble as them, ready and willing to travel in a Janata class railway compartment and at ease with Bharatwasi, the local people. It was a far cry from our tailor made excursions, in an air-conditioned, some what a private compartment with NRIs as our fellow passengers.

After a week, we left Baroda by air for Bombay. When we opened the case in Bombay, we found Lord Krishna's murti broken, in two pieces. It broke our heart but we were told that such images, made from chalk, although very artistic and beautiful, are very delicate, only made for local use. That is why they are not exported to Britain. It was a miracle that it survived the train journey from Surat to Baroda, especially as the compartment was overflowing with humanity.

We left the broken murti with Pujari, a priest at the local temple, with a request to immerse Lord Krishna in the holy waters of Jamuna or Ganga River. Although the above episode happened some ten years ago, the experience is still vivid in our mind.

Whenever we visit Hare Krishna temple in Watford, look at the beautiful images of Lord Krishna, the memory of this epic train journey comes flooding back, becomes alive and there is bhagwa vaster, the saffron cloth given to us by Panditji, to remind us of our involvement with kind and noble Kersavak.

This may not be an epic journey in distance or the awesome scenery that we normally associate with a train journey, such as crossing Canada, from Toronto to Vancouver, taking in the breath-taking scenery of Rocky Mountains, ice glaciers and vast tundra plains but it was memorable in many ways.

It took us back to our roots, to our culture, our tradition and showed us the true human face of my mother country Bharat. It was our pleasure, our pride and indeed our good luck to be a passenger on this compartment full of Kersavak.

****

ANAND

Today was the ninth and final day. The Shastriji (preacher) would finish reciting Ramayana tonight and will leave the town, to the regrets of the town folk of Palanpur, early next day.

Shastriji has captivated the town folk with his reciting of the epic tale of Ramayana. There was no mystery in why the town folk were so mesmerised. Shastriji had such a sweet voice, the sadness, the loneliness and the pain that his reciting conveyed to his audience, was a genuine one, oozing from his heart.

May be it was the result of a tragedy in his own personal life that he was reliving, with tears running down his weather beaten, bearded face, every time he recited this sad episode of Ramayana.

The heart broken Mata (mother) Kaushalya, bidding farewell to his favourite son Lord Rama, which has made this epic, holy book a household name, even among the Western culture, became alive when listening to Shastriji. He gave the story heart and soul. It became alive, like watching a tragedy on a big screen.

When he described the abduction of petite Sita by the evil Ravan, the banishment of Lord Rama to the forest for fourteen years, tears flowing from the eyes of the distraught Mata Kaushalya, while bidding farewell to Rama, to let him go to Van (forest) to fulfil his father King Dashrath's promise to evil queen Kaikai, Mata Kaushyala's pain, her tragedy, her heartbreak was shared by every one in the audience.

The audience unashamedly wept with Shastriji. Mata Kaushyala's heartbreak, her pain, her sorrow at losing her husband King Dashrath, who could not bear to see his favourite son Lord Rama, the heir to the crown, banished to forest, his heart just stopped beating. Her pain, her sorrow became every one's pain, every one's heartbreak, their own personal tragedy.

There was hardly a dry eye among the vast audience, even among male devotees, those who have heard the story so many times before but never recited in such a touching, tragic manner that it became a personal tragedy for every one present in the audience.

Shastriji's pain, his tears became my tears, every one's pain. It touched my heart, someone like me who could sit through a tragic Indian movie without shedding a single tear, was crying unashamedly, like a child, along with most of the audience. It was like a little girl who was about to be parted from her mother for the first time.

I would never have believed that listening to someone reciting the epic story of Ramayana could touch one's heart so deeply. His sweet, kind yet authoritarian voice had the ability to convey pain, touch the inner most corner of your heart and make you feel part of the audience that was watching Mata Kaushalya weeping uncontrollably while bidding farewell to Lord Rama, his wife Sita and brother Laxman, on the streets of Ayodhia, believing that she may never see her beloved son ever again. After all, fourteen years is a long time, especially when confined to a forest, with danger lurking at every corner.

This was the first time I had the opportunity to listen to Shastriji. I had never met him, nor heard of him before he came to our town. But somehow, deep in my heart, I always felt and thought that this was not our first meeting. Our path has definitely crossed before, may be more than once. But where and when I could not determine.

I felt that Shastriji's voice, his face hidden behind his beard, was familiar but however hard I tried, I could not place him or even guess where and when I may have met him. I felt frustrated, even angry with myself but all I can do was to wait and hope that my memory will not let me down. One day I may wake up and realise who Shastriji really is.

Every evening, from 7pm to 9pm, Shastriji would recite Ramayana, as it is in the holy book, without mixing or diluting the script or the atmosphere with his own comment, jokes or bhajans (devotional songs) that most other preachers prefer to do.

This was a pure Ramayana, as written by sage Valmiki, some ten thousand years ago, without alteration, addition or deviation.

After performing the arti, a short prayer to mark the end of the session, when most of the audience has left, he sang bhajans for the benefit of few of us who were more interested in listening to his bhajans than the main episode, the reciting of Ramayana.

The bhajans that Shastriji recited, sang with devotion, were the type I appreciated most, that of Meerabai, Sant Kabir, Kavi Pradeepji and the old traditional ones of Lord Krishna that has stood the test of time, remain popular for the last few hundred years.

I felt Shastriji had a soft corner for me, as he would, without fail, sing my request. Some how he knew what type of bhajans I like. May be it was my imagination, as I was crazy about Shastriji's bhajans.

Every one who listened to his bhajans, in his deep, heavy but sweet and authoritative voice, not too dissimilar to my favourite Indian playback singer S.D. Burman and Mukeshji, which he sang with emotion and dedication, conveying the pain, recreating the atmosphere the composer would have encountered, when writing these bhajans hundreds of years ago.

We all felt that if Shastriji had lent his voice to film industry, he would have rivalled Mukeshji and made a name for himself. But he had no desire for fame, money or position in life, in the society. Perhaps one person with whom he would have shared his life, his success, may have betrayed his love, his trust and left him with broken heart. After all such talent, such devotion usually is the result of a sad event, betrayal in love, in real life. It seems Shastriji was a classic example.

As today was the last day, I had brought my tape recorder with me. I wanted to tape Shastriji's bhajans, as a reminder of this occasion, nine wonderful days in the life of the town folks, who do not experience much excitement in their dull and routine life.

When arti was finished, I asked Shastriji for his permission to tape the bhajans. He smiled and readily agreed to my request. When bhajans were over, I gathered my tape recorder and seek Shastriji's permission to leave.

Stopping me with a mischievous smile on his face, he said, "Nayanbhai, would you not let me hear my own bhajans?"

He talked to me in such a familiar way, as if we have known each other for a very long time. I rewind the tape and pressed the play button. My joy turned into sadness, as the recording conveyed more noise from the audience than the bhajans I wanted to tape.

I felt disappointed and the sadness was clearly visible on my face. Looking at me, Shastriji knew how disappointed I was.

He said in a casual voice, "Nayanbhai, let us go to my flat. I have some cassettes professionally taped. If you like them, they will be my present to you."

There was sweet but mischievous smile on Shastriji's face, a familiarity, warmth in every word he said. I was surprised, confused but felt privileged. Not only Shastriji knew my name but spoke to me as if we have known each other for a long time. Perhaps it was not my imagination when I felt I knew Shastriji well.

Shastriji, with his entourage, was staying in a flat, in the temple's ground. The town folk had built a modern and very comfortable Dharamsala (guest house) with a couple of VIP flats, with en suite bathroom and a balcony, built with the money donated by NRIs, as most of us had our children settled in USA, Canada and Britain.

Within five minutes, we were at the flat. I took a seat and Shastriji sat in front of me. Before I could say any thing, Shastriji said, "Nayanbhai, don't you recognize me?"

I took a long, deep breath but however hard I tried, I could not remember where and when I may have met Shastriji.

Not keeping me in suspense any longer, Shastriji said in his usual, kind voice, "Nayanbhai, I am not surprised that you could not recognize me. I left Palanpur some thirty five years ago. This beard, bhagwa clothes and heavy body, I would not be surprised even if my own parents could not recognize me. But Nayan, you know there was a time when a day would not pass by without us meeting, usually in your house, especially in the evenings and at weekends."

ANAND .... I cried out loudly and we both got up and hug each other. Tears were flowing uncontrollably from our eyes, especially from mine.

Shastriji, who made us cry every day, was himself crying but these were the tears of joy. After few minutes, when we reconciled ourselves, we started talking. There was a lot to talk about, accumulated over thirty five years of unplanned, painful separation.

By the time we ran out of topic of conversation, it was dawn. On Anand's request, I slept on the comfortable sofa bed. When I closed my eyes, my past came alive, as if I was watching it on a cinema screen.

Anand was my childhood friend. We were like twins, inseparable. After passing our matric (form 4) examination, we went to college in Rajkot, as there was no facility for further education in Palanpur. We used to leave our small town at day break, by bus and return late in the evening.

It was a long and tiring journey but full of youth jubilation, mischief and euphoria. After a year, Anand got a place in the college hostel. So he settled down in Rajkot but we used to meet without fail in the college and at weekends.

Anand had lost his mother when he was only ten years old. His father got married again, within one year of her death, even before her ashes were cold. Thus Anand lost the love of both of his parents, within a very short time. Anand could not get along with his young, beautiful but authoritative step mother. So he used to spend most of his time with friends, especially with me and at the Radha Krishna temple.

With his mild, obliging nature and work ethic, Anand was welcomed in our homes. But he used to prefer spending every spare minute in the temple, on the outskirt of Palanpur.

The temple's Pujari (priest) was Premjibhai, a kind and a considerate person. His son Manu was of the same age as us, living in the temple's quarter. The temple had a vast compound, a ten acre plot with cluster of mature fruit trees, which include mangos, guava, coconuts, eucalyptus, whistling pine, babul, bamboo, banyan, birch, cedar, conifer, flame tree, papal, almond and many more.

Premjibhai, by profession, was a farmer with vast knowledge of forestry. He created a flower garden, a Vrindavan, Lord Krishna's favourite place, with our help and hard work. This garden was Anand's favourite place, as it was, more or less his creation, planting beautiful flowers of all colour, size and shape.

The flowers that Anand prefer were African and French marigold, periwinkle, camomile, daisy, jasmine, michelia (champo), pink rose (Karan) Oleander and water lilies, deep or purple red, snow white and sky blue in colour, in the vast and deep pond, which was a nature's creation, was there even before the temple was built, fed by the under current.

Although the climate was not suitable for roses, Anand had managed to create a small rose garden, with sheer hard work, dedication and knowledge of plants, creating a natural shade to protect the rose bush from the heat of the mid-day sun. Gardening was his passion, his hobby, his enjoyment in life.

Our hard work also provided a perfect heaven for birds, butterflies and insects. In a way this place was a refuge for tortured souls, lonely hearts and a heaven on earth for the rest.

In the evening, four of us, Anand, Bina, Varsha and me, used to get together at my home or at the temple, without fail. As our four families were close, even in a small town like Palanpur, our friendship was not open to question or would set tongues waging.

Bina, whose real name was Bansri but we all call her Bina, was the only child of Sheth Shantilal and Sarlaben. Anand and Bina were close friends. They were both outgoing persons. They liked sports and share the same interest and hobbies, like acting in school plays and dramas. They both had sweet voice and hardly any function can materialize without their active participation.

On the other hand Varsha, like me was a quiet and some what reserved person. We used to go on a college picnics and participate in sports, on the insistence of Anand and Bina. But compared to them, we were a docile couple, although I was good at writing poems, plays and short stories, which were in demand for the college magazine as well as local papers and periodicals. Varsha was good at painting and beauty therapy, the usual ladies hobbies and interest.

Even when Anand moved to college hostel, there was no ebb in our friendship. We were not able to meet in the evenings like before but we always got together at weekends and in holidays.

Our friendship blossomed until we finished college education. On acquiring B.Com. Degree, I joined the local bank while Anand became a school teacher, after passing his BA exams. In a small town like Palanpur, there was not much choice on the job front. It was school, bank or the local government that provided desirable and secure jobs.

Bina and Varsha were now talented, young, physically attractive, matured women. It was no longer possible to meet each other so openly in the town. But our friendship, especially mine and Varsha's grew stronger and our innocent childhood friendship inevitably turned into a physical attraction, a love match.

We used to meet outside the town, at a lonely place or in the vast temple compound, for a cuddle and comfort, plan our future, chart the course of life and lost in our own, make believe world. Without any doubt, these were the happiest days of our lives.

I made good progress in my job, especially after passing my Charted Institute of Bankers examination, acquiring the right to put MCIB after my name. Our two families were more than happy to let us join in holy matrimony.

Our wedding day was one of the happiest occasions for all of us. Our childhood friendship, our young love came to a fitting and a happy end.

Unfortunately, Anand and Bina's friendship, which was full of twist and turn, took a wrong path. Bina was the only daughter of a respectable and wealthy family. After acquiring her BA, she stayed on at the college to do her Masters.

Bina's parents were not keen on Anand. His teacher's job would not put Anand on the pinnacle of social ladder, nor would he be able to keep Bina in comfort she was accustomed to.

Moreover the atmosphere in Anand's house was always stressful. The clashes with her step mother, his half brother and sister were a taking point in a small town like Palanpur.

But for Anand, Bina was the only bright spot, only hope in his tortured life. She was his heart and soul, his future happiness, the only ray of sunshine in his topsy-turvy life. Anand was deeply in love with Bina. He was trying to seek the affection, companionship and love from Bina that he was denied, could not find from his own family.

But this ray of hope extinguished rapidly when Bina joined MA classes and was offered a place in the college hostel. Moreover Bina found Anand's love, attention and attentiveness a hindrance to her free spirit. Bina, being the only child, was brought up in the lap of luxury where her every wish, her every whim was attended to without any question.

Bina started spending more and more time in Rajkot, with her new class mates of equal status, rich, influential and social climber. The unthinkable, what I and Varsha were afraid off, even dreading to think, happened.

After completing her Masters, Bina got engaged to Parash, the only son of the famous surgeon Dr. Raj Mehta. Within three months, Bina got married and left Palanpur for good. Her wedding was an event of the decade. Bina and Parash were the only heir apparent to their family fortunes.

No wonder their wedding was the event of the century for a small town like Palanpur. Their parents made sure that no expense was too much for the wedding feast. The whole town was invited and the festival lasted a week.

While the whole town was celebrating this auspicious occasion, Anand's life was in turmoil. His dream turned into a nightmare. The only light, the spark in his life was now extinguished, never to reignite again. It was practically impossible for any one, including me and Varsha, to imagine Anand's heartbreak, his agony and his shattered dreams.

Anand avoided us all; spend most of his time at the temple, in the company of the temple priest, Premji Maharaj (priest) and his son Manu, tending the Rose garden or playing his favourite musical instrument flute. But alas, our Krishna had lost his Radha. She was not there to praise, appreciate his talent.

I knew what Anand was going through and was worried what effect this sad and tragic event would have on his life. After all we were childhood friends. But however hard I tried, begged him and the God is my witness, he would not confide in me, let me share his pain or for that matter any one else.

He avoided us all, may be afraid of breaking down in front of us. Anand, if anything, was as strong as it comes. I have never seen him cry or shed a tear, except when his mother passed away. He would bottle up his feelings, his emotion and retreat into a cocoon of silence, solitude and self recrimination.

At the time Bina was getting married, Swami Devanandji's sangha, caravan, was passing through the town. At any other time, this would have been a major event in the life of the town folk but not this time.

For three days, Swamiji entertained the town folk with his pravachan (teachings), on Gita, on the life of Lord Rama and Lord Krishna. The conversation between Arjun and Lord Krishna when on the battlefield, Arjun's reluctance to fire the first shot at his opponents who were all his relatives, close friends and his elders like Bhishma, Karna and Acharya (guru) Dronacharya, was and still is legendary. This is Hinduism at its best, the most sophisticated culture in the human history.

How can he fire a shot, release his arrow that may kill Bhishma Pita, a fatherly figure under whose guidance, love and encouragement they all grew, matured and became fine, feared warriors. Bhishma was the noblest human being that ever graced this planet. Arjun would rather sacrifice his own life than take his. Would he ever forgive himself if his arrow penetrates Bhishma's heart?

Swamiji put forward Lord Krishna's argument, his words of wisdom, in such a forceful and convincing manner that every one in the sparse audience was as convinced as Arjun, when he raised his dhanus (bow) and fired the first shot, in the most destructive war the world has ever seen, experienced. It was a nuclear holocaust.

Swamiji was a God sent gift for Anand. He was at his side from the beginning. He sang bhajans and accompanied Swamiji on tabla (Indian musical instrument, like drum) throughout his programme.

Anand, rejected by his sweetheart Bina, and his parents, sought salvation and comfort under the shade of the Sangh which was always looking for young recruits, especially educated and talented ones, so often disappointed, rejected people like Anand.

When Swamiji left Palanpur, Anand joined them. He left us, his job, family and his place of birth, without a word to any one. He cut off his relations with the town, at a stroke and no one was the wiser.

I was very hurt that Anand did not even confide in me. I had tried my best to comfort him, share his pain but he did not let me near him. But how can I blame Anand? Every one he trusted, loved or depended upon, betrayed him and deserted him in his hour of need. None of his cloud had a silver lining. There was no pot of gold at the end of the rainbow. All the Greeks who came to him bearing gifts, turned out to be Trojan Horses.

Anand found the home for his talent, true happiness, appreciation and understanding in the company of Swami Devanandji and his sangh, the happiness that eluded him in life, in sansar. Anand soon became Swamiji's favourite disciple, his right hand person.

Anand devoted all his energy, his entire life to Swamiji's cause and soon captured the heart and soul of every member of the sangh, numbering over one hundred devotees. As there were not that many well educated members of

Anand's calibre, Swamiji took Anand under his wing and made him his heir apparent.

As we say, time is the best medicine for healing painful wounds. So in a couple of year's time, every one in Palanpur forgot Anand and he in turn, never made any attempt to get in touch with any of us.

Now today, after some thirty five years, my best friend Anand was standing in front of me, as a swami, dressed in bhagwa lebas, holy clothes. No wonder I could not recognize him.

Even his own father and mother would have failed to recognize him, had they been alive. No one from the town's population even had inkling about Swamiji's identity, that this Swamiji is the son of the town's prominent resident Bipinbhai, perhaps with the exception of one person, which was me. I always had inkling that I have met Swamiji before but heart's familiarity did not extend to the brain.

Throughout his nine day stay, Anand had not raised his eyes or looked at any one with interest or acknowledgement. His step brother and sister, as well as life long love Bina were in the audience. But he ignored every one of us.

Anand found the love, happiness and contentment in the vicinity of Swamiji, the happiness that eluded him in sansar. Anand became his favourite pupil and within five years, working fifteen hours a day, Anand mastered Ramayana, Mahabharata and Bhagwat Gita.

Anand's voice was even sweeter and authoritative yet full of emotion than that of Swamiji. Life's tragedies, like Lord Rama's Vanvas (banishment), Kuvarbai's Mameru, Arjun's reluctance to fight his elders, family's betrayal and failure in love, when recited by Anand, were more tragic and penetrative. It kept the audience spell bound and even Swamiji's eyes used to get wet, shed a tear or two, along with every one else's in the vast audience.

Some ten years ago, Swamiji passed away. Anand was his heir apparent and was unanimously elected to take his place. Anand could not let down the Sangh members or the Swamiji's wishes who had taken him under his wing and gave him a purpose in life, a reason to live when he was down and almost out.

Anand reluctantly accepted the responsibility of leading the Sangha and acquired the name of Swami Akhandanandji. This was the life story of my childhood friend Anand.

I began to summarize my own life. Anand had done his duty, his kartaya. (Obligation) His mission in life was fulfilled. He obtained his moksh (enlightenment) and was ready to meet his creator. But what have I achieved in life?

I must admit I had lived a relatively contented and happy life with Varsha, whose kind and considerate nature, her devotion and love for me, had kept stress and unpleasantness out of our sansar. (Family life) She also gave me two beautiful children, son Mayank and daughter Mansi.

Mayank, after qualifying as a doctor, passed his entrance exam for America and went to New York for permanent settlement. Mansi followed him. They are now happily married and well settled in America.

Five years ago, Varsha left me, after a short illness. Her departure shattered me, turned my life upside down. I was completely lost without her. We were together from childhood. I had never imagined life without Varsha. She was the reason for my existence. In many ways I was a broken man, a soul lost in the maze, in the labyrinth.

After Anand's sudden departure, Varsha was, besides being my wife, also my best friend. We were a couple in a million. Today I am all alone in Palanpur. There is no one I can really call my own in this town, my birth place, although I am surrounded by familiar faces.

I feel I am in a desert, in an oasis of unfamiliar familiarity. I made up my mind. There was nothing here to keep me, to bind me to Palanpur. It was time to bid farewell to Palanpur, the place of my birth and once again to join the world of my childhood friend Anand.

So, when Anand came at mid-day to say goodbye, I was ready, with my small suitcase packed, to bid farewell to my beloved Palanpur. I left the town like Anand, without saying a word to any one. Like Anand, I cut off my link with Palanpur, at a stroke, without informing a soul.

On reaching the outskirt of Palanpur, Anand gave me a fist full of earth and said, "Nayan, keep this earth in a safe place. This may prove to be the last link with your beloved Palanpur. I set foot in Palanpur after thirty five years. Don't be surprised if we never set a foot here again.

I have never forgotten your love or your friendship. Deep down in my heart, I had a wish to meet you, for the last time, before I make my peace with my creator.

I knew I had hurt your feelings by not confiding in you when Bina deserted me. It was not your fault. In fact no one could have done more than you and Varsha to cheer me up try to share my pain but I had no strength, no desire to confront my problem.

I was down and angry with the world. I felt I was dealt a rotten hand; everyone was kicking me when I was down. I asked the question, why me, a thousand times.

Swamiji gave me a choice. He threw a lifeline to a sinking man, offered me an escape route which I readily accepted. Perhaps this was the best decision I ever made, even though it was made in anger, on the spur of the moment. I had a wonderful life; the best years of my life were with the Sangha.

To atone my one mistake of hurting your feelings, I accepted the invitation of reciting Ramayana in Palanpur, hoping to meet you and say how sorry I am for not confiding in you when I was leaving Palanpur. But I never thought for a moment that when I leave, you my best friend will accompany me.

Nayan, you have to visit so many places, go on a pilgrimage to Kashi, Amarnath and Man Sarover in Tibet. We are not spring chicken any more. There is so much to do in such a short time. So do not expect to see your beloved town, your birth place again.

I gave the last glance to Palanpur, the place where I had spent sixty happy years. My beloved Varsha's ashes were scattered in the temple garden, created by Anand, where my two children were born.

My heart was heavy with emotion. I knew I would never have left Palanpur if my beloved Varsha was still with me. But after her sudden departure, my life had no meaning. Palanpur had lost her charm. I was sure my Varsha would have approved this decision of mine. She would indeed be happy that I was once again united with my friend, my soul mate Anand.

My eyes were shedding tears by a bucketful. My heart was in turmoil, leaden with emotion but I was not sure whether the tears were of sadness, as I was leaving behind my friends or they were tears of joy, as I was going to spend the rest of my life in the service of the Lord who gave me this opportunity to do some thing useful for the humanity at large.

Only the time will tell whether I made a mistake or took the right decision.

****

TIME MACHINE

I was trying to do my home work, a project on "Stone age people." But some how I was not making any progress. May be this new house we just moved in recently did not make me feel at home.

Our new home, actually it is more than seventy years old, is situated in a sought after, prestigious area of Barnet, just off the famous Bishop Avenue, a millionaire's row, if ever there was one.

It is a magnificent six bedroom, detached property, built on a vast, three acre plot, with a large, well stocked garden, a pond and a tree corner, with Oak, Sycamore, Pine and Silver Birch trees, our own mini forest and a bird sanctuary.

My parents are a devoted naturalist. So our garden has always been a heaven for wildlife and indigenous flora and fauna. The trees were full of artificial, wooden bird nests, ready made homes for sparrows, black birds, robins, starlings and kites. But small enough to keep big destructive birds like wood pigeons, sea gulls and crows out of this beautiful natural habitat for the wildlife.

As I was not making any headway, I decided to explore the large attic, hoping to find some old books, pictures or any items that may help me with my project. I knew from my dad that the vendor had left the junk in the attic, untouched for a very long time. Who knows, it may turn out to be Aladdin's Cave after all.

My mum was going out shopping to West End with her sister. They loved shopping, especially window shopping. So I knew this will give me at least four to six hours of undisturbed browsing time, to go through every item in the loft.

As this was my new school, I was hoping to make a good impression, not only with my teachers but also with my project partner, a tiny, pretty, petit girl with a lovely name Chelsea, the name of my favourite football club.

That is why, on such a warm, lovely Saturday morning, I was rummaging in the old cardboard boxes, expecting to find what, I had absolutely no idea.

As I moved some boxes and a big screen, I saw a big object covered by dust sheet. When I removed these covers, I was staring at what could be loosely described as TIME MACHINE. May be last used by Dr. Who, who else?

I looked at it with curiosity and anticipation. I opened the door and sat down in the cockpit, facing a panel board full of multi-coloured buttons. There was a key in the ignition but I failed to get any life. I got out to see if there is any battery but I saw an electric wire with a plug. I plugged it in and switched it on.

When I returned to the cockpit and turned on the ignition, all lights started flashing. I stood or rather sat there gasping at this wonderful toy, perhaps a toy more suitable to elders. It was some thing, some gadget like out of the movie, "Back to Future"

There were buttons every where. Some were labelled with periods and important events in the history of the world. There was Roman Empire, Alexander the Great, Lord Rama, Krishna, Buddha and Jesus Christ and the crucifixion, Julius Caesar, Mahabharat, and Napoleoniac war, Intergalactic travel and Stone, Iron and Bronze Age.

I was excelled with joy and without thinking of the consequences, I pressed the button marked "Stone age." On the ceiling of the machine which I would like to call Budgiecoptor, all hell broke lose. Lights started flashing and ear piercing noise made me close my eyes and cover my ears. The machine started whizzing round and round in circles, gaining speed and creating weightlessness, as if escaping the earth gravity. It was unbelievable, unreal.

The flashing lights and ear piercing noise made me close my eyes, as the machine gained momentum, impetus and power. It may have lasted less than a couple of minutes but it seemed a long time. When the noise stopped, I slowly opened my eyes but the bright sunlight was too much to take in.

I closed my eyes again and waited few minutes before opening them again. But this time very slowly indeed, a little bit of a peep at a time.

The Budgiecoptor had landed with a thud in the middle of no where. The landscape was like a lunar surface, covered with volcanic rocks and dust, completely devoid of any vegetation.

It reminded me of my holidays in Tenerife, particularly the excursion we undertook to Mount Teide, an extinct volcanic crater covered with rocks of every shape, size, dimension and description, containing metals like iron, zinc, silver and magnesium, in tiny proportion, not worth commercial exploitation.

The land was flat as far as eyes could see, on three sides but in the West, looking deceptively near, I could see a mountain range. Some peaks were covered with snow. It was a magnificent view.

While I was digesting this beautiful scenery and enjoying the sun and the open space, having come out of a crampy cockpit, I saw some people, men women and children. They were dwarfs, pygmies. No one was more than four feet tall.

At first I wondered why. But then I remembered that even some two hundred years ago, the average height of British people was just above five feet, compared to our average height of six feet, among men. Going back perhaps one hundred thousand years, four feet seems reasonable.

When they came near, I could see that they were Stone Age people, wearing practically next to nothing. Women looked like Rachel Welsh in the movie A Million Years BC wearing the tiniest bikini, actually an animal skin loosely wrapped round their waist line but otherwise topless and men looked like mini Tarzans with loin cloths wrapped around their waist.

Children were completely naked, so were old men and women. It seemed the animal skin was in short supply. So only young men and women were wearing them. Could it be out of modesty or there could be some more rational explanation?

"Hallo, my name is Rishi." I said with as much dignity as I could muster. The situation could not get any weirder. I pinched myself to make sure I was not dreaming.

"Welcome to our land." Uttered one man who seemed to be the leader of the group of some fifty people in all. They were actually speaking a very primitive language which sounded like English but could be any primitive language, mixture of Greek, Latin and English. I was able to pick up a few words. They were using peculiar animal noise and sign language more than words, as the vocabulary was very limited.

I extended my hand in a friendly gesture with a big smile but there was no response except the briefest of a smile. Finally I said "I have come to see you and how you live."

"Come, our settlement is just beyond those mountains." I climbed into a cart or a barrow, without wheels but a sledge like smooth under surface, drawn by an animal that looked like a big goat. There were only a few of these carts, for old people and children. The young ones walked and ran.

We started moving towards the mountain. It must have been a very tiring walk. The sun was breathing down on us and the land was littered with rocks but there were paths covered with sand which may be regularly used by these people.

There was primitive vegetation of coarse grass and moss was visible. We also passed an oasis, having an underground supply of water, with small palm like trees, desert thickets and coarse grass where strange camel and goats were grazing on the rich grass.

The oasis was inhabited by pygmies who greeted us with enthusiasm, gave us water to drink and fruits to eat. After a long and tiring track, we came to the base of the mountain. Some more pygmies joined us as we entered a long and narrow cave, the entrance was well guarded with trap doors, pitfalls and fire traps. It would be difficult for any one to enter the cave without the knowledge of these obstacles. It was a primitive but never the less a genius work of engineering.

This was our night camp. A fire was lit. They cooked some vegetables, something resembling to potato, cassava, carrot and cabbage. It was served with a strange tasting meat, on a rough wooden plate and a hollow stone beaker to drink water from.

After the meal, I fell asleep, ahead of them, as I was so tired, even though I had hardly done any walking. These pigmies were hardened people. The bed was made of straw with birds' feathers to make it bearable. I was so tired that I could have slept on a bed of nail without a murmur.

In the morning, the noise of the children woke me up. It was bright and warm. I got up and wandered around but the cave was practically deserted with the exception of children and few old women.

Around midday, the gang returned. We gathered the few possessions we had and made a hasty retreat. The pygmies were in an excitable state, talking to each other, mainly in sign language and gestures only.

We travelled deeper in the cave which was curving like a snake. Some times the ceiling was so low that we had to walk on all fours to avoid the bump. The dark passages were navigated under the light of burning straw torch. After walking, climbing and crawling for hours, we came to vast open land.

It seems we had crossed the mountain through the network of natural caves and men made tunnels. It was a magnificent journey, just like in the movie, "Journey to the centre of the earth" based on the novel by my favourite author Jules Verne.

We emerged from the semi darkness of the cave to a bright and extremely sunny atmosphere, without a cloud in the sky. In fact I was wondering whether the sky was permanently cloudless, as I had not seen a single cloud in the clear blue sky.

Emerging out of the cave, I was greeted with the most magnificent sight I am ever likely to see, even if I live to be hundred years old. Every where you see, there were mountains. We were on some kind of plateau, completely surrounded by high, snow bearing mountain peaks, resembling Alps in Switzerland and Austria. This reminded me of my holidays in Interlaken in Switzerland.

It seemed the only entrance may be through the narrow passage we had just navigated. It was like a heaven on earth, the monastery at Shangri La in central Tibet, surrounded by the most majestic Himalaya Mountains, as described in my favourite book, "The Lost Horizon" written by the popular author James Hilton.

The landscape was in complete contrast to what I saw on the other side of the mountain range. The climate was cooler and tolerable, especially for people like us who live in England, a much cooler place than tropics.

The land was green with water every where, small streams constantly fed by the melting snow. The plateau was alive with birds and small animals resembling rabbits and squirrels. The trees were of all shapes and sizes; some were loaded with fruits similar to our mangos, oranges, guava, apples and pomegranates, a strange mixture of tropical and temperate fauna and flora.

There were also some vegetables growing wild, cabbage, cucumber, radish, muli, aubergine, okra and Brussels sprouts. I do not know what was edible and what may be harmful. But Pygmies were knowledgeable and made the most of this free harvest, as meat was in short supply. We had a picnic type vegetarian lunch, a healthy diet indeed. No wonder these pygmies were super fit who could run a marathon on a daily basis.

Even in this paradise, pygmies were moving around with great care, not letting down their guard even for a moment. I soon found out why. I heard a scream, a warning of approaching danger. It came from the sky. A large, ugly, vulture like bird, some thing I have only seen in a movie like Jurassic Park and Lost World, swooped down from the clear sky.

Every one took cover but unfortunately a woman with a small baby was not quick enough to escape this vulture. It grabbed the tiny baby, like a kingfisher with a tiny fish in its beak and was gone in a flash.

There was nothing any one could do. We threw stones and sticks but to no avail. I thought of teaching these defenceless pygmies how to make nets and bows and arrows which would protect them from the menace that descended on them from the sky. But it would take a long time, even if we could find suitable materials for making nets.

Apparently for these pygmies, this was an every day occurrence. Soon every one went back to their normal routine. These were hardened people who deal with deaths every day. My dream of a paradise was shattered in a minute. As the night was approaching, we headed back to the safety of the cave.

Every one was in sombre mood. We had an early dinner, mainly fruits and vegetables. I had a strange root beer like drink, perhaps alcoholic. I fell a sleep practically as soon as I finished my dinner and the drink, although I was not that tired, just excited.

When I awoke, my real nightmare began. I felt as if I was under some oppressive or stupefying influence. I was in a giant cooking pot, carved out of a big stone, which was filled with water, which was getting hotter by the minute. I was also surrounded by big carrots and potatoes like vegetables found in abundance.

I was horrified. These friendly looking pygmies were in fact cannibals. I may already have eaten human flesh. The thought horrified me. I started praying, although I am not a very religious person. I cursed myself for not listening to my mother and visiting our Hare Krishna temple on a regular basis. Then most people only remember God when they are in trouble and I was no exception.

Suddenly a miracle happened. A tall, bearded man, in fact a giant, some seven feet tall, looking very much like Bhim, a gentle giant figure in our holy script of Mahabharata, who always come to the rescue of the old and infirm, holding a weapon which looked very similar to gada, a thick wooden or metal stick, some four feet long, with a big, round cone at the end, a favourite weapon of my hero Bhim.

He was shouting and cursing these pygmies, who at once kneeled as if praying to a Lord. He swung his weapon with all his might. The pot cracked with a loud bang. The gushing water extinguished the fire and threw me out with a force. I hit the ground with a thud. My head hit a sharp rock and I lost consciousness.

When I woke up, it was dark and cold. I was still in my attic. My Time Machine was flashing bright lights. I thought I had a nap and had a bad dream. Surely it can't be true. There is no time machine or is there?

Then I instinctively put my hand on my forehead to find out the cause of my pain. My hand got covered with blood, the wound I sustained when I was thrown out of the pot. Even before the shock could subside, I noticed that I was holding a greyish coloured carrot, the favourite food of pygmies. My cloths were soaking wet and I was shivering in the cold, damp atmosphere of the attic.

I quickly switched off the Time Machine and climbed down the ladder, in case I lose consciousness. I still have my Budgie copter in the attic, in case a reader wants to take a trip in the past or future. Just give me a ring?

I will always wonder how and why I was allowed to return, that is if I ever left the attic. It could be some sort of hallucination, a device that could turn an illusion, a wish and an intense desire into reality, in our sub consciousness mind. But somehow I doubt it. I never told this story, my strange experience to any one, not even to my parents, as no one is going to believe me. But it is needless to say that my assignment was widely acclaimed, came first, top of the class and my project partner Chelsea was most impressed. So in a way, it was an all round success, thanks to Time Machine!

****

HOW TO TRIUMPH OVER ADVERSITY

Going on a holiday for a disable person is a real challenge, but then life it self is a challenge in this fast changing world where human values are in the decline and the survival of the fittest is the norm.

Any challenge can be overcome, conquered and be victorious to a certain extent, even making the adversity work in your favour if you have courage, determination, foresight, imagination and especially an understanding partner but a bit of luck always goes a long way.

After all every cloud has a silver lining, although some times it may be invisible to all except to the most optimistic persons. It is important not to lose one's perspective, goal, purpose and ambition in life. That puts us the humans, one step above all other living creatures and makes our lives worth living.

We have been going on holidays for the last twenty years. In the beginning, in common with most hard working people, our holidays were modest, to Wales, Lake District, Devon and Cornwall, Isle of Weight and such other local destinations, for a week in summer, driving to a rented cottage in our old banger. But they were as enjoyable as any holidays we undertake today.

We used to go as a joint family, even our parents joining in, that gave them a quality time with their grand children. In fact these holidays, in a way, were more complete, more gratifying than the global trotting of later days when we were mostly on our own, although making friends with our fellow travellers was not that difficult for us.

As years went by, with rising income and reducing expenditure, as well as good luck on investment front, we were able to take several holidays a year, visiting far flung corners of the world, from Canada, USA to Kerala, Goa, Sri Lanka, Kenya and Tanzania, the land of our birth.

That gave us the opportunity to visit exciting places like Niagara Falls, Grand Canyon, Sailing eco friendly Kerala backwaters where you are cut off from the world and majestic Western Ghats with romantic hill stations like Munar and Ponmudi.

But above all the Ngorongoro Crater, the lost world of Africa, is our most cherished destination. It is a natural wonder on par with the Great Barrier Reef and Ayers Rock in Australian desert, not forgetting a gem of a destination on our own doorstep, such as the floating garden island of Madeira, still relatively safe from mass tourism.

Another fabulous island is the desert island of Formentera, yet undiscovered by the mass tourism and for that we thank the All Mighty, as these are our favourite destinations, that we visit again and again. But I wonder how long they will remain hidden from the hoards that descend on Spain and Portugal. Perhaps the present trend of travelling further and faster may leave these gems on our doorstep alone for us, the oldies to enjoy and cherish.

Formentera is a millionaire's paradise with shallow seas that surrounds the island, jammed with luxury yachts but the island is still within reach of ordinary people like us. It was and still is a favourite place for recluse, artists, painters and writers where my favourite and one of the most famous French adventure writers Jules Verne wrote most of his books, especially "The 20 Thousand League under the Sea" in 1870.

We visited the exact place, a high cliff with a sheer drop of some 600 feet, a favourite suicide spot for failed lovers who are unable to unite in this life and seek salvation, unity in heaven, where Jules Verne used to sit and gaze out to the vast open, endless sea, a desolate, an isolated place far removed from civilization with haunting aroma of loneliness and shrieks of sea gulls to break the death like silence.

It is still a real frontier outpost with less than a dozen houses and no one under the age of 70 among the residents, as if waiting for the final roll call.

But our wondering lust came to a sudden halt some years ago when Bhupendra went into hospital for a minor liver biopsy with a three hour stay in a day care ward, which due to a blunder by the doctor, ended in a major, life threatening emergency, a twenty two day stay in the hospital, undergoing a four hour long surgery with a loss of perfectly healthy gall bladder.

Every thing that could go wrong did go wrong. How he survived is a minor miracle and I feel our strong faith in our noble Hindu religion, especially Bhupendra's affinity with Lord Krishna, saved him in the end. Perhaps hope, faith and strong belief triumphed over failure, frustration and defeatism.

But this has changed his life, our lives for ever and beyond recognition. He is unable to leave the house for more than a couple of hours and that is also on a good day which are getting fewer and far in between as the time go by. So we have to make the most of our limited opportunities as and when we can.

Luckily he has his writing to keep his mind occupied. He has now become a prolific writer, writing some two to three pieces every week. It is possible, as he writes on all sorts of subjects, including poems, short stories and interviews with leading personalities, mainly politicians.

Exotic holidays to far flung corners of the world are no more than a dream now. He feels bitter that we missed out on destinations we always wanted to visit, that include Nepal, Singapore, Bali, New Zealand and crossing Canada from East to West by Transcontinental railway, passing through majestic, snow covered Rockies, breaking the journey for a day or two, to visit lakes, rivers and woodlands, beaming with wild life, one of the most beautiful place on earth and finally ending it with a cruise to Alaska, the last wilderness. Well, it will now remain a dream to be taken to the grave.

The only holidays that we can now take, that Bhupendra can endure, should be within three hour's flying time, to Spain, Portugal, France and such destinations. Even that involves taking special medication before hand and getting all the help from the airline and the tour operator.

That involves wheel chair assistance, boarding the plane by lift, special seating and quick taxi transfers. As we have been taking our holidays from the same tour operator for a very long time, we are their special clients and get a VIP treatment, all the assistance we need. It is heartening to know that there is still compassion left in the travel industry which is not so prevalent in other walks of life, especially if you suffer from a debilitating condition that is not so obvious at first look.

Before when we visited a new destination, we used to spend most of our time touring the place, meeting local people on their own turf, in their backyard, in their homes, fields and orchards, soaking the local culture and enjoying their hospitality in their own home.

Bhupendra even learnt to speak Spanish, the country we visit most, so that he can speak with the locals in their own tongue, which is very much appreciated in Spain. So often Bhupendra is told by the Spaniards that he is the only Englishmen they know who can speak Spanish?

We the Brits are considered to be lazy at learning other languages, as we expect others to speak English. But now he has to spend most of his time in and around hotel, on the beach, under a shade or beside a pool, reading and writing, with occasional half day excursions when Bhupendra is felling well.

We have just come back from our latest holiday to Ibiza and Formentera. In our Ibiza hotel, in the resort of Playa den Bossa, where we have stayed several times before and know most of the staff, we met Fabian, a barman and an old friend.

He is married to an English girl whom we would like to call by her Spanish name of Pillar, a very popular and holy Spanish name, similar to our English name Mary. She also works as a receptionist in the same hotel. They are a husband and wife team who have looked after us so often.

As we did not see Pillar for a couple of days, we enquired about her and were told by her tearful husband that she is off sick for the last two months, suffering from breast cancer. As Ibiza is a small place with limited medical facilities, serious cases are referred to Barcelona.

Some 65Km from Barcelona, in the mountains of Sierra del San Geronimo, there is a famous Christian holy place called Montserrat, on par with one of the holiest place in the Christian calendar, the village of Lourdes in South West France.

Montserrat is famous for the statue of Virgin Mary, known as the "The Black Madonna of Montserrat" with miraculous healing power. It is a wooden statue that has darkened a bit, as candles have been lit at her feet for hundreds of years. Now it is kept in a glass cage, with only her right hand extending outside so that we can hold it and make a wish.

We had been on a pilgrimage to this holy place in May 2004 and as Bhupendra wanted to write an article on Black Madonna, we were encouraged to go on this eight hour excursion by our friends in the hotel, providing us with all the facilities, such as a wheel chair and a sleeping berth on the coach. It was a minor miracle for Bhupendra to survive such an arduous and exhausting pilgrimage, as there was so much climbing to do, slopes and steps to negotiate. Looking back, it was most foolish thing to do but some times our hearts over-rules our minds and sanity goes out of the window.

As Pillar was going to Barcelona, we gave Fabian a copy of our article for her to read and to encourage her to visit Montserrat. After all she has nothing to lose. Pillar was so grateful and impressed with the story of Black Madonna of Montserrat that she invited us to their home.

One evening Fabian took us to their home to meet Pillar, to have a dinner and to say thank you. We felt guilty for imposing ourselves when she was so sick but it seems our visit may have been a tonic to her. She looked so cheerful when we left. I hope, with a bit of luck and the blessings of Virgin Mary, the Black Madonna of Montserrat, she will be cured and on her desk by the time we visit Ibiza again.

Such touching moment, hospitality, admiration and friendship we receive, sometimes from complete strangers make us feel that all the hard work Bhupendra puts in his writing, even when he is not so well, is worth the effort.

It brings us blessings and an uplifting and humble reward from God. This is our triumph in adversity, a silver lining to a black cloud that descended upon us on that fateful day in the hospital.

Well, what more we want from life except blessings and goodwill of people like Fabian and Pillar whom we meet once in a while but are like a family member whom we look forward to meet on our next visit.

****

BLACK MADONNA OF MONTSERRAT

Our experiences have made us realize that the best enjoyment, most memorable moments, enchanting or unforgettable events in our lives happen when least expected. It is just like falling in love without a warning, without a premonition.

One can not plan, instigate or choose the time and the person to fall in love. It just happens, so often when least expected. Otherwise we will all be marrying Ashwaria Rai, Rani Mukerjee, Karina Kapoor, Jacqueline Smith and pretty woman Jody Foster.

So when we booked our annual holiday to Costa Doroda, one of the most beautiful parts of Spain, we had no idea, no inclination that one of the most revered Christian holy place, "The Monastery of Montserrat with the famous statue of Virgin Mary, popularly known as The Black Madonna will be on our door-step.

Montserrat means a shorn off mountain and looking at the sheer cliffs surrounding Montserrat, one can understand why it is called Montserrat. Black Madonna is a patron saint of the people of Catalonia and is said to have a mystic healing power. Madonna is a beacon of hope and joy to millions of her worshippers among all faiths.

We only came to know that a visit to Montserrat is one of the excursions on offer when we attended the get together meeting on the next day of our arrival, a normal practice on a package or all inclusive holidays.

As we have lived happily and prosper in England, a Christian country, for the past thirty five years, we consider ourselves honorary Christians. The beauty of Hinduism is that we can be flexible and can accommodate, mingle with and even participate in the holy, religious rituals of other religions, especially Jainism, Sikhism, Buddhism and Christianity, without diluting our Hindu faith in any way. We feel at ease in any religious confinement and that is the greatness of our culture, our up-bringing and our noble, all accommodating Hindu religion.

The three most important holy places on the Christian calendar, at least for me, that we wanted to visit are, the Lourdes in South West France, again a world famous Christian shrine dedicated to St. Bernadette which has a reputation for miraculous cure, which we visited back in 1974.

Our second choice was The Basilica of Bom Jesus, in our favourite holiday destination of Goa which we visited in 1996. The basilica contains the tomb of St. Francis Xavier in a glass cabinet and is lowered for public worship every four years. To be present on this holy occasion with a million people who come from all four corners of the world, gathered outside to witness this miracle. This is an unforgettable experience difficult to describe. One has to be there to catch the spirit, the atmosphere and the rituals.

And now in 2004, we have fulfilled our last desire, to visit Montserrat and hold the hand of holy Madonna. Perhaps we left it last, as it is on our door-step and with all the globe trotting, we can now appreciate it better than at any other time in our life, as Montserrat is the centre for dissemination of culture.

The Excursion:

So the first excursion we booked was naturally to Montserrat. I was a bit apprehensive as the excursion was a whole day outing, lasting some ten hours and a bit exhausting, especially for me as I suffer from M.E or more commonly known as chronic fatigue.

The long steep walk and numerous steps would not help me but our rep, a lovely girl called June, when she learnt that I am a hobby journalist and would like to write a piece on Montserrat, assured me and even arranged for a wheel chair to be on the coach, in case it is needed.

But I should not have worried or harbour any reservation. With my unshakable faith in my noble, culturally rich, tolerant, progressive and peace loving Hindu religion, as well as faith in Christianity, which incorporates all the noble characters of Hinduism, besides having their own noble traditions, I should have known that I will come through this ordain with flying colours, with a bit of help from above, from Virgin Mary, The Black Madonna of Montserrat.

On The Road To Montserrat:

The coach arrived outside our Donaire Park hotel at 7am. After collecting passengers from several pick-up points in and around La Pineda, we were on our way to Montserrat by 8am taking the coastal highway, passing by the coastal resorts of Cambrils, Salau and Tarragona, the ancient capital of Spain and still a thriving city with numerous historical sights worth a visit, that include amphitheatre and Roman ruins dating back 2000 years.

Our guide was a lovely young and beautiful Catalan girl named Pillar, a very popular Spanish name. It seems every other girl is called Pillar in Spain.

She was a walking encyclopaedia and like most guides, she loved to listen to her own voice. I must admit her voice was sweet and sensual and as she had lived in London for few years, she spoke perfect English.

When she saw me taking notes and when I introduced myself in perfect Spanish, may be not so perfect, I instantly became her favourite disciple, most favoured passenger on the coach, allowed to ask any question, on any subject, although my favourite subject was Montserrat throughout.

Pillar even had a good sense of humour. She told us her favourite comedy programme in London was Faulty Towers and she introduced the coach driver as Manual from Barcelona?

The History and Evolution That Created Montserrat:

The area of Montserrat was part of the Mediterranean Sea some 25 million years ago. Gradually the sea retreated, dried up and rock formation was created, so often accompanied by volcanic eruption and violent earthquakes, which was an every day occurrence in the beginning. The present day Montserrat is a long process of evolution, perhaps a minor miracle for Virgin Mary?

The incomparable mountain of Montserrat is unique in the world, in its particular silhouette and formation and stands some fifty kilometres from Barcelona, the most beautiful city in Spain, if not in Europe.

As Montserrat is practically on the French door-step, it has a troubled history. Our guide Pillar, a Catalan patriot, did not mixed words when she narrated history. She described in detail how French army, under Napoleon Bonaparte, the Emperor of France who introduced centralised despotism and ruled France with an iron fist, destroyed Montserrat more than once and converted the buildings into a military fortress.

Montserrat is perched on a precipice with a bird's eye view of the plain below and can be easily defended from the rampant, patriotic Catalans who hated French. The French army vandalised the monastery and destroyed not only the monastic life but destroyed and looted the artwork; ancient treasure and burnt thousands of books, along with the library buildings. French destroyed in just two months that has taken centuries to built. It was a mindless, thuggish and unwarranted act of vandalism akin to the rule of Attila the Hun.

The statue of Black Madonna which has been carved out of Oak wood was taken to Barcelona for safe keeping. It took another thirty two years to rebuild Montserrat which became an abode of monks who were erudite historians, physicists, students of science, music and philosophy.

The popularity of Montserrat, the culmination of this period of splendour for the holy place was reflected into the construction of new monastery buildings to accommodate the growing demand from the modern day pilgrims.

Being a Hindu, I know that no Hindu king would ever destroy a Hindu temple, a Hindu place of pilgrimage where other Hindus worship. There are so many sects in Hinduism, worshipping different deity but there is no conflict what so ever between them. So I was at a loss to understand why a Catholic king of France would destroy another Catholic place of worship where Catalans pray.

So when I asked this question to Pillar, she had no logical answer, an acceptable explanation except that Napoleon was not a religious person and the military conquest was more important to him than religious sentiment.

Moreover it was the character, the requirement and the tradition of the time when colonisation was a byword for progress.

Nearing Montserrat:

By 10am we were within the striking distance of St. Jerome Mountain and the mass of sandstones and conglomerate rocks with a serrated spine rising to some four thousand feet above the surrounding plane.

This is where Montserrat is located. The last half an hour's drive took us through turning and twisting narrow roads with breathtaking scenery, deep valley on one side and steep rock-face on the other. Fast flowing tiny rivers and picturesque chocolate box hamlets that look so enchanting from a high vantage point.

Where the land was not cultivated, the valley and the mountain slopes were covered with Alpine pine, ash, birch and maple trees. As we go higher, the vegetation became richer, varied and dense. I wonder what animal life cohabit these mountains.

Our guide Pillar pointed to various rock formations that resemble to a monkey, a gorilla, a maid and a bull. If one has a varied imagination and some faith, then it is not impossible for you to see a rock formation resembling our favourite God, May that be Lord Krishna or Lord Rama.

In my case I saw Lord Krishna in a rocky Vrindavan. Perhaps I was the only one to see an image of my favourite God Lord Krishna among all those rock formations. Well, if it provides solace, comfort and alleviation, then why not?

In Montserrat:

Our coach was in its parking slot by 11am. There is a long walk from the car park to the Montserrat Complex. As we were going to spend some four hours here, our pace was leisurely. We were lucky that our guide Pillar accompanied us throughout and continued to give us the benefit of her immense knowledge of the area.

The roads, lanes and foot-path surrounding Montserrat have existed ever since the mountains were inhabited by humans dating back some two thousand years, around the time Lord Jesus was born.

But Montserrat became a holy place, a spiritual centre for Christianity when a monastery and a basilica were completed in 1592, although the foundation of the faith was laid back in 1025AD.

The basilica is the home of La Marc De Dev, the mother of God. It is a small wooden statue no more than five feet high, blackened by the smoke of millions of candles lit at her feet over the centuries.

That is why it is known as The Black Madonna of Montserrat. The statue is kept in a glass cabinet but her right hand is outside the cabinet so that a pilgrim can hold her hand and make a wish, in the privacy of a tiny cabin that can accommodate only one person at a time.

It is said that if you are sincere and have faith, your wishes may be granted; your dreams may become a reality. That is why so many sick, disabled and disappointed pilgrims make this pilgrimage. It is famed of rumours that include cures for the sick and dying. Some pilgrims have been so impressed that they abandoned their worldly possessions, gave it all to the Montserrat and went there to live, devoting the rest of their lives to Virgin Mary and to serve humanity.

By the time we reached basilica, there were already 200 people in the queue, which means a waiting time of over three hours, even if each pilgrim takes only a minute to pray at the foot of Black Madonna. Fortunately our wheel chair and people with crutches gained us an instant entry.

It was an emotional moment for me when I hold the hand of Black Madonna, prayed and made a wish, although I would not like to disclose what my wish was and to what extent it was fulfilled. The fact that I have faith is my reward and the fact that I was able to undertake and complete this gruelling and extremely exhausting excursion without any ill-effect was a minor miracle in itself. I feel that I was blessed by Virgin Mary, the Black Madonna of Montserrat.

Even today one can light a candle, not at the foot of Madonna but a few feet away, in a basement room, where hundreds of candles are laid out, along with postcards and such other items for the use of pilgrims, with a suggested price list and a donation box.

While in the basement, I met a young, tiny and beautiful Afro American girl named Monica, who had converted to Buddhism and taken up the name of Meera.

She was very intelligent, charming and a highly educated person, with a PhD in Economics, working as a professor in one of the Deep South Universities.

It was her routine to visit every year, Lumbini in Nepal, Lord Buddha's birthplace and Buddh Gaya in Bihar, Bharat where Lord Buddha became enlightened while meditating under a banyan tree and of course Montserrat where she feels at peace with herself and the world. She was on her own.

It was a chance meeting, as we were the only non white pilgrims in the sea of humanity. My curiosity to know her overcame my shyness and when she realised that, like her we were non Christians, she was as eager to know about us as I was about her. But alas! We had only twenty minutes together before we had to Part Company. Who knows, one day we may meet again, as she visits Montserrat every year.

After lighting the candle, we came out from the back door. By now I was dying to know more about the statue of Black Madonna and Pillar obliged me with the following story:

The statue was carved by St. Luke and brought to the region by St. Peter. When Moors landed in Spain in the 8th centaury, the statue was hidden in what is now called Santa Cove (Holy Cave) when discovered in AD 880, it could not be moved. A shrine and a chapel were built to give her a permanent place, that is until AD 976 when Benedictine Monastery was established which has now become an influential centre of culture and religious activities par excellence, with donations pouring in from all over the world.

The Complex, which is being extended and improved regularly, has an accommodation for 300 resident monks and their visitors. There is also a hostel, shops, restaurants and other modern comforts that the present day pilgrims need and expect.

La Escolania Choir:

After the reopening of the monastery, the music school did not function until the arrival of Father Gozman who was responsible for the reconstruction and restoring the fortune of the music school.

The monastery is also the home of thirty young boys who sing in the Boys Choir known as La Escolania Sings.

It is a privilege and an honour to listen to these boys who are not only so talented at music but are the best brain in the region. Most of these boys go on to climb great heights and make themselves famous in different walks of life.

May be the Monastic discipline and the holy atmosphere is responsible for their progress in life, not forgetting the blessings of Virgin Mary, the Black Madonna of Montserrat. It is no wonder that a place on the choir is most sought after and so often accompanied by a large donation to the monastery?

The Library and the Museum:

The library, with some two hundred thousand books, some older than the monastery it self, is the hub of activities for the young residents. The walls of the museum and the art gallery are tastefully decorated with the works of Caravaggio, El Greco and other great artists, past and present. The painting by L. Limona depicting the adoration of Catalonia for La Morenta, the Black Virgin of Montserrat is in itself worth a visit.

It is a wonderful recovery in the prosperity and popularity for a monastery that was so often looted and destroyed, community dispersed and the sanctuary abandoned. It is the reputation of Black Madonna's healing power and the attraction of the monastic life in an ideal location that has restored the reputation and the popularity of Montserrat. It is indeed a Sangri La of the Christian faith that even the mighty Napoleon failed to destroy, one of the most destructive force in the European history.

Montserrat is more than a mere mountain. It is the spirit, the soul and heart of the Catalan people. Now Montserrat, just fifty kilometres away, can be reached by train from Barcelona. It is also possible to spend a few days in the comfortable hostel and young couples even come here to get married and spend their honeymoon. It is said that a marriage blessed by the Black Madonna rarely ends up in divorce? This in it self a minor miracle and worth the expense of getting married in this idealistic place. But faith is the all important ingredient. Faith can move a mountain.

We took a vertical cable train that took us to the highest point, with most magnificent views of the surrounding countryside, as far as eyes can see.

The End of a Dream:

By 3:30 pm we were ready to leave, albeit with heavy heart and every bone in my body aching, as I had not walked so much for a very long time, even with the help of crutches but our spirit was lifted, having fulfilled one of my main ambitions, that of holding the hand of Black Madonna of Montserrat and making a wish.

The second part of our excursion took us to one of the largest plantation in Europe, growing grapes that produce Spanish champagne, popularly known as Cava. The underground storage space where the wine is left for a long time, until it acquires maturity, taste and aroma of true champagne. But after Montserrat, every excursion was an anticlimax.

My one disappointment, point of contention was the lack of facilities for the sick and the disabled pilgrims, some of whom were suffering from a terminal illness. As Montserrat is visited by more than a million pilgrims and donations are pouring in from every corner of the world, I sincerely hope that the authority will rectify this glaring fault, in their otherwise perfect management of Montserrat.

We were back in our comfortable hotel in time for the evening meal and the soft, comfortable bed that was awaiting us.

****

DOWN MEMORY LANE

I was setting foot on the sacred soil of my motherland Bharat, after a very long time. I was born and brought up in East Africa, where I spend my entire childhood and the adult, working life, the best years of my life.

The only exception was a short break, of four years to be precise, which I spent in Bombay, acquiring further education, where I gained my BA degree in economics, from the famous, desirable and prestigious St. Xavier College.

When the East African countries of Kenya, Uganda and Tanganyika became independent, there was no place for some what elderly people like us, who were surplus to requirement. I was obliged to retire from the Civil Service, in the name of Africanization, what ever it meant.

One was judged to be an African, from the colour of the skin, not where one was born and brought up and the family may have lived for generations. Yes we were given local citizenship if we gave up our British or Indian passports but not equality or equal treatment on job front.

Then again, African people had a lot of catching up to do. During the colonial rule, education was denied to the masses, unless they embrace Christianity and went to school, so often run by religious establishment.

There was a big economic gulf between the Africans and the rest of us. Surely no independent country can tolerate such a wide economic gulf, disparity of living standard for long.

The wind of change was blowing throughout the dark continent of Africa. The Western colonial powers, like Britain, France and Belgium, were in a hurry to leave Africa, the so called white men's burden.

Communism was not a welcome word and the departing colonial powers made sure of it. But on the other hand, Socialism was made popular, desirable and even fashionable by the idealistic but not realistic, non practical or pragmatic African leaders like Nkrumah, Nasser and our own saintly leader Malimu (teacher) Julius Nyerere.

Nyerere introduced Ujama, which means co-operative farming, mainly in the villages, splitting up big plantations, which were so effectively and efficiently run under colonial rule but proved to be a disaster under Ujama. Mughabi of Zimbabwe made the same mistake. Now people are starving in a land which was once considered a bread basket of Central Africa. Then Africa is full of mad rulers like Idi Amin, Mughabi, Mobutu and many more, some in the pocket of their former colonial masters.

If you add the names of Nehru, Tito and Sukarno, then socialism indeed became a byword in political freedom, political independence. Some of these leaders ruined the economy of their countries so badly that they were overthrown by their own army, as people were denied the opportunity of changing the political rule by democratic means.

Some countries are still suffering from their misrule. Then perhaps, I am trying to be wise after the event, as our own Saint Mahatma Gandhi was one of such personalities, revered by all, from all walks of life, culture and religion.

Communism, Socialism, Co-operativism, whatever you may want to call it, did not go hand in hand with our life style, evolved during the last five thousand years and weathered, survived, even flourished so successfully, first under Mogul and then under British rule.

Our lifestyle was easy, carefree and based on joint family tradition, of educating our children, looking after our elders, improving our economic standing in our close-knit society but to the detriment of our political, social and religious well-being.

It was difficult for people like us to maintain our lifestyle or be part of the fast changing world of the post colonial era. One has to be young, adaptable, idealist and full of energy and zeal to be part of the ever changing face of the new era, new dawn, new world.

Our only option was to go to Britain or come to Bharat, where the cost of living was low enough for us to be able to live comfortably on our meagre pensions and some savings that most of us have accumulated over the years, which may mean very little in European countries like Britain but more than sufficient for the Indian life style.

Today, I had completed six month's stay in Bombay. Children had already settled down in the college but our flat, although spacious by local standard, was some what cramped and in a densely populated area. We missed the open air living, atmosphere of natural beauty and affluence that we enjoyed in Africa, a sparsely populated country with an unimaginable landmass and natural beauty to match its wonderful lifestyle.

We used to spend most of our spare time under the sun, moon and the stars, picnicking on the beautiful beaches and the small islands of the coast of Tanga and our various trips to the nearby hill station of Lushoto.

Of course, it would be impossible to find such a life style in the over crowded city of Bombay, with a population of some fifteen million people, more than that of our country of Tanzania at the time of independence.

I would have preferred to settle down in a small town like Rajkot, Jamnagar or the seaside town of Porbander, the birth place of my namesake Mahatma Gandhi where we could have open air, open space and the beauty of Indian Ocean on our doorstep and certainly a life without hassle.

But in the end, the educational requirement of our children took precedent, who may one day want to settle down in America, Canada or England. They needed Bombay University education, with English medium that was considered to be the best in India at the time. We had, along with most Indians, retained our British passports.

Life in Borivali, a suburb of Bombay, was not half as hectic as life in the proper Bombay. But the train journey, especially in the rush hour, was a murder. As I was leading a semi retired life, my off peak travel was reasonably comfortable, under the circumstances.

To-day I caught the noon train, which was nearly empty, as it started from Borivali. It was hot, unbearably hot. The sun, from the cloudless sky, was throwing the heat by bucketful and the sunlight was in abundance. The land, parched and dry, was as hot as oven, throwing the heat back in the atmosphere.

I took a seat in the shady part of the compartment, open my newspaper, Hindustan Times and started reading the sports pages. As MCC was touring India, sport pages were full of cricket news.

With Vinu Mankad, Manjaraker, Chandu Borde, Ramakant Desai, Pankaj Roy and the spin wizard Subash Gupte, Gulam Mohamed and young Bisen Bedi in the side, there was hope. But with the retirement of Mantri, Nari Contractor and Polly Umrigar, the batting was a problem. The English team, with players like Bailey, Barrington, Cowdry, Evans, Jim Laker, Tony Lock, Tom Graveny, Freddie Truman and Bob Appleyard, were the favourite to take the series.

The train was taking passengers at every station and even in my first class compartment; seats being filled up rapidly. Soon every seat around me was taken. After half an hour, I put down the paper, to give rest to my tiring eyes.

On looking left, I saw a middle-age woman, sitting next to me. She must be in her mid fifties, with plump, puffy, swollen body, a face that always carries a smile, a fair but weather beaten, neglected skin, hair going grey at the roots. It was obvious she was someone who must have been very charming, beautiful and a friendly person, when young, in the prime of her life, the prime of Miss Jean Brodie. Then we are all reasonably charming and attractive in our young age, aren't we!

Her face was somewhat familiar but the familiarity of the heart did not extend to the brain, which was as blank as it could be. She was looking at me intensely and to lighten the atmosphere, I gave her a smile.

She smiled in return and said, "Aren't you Anilbhai Shah from Tanga?"

"Yes, I am Anil and I do feel that we have met before but where and when, I cannot remember." I said politely with a smile in return.

"Anilbhai, I have changed so much during the last forty years that my own parents would hardly recognize me. I am Anjana, Shantaban's daughter. Remember our childhood in Tanga?" She said in some what sad and emotional voice.

"Who, Anju? You have really changed." I exclaimed unintentionally. My school days, my early life in the beautiful seaside town of Tanga came alive.

Our two families were living in the same compound. The early period houses in Africa were some what primitive. They were more like a commune than an individual home. Some ten to twenty flats were built, either in a square or circular building, with a huge compound in the centre.

There was only one entrance to the compound. All exit doors face the compound. So once the compound entrance is locked, it was safe for children and the ladies. The courtyard, most often used to have trees, especially big mango trees, under which ladies sat in the afternoon and do their chores and most used to have deep wells as well, as water was scare during the hot summer months.

It was like a kibbutz or may be a fortified settlement, where people were friendly, shared most things but there was no privacy of any kind. In those days, even a radio was a luxury and only one in ten family used to have it.

But I must stress there was hardly any crime. Even though people were much poorer than today, there was honesty, honour, comradeship, love, brotherhood and communal harmony that is hard to imagine today. People would be at each other's throat, if we have to live under such a close proximity today. How the priorities, preferences and values have changed!

Anjana and I were brought up in such an atmosphere, a one big happy family, caring and sharing was a way of life, a daily routine. As there was no social security, pensions or savings, as most used to live hand to mouth, this kibbutz type lifestyle evolved over thousands of years. It made sure that no one went hungry or felt neglected.

Anjana's father was a Custom Officer, working on the port, collecting duties on the imported goods. My father had a small grocery shop. Although Anjana was some three years younger than me, we used to get on well. May be I was the older brother Anjana never had.

She was a really clever and a charming girl, with a permanent smile on her tender and pretty face. She was also a chatter box. She was tall with slim body, baby face, to go along her long, light brown hair, sharp, inquisitive brain and helpful nature. No wonder she was every one's favourite person.

Anjana was very friendly with me. It was a pure, innocent friendship between us. I suppose living in a kibbutz atmosphere and attending the same school, the only school, as Tanga was a very small town in those days, such a friendship was inevitable. Perhaps she was looking up to me as her elder brother.

Tanga, having a small Indian community, was blessed with total unity among the Indian community, which one may not find in a large town, where Indian community was divided on the caste basis.

These were the romantic, idealistic days. The war in Europe was coming to an end and India was moving towards independence and the inevitable partition, under the theory of two nations, with Jinha and Gandhi leading their respective community, one committed to his culture and religion while the other wanted a secular humanist constitution for Bharat. What a big mistake it has turned out to be? Today Bharat is a hot bed of communal violence and the progress of the nation is thawed by a tiny religious minority who are holding back the majority Hindus community who are on most part well educated, industrious and law abiding.

Anjana was the hub of the social activities. School plays, garba ras, dandia ras or any such activities would not take place without her active participation. So often in the school drama, we used to end up playing the roles of a brother and a sister, even husband and wife and always partnered each other in garba ras competition.

It was a pure and an innocent friendship, a sign of the age when any other type of friendship between a boy and a girl was unheard of. We were able to go on picnic, meet any where and do everything together.

We did not realize at the time but during such functions, playing dandia ras, the young and unmarried girls were some what scantly dressed and Anjana was no exception. Remembering later, she indeed looked smart and sexy in her sleeveless blouse, most often worn without a bra, exposing with ease her milky white but some what under developed bosom, as bra was an expensive piece of clothing, unless made at home.

Our friendship lasted nearly ten years, until we were teenagers, when Anjana's father was transferred to Mombassa, the main port, serving Kenya and land locked Uganda. Within three years, Anjana's father retired and moved to India.

In the beginning I received letters from Anjana at regular interval but they soon stopped. The last time I heard from Anjana or rather from her father, was when she was getting married. It was just a Kankotri, the traditional Indian marriage invitation card. Anjana had scribbled a few words, expressing her wish to see me at her wedding.

By this time, my father had passed away and I was myself a civil servant. I was also engaged to Bhavna and about to get married when I received the news of Anjana's impeding marriage.

The friendship between me and Anjana was not the type which should make me jealous and we both have moved on since those early, carefree days of our innocent childhood friendship, a very long time ago. But in reality, I had never forgotten Anjana. Perhaps she was my first love, the romantic feelings being suppressed by the prevailing social atmosphere. Anjana was lurking like a shadow, at the back, deep inside my sub conscious mind.

I must admit, for few days, I felt sad, as if I was going to lose something precious. Even felt jealous of Anjana's fiancée. I am sure everyone who had come in close contact with Anjana must have experienced similar feelings, undergone the same, soul searching sentiments.

I was closer to Anjana, a girl in a million, almost a perfect life partner than to any other person. She was beautiful beyond description, a tall, slim figure with alluring, lovely milky white complexion, almond shaped eyes and long, dark brown hair. But above all, she was a happy go lucky girl with kind, joyful, considerate and helpful nature, to accompany her sharp and inquisitive brain. Anjana was almost too perfect a girl to be true. She was a princess residing in the heart of every boy, every young man.

I was sure life with Anjana would have been a heaven on earth, without strife, without complications and certainly full of love, romance and a bundle of innocent fun and laughter.

I had spent ten years of my life in her company. They were the best and the happiest years of my life. I am sure Anjana will agree with me without any reservation at all.

Sunday picnics on the sandy beaches, especially our favourite Raska-Zone beach, washed by the warm waters of the Indian Ocean and the island of Pemba, with abundant wild life, a retreat fit for a king, our family outings to a small, in fact a tiny village of Lushoto, with rose gardens and the sulphur springs of Amboni as well as our joint participation in plays and Ras garba was an unforgettable, most happy, memorable and enjoyable period in our lives.

We had a wonderful life, a happy childhood and dare I say we were deeply in love without ever realising it? The three year age gap was a blessing rather than a disadvantage. It would be difficult for any youngsters to understand such a friendship, especially here in the Western world where moral standard is so different; almost non-existence compared to our era dating back more than half a century.

I soon got married and Anjana was, more or less forgotten during the last thirty years or so. No wonder I could not remember or recognize her today, a chance meeting in more ways than one, a happy and fruitful one or not, only the time will tell.

I was lost in my thoughts when I heard Anjana's soft and still sweet voice. "Anilbhai, what are you thinking?"

"Well Anjana, I remembered our childhood, those happy, carefree days, full of innocent mischief." I said in a sad, heavy tone. The pain or rather disappointment was obvious in my voice.

"Yes, Anilbhai, how can we forget those days? It was a heaven on earth. Those days were unique, never to be repeated again. A life full of hope, expectation and happiness knew no bounds. Whenever I think about those days, it brings sadness, tears in my eyes. My heart cries from within. Well Anilbhai, we made a very big mistake and let the heaven slip through our fingers." said Anjana with tears running down her pale, white face.

Pain in Anjana's voice was undisguisable, raising a question in my mind as to what mistake she was referring to. After a few minute's silence, She said, "Anilbhai, when did you came to Bombay?"

"Nearly nine months ago and I placed my card in her hand."

"Does this mean you have come here for good?"

"Yes Anjana, I have left Africa for good" and we talked until she got off just before Bombay Central, the station where I was going to meet my publisher.

Now Anjana knew everything about me, my wife Bhavna and our two children. But before we parted, she extracted a promise from me to have the Sunday dinner at her place.

As usual, no one can say no to Anjana, when she uses her charm. That gift was still with her today. I was thinking about her until I got off the train. How cruel the fate had been with Anjana. It was even difficult to imagine.

Anjana was living only half an hour's taxi ride from us. We were at her place, early on Sunday afternoon. I had told Bhavna everything about Anjana. So she was as eager to meet her as I was.

But it was difficult even to imagine the childhood Anjana, looking at her now. There wasn't a trace of that spark, spirit, beauty or mischief left in her today, except may be her sweet, innocent smile.

It didn't took us long to find her place. She was standing outside her tiny flat, awaiting us. Bhavna and my daughter Sharmila were soon at ease with Anjana and her two daughters.

Anjana's flat consisted of two tiny rooms. The kitchen was at the end of the narrow passage and as usual in such overcrowded block of flats, the bathroom and toilet facilities were for common use. This was a stark reality of a family languishing in the grip of poverty.

Anjana had five children, three girls and two boys. If she had not taken the drastic step of making herself sterile after the birth of her fifth child, there would have been, without any doubt, an addition to the family.

Anjana's twenty two year old daughter Rekha was a carbon copy of her mother Anjana. The same slim figure, blue eyes and milky white skin, the face with a permanent smile, a duplicate of young Anjana. But due to poverty, her figure was not that well developed nor was there that mischief, anticipation and happy go lucky attitude of her mother. But she was without any doubt, young looking, attractive and beautiful, even without any makeup.

I couldn't resist giving young Rekha a big smile and firm hug, unwilling to let her go; nor could I control my thoughts that Rekha could and should have been my daughter.

Anjana's husband Ramesh had a small book stall, which was open seven days a week yet hardly provided the family a decent living standard. When Anjana got married, the family was reasonably well off, with a big book store in the most desirable part of Bandra. The business was booming with contracts to supply books to local schools and libraries.

Ramesh, along with his younger brother and the father, was involved in the family business. Unfortunately Ramesh's father got cancer. The sickness, this terrible tragedy, lasted five long years.

In a country like Bharat, there is neither social security nor the free national health we enjoy in this country. Sickness like cancer may consume family's entire wealth. By the time Ramesh's father died, the family was ruined and financially bankrupt.

Ramesh was neither clever nor that well educated to earn a decent living. Anjana was really devastated. The fate had dealt her a very cruel blow, played a dirty trick on her. What a tragedy! She passed many a night crying to sleep. When young, Anjana was ambitious and wanted to qualify as a doctor but she even failed to make to the college.

It seems leaving Africa so early was the biggest mistake Anjana's father made. Soon after coming to Bombay, Anjana's mother became a victim of stroke. Looking after her bed ridden mother and the general household responsibility, put paid to her ambition of becoming a doctor. Anjana got married soon after her mother passed away.

Even today, when Anjana gets fed up with her life, she cursed her father for her misery. Anjana was willing to continue her studies, even after a break of four years, after her mother passed away. But her father wanted her to get married, to fulfil a promise he made to his dying wife.

Where would Anjana be today, if she was allowed to continue her education and had qualified as a doctor? She was a brilliant student. There was no goal she could not achieve, no mountain she could not climb on the educational front. I could vouch for that.

Although Anjana was now used to her life, her struggle, there was no joy, no passion, just passing time. Her life was centred on her children who were all brilliant at studies. She was determined to let her children, especially her daughters, to study as much as they would like to.

Rekha, like young Anjana, was a brilliant student and already in her last year at the medical college. The community scholarships were helping her children to attend colleges which would be out of bound without this financial assistance.

Although I met Anjana after such a long time, there was more sorrow than happiness in our chance meeting. Looking at Anjana's life, I felt depressed. It would have been better if I had remembered Anjana, preserved her memory in my subconscious mind, as she was in her younger days in Tanga, a young, ambitious, kind, considerate, clever and a very beautiful girl indeed. In fact she was one in a million.

Looking back at my own life, I could give a smile of satisfaction. In Bhavna, I have a lovely wife. Both of my children are already climbing the educational ladder. My son is on the way to becoming a Chartered Accountant while my daughter was writing a thesis to gain her PhD in economics. They are both clever and wonderful children, a pride and joy of our family.

Although I am not a rich person, our financial future is secured. Now I am able to pursue my life long ambition of becoming a writer. While in Africa, I had already written a couple of novels which I recently finalised. The first one, "Atham Ta Surya Na Keran (rays of the setting sun) was published six months ago, with rapturous reviews.

The second one, "Ganga Na Vahata Pani" (Flowing waters of river Ganges) was with my publisher. I am already working on the third novel. It seems my publisher is keen to encourage me to write as many novels as I can. The life could not be sweeter.

It seems my goal in life was more or less fulfilled. Everything else I may achieve, accomplish from now on is a bonus, especially on the financial front social front.

When taking leave of Anjana, I pressed a hundred rupee note in the soft hands of Rekha and promised to attend her graduation when she qualifies as a doctor. Some how we were able to establish an instant affection between us.

On the way back, my heart was heavy. I could hardly hide my pain from Bhavna. I wondered how many such Anjanas, suffering from the middle class poverty, are there in our society and what would my life be if the fate had not separated me from Anjana.

****

Epilogue: I am a firm believer in fate, that every cloud has a silver lining. There is some reason, some purpose for everything that happens to us, occurs in our lives. Three years after my chance encounter with Anjana, on a suburban train, my son Rakesh, a Chartered Accountant, got married to Rekha, a doctor. What we could not achieve in our life, a union of two souls, our children could and did. It was the happiest day in the lives of our two families. A permanent bond was established between our two families that will last until death do us part. Well, all's well that ends well.

****

HEAVEN ON EARTH

As a regular contributor to various newspaper and magazines, I often receive request to write on various tropic and subject. One request that I receive more often than most is to write about our happy and carefree days in East Africa, particularly in Dar Es Salaam. Most of us till consider it a heaven on earth, even after leaving the place, some what in haste, well over thirty five years ago.

In this piece, I would like to go down the memory lane and rekindle the nostalgic era for the devoted and loyal readers who came here from East Africa, leaving behind a carefree, happy and may be idyllic life, due to the rapid political, social and economic changes which made our lives difficult and the future of our children uncertain.

Perhaps our pioneering spirit, wondering instinct, Gypsy Romany nature that was inbred in all East African Asians but especially more in Gujaratis, was too strong to hold us back. The imminent departure of the British under whose shadow, under whose protection, under whose wings we had lived for centuries, unconsciously made us seek shelter in countries where British influence was still a dominant force.

The young and youthful East African Indians, who emigrated to the West, just before or after these countries gained independence, can be divided into two categories, the one who remained in Dar after passing their Senior Cambridge examination, joining local civic service or the Common Services which managed ports and railways throughout East Africa.

In the second category fall youngsters who went to India and U.K. for further studies after completing their secondary education. This group, especially those who went to UK, with a few exceptions, did not return to Dar except on holidays or to meet their families, may be to get married or to introduce their English girlfriends to their family members and friends. It was a trend, a fashion to get married to these charming young, pretty English girls.

During fifties and early sixties, a marriage to an English girl was a step in the right direction, a climb up the social ladder and an envy of those who were stranded in Dar but to be truthful, these charming, beautiful and idealistic English girls, on their part, made tremendous effort to learn our culture, our tradition and to adopt our way of life.

In most cases they even mixed and integrated with ease in our joint family life that was the hallmark of our culture. How the times have changed? Now a days even our own Indian girls are unable or unwilling to mix and stay in a joint family.

Those who were returning from India made Dar a transit camp, which is until they were able to emigrate to UK, USA, Canada or Australia. This group had less attachment, were less nostalgic than what I would like to call the indigenous, autochthonous Dar residents, who had never been out of Tanganyika until they were forced to leave the country, to emigrate after independence, due to fast changing topography of the region.

The civil war in the former Belgian colony of Congo, the bloody overthrow of the government in Zanzibar and the brief army mutiny in Tanganyika, put down with the help of British marines, did not inspire much confidence in the emerging countries of Africa.

Now that we are here and well settled, some of us, especially the retired older generation, while sitting in our rocking chairs, watching endless and meaningless Indian movies, in a pin drop silence, occasionally shattered by the harshness of a telephone ring, in a dark, gloomy, cold and damp winter atmosphere, a hallmark of the unpalatable British weather, unwittingly make us compare our shallow, day to day existence in this country, with that of our carefree lives lived to it's full potential until the end, a time to reunite with mother nature, dust to dust, ashes to ashes, on the shore of the vast and romantic Indian ocean.

I can still remember, without exerting my vivid imagination, the evenings and specially the week-ends, mostly Sundays that we spent on the long, sandy beach, as a child and as emerging teenagers, young men, playing in the soft, warm and silky sand of Oyster bay, Kunduchi, Bagamoyo or the small island of Magogoni, just across the Dar harbour. Dar Es Salaam is an Arabic word which means Gateway to Heaven. Well, it sure was to most of us but we did not appreciate it at the time.

Magogoni is the place where we used to go on picnic most, in the fifties, in a large group, often spending a night or two on the beach, under the moonlit, star-studded night, with lovely turquoise sea water, frothing waves reflecting and magnifying every twinkle of the distant star, every moonbeam a thousand times. It was a twinkle twinkle little star, like a diamond in the Dar sky?

East Africa was a Jules Verne world, a lost continent, James Hilton's imaginary Shangri La, the place where time had stood still for the last two centuries, just like the place set in the isolated, impregnable plateau of the lost world of ancient and mysterious plateau of Tibet, the most elevated land mark in the world, known as the roof of the world.

The rustic atmosphere was wrapped in silk cocoon and isolated from the rest of the world, protected from the turmoil of the aftermath of the most gruesome Second World War that killed some thirty million people and set alight the entire continent of Europe, the Pacific Rim and the Indian sub-continent, a scale of men made destruction the world has never seen before nor is ever likely to be repeated.

Waking up early in the morning, with the sound, coos and chirps of birds, mostly seagulls, cranes, wild pigeons, ducks, skylarks, various types of sparrows, grey parrots (kasuku) and the flocks of noisy parakeets, capable of disturbing the sleep of even Kumbkarna, was indeed an unforgettable experience, a part of our life that made Dar a heaven on earth.

Bathing in the warm, crystal clear water of this mighty and romantic Indian ocean, with white, powdery sand under one's feet that made walking a surprisingly pleasant pastime or bathing in the fresh water stream, water being magically sprouting and unceasingly flowing all year round, even during the dry summer months when the temperature soared above 120ºF, from a shallow basin of sand, feeding from the underground stream, perhaps a big reservoir, water being so clean, pure and sweet that we used to bottle it and take it home with us?

It seems the sandy beach on the island extended well inland, covering the whole island with soft sand, with sweet water stream running underground, surfacing at regular interval, forming a tiny reservoir of fresh water for human consumption, as well as for irrigating the small patches of sandy but fertile land.

The whole island was a one big natural park, covered with all kind of fruit trees, mostly coconut lagoons, grove of fruit trees which include mango trees, guava, black plum (jambu) cashew nuts, oranges, sweet berry (Chania bor) papaya, musk melon, sweet ambli, mulberries and many a fruit with only Swahili names.

Our early morning breakfast was made up of sweet coconut water or if we were lucky, fresh goat milk, the goat being milked right in front us, with banana, pawpaw and half baked roti cooked by us on a smoky fire. Take your pick. It does not sound real? May be it was all a big hallucination. When the tide ebb; it was possible to walk from Magogoni to a tiny island just a mile off shore. But it was a dangerous adventure to undertake, as the tide would rush in and cut off the retreat. As we were all born in a seaside town, we were taught from childhood to treat the sea with great respect. Still occasional drowning of young, fool hardy children was unavoidable. But in a small, close nit community like ours, it was a tragic event indeed, which would put us off, going into the sea for few weeks.

Still it was wonderful to walk, mile after mile on wet sand and observe the sea life trapped in a shallow puddle made by retreating tide. These puddles provided a feast of palatable sea food for gulls and other marine birds. Some of these puddles were big and deep enough to provide a safe bathing place, especially for the young and those who were not proficient swimmers.

Dar was a place where sun always shone brightly, sea water was always azure blue, warm, comforting and indeed inviting. Even the scorching heat of the mid-day sun was not a deterrent enough to dampen our spirit or to keep us indoor, as there was neither air-conditioning nor the dreadful TV that keeps most of us indoor in this country. The seaside was the best place to be in such a hot and humid atmosphere.

The other enjoyable aspect of our life were the cricket matches, teams being organized on communal basis, with few exception, notably P.W.D. and Customs, where some of our best players found a natural home but weakening the Hindus team in the process. These matches gave us the most thrills. The rivalry, although intense on the field, was friendly and accommodating off the field, without any ill-feeling once the match was over.

The seeds of cricket mania were firmly planted at school. Who can forget the Oxford and Cambridge type rivalry between the two leading schools, the Indian Secondary School and the Agakhan School? Making to school team was more important than passing one's Senior Cambridge exam with flying colours or winning a lottery of any kind. Even teachers would like to be in good books of those high flying student cricketers and who can blame them?

My Indian Secondary school was blessed with players of the calibre of Shashikant Patel, Rajni Mehta, Navin Patel, Vinu Valambia, Chuni Vaghella, Ramnik Modessa and our commerce teacher, the only teacher who played cricket for the school team.

No wonder our school used to have an upper hand most of the time. But in Mamda Kassam and for a short period, John Solanki, Agakhan School had a potential match winner who could change the course of the game single-handedly.

I distinctively remember fast bowler Shashikant Patel and spin wizard Mamda Kassam embarrassing the visiting MCC team, when they were bundled out for just over one hundred runs, although I suspect the real culprit was the scorching December heat with temperature touching fifty degree mark, most MCC players were suffering from dehydration and nose bleed?

All these schoolboy heroes went on to play for their respective teams and produced some scintillating matches, playing alongside such famous and legendary names like C.D. and R.D. Patel who had played Ranjit Trophy Cricket for Baroda, Babu Chauhan, Bharadia Brothers, Karim, Ronaldson, Meredew and many more.

John Solanki even played county cricket for Glamorgan. These were the days of true chivalry, on and off the cricket field. Looking at today's younger generation, it pains me, saddens me that they do not have even a fraction of our passion, love, attachment, fondness or romantism that made our childhood so special, so unforgettable.

The late forties and the fifties were the era of romance, expectation, achievement and every one of us had a dream of doing something for humanity; make the world a better place for everyone, to eradicate disease, poverty and illiteracy, even the religious differences!

It was the era of peace crop volunteers who came to Africa, all the way from America, Canada and England, living in isolated villages and tiny settlements totally without any facilities, many of these fine and idealistic young men lost their lives, falling the victim of malaria, TB, Cholera and other hazards associated with developing countries. It is a pity that the then government of emerging African countries never understood or appreciated the efforts of these idealistic young university graduates.

The hatred for the white people and colonialism was so intense that they were unable to see the better, humane side of the peace crop volunteers. But I admit, our leader Malimu Julius Nyerere was an exception.

That idealism, our intense desire to serve humanity took so many of us all the way to India and England for further studies and became doctors, lawyers, accountants and teachers. In comparison the lives of our youngsters here seems to be shallow and aimless, with enjoyment and accumulation of wealth uppermost in their mind.

The film industry was at its nostalgic best, producing in keeping with the era, some of the most haunting, evocative and memorable films, like Kismat, Awara, Andaz, Mother India, Madhumati, Pakiza and many more.

Film stars like Raj Kapoor and Nargis, Dilip Kumar and Meena Kumari, Dev Anand and Kalpna Kartik, Ashok Kumar, Madhubala, Geeta Bali, Mukesh and my favourite Vijayantimala were the household names, by-product of the romantic era, which every youngster wanted to emulate.

Retrospection brings with it the sense of nostalgic era. All these experiences will be a fading memory that will only remain alive in our deep subconscious mind, as we slowly but surely grow old and senile. But as the saying goes, old soldiers never die, they only fade away, but let us hope and pray that the fading process for us happens very slow indeed.

Perhaps growing up in Dar, in the idealistic fifties was a God's gift, a unique experience, going through the excitement of India gaining independence in 1947, Gandhiji being murdered in 1948 and living in Tanganyika while the country was going through political as well as social upheaval. This made a major difference in our lives and the lives of others that we were associated with.

In Tanganyika we had a wonderful political leader in the late Malimu Julius Nyerere, a kind considerate, highly educated man of integrity and honour, a man in the mould of Mahatma Gandhi, Martin Luther King and Nelson Mandela.

I consider a great honour, a great privilege that I was able to meet this saintly man several times, while working as a civil servant in the independent Tanzania.

It is difficult to acknowledge that we, who only a few years ago, were in our prime, enjoying the robustness of youth, the vitality of young age, are now old-age pensioners, getting old and have already lost some of our best, childhood friends and relations.

I was perhaps most attached to Dar, as I was not only born there but I spent the first thirty years, the best years of my life in Dar as well. My father, Mohandas Gandhi, no relations to Mahatma, after retiring from the Post Office in 1947, opened **"Sunrise Store"** similar to a mini supermarket. It was a pioneering experience at the time which put bread and butter into our homes, Hindu homes, thus giving a free evening to our ladies on Sundays.

My inner friend circle was made up of Dariave Rathod, Rajni Popat, Janu Bakhda, Shashi Vasani and Pravin Barot. The first three, who were closest to me, have already passed away, at a relative young age of mid fifties and I am out of touch with most of the rest.

That makes me wonder how much time we have and how to make the best use of our remaining, borrowed time? It is time to come out of our petty jealousy and do something worthwhile that may leave our footprint, our mark, after we are gone for good.

I retired at a relatively young age and I feel I am at least making good use of my time, learning a new language, teaching youngsters, helping the community members in my area of expertise, travelling overseas at every opportunity and writing extensively in various newspapers and periodicals which are very much appreciated by readers, people at large.

I am trying to put something back into our community which has given me so much. I hope my friends will remember me for this contribution which has also made me some very good friends in deed, some in high places.

My faith in my culture and religion helps me to maintain the high moral standard and the self belief that is so vital as you grow old, so do the frequent visit to my beloved Hare Krishna temple in Watford, which resembles Vrindavan, at least during summer months, where I get my inner peace and be one with mother nature.

The main satisfaction is to feel contended in life. I am lucky to have a vast circle of friends and all my family members are in London which enables us to carry on the close family tradition. No wonder people of our generation want to keep in touch and share memories while we can, as we are a fast disappearing breed, the like of which may never emerge again.

Perhaps that may be the reason why Dar Reunion, whether it takes place here in London, Toronto, Mumbai or in Dar itself is so well attended by the older generation, where we meet long lost friends, in some cases after almost four decades, reminisce our common and romantic past, with the people of all caste, creed, status and religion, immersing our soul in the sweet smell of nostalgic past.

May be our happy go lucky, carefree, idealistic life was an exaggeration, a fiction mixed with some reality. Given the gloominess of the weather in this country, especially in winter, it is no wonder that the sunshine of East Africa and the warm waters of the majestic Indian Ocean look tempting beyond reality, beyond possibility.

The only people who return to Africa, on a regular basis, with little exception, are those who have relatives still living there or have some business connection. The rest of us prefer the beaches of Maldives, Goa and Kerala which are a well established tourist destination.

I genuinely feel that almost all of us would like to revisit our place of birth, at least once before it is too late, taking in the wonders of Lake Manayara, Serengeti Plain and the Ngorongoro Crater, a natural wonder, on par with the Grand Canyon, Kerala Backwaters and the Great Barrier Reef off the coast of Queensland, Australia.

I performed this nostalgic pilgrimage a few years ago which gave me a sense of satisfaction and contentment, as if I have done my duty, performed the last rights and I am now ready to meet my creator, join my childhood friends.

We may not like to admit but the old romantic atmosphere no longer exists in Dar. Yet life is still stress free and going at a leisurely pace, that is compared to our lives here in London.

When I was in Dar, I expressed my desire to visit Magogoni Island. I was told no one now a day goes there. It was too dangerous to venture over there, my favourite picnic spot? I suppose Tanzania has moved on, along with the rest of the world and it is time for us to move on as well or may be not?

It would do immense good, if we show our youngsters, those who were born and brought up in this country, the place of our birth, where perhaps we spent the best years of our young, youthful and ambitious life, where we received such a wonderful education in every sense and made us kind, considerate and better human being, prepared us so well to enter the Western world with full vigour and enabled us to make our presence felt, led us out of puddle to the ocean of knowledge, wisdom and truth.

Such a reunion, the holy resurrection brings with it the sense of nostalgia, the craving and longing of the real as well as imaginary past, may be distortion of reality but as long as it serves the purpose, some event to look forward to, bring us all together, why should we care?

Quoting the late Mukeshji's song, "Do din ke lea meheman yahan, malum nahi manzil ha kaha." (We are here, on this earth, a guest for few days but we don't know what and where our final destination is.)

I have expended a lot of time, a sea of feelings and emotion, digging deep to bring up some of the long dormant and forgotten memories, to enable me to write this nostalgic piece. I will consider the effort well worth if it puts me in touch with a few of my long lost friends.

I hope the readers will enjoy reading this piece as much as I enjoyed researching and writing it.

****

LOST HORIZON

NGORONGORO CRATER is a land that time forgot, well almost, that is until recently when it was rediscovered for the benefit of Western tourists, who flock the Sub-Saharan Africa in search of wild life adventure that has put Kenya, Tanzania and now South Africa on the world tourist map.

Fortunately, Tanzania which is blessed with the best game reserves has not yet joined the mass tourist market and the package holiday industry which has so often proved a disaster in disguise, eradicating flora and fauna of a particular region which is normally unique to that region, endangering the whole ecological balance in the process.

Ngorongoro Crater is one of the seven natural wonders of the world. The other six are, the Grand Canyon in Arizona USA, Niagara Falls in Canada, the Great Barrier Reef, off the coast of Queensland Australia, Ayers Rock in Northern Territory of Australia, Kerala Backwaters in India and Mount Everest, which does not need any introduction.

All these natural wonders are breath takingly beautiful and unique in their own right, in their sphere but Ngorongoro Crater is the only one still untouched and commercially unexploited so far by the human greed.

One early August morning, we landed at the Kilimanjaro International Airport, under two hour's flight time from Dar Es Salaam, in a Fokker Friendship aircraft, still in use at the time in Tanzania, although confined to a museum in Europe.

This was our first visit to Kilimanjaro region, having flown all the way from London to Dar, to go on a safari of a lifetime, visiting Lake Manayara, Serengeti National Park, and Lobo Lodge and of course **Ngorongoro Crater.**

On stepping out of aircraft, we were greeted by our tour guide and driver who introduced himself as Omar but no relation to Shariff, in his own words. We liked his sense of humour. The Toyota mini coach was equipped to take nine passengers in comfort but we three were the only occupants, as the safari was tailor made by Kearsley Travel and Tours Ltd.

On leaving airport, we drove straight to Lake Manayara hotel. It was a four hour drive, passing through some ruggedly beautiful countryside, small plantations growing coffee, banana, mango, pineapple and such exotic tropical fruits we like most.

The hotel was a one story building, not particularly beautiful or impressive but rooms were spacious and comfortably furnished.

Next morning, after heavy breakfast, we left the hotel at the crack of dawn, half a sleep, in our empty mini bus, especially as the drive to Lake Manayara was not particularly eye catching. But it was a completely different ball game when we reached the lake. It was wild and exciting.

The lake was overflowing with water due to unseasonably heavy winter rain that had soaked the land only a few days ago. Some crocodiles were basking in not so warm early morning sun, not too far from us. May be waiting for an unsuspecting tourist to walk in her dinner plate?

The place was full of tourist coaches, so we left within half an hour. On our way we saw what we had come for, a pride of lions monopolising the surrounding thorny Acacia trees?

It was once in a lifetime experience. So we made the most of this nature's trapeze artists at work, showing off their natural skill to the world wide audience of Americans, Australians, and Germans and of course us the Brits?

We stayed there for an hour, taking photographs and soaking in the natural surrounding, a complete contrast to European landscape we encounter on our local outings to Spain and Canaries?

We drove on to Arusha and to Ngorongoro Crater, passing through the North East boundary of the Serengeti National Park. The park is an immense landscape, as flat as a football pitch, extending into Kenya, forming part of Masai Mara game reserve.

The beauty and uniqueness of Serengeti is in its vastness, miles after miles of flat, undulating billowy grassland with rolling hills on the distant horizon, bigger than Wales and Scotland put together, covered with savannah grass stretching to the horizon in every direction.

It is an unforgettable experience to watch the never ending expanse of wildebeest, intermingling with zebras and Thompson's gazelles, from one end of the horizon to another.

Big cats are always around these herds and we saw plenty of lions but had to search for Cheetahs and leopards as they are shy, solitary and somewhat elusive creatures. We had to enter and leave Serengeti National Park before we came near to a conspicuously visible **NGORONGORO CRATER.**

The last half an hour's drive to the crater was breathtakingly beautiful. The rim of the crater, in some places, is over five thousand feet high, with a sheer, veritable drop that no vehicle could survive.

August is the best month to visit the Crater, being winter and before the summer excesses which often turns this part of Africa into a parched land. After a long, hard, brutal and savage summer, the arrival of rainy season, the monsoon comes as a breath of fresh air.

The parched land, a feature for a long time, turns into an eye pleasing, mind soothing green pasture, a green carpet, covered with beautiful wild flowers of all colour and size. It was like a perpetual garden, a garden of Adam and Eve. I must not let my imagination stray too far away from reality but then in this part of the world, there is a very thin line between reality, imagination and dream world?

The evening was setting in and the mist had descended in abundance. Visibility was practically nil. We avoided running into a bull elephant by a whisker who was crossing the road. Our driver exclaimed in an irritated voice, "These damned elephants never use Zebra Crossings." I could not help but laugh.

It was chilly and getting very cold and dark as we climbed to the Crater's edge, well over 5000ft. high. It was a relief when we reached our hotel, "The Ngorongoro Wildlife Lodge" situated at the very edge of the Crater, with scenery out of this world.

It is a very impressive lodge with a large wooden arch fronting the entrance. The dining room is very scenic with large glass windows overlooking the Crater. So often, from these windows, we can see, observe wild life, dangerous animals, such as buffaloes grazing right underneath.

No wonder window seats were always taken but it was not difficult to reserve such a seat with baksheesh. (Gift or a big tip) The food and service were excellent, including vegetarian food and wild life meat dishes.

Early next morning, as we were getting ready, we heard a commotion downstairs and on inquiring, we were told to stay in the hotel, as two bull elephants were browsing in the courtyard. They looked so near from the first floor windows that we felt like touching them.

After the usual breakfast, we got into a four wheel Land Cruiser and a new driver called John. Only 4 wheel drive vehicles are permitted to enter the Crater with a specially trained guide cum driver. We soon find out why? The dirt road or rather a track was cascading from the rim to the Crater floor, a drop of over four thousand feet, with alarming steepness.

You take the ride or rather a free fall with your heart pounding and brain half paralysed, partly due to fear of plunging to the bottom but mostly due to unforgettable experience you are going through. The feeling and the changing scenery is indescribable. It took us just under two hours to reach the bottom, as the vehicle was crawling most of the time but it felt like a lifetime?

The Crater is a wondrous dreamland, with a ten mile radius, a land covered with lush green vegetation, carpeted by millions of colourful, eye catching flowers, which include wild orchids, a really pleasing and soothing sight for a sore eye or even a throbbing, raging heart?

The Crater is a perfect habitat, a Garden of Eden, a heavenly retreat for wild animals, most of whom were born and will die in the Shangri La Crater, an imaginary heaven created by my favourite author James Hilton in his equally famous novel Lost Horizon, based in the remote part of Tibet, without ever leaving the Crater.

This extinct volcanic crater provides all year round pasture to grazing animals of all shape and size, elephants, buffalos, endangered African black rhinoceros, wildebeest, zebras, gazelles and antelopes, as well as hippopotamus who completely monopolised one pool.

They remain submerged throughout the day, with only their nostrils and tiny ears visible above water surface, coming out at night to feed on the green grass surrounding the pond.

Where there are hoof animals, there are inevitably big cats like lions, leopards, cheetahs and to take advantage of their kill, who else but Africa's own scavenger hyenas, a most famous carnivorous quadruped of African Savannas.

There are over a million animals in an area not much bigger than Birmingham, so you do not have a time even to blink. Lions were so plentiful that we nearly ran over one who was asleep in tall, golden rippling grass.

Elephants were mainly on the other, northern side of the track, on the edge of Leary Forest. We encountered a herd of some 20 elephants, mostly young females and a couple of bulls. But there was a female with unusually two calves, may be a surrogate mother to an orphaned baby elephant.

Our driver turned the vehicle off the designated track and on to wet slippery grass, to take us closer to the herd. These animals are normally docile and used to human company but one young bull took a dislike to us or may be guarding his offspring, came towards us with ears flapping, trunk waving, land shaking and trumpeting to awaken the dead.

It was a fearful sight, not for those with a weak heart or nervous disposition, with a desire for a long and peaceful life. They say that most elephant charges are mock; a test of will, show of strength and it will come to a sudden halt a few yards from the vehicle.

But wisely our driver did not wait to find out what the elephant's intentions were. He reversed the powerful Land cruiser off the grass and on the dirt track and took off at full speed but not without a scare. Initially the vehicle slipped on the wet grass but the skill of our driver saw us safely home that is to our comfortable lodge.

After the above adventure, we went in search of black rhinos. There were only ten in the crater at the time, living in three separate groups. We found one, a herd of three, with a calf. We had to watch them from a distance but with the help of a good pair of binoculars, they did not seem far at all.

Over one third of the lake is covered with shallow water, no more than three feet deep. The thriving bird life is centred on the lake but the lake is particularly famous for thousands of pink flamingos who monopolize the lake all year round.

There were many varieties of birds, including many types of geese, cranes, fish eagles, woodpeckers, whistling teal, common pariah kite, goshawk and many we could not identify, at least not without the help of our guide. We had so little knowledge of African bird life. After all we were born and brought up there.

We spend some four fascinating hours on the crater floor and there was not a minute's gap when some wildlife was not in sight, on view. We did not know at the time that there is a night camp facility available on the crater floor.

It would have been wonderful to spend a night, under the clear sky, with masses of stars twinkling at us, telling us how they wonder where we are and to wake up early in the morning, to the sweet sound of tropical birds and to watch the animal at the break of dawn, the best time to watch wildlife.

We left the Crater late in the afternoon. The return journey was without incident, nevertheless nerve shattering. We reached our lodge late in the evening. The hotel management had put up a floor show of African dances and traditional ngomas to entertain the overseas guests but after the day's outing, we were shattered mentally and bone tired physically.

We had to make an early start next morning, a very long drive to Serengeti Wildlife Lodge. So we made an early retreat after dinner. We spent two more days touring Serengeti and Lobo but after Ngorongoro Crater, every thing else was an anticlimax.

****

THE LAST FRONTIER

One of the most adventurous, exciting and rugged train journey one can undertake, enjoy and treasure for life is to travel by "The Ghan Express" (shorten from Afghan) I would not say that Ghan is as romantic, comfortable or scenic train ride as the Trans Canadian Express that passes through one of the most beautiful, scenic part of Canada, the Canadian Rockies, full of swift flowing streams, lakes and snow covered mountain peaks with forest and wildlife that is out of this world.

What Ghan lacks in beauty and comfort makes up in frontier spirit, friendliness, comradeship and unique atmosphere that is difficult to describe and can not be found in any train journey any where else in the world. Not even in India, a country famous for some of the most romantic train journeys in the world, like Maharaja Or Rajasthan Express, a five star hotel on wheels, hustling through the historic, romantic desert landscape of the run (desert) of Rajasthan.

The Ghan recreates the frontier spirit that was so much part of the culture of the early American settlers who endured untold hardships, from harsh winters, illness to conflict with Native Americans. Their story is so ably personified and embodied in the legendary heroes like Bill Cody, a genius scout and popularly known as Buffalo Bill, Erap Wyatt, General Custer, Billy the Kid and Doc Holliday, a few among many.

These frontier men are immortalized by great Hollywood actors like John Wayne, Paul Newman, Gregory Peck, Kirk Douglas, Burt Lancaster and many more, in films like Shenandoah, How the West Was Won, The Last Frontier, Shane, The Wagon, Butch Cassidy and the Sundance Kid and numerous Hollywood hits that kept the legend alive.

The Early Settlers:

The early British settlers battled heroically against the most inhospitable landscape in Australia, the rust-red desert where it rains once in ten years and occupies the vast areas of Central Australia bigger than France and Spain put together, crawling with snakes, scorpions and wild dingoes that hunt in packs and would bring down any animal.

Australia is, in many ways a pre-historic land, a lost continent, cut off from the rest of the world, with some of the most unique and pre-historic wildlife in the world. Indeed Australia is a giant Jurassic Park, still unexplored in many ways. The geological isolation of Australia has helped to preserve the prehistoric animals and plant life that is unique to this part of the world.

The early settlers used hardy Afghan camels to open up the hostile interior. A narrow gauge Steam Ghan, a rickety slow railway travelling at just 15mph was built from Adelaide to Alice Springs, although the train did not reach Alice Springs until 1929, then a remote telegraphic station around which settlements were being established.

These settlements were served by the camel caravans that brought in every day use essential items, such as food, medicine, barbed wire to fence off their land and wooden sleepers for the railway tracks. On return journey, they would take back wool, animal skin and fur.

The Ghan Story:

In the beginning the Ghan journey was unpredictable and hazardous, as termites would eat wooden sleepers or the flash floods would wash away the tracks and as a result Ghan would get stranded for up to a week and more. The guards on the train had to carry riffles so that they can hunt wild animals and provide fresh food to stranded passengers.

But in those days time had no meaning, the pace of life was slow and leisurely. Travellers would willingly spend six months to a year on a ship, travelling to India, Far East, Australia and New Zealand. The ship captain was so often called upon to perform marriages, christening and read the last rights, read the holy Bible for those who were buried at sea.

The tracks were re-laid to a standard gauge in 1980 and now extended all the way to Port Darwin, a journey of some 2000 miles, a great engineering feat not much publicised in the West.

We boarded Ghan at Adelaide, a popular tourist destination and only 200 km from Melbourne, home of the most popular Australian export, "The Neighbours." Our train slid out of the clean and busy station in the mid-morning, among scene of euphoria, joy, emotion and tears.

Most of our fellow travellers were elderly, retired Australians who are all eager to make this dream journey, almost desirous to cross the continent by Ghan. One attraction to postpone this journey until retirement is that retired Australians get up to 50% discount on their train fares. So they leave this adventure for their twilight years, although most Aussies are as fit as a fiddle even in their seventies.

The station was crowded with their children and grandchildren who were there to see them off. The commotion was more akin to a fish market than a railway station. This reminded me of our boat journey, from East Africa to India, when practically all family members would come on board the ship to see us off. So often some people were stranded on the ship and in the end only the passengers were allowed to board the ship?

The Ghan Express is not a luxurious train. It is more like a 2* hotel on the wheel. A sleeper in Red Kangaroo is much cheaper than a Gold Kangaroo Cabin with your own private facilities. It would set you back some £800 with basic food which we found most unappetising. It was a frozen meal reheated in a microwave, a far cry from the luxurious meal served on the Orient Express or a freshly cooked 5 course meal served on most Indian trains that cater the needs of the Western tourists, such as Maharaja or Rajasthan Express.

The Ghan is some 490 feet long with many coaches and three dinning cars and a bar that served cool drinks, especially famous Australian beer that is so popular with us the Brits. It was more like a snug bar in one of our friendly English pub, a tavern where people were friendly and it was easy to make friends.

On Board The Ghan Express:

There were some 200 passengers on board, most of them much older than us. But we felt we were in a Retirement Home, a Sheltered Accommodation on wheel, until we met a young English couple from Liverpool, David and Nancy who were both university graduates and were on an extended working holiday before they settle down and tie the knot. Working holiday is the only way one can see this vast country without spending a fortune.

There were also two young girls in their company, Mary and June, one a nurse and the other a secretary who were on a career break? We really enjoyed their company, as they were our fellow Brits and made us feel young at heart.

Soon after slipping out of the Adelaide station, we crossed the Adelaide River. Some of the stops between Adelaide and Alice Springs are Port Pirie, Port Augusta, Cooper Paddy, Codney Park, Marla, Erldunda and many tiny settlements where the train would just slow down rather than making a stop.

Our guide book told us that the north of Adelaide, with lush green countryside, is a home of herbivorous Emu and hairy nosed Wombat, a prehistoric animal life unique to this region that has High Mountain with white Cyprus pine, oak and maple trees.

The ever changing landscape was a pleasure to watch. The evergreen lusty vegetation with numerous small rivers near Adelaide and the coast soon gave way to a barren parched interior with huge termite towers, low bushes with thick leaves and thorny cacti and kangaroos, pack of vicious dingoes and wild camels that number over half a million and in need of culling.

If no action is taken, as some nature loving Australians would prefer, the native fauna and flora will completely disappear and ultimately camels would die of starvation, a calamity for nature that may change the face of this land for ever.

These camels are the descendant of the Afghan camels set free when they were no longer useful as a beast of burden. Now some of these camels are also exported to Middle East and North Africa.

We disembarked at Alice Springs with many of our fellow passengers who wanted to fly to Ayers Rock, a 400 miles journey to the largest rock formation in the world and a sacred Aboriginal sight. But now a popular holiday destination that is fast becoming the most visited place in Australia.

But we just wanted to spend few days in Alice Springs, a place I always wanted to visit, an isolated, mystic place with the spiritual apprehension of truths and beliefs beyond the human understanding, that caught my imagination the day I read the novel "A Town Like Alice" when I was still at school and the author of the book Neville Shut also became my favourite author. His books touched and fascinated me and perhaps encouraged me to write.

In Alice Springs, we wanted to see the dry river bed with hidden water, which is so often used as a race course, visit a remote sheep farm with deep artesian well, where the water rises to the surface by natural pressure through a vertically drilled hole.

This source of fresh water has become a life-saver for the sheep farmers in the Australian outback. We also wanted to enjoy, experiencing the sheer isolation, the wilderness and emptiness of this fascinating continent, one of the most desolate place on earth.

Paddy's Hideout:

We spend a couple of nights on an isolated sheep farm, appropriately named Paddy's Hideout, with the courtesy of my Australian pen-friend John and his wife Ester with whom I have been corresponding since early fifties and met them in London twice when they visited Europe.

It seems most Australians visit Europe, especially those who fought in the Second World War and were stationed in England. But I never expected to meet them in Melbourne where they live. Australia is a place once considered to be out of bound for most of us, some place on the moon rather than down under.

On this farm we had the opportunity to ride camels. Each camel was given a name of a famous person. The camel I rode was called Camilla, a gentle lady of advancing age. After whom she was named I can only guess. Kumudini rode the handsome Rock Hudson and others were Bill Clinton, Monica, Regan, Diana and even Churchill but mercifully no Sonia Gandhi?

It seems Gandhi name has not yet reach the outback. After spending a few days and recharging our batteries, we were ready to board The Ghan Express again and resume our unique train journey to Port Darwin. We soon settled down in our Gold Kangaroo Cabin with faux Oak panelled walls, a cold drink and saw the harsh, some what lifeless desert go by.

The merciless sun in the cloudless sky would soon drive out the desert night chill and heat up the desert to an uncomfortable 40c to 45c in the shade.

Katherine, the Last of the Frontier Town:

Our next important stop before Darwin was a small town called Katherine, with a tiny airport and the famous 25 million year old Katherine Gorge, which may, one day rival Ayers Rock for attracting tourists. The people here got rich making concrete railway sleepers which were replacing wooden ones, a favourite munching snack for the termites.

Here we had the opportunity to see the town, visit some shops and markets selling home grown tropical fruits like mangos, papaya, guava, sugar cane, banana, Jack fruit and green coconuts, my favourite fruit and drink. We also visited a Rodeo Park and the gorge. The local wild life included blossom bats, slow moving Aussy lazy lizards, a nice way to pay back Aussies who always called us Pommy and a mass of colourful tropical birds with green parrots, budgies, wood peckers and usual town birds such as pigeons and sparrows.

This is indeed an interesting corner of Australia with tropical climate, completely different from South Australia with mild temperate climate and big cities like Sydney, Melbourne, Canberra and Adelaide that most European settlers prefer.

By the time we disembarked at Port Darwin, we had spent ten wonderful days on this unique journey, the experience which we are never likely to relive or experience again. It also gave a new meaning to our most popular advertising slogan, "Let the Train Take the Strain."

****

A CHANCE ENCOUNTER

Our last holiday to the island of Lanzarote, where we go on holiday practically every year, was a memorable one, in more ways than one. We were flying to the picturesque, lunar landscaped island of Lanzarote, in the Canary group of islands, a heaven for winter sunshine and for film makers, especially if they need a lunar landscape.

The film "A Million Year BC" with Rachael Welch, in her famous animal skin loincloth, which started a trendy fashion in skimpy bikini for the Hollywood film industry, was filmed here, on the Lanzarote Island.

It seems our holidays are rarely dull or without unusual happening, incident. So often it starts while we are standing in a queue at our local Luton airport. To-day was no exception. The couple in front of us, with three children, whose luggage was being weighed, found that one of their suitcases exceeded the weight limit for a single item of luggage, which would not be handled by the baggage staff.

So they had to open the suitcase to remove some of the heavy items. To the surprise of airline officials, they found a couple of real looking but plastic toy guns, amongst other toys. Although these were harmless toys but after the 9/11 scenario, an unprecedented terrorist attack on America, the most powerful nation on earth, it was foolish, to say the least to pack toy guns in your luggage.

The family was taken on one side and all there suitcases were thoroughly searched, offending items removed. This incident held us up for half an hour. But it gave us the opportunity to converse with a couple who were standing behind us.

As we were standing along side them for a long time, we were already feeling at ease in their company.

They were a young couple, an Englishman married to an Indian girl. I would like to call them Peter and Priya. As we go on holiday all the time, it is easy for us to make friends. We have learnt the art of making friends while on holidays. This was a lucky break for us, as they were staying in the same hotel called Paradise Island Hotel, as we were.

Our plane was a Boing 747 with 320 seats but hardly half full. This was the time when people were still reluctant to fly. So we had plenty of space and empty seats to lie down. It is a great bonus for me, as I suffer from chronic fatigue.

As there were so few passengers, we certainly got a VIP treatment from the cabin crew. We had a near perfect landing at Arrecife airport and a relief that we have seldom experienced.

Our journey, from airport to our hotel was uneventful. Normally we make friends at the reception, which is held on the next day after our arrival, when the tour rep gives us all the information and try to sell us as many excursions as he or she possibly could. In the cut throat business of package holidays, revenue generated by selling excursions is a welcome side business.

Peter and Priya were a lovely couple. Both of them were solicitors, Oxbridge graduates. Considering their intellectual and professional status, they were down to earth couple, a bit reserved, that is until you gain their trust.

We had an opportunity to be friends even before our holiday began in earnest. Although we are old-age pensioners, we are young at heart tourists. We do not spend most of our time sitting near the swimming pool, reading books. We do it occasionally, sitting in a shaded place, a garden, when we are recovering from a long and tiring excursion.

Peter and Priya had a similar taste and when they realized I am a hobby journalist, a writer, specializing on holidays, they borrowed the book I had written on my travels to Goa and Kerala. From then on, we were their equals on the intellectual side at least and as elders, we were accorded the respect and dignity our seniority, my silver hair deserved?

We had a wonderful holiday together, especially as Priya and Kumudini got on so well, visiting so many places, by bus, by coach and by car. Our friendship continued unabated when we returned home.

Normally holiday friendship, like a holiday romance is over when we return home. But once in a while we do meet people who keep in touch well after the holiday is over. Peter and Priya proved to be such a couple, along with another good couple, Michael and Marlina, whom we met in Kerala.

Another advantage was that, like us they live in London, not too far from where we live. Although we did not meet that often, we kept in touch by phone and email, a wonderful invention for the busy and the less mobile people. My travel brief on Lanzarote will never allow them to forget us.

A year after our chance encounter at the Luton airport, I got an email from Peter that his eighty seven year old father had a heart attack. We went to see his father at the London hospital, in the East End. This was our first meeting with Peter's parents.

When I gave him a get well card, with my full name in it, "Bhupendra Mohandas Gandhi" he gave me a look, a smile that said a thousand words, as if we have known each other for a long time.

I thought nothing of it at the time, until I met Peter and Priya after six months, at his father's funeral. Peter said to me, "Bhupendra, you know your get well card brought some childhood memory flooding back in my father.

In the twenties, when my father was a young boy aged ten, he used to live in Forest Gate. At the time it was a rural area, with farms and animals. We had some goats and the goats' milk was as popular then as cows' milk is today.

In 1926 Gandhiji came to London for talks with the British government. He was staying in a private house in the Mile End area. My father, as a little boy, was given the responsibility of delivering two pints of goat's milk to Gandhiji, at 6am in the morning.

Gandhiji stayed in London for a week. He got his milk on time, everyday. My father used to get up at four in the morning, milk the goat, cycle some seven miles in order to deliver milk on time. My father, as a young man, served in India, during the Second World War and came to realise what a great man Gandhiji was.

He was glad that God gave him the opportunity to serve such a noble, saintly man. It was like serving Lord Jesus Christ, although he was too young to realise that at the time.

When you gave him the get well card in the hospital, he was surprised to read your name. For a second, he thought you were Gandhiji's son or a grandson and all the old memories, which had laid dormant all these years, came flooding back. We are all very grateful to you that you came to see him in the hospital. It did cheer him up to no end."

Before we left, Peter gave me an old, sealed envelop and asked me to open it when we reach home. I had no idea why he gave me such an old envelop. So I was eager to get back to our home. When I opened it in the comfort of my house, I was speechless for a while.

It contained an old, black and white, yellowing photograph of Gandhiji and at the back, Gandhiji had written in his own handwriting, "To my son Mark, for looking after me and giving me the most delicious goat's milk I have ever tasted.

"Signed Mohandas K. Gandhi".

There was a short note from Peter, which read, "Dear Bhupendra, my father has requested me to pass on this photograph to you. It was his prised possession and I hope it will be yours as well. Look after it. Best wishes and hope to see you soon."

I was speechless for a time. My heart was filled with joy and a sorrow of a kind, as if I had lost someone close to me, yet I had met Mark, Peter's father only once, in a hospital and for some half an hour.

I wish I had met him earlier, known him better and talked about his chance encounter with the noblest person that graced mother earth, since Lord Rama, Lord Buddha and Lord Jesus Christ. The photograph will always remain my proud possession as long as I live.

We are still in touch with Peter and Priya. Even if I never see Peter again, which is more than likely? As the time passes by, the old memory, old friendship and old, first love always fades away. But the photograph will always remind me of Peter and his father.

Life is full of coincidences. A chance encounter with Peter and Priya has brought me so much joy and happiness that would be impossible for any one else to understand, to comprehend. Perhaps as a writer, I have a vivid imagination and a soft heart, an emotional outlook. But I would not have it any other way.

Before this chance encounter, I only shared my surname Gandhi with Mahatma but now I feel analogy, affinity and similitude with this great man who was voted the personality of the 20th Centaury.

Now I am proud of my surname and the fact that our families came from the same village as Mahatma Gandhi. It took an Englishman to make me realise my great heritage and how great Gandhiji was, a real Lord Rama of our time.

****

TO HELL AND BACK

Most of my short stories have a nucleus of personal experiences, mostly my own but so often that of a friend or a family member. So this story is no exception, except in one way, that I have not in any way modified or sensationalised it in order to make it more interesting, more exciting and reader friendly, which is the norm for every writer when stories are based on factual accounts.

This was such an unusual, unbelievable experience that I would not like to spoil it, dilute it in any way but to describe it as it happened. Moreover there is nothing I could add or exaggerate that could make it more extreme. The facts themselves are unbelievable, especially for those who never had such an experience in their lives. So often facts are stranger, more unbelievable than fictions. This is one such case.

It was a bitter sweet experience, although it is most inappropriate to describe such a painful, soul destroying experience in any way sweet. But then every coin has two sides, every cloud has a silver lining and it was no different in this case either. This experience made me a better person, a kinder person, a considerate and an appreciating person. It made me realise what a wonderful friends, devoted family members I have and how much I am appreciated and what a wonderful blessing Lord Krishna has bestowed upon us.

It was a fateful morning when I walked into a hospital day ward, to keep an appointment to undergo a liver biopsy, a minor procedure that would take only some twenty minutes to complete and no more than three hour's stay in a day ward, that is according to my consultant, who was so eager for me to undertake the biopsy.

Somehow I was feeling uncomfortable, with a desire to walk away, when I entered the ward. I felt a strange kind of bone piercing chill. Perhaps it was a premonition or just a fate or may be I was trying to be wiser after the event. With hindsight, I feel I should have listened to my inner voice but as I was a regular visitor to NHS hospitals for the past thirty years, undergoing numerous investigations without any mishap, I had full confidence in my doctors as well as in hospital procedures.

How wrong I was, how misplaced was my confidence became obvious, became crystal clear, within the next few hours. Normally such a liver biopsy is performed under ultra scan, so that the doctor can see where he is putting, the needle, can guide it to the right spot.

But in my case it was done without the help of a scan, a blind biopsy may be to save a couple of hundred pounds or to give the young doctor some practice. But in the end my 22 days stay in the hospital must have cost NHS more than fifty thousand pounds and taking into account life long drug dependency and frequent check-up, the cost would easily exceed half a million pound?

Anything and everything that could go wrong did go wrong, with disastrous consequences. As soon as the needle was inserted, I started experiencing an excruciating pain. The doctor, at first put it down to local anaesthetic not working in the inner part of the abdomen but he soon realised it was more than just anaesthetic not doing the job, when he saw the pain, the anguish and the agony on my face, along with my screams which obviously unnerved him.

The pain was unbearable, breathing was difficult and I collapsed. I was sweating buckets, as if I was under a shower. I must have lost a pint of body fluid in less than fifteen minutes.

I can not imagine what these screams must have done to Kumudini, who was sitting on the other side of the flimsy curtain that separated us. Later I learned that she feared the worse, thinking the doctor may have punctured my lungs, causing pneumothorax.

The doctor, whom I would like to call Dr. John, was soon on the phone, summoning help. In no time three doctors stormed in the tiny cubicle where I was being treated. As I was in great pain, they gave me pethidine with stemetile, a strong pain killer to start with and morphine injection every few hours.

I was detained overnight; a three hour stay became a twenty four hour stay before I was discharged the next day. But this was just the beginning, not the end of my nightmare. I was not feeling well at all. My stomach was distended and I was in constant pain, hardly able to walk. We even enquired whether it was necessary to have an x-ray before I go home.

I was assured that it was a normal pain associated with such a biopsy and I will be fine within the next 48 hours, word of wisdom that sounded like a death sentence when the reality dawned upon us. So I was discharged with some strong pain killer tablets.

At home, my condition kept on deteriorating. I was unable to eat, drink and always in severe pain. The next day we went to our GP with a sample of urine. On examination, the urine was found to contain ketone, blood and protein. My GP, who is such a caring person, was worried and after being on the phone for a long time, she managed to contact my consultant. I was rushed to hospital by an ambulance. So I was back in hospital within 48 hours.

This time the whole team, including my consultant was there and I was admitted to a ward within two hours of my arrival. The surgical team was also put on standby, just in case an emergency surgery was needed. Within an hour I was given a thorough examination, which included chest x-ray, ECG, blood test and even CT scan of the liver and the stomach.

I was also put on a fast drip as I was badly dehydrated and it was difficult to draw blood. I was given saline, stemetile, antibiotics and some more drugs when I was in the casualty, before I was transferred to a ward.

The prognosis was that the needle had penetrated right through and punctured the gall bladder which lies just behind the liver?

The gall bladder was leaking badly, pouring bile and some blood in the abdominal cavity. My eyes and forehead looked jaundice and I was passing bile and blood in my urine.

I was in agony with temperature and blood pressure going up and down.

The next day was Saturday and for the first time since the biopsy, I felt much better. I thought I was on the way to full recovery but it proved to be a false hope, a mirage in the desert, not an oasis. Perhaps it was just a last flicker of a dying wick which always seems bright. From then on, I began to deteriorate, slowly but surely.

I was in severe pain and discomfort due to diarrhoea, caused by strong pain killer tablets, acidity pain, high fever and high blood pressure fluctuating all the time. I was given panadol, gaviscone liquid, nizatidine capsules and tamazopan at night to help me go to sleep, as well as pethidine injections and all sorts of antibiotics through intravenous feeding.

Chest x-ray and C.T. scan were done every two days and as it did not show any abscess, the same treatment was continued, in the vain hope that powerful antibiotics would somehow heal the wounds, seal the puncture. But I was getting worse day by day. Bile was still leaking, forming puddles in the abdominal cavity. Constant morphine injections could only provide a temporary relief.

After some eight long and morale sipping days, it was clear, at least to me, that the treatment was not working. The only alternative, albeit a drastic one, was to undergo a surgery with inevitable loss of a perfectly healthy gall bladder. This was not only our, mine and Kumudini opinion but that of all the nurses who were involved with my case, looking after me.

Next day when my consultant came to see me early in the morning with her team, I had a bad, sleepless night and I was completely demoralised, depressed with tears flowing down my unshaven, weathering face. I begged her to consider an alternative treatment. She looked at the chart, the scan report and straight away asked her surgical team to have a look at me.

It was Wednesday. The surgical team, consisting of three doctors and an anaesthetist, visited me late in the afternoon. They all agreed that I should have an operation and it would be done on Friday, early in the morning.

On Thursday, late in the evening, the head of the hospital's surgical section, whom I would like to call Mr. Parkinson, a leading and renowned surgeon in his field, came to see me. I thought it was a routine visit, to give me a pep talk before an operation.

While trying to explain my predicament, I completely broke down. He explained to me that he has postponed my operation until the next day, which is Saturday, as he would like to do it himself. He would also like to study my x-rays, frame by frame and as he was fully occupied on Friday, he would come in on Saturday, his day off, to perform the surgery. He wanted to devote his full time and complete attention to my case.

This was indeed a minor miracle, a famous surgeon, an authority in this field, giving up his free day, which they normally spend on a golf course, to treat a NHS patient? It was a wonderful gesture on his part. I was very much impressed with his manner, his detailed observation and the way he explained the surgical procedure.

It was so reassuring and made me feel at ease. It lifted my spirit to no end and gave me hope where there was none. After all, this black and gloomy cloud had a silver lining? I saw the light at the end of the tunnel.

Mr. Parkinson carried out the three hour operation, laparoscopy, peritoneal washout and cholecystectomy on Saturday morning. He was unable to save my gall bladder, a difficult organ to heal, which was leaking badly. He thoroughly cleansed and washed all the organs with saline water which were immersed in bile. The operation was a complete success and I had a very peaceful Saturday and Sunday nights, in an ICU ward.

It was a major operation and normally a patient has to be in a reasonably good health to undergo such a demanding surgery. But in my case we had no choice. I was getting worse day by day and we may have already delayed the operation too long.

After a couple of days, the toll on my body began to tell. During the last ten days or so, I had hardly eaten anything. I had lost over a stone in weight, due to continuous diarrhoea. I was in constant pain, my guards were down, my body was weak and finding it difficult to cope with the strain of such a major surgery. Now I understand why most surgeons refuse to carry out a major surgery, such as organ transplant, on older people.

From Monday to Thursday, I had the worst four days of my life. I had high fever, stomach pain, along with anxiety, depression and my blood pressure shot up to 210. Every day my hands were punctured several times to draw blood but my veins have collapsed which made it very difficult and painful to find a blood vessel that would yield blood or hold a drip for more than a day.

It was a sheer torture to get through a day, especially night. All doctors were wonderful but I could not say the same about some agency nurses, who were on duty mainly at night. My surgeon came to see me every day and so often had a lengthy discussion with my wife, especially when he knew that she is a qualified nurse.

It was sheer torture and however hard I tried, I could not contain, held back my tears. I thought I was fighting a losing battle. My heart was bleeding from inside and I thought I am not going to make it. I had given up physically and mentally. I had no desire to get better or to live. Relief would come only in death. If there is hell, this was it.

One night, I started hallucinating, while drifting in and out of sleep, feeling happy and contended in a strange way, knowing that this pain, this suffering would soon come to an end, seeing my mother who was talking to me, telling me there is nothing to fear or to worry. Some of my childhood friends were waiting at the gate of heaven to welcome me. It was a strange, a bizarre feeling that is difficult to describe, difficult to put into words or for any one to understand.

In the morning when I got up, I was calm and contended, as if the present situation, this predicament does not matter at all. When Kumudini came in early in the morning, I was calm and at peace, telling her about my wonderful dream, talking to my mum.

I expressed my desire to see all my family members, especially children. I was no longer in pain. There was even a smile on my face, perhaps a mischievous smile but this did not reassured Kumudini at all.

Being a nurse, she has come across such a condition, seen patients who have lost the will to get better, lost the desire to live. She realized that I was giving up fight. This is the worse scenario. If a patient gives up fight, lose the will to live, to get better, then no doctor, no amount of medicine can help him.

Kumudini has been by my side from day one, not only looking after me physically but encouraging me, giving me hope that I will be fine. It is only a matter of time. She is a strong willed person, bearing the strain of the last few days with courage and dignity that only a trained professional can muster. It is also a hallmark of most Hindu women.

But my calmness, lack of desire to fight back brought tears in her eyes, which made me feel guilty, especially when she told me that she would like to see me back in our beautiful house, our Vrindavan like garden, the abode of Lord Krishna. But it would be hopeless, near impossible without my help, my burning desire to get better, to fight with all the strength that I could muster.

I knew I could never let down one person who has done so much for me, who has suffered as much, if not more than me. In the afternoon I dozed off for an hour or so. In my dream, which I still feel was more than a dream, a real experience, a divine intervention, I saw myself in my beloved Hare Krishna temple in Watford, which we visit practically every Sunday in summer.

It was a Sunday afternoon. The noon arti was just over and all devotees had departed. There was a heavenly peace. I was standing in front of Lord Krishna's image, eyes closed. Suddenly I was blinded by a flash of light, a thunderous light that brightened the whole temple. Lord Krishna, emerging from the image, came to me, some six feet tall, with a smile that said a thousand words. He did not utter a single word but his message was crystal clear.

I was humbled. Could it be possible for me or even any one else to see Lord Krishna in person? Was it a dream, a mirage or a hallucination? I pinched myself and feel the pain. His message was for me to get better. It was my duty, my obligation to my family, especially to Kumudini and to Lord Krishna.

How can I even think of abandoning my Vrindavan on this earth? My mum, my departed friends and family members will always be there for me at the gate of heaven. I can and I will meet them but only when the time is right. Was it Lord Krishna preaching to his favourite disciple Kunti putra Arjun or giving darshan to Meerabai, his famous disciple?

This dream, this divine message was so clear that I had no choice; above all I was convinced I will get better and go home to my family, my beautiful garden and to Hare Krishna temple.

When I opened my eyes, I saw Kumudini standing over me. I gave her a smile which said every thing. We both knew instantly that I will be going home and very soon indeed.

Next day when Mr Parkinson visited me, he was surprised to see me so positive, so well under the circumstances. My stitches were removed the next day and I was home within three days, when I was expected to stay there for at least a week more.

This was the first time I saw a ray of hope where there was gloom and doom, despair and darkness.

Although I am proud of our noble, peaceful and secular Hindu religion, our deities, avatar (reincarnation) of Lord Rama and Lord Krishna, our rich and superior cultural heritage that goes back to ten thousand years.

I would not consider myself a superstitious person nor do I believe in miracles but I do feel that there is a divine figure, a super power up there that looks after us. Some may call him God and worship him through his disciples, call him Lord Rama, Lord Krishna, Lord Buddha, Guru Nanak Lord Mahavir or Lord Jesus Christ.

I believe that it is better to have faith, believe in God and his disciple Lord Krishna. Faith can work wonders when we are in no win situation. I believe, rightly or wrongly, that I would not have come out alive from my ordeal without my faith, my belief and my trust in Lord Krishna.

This is such a painful and personal experience that I have hesitated a long time before putting it into print. I feel it is my duty to share it with my fellow Hindus so that they may come to appreciate our noble religion as much as I do.

****

IS THERE A GHOST?

It was exam time once again. Well, it was difficult to escape exams when one is studying medicine, the most difficult, extensive and thorough course one can undertake.

Then we are well rewarded when we qualify. It brings not only financial reward but social standing that is second to none. If you play your cards right, the word Doctor in front and the letters such as MBBS, MD, FRCS behind your name normally works wonders and will open all doors.

When it comes to marrying a young, beautiful, well educated girl from a wealthy and respectable family, there is no competition.

After all doctors are only second to God in our ultra conservative society. It is not too difficult to imagine what lies at the end of the rainbow. Five of us, I, Rishi, Ravi, Nikhil and Nayan had made Rishi's one bedroom flat, with a lounge and a kitchen, our headquarter for the duration of our exams. After all rest of us were living in a tiny bed-sit where we had to share all facilities.

As Rishi's family were in the property letting business, it was possible for Rishi to have such a luxurious flat in the heart of Bombay.

Ding .... Ding .... Ding .... ancient clock on the wall struck twelve, the midnight. As we were at it for the last five hours, it was time to take a break. As Rishi was the host and some what domesticated, it was his responsibility to provide tea and some bitting.

Rishi reluctantly went to the kitchen and within fifteen minutes came back with a tray full of teapot, milk, sugar, some biscuits and Bombay mix that was every one's favourite.

This was the standard diet for college students, as it was cheap, easy to prepare and above all labour free, although not so healthy. Sandwiches were not yet on the market nor were pizza, Chinese or Indian takeaway. Microwaves were not even on the drawing board.

But when we are young, healthy, virile and full of energy, healthy diet is the last thing on our mind. In those distant days we were not as health conscious as we are today. I distinctly remember every one in my family used to smoke while today no one does.

While drinking tea, we started talking. Our favourite topics of conversation were films with Meenakumari, Madhubala, Vajayantimala, Nargis, Raj Kapoor, Ashok Kumar and Dev Anand who were our favourite actors. Cricket and girls came close second.

"What movie we should see this Saturday?" As usual, it was Ravi's question. No matter what, we must go to a movie either on Saturday or Sunday. It was cheap, long lasting and the theatre was just round the corner, saving us the bus fare. It was a routine for most of the collegians.

"There is a double bill of Dracula and the Revenge of the Virgin Vampire". Pressed Ravi. No matter what, Ravi must have his weekly fix. It was like an addiction for him.

"Count me out." Said Nayan in a soft, almost apologist voice. "I do not enjoy such horror movies."

"Why? Don't tell me that you are scared." Ravi was sarcastic. "I find it difficult to believe that any one can take these movies seriously.

They are meant to provide a cheap entertainment, nothing more. Could there be any other reason, such as you would like to revise while we are at the movie?" Ravi wanted to put Nayan on the spot and he succeeded.

"I do not like these kinds of movies." It was Nayan's curt reply.

"No, that will not do. If you do not want to come, you have to give us a better, believable reason." Ravi would not let it go.

"Well, I know you boys would not rest until I come clean. Well, this is a long, sad and perhaps unbelievable story that is unless you have experienced some thing similar. It won't be fun, especially for me. But I am willing to share my bitter experience with you all." There were tears in Nayan's eyes. So we knew we are in for a long and rough night.

"This incident goes back some six years. I had just joined the college. Like every young entrant, we were full of big talk, high hope, proud and some what naïve and foolhardy as well; ready to take any challenge, no matter what the consequences may be.

In the summer vacation, I and my nephew went to Devital, a small village at the foot of Nilgiri mountain range. It has a cool, tolerable summer climate, a place where any one would like to spend his summer vacation.

My grandmother was living there. So I used to go to Devital now and again.

This year four of us met in Devital. It was our plan to explore the mountain, learn about the flora and fauna of this region, make note, sketch plants, flowers and birds, take some photographs, as some in our group were studying agriculture, forestry, wanted to become naturalist and botanist.

We could kill two birds with one stone, study, have some fun and experience an out door life; learn how to survive in wilderness. Well, watching Tarzan movies, Johnny Weissmuller and Jane in loin cloth and skimpy bikini had made us all aware and fond of Jungle life.

On one of our outings, we sat down outside a log cabin, built on an elevated ground in front of a fast flowing but a shallow stream. Such well built, sturdy and spacious log cabins were located all over Nilgiri hills, especially at the foothills.

These cabins were well stocked with firewood, tined food, lentils, water and cooking utensils, as these cabins were used by the forest officers but were not out of bounds for the local shepherds who herd their goats on the slopes of these hills or for novices like us, who just want to wonder, explore these hills and spend a night or two.

The only condition was to leave it clean, tidy and as well stocked as you find it. These were the times when people were honest to a fault, especially in villages where no one had to lock their doors and women can go out at any time of the day or night without any fear. Old people were considered wise, knowledgeable and worthy of respect. How the time has changed?

We lighted a fire and warmed the food while drinking tea from the flask we always carry with us. This masala or spiced tea really acts like a tonic, as effective as a peg of brandy or whisky to fight the cold.

Our food was roti or Nan, a kind of Indian bread which is cooked in special earthenware over a log fire, from the locally grown wheat, hot, dry Karai potato curry, green salad to be prepared from onion, cucumber, celery and half ripe tomatoes, a pot of yogurt and hard cheese made from goat milk. The food was good enough for a royal feast. After a hard day and a long walk, this food was God send to wet our appetite, simple but surprisingly tasty and nourishing.

Today we were six of us, as two local boys had joined us on this special expedition. We though their local knowledge of the area, especially the mountain and their experience will be valuable to us, as we were going to spend a night or two in wilderness.

Our after dinner talk, round a log fire with open sky full of twinkling stars hardly seen in the polluted city sky, some how turned to ghost. Could it be true, do ghost exist or was it an old wife's tale, a vivid imagination, a weakness of mind? It is an age old question no one has managed to find an answer. Is it chicken or the egg that comes first?

In our group there was a young man called Kishan, who was like us in his final year of medicine. Being born and brought up in Bombay, in an upper middle class family, he was of the opinion that all those who believe in ghost, in such mumbo jumbo were halfwits and should be locked up.

Our discussion turned ugly. Kishan, I and Raj were on one side while Amar, Milan and Shyam were on the opposite side. Not only they believed in ghosts but were willing to provide the proof and make us change our mind, our belief in the existence of ghost.

It was a common and well known story amongst the residents of Devital that the derelict building, once a beautiful bungalow on the outskirt of the village called "Madhav Nivas" but now a deserted, neglected building, was the haunt of the departed souls of a beautiful girl Meera and the son of the village elder Madhav.

It was decided that four of us who were from Bombay should spend the Saturday night at the haunted house. If we survive the night unscathed we won, otherwise we have to concede that ghosts do exist, that there is a supernatural power that may affect our lives.

The story behind this Laila Majnu episode was as follows:

"This incident happened some fifty years ago. At the time Devital was even a tinier village than today, with just two hundred inhabitants. The Mukhi, the village elder was Pitamber Patel who had a young and beautiful sixteen year old daughter who had become a widow.

As most of the girls used to get married in their teens, before their bodies were even properly developed, before beauty had the chance to emerge, a bud to open into a blossom, a sixteen year old fully grown and well developed girl in her prime was a rarity and an attraction to young and the old alike.

No wonder she was the most beautiful girl, the object of every one's desire in the village. At the time it was a taboo for a widow to remarry. No single, unmarried man would touch her with a bargepole. Some how these young and healthy widows were considered evil, responsible for the death of their husbands. They were forced to return to their parent's homes who were obliged to take them in but certainly not welcomed, especially if they had other unmarried daughters. They were destined to spend the rest of their lives alone, mostly confined to their tiny rooms.

Fortunately for Meera, she was the only daughter, with three big, strong and easy going brothers. Moreover being a Mukhi's daughter, she had more freedom than normal under the circumstances.

She was not obliged to shave her head or unable to leave the house unaccompanied. So she was known to every young and eligible bachelor in the village, although there were only a handful of such youngsters in this tiny village to match Meera in age and physique.

A widower can easily find a young, virgin girl but no young, single, unmarried man would extend his hand in marriage to a widow. But Madhav, the son of the Mukhi of the neighbouring village, three times bigger, more populous than Devital, was all together a different proposition.

He had lived in Bombay, although for a year only. Yet he was headstrong, independent minded and adventurous in every way. No wonder he was single even at the age of twenty.

Madhav and Meera met by chance at a village fair. She was with her two brothers but got separated in the melee. Seeing her alone, a couple of thugs tried to molest her when Madhav came to her rescue. Like a gentleman, he delivered her safely to her grateful brothers.

But Madhav some how fell head over heels in love with Meera, a love at first sight. Meera could not help but oblige, reciprocate his attention. No matter how hard Meera tried to keep away, she could not banish Madhav from her thought, her heart and her cogitation.

Soon they started meeting in the nearby forest, isolated huts on the mountain slopes and in the vast temple ground. It would be impossible not to attract attention in such a tiny place. Soon their romance was the topic of gossip, sweet, juicy piece of conversation on the lips of every one, young and old.

Although this relationship, a marriage would have been acceptable to Meera's father Pitamber Patel, the way this relationship started, blossomed into love was more than any one could bear.

But it was a completely different kettle of fish for Madhav's father. His family was superior, wealthier and he was the Mukhi of a village that was three times more populous than Devital. Madhav could marry any girl, a sweet sixteen year old girl from his village, a virgin, respectable and his equal.

The situation turned ugly, into an open warfare where there was only one loser and that person being Meera's father Pitamber Patel.

He was obliged to give his daughter Meera in marriage to a forty year old man from a nearby city who was a father of five children and only wanted Meera as a housewife, a servant, a baby minder and perhaps as a sex slave, to keep his bed warm.

Madhav tried his best to rescue Meera, his sweetheart, his life, his reason for living but all to no avail. He could not fight, not only against two powerful families but also against every person in both the villages.

It was a fight no one could win; no one could even dare to come to their rescue, not even Meera's three brothers who were very fond of Madhav and knew deep inside their heart that Madhav is the right person for their sister, who would make her happy, fulfil all her arman (desire) dream and ambition. It was too much for Madhav. While Meera's palkhi, (a wooden structure carrying bride and bridegroom and lifted by four strong men) was leaving the village with her husband to start a new life in the city, Madhav hanged himself in an empty bungalow, on the outskirt of the village, belonging to a rich village family residing in the city.

When Meera learnt about Madhav's suicide, she could not bear it. She ended her life by jumping into a deep well and drowning herself. This is the sad story of two young, hopeful lovers, Laila and Majnu, who were cruelly separated by the orthodox and ultra conservative society.

Since Madhav's suicide, the bungalow came to be known as **"Madhav Sadan"** a residence for Madhav. No one is able to live there, even spend a night there without experiencing some sort of turbulence, even seeing Madhav and Meera, listening to their laughter, chatter and heart shattering grief, cries and mourning. We were challenged to spend one night, a Saturday night in this ruin that was once a beautiful bungalow but now more of a Dracula's abode. I was not so keen but Kishan would not listen. He was determined to prove to every villager how ignorant they were; that the ghost only exists in their imagination, a housewife's tale, a product of weak mind and superstitious beliefs.

Our hot discussion, our determination to spend a night at Madhav Sadan spread like wild fire. No one from the village would go within a mile of these ruins during the night.

Villagers pleaded with us, warned us, even threatened us but to no avail. Kishan would not listen to reasons. He was willing to spend the night alone in

Madhav Sadan if we opt out. How could we abandon Kishan? We were all in it together, sink or swim, succeed or fail, live or die. We have to show solidarity, loyalty in Kishan's hour of need.

Only regret I had was that of upsetting my grandma. She was almost hysterical. At last our day of destiny arrived. Four of us left the village before sunset. We were fully prepared for all eventualities.

We had food, tea, coffee, matches, lighter, torch, cigarettes, two lanterns with enough kerosene to last several nights, playing cards, carrom, a typical Indian board game, gramophone with several records, even pills that we normally take during exam time to keep us awake all night, first aid box and dressing. After all Kishan was almost a doctor. We did not leave any thing to chance. How could we? It was a question of survival?

After an hour's walk, we arrived at our destination, in more ways than one.

We chose the best, the biggest and least damaged room, as the rest of the building was almost overrun by weeds, covered with rubbles and bird's droppings. We spread our waterproof sheets and blankets, collected firewood to last the night and started a small fire.

There was plenty of food. Yet we tried to roast chestnut, Indian cassava, Corn on the Cob to create a picnic type atmosphere, but to no avail. No one was in that sort of mood. We kept on sipping tea and coffee which is good enough to keep us awake.

There was tension, tautness, strain, unease and hidden fear in the air, in the atmosphere that no one was willing to talk, to admit. Certainly silence was not golden. We could almost cut the heavy atmosphere with a knife? Our mind was wandering, thinking about Meera and Madhav. We were even short of conversation, something that has never happened before?

Within a couple of hours we realized that this was a big mistake but again no one was willing to admit and say lets go back! Any how it was too late, as darkness and dense fog had descended on these mountain slopes like a locust on a green field.

In any case, it was too dangerous to walk in this dark, clouded, moonless sky, with boulders, ravines and gullies spread all over the place. The sky was even without stars that normally shine brightly in this part of the country. It seems the nature has conspired against us, against our foolhardy adventure. We were trapped in Madhav Sadan.

Although these were summer months, climate on the mountain slopes get cold at night, especially if there is a dense fog in the atmosphere. So it was important for us to keep the fire going.

We had a light supper as no one was really hungry. By now it was pitch dark with cloudy, heavy and moonless sky. Even the light from the two kerosene lanterns and the log fire could not lift the gloom and the darkness that was so wide spread.

When we ran out of conversation, we tried playing cards, carrom and listening to records on the gramophone. But the howling wind and strange noises of nocturnal insects and animals like foxes, wild dogs and occasional howling of wolves drowned the music from the gramophone.

As the night progressed, the tenseness in the atmosphere became almost unbearable. The light from the lanterns attracted various types of insects, especially bats, reminding us of the dwelling of Count Dracula. There was frightening silence, blood-curdling, creepy and mind disturbing silence in the atmosphere.

The clock was slowly ticking on. When it struck midnight, I along with Kishan were the only ones awake. I was surprised. How come our partners in crime were so fast asleep? These were the students who can keep awake night after night, even without the help of the pills. Yet today nothing seems to work, tea, coffee or pills could not keep us awake.

When I went to sleep or rather lost consciousness, Kishan was the only one awake. But there was fear, fright, terror and even horror on his face. I had the premonition of the terrible event that was about to unfold. I tried my best to keep awake and give Kishan the company, the moral support that he deserved in his hour of need but all to no avail.

I was the last one to fall a sleep except Kishan. Early in the morning I had a terrible, frightening dream. It was so frightening that it is difficult to put into words. I saw Yamraj, the messenger of death. He was wearing a necklace made of tiny skulls, decorated with red and white flowers that spell doom and gloom. He had come to take away Kishan.

It was raining hard but it was raining blood not water, with lumps of human flesh as big as a brick falling all over Madhav Nivas. Flesh eating birds like Vultures, kites, peregrines and falcons were having a field day, so were Wolves and hyenas.

Witches were having their convention in the house and there was only one agenda on their rostrum, the death of Kishan who had defied and made fun of them. Revenge was in the air.

No .... No.... No ... I shouted with all the strength I could muster, waking everyone up.

I was shaking like a leaf, all my clothing were wet with perspiration.

Everyone surrounded me, asking me what the matter was. I said I had a bad dream but as the night was over, we felt relieved. The log fire was out, so were lanterns, although they were more than half full with kerosene.

The wind had died down and the sky was getting clear, although the mist was still lingering in the air, as if reluctant to let go her domain. It was cold and the atmosphere was damp, as the sun was just over the horizon, trying hard to break lose from the morning clouds that normally hug the mountain slopes early in the morning.

Birds were singing and even the peacock sound was audible in the distance.

In the pleasantness of the morning, it was difficult to imagine the horror of the last night. Looking at Kishan's sleeping bag, it was empty and probably unslept.

We thought Kishan must have got up early and gone for a walk. He was a light sleeper in any case. We all got out of our sleeping bags and with a bawad stick in our mouth; bawad is a tree that provides thin branches which acted as a tooth brush in those early days. We left the room to enjoy the fresh air.

When I came to the entrance hall, I gave a cry, with every ounce of strength I was left with, after the tormenting night I had, a snivelling that shattered the peace, the early morning tranquillity and startled everyone who came running to the hall, to my assistance.

I found it difficult to breath and lost consciousness for few minutes. If Amar had not get hold of me, I would have fallen down on the stones, boulders and the rubbles that littered the floor, injuring myself badly.

It took me a few minutes to regain my composure. But the ghostly sight, the dangling body of Kishan, that was in front of us was so terrible that even today, after some six years, it is still in front us, still haunts all of us who had witnessed it. I wonder whether it would ever leave us alone.

We cut the rope and gently lowered Kishan or rather his lifeless body which was now ice cold. It was obvious that he had died a few hours ago. His eyes were wide open. There was a fear on his face as if he had seen a ghost? It was the face of a tormented soul.

Kishan had chosen the same spot, the same beam that Madhav had chosen.

It was a copycat suicide. We were told later on that it was the same day and date, exactly fifty years on?

Going through Kishan's pockets, we discovered a letter, written at half past midnight and addressed to all of us.

Dear Friends

By the time you find this letter, I would have departed, left this world and perhaps joined Meera and Madhav whom I treated with scant respect, made fun of. I am the only person responsible for my death.

This tragedy was of my creation and it is just that I have to pay the price, the ultimate penalty. So please do not feel bad. Go on with your life but I hope you will forgive me and perhaps remember me with fond memories, with the passage of time, when your wounds have healed.

I had no choice but to commit suicide, bring my life to an end. By the time it was midnight, all of you went to sleep. Nayan was the last one to fell a sleep, although he tried his best to keep awake and give me a company.

While you were dropping off one by one, as if you all have taken sleeping pills, I could not take even a wink, as if sleep had deserted me. The atmosphere was really frightening, with bats flying in and out, wolves hauling and the air was thick with Meera's laughter and Madhav's murmur.

Their shadows were running wild, some times clearly visible but most of the time remaining in the background, making love?

Both the lanterns were out, as if extinguished by a ghost. The log fire was also rapidly losing its sparkle. All around me was the pitch darkness, the glum, the grief and despondency we associate with Kabrastan, Smashan and the Cemetery.

Perhaps this was my imagination, may be my punishment. I could not determine. I was unable to bear this torture all alone. I tried my best to wake you up. I poured cold water, even used the burning log on you which would normally wake up even a Kumbkarna, the patriot Saint of sleep, all these to no avail. You were all motionless like logs as if there was no soul in your bodies.

I was fast losing my mental faculty, my sanity. Some unknown voice, spirit or perhaps ghosts of Meera and Madhav were urging me to kill one of you.

That was the penalty I had to pay for making fun, violating their abode, to unable me to live.

How can I decide whom to kill? After all every one of you is my friend. As I was responsible, I was the main culprit for this venture, I had to make the ultimate sacrifice and save you all.

I hope you will understand me, my action and forgive me for involving you all in this misadventure. Lastly I have to ask you to perform the unenviable task of informing my family.

Yours unfortunate friend Kishan."

As soon as we finished reading the letter, we all examined our legs. Surely there were severe burns where Kishan had touched our legs with the burning log. Every one had one but I had two, one on each leg.

We realised what a price Kishan had paid for this misadventure and to save us all by sacrificing his own life. We bowed our heads in admiration for the sacrifice Kishan had made to save us all. Could I have been next in line if Kishan had not given his life? The thought still lingers my mind.

We were so overwhelmed that we could not even cry. How did we managed to return to Devital is still shrouded in mystery.

For months, we were unable to sleep at night and even when we managed to sleep, take a wink, we were haunted by this tragic event. Meera, Madhav and Kishan were not far from us. How did I or any one of us managed to stay sane is a mystery." On completing his story, Nayan showed us the spot on his legs caused by the burning wood. They were still relatively fresh, although completely healed.

"Well Nayan, your story is indeed tragic but that does not prove that there is ghost, that ghosts do exist. It could be the weakness of Kishan's mind, the lonely, deserted atmosphere that may have played a big part in this tragedy." Ravi commented.

"I can understand your doubt, your scepticism and your apprehension. But after this experience, you have to understand why I would like to keep away from all such stories, discussion, including horror movies. So watching Dracula and the Revenge of the Virgin Vampire is out of bound for me, now and for ever.

There will always be those who passionately believe in God, Ghost, UFO and life after death, in reincarnation but equally there are those who refuse to believe in this nonsense. This question, belief will remain with us as long as human civilization exists.

Moreover why did I get this terrible dream, saw Kishan's death and above all why we all fell asleep, why Kishan could not wake us up, even a bucket of ice cold water and a burning wood had no effect on us?"

No one could reply, supply a valid explanation to Nayan's question.

The clock struck five, early in the morning, a time when our favourite restaurant, Irani Café open. It was time to pack up, call it a day and go for an early morning breakfast to our favourite place, the abode of barvatias, the outlaws, that is us, the medical students.

****

RUPA

The train was slowly slipping away from the Bombay Central station. This train journey from Bombay (Mumbai) to Chital was a slow, long and some what tiresome, especially as only a slow train that would stop at any and every station, like a local bus, would take me to Chital, a tiny village some four hundred kilometres from Bombay.

Since the introduction of first class compartment with air condition and a sleeping berth, the journey had become tolerable, comfortable and even pleasant, especially if I get the right company, those of NRIs from East Africa and occasionally from England, who always travel by first class.

It was a full day's journey. For once the train was on time and we slipped out of the Bombay Central like a serpent, in the late afternoon. Once we left behind the sprawling suburbs of Bombay and entered the rural area, a pastoral, rustic countryside, the scenery changed dramatically.

The mass of humanity gave way to nature, with coconut groves, banana and sugarcane plantations and fruit orchards, interwoven with wheat and occasionally paddy fields that looked pleasing to my sore city eyes where concrete jungle was more visible than a green one created by nature.

As I take this route, travel on this track every year, it was normal scenery for me. I get more excited when we pass through a jungle, ravine and a gorge and over fast flowing rivers. But unfortunately forests were fast disappearing, being replaced by fields and human settlements. Whenever I go to Chital, I always take a bag full of books, which include books by my favourite authors, Sir Arthur Conan Doyle, James Hilton, Jules Verne, Agatha Christie, Nevil Shute, Bronte sisters, Charlotte, Emily and Anne, Leo Tolstoy and my favourite Gujarati author Ramanlal Vasantlal Desai.

I feel the books I read as a youngster, The Lost Horizon, A Town like Alice, For Whom the Bells Toll, Wuthering Height, Dr. Zhivago, Anna Karenina, The Great Expectation and Twenty Thousand League Under the Sea, Hounds of Baskerville, a few amongst many, some how shaped my life, made me what I am today.

The dining car on this train was primitive indeed but fortunately the food was fresh and tasty. Any way Rs.20 tip would do wonders, as it was more than a day's wage for a chef in those distant days when money really had a value and a tip was appreciated, a bonus rather than an obligation.

After a long and enjoyable dinner, with a bottle of local beer, Kingfisher beer was not available at the time, I retired early. My eyes were tired with constant reading.

Somehow I always sleep soundly like Kumbkarna on a train. The rhythmetic noise of the running train is some how music to my ears and acts as sleep inducing tonic for me. Then again, I always sleep well no matter where I am.

The simple breakfast of coffee, hard boiledd egg and toasts was provided in our compartment. After lunch, we entered the hilly country. After all Chital is a hill station, although still undeveloped, mainly due to lack of infrastructure and the fact that it was in the middle of nowhere.

The scenery changed dramatically. The dry, parched and flat land gave way to lush green vegetation with rolling hills in the background, tiny fast flowing rivers and ponds, lakes and check dams.

Ponds were covered with white, red and purple lilies, my favourite flowers, symbol of Goddess Saraswati, the Goddess of education, knowledge and wisdom.

The hill slopes were covered with forests and trees like Pine, eucalyptus, silver birch, Indian Oak, Pipal, Banyan, Jack fruit trees and sycamore were prominent.

When the train passed by the vast Viral lake, I knew Chital was within a striking distance. The sharp whistle of the train broke my chain of thoughts, letting me know, reminding me that we have at last arrived at our destination.

Chital is a very small, rather a time wrapped tiny village that has not changed a bit during the last thirty years or so. The progress was slow; even non-existent in those peaceful era when time had no meaning, no significance and certainly did not rule our lives.

The station was no more than a short platform, with a wooden building that would give some what misleading impression that it would collapse at any time. But it has been there as long as I can remember. So it was a deceptive appearance.

It was the month of October, the beginning of winter but for Chital, a hill station some four thousand feet high; the chill was already in the air. The cold, chilly wind made its presence felt in no uncertain terms.

The sun was in a hurry to go home, to disappear behind the distant peaks.

With the melting of the sunlight and diaphanous warmth, it was time to be indoor as soon as possible, with log fire to warm and replenish the body heat. I was greeted by the station master, Karimchaha to me, an old family friend who was as much part of the station as the old building.

I was the only passenger to disembark at Chital and the train departed as soon as I disembarked, as if in a hurry to make up for the lost time. Perhaps the train driver had his home at the end of the line, where his family, perhaps his sweetheart may be eagerly waiting for him.

Luckily a horse-carriage was waiting outside the station. Without asking me, an oldish looking person took my two suitcases and put them at the back of the carriage, while I took up the seat in front. As soon as I sat down, he drove off, as if he knew exactly where I wanted to go.

"You are Pareshbhai, son of Jayaben, aren't you?"

"Yes uncle but I do not remember you?" I said in a polite voice. His grey hair and advancing age demanded some respect from a young person like me.

The uncle was obviously impressed, taken back by my mild manner and the respect I accorded to him.

Perhaps most, if not all Bombay babus (young men) were arrogant when it comes to dealing with some one in a village. But educated persons like us should not forget either our background nor should we use our knowledge, opportunity and upbringing to look down on others.

That was the discipline installed in me by my parents from the childhood and I must say it has stood me in good stead in a city like Bombay where civility is in short supply.

"Son, I have moved to Chital recently. The station at Ramper was getting crowded. It was getting difficult for an old man like me to compete with the young and aggressive motorised Rickshawalas. There was a pain in his voice, a reflection of bad experience he may have encountered while dealing with the youth of today. Who can blame him?

I deal with such rowdies every day, so often I have to defend them in court, even though I know that they are as guilty as hell. With rich and influential parents, they literally get away with murder.

This is our modern day Bharat where decency, honesty and respect for the elderly, the sick and the disable have been consigned to the dustbin.

It is the survival of the fittest, a jungle law where might is right. It is not what you know but whom you know that counts.

Maji (mother) told me a couple of days ago that Bhai (brother) will be coming from Bombay. So I was here to meet you. Within twenty minutes, we were at Ganga Mahal (Holy Ganga River Cottage) my ancestral home where my father and I were born and brought up, where I have spend some of the happiest days of my young life.

On hearing the sound of the approaching carriage, my mother came running out or rather limping out, as due to her old age and the onset of arthritis in both her legs, her walking, her movements were severely restricted.

I was setting a foot in my childhood home after a long time. Although this was a spacious three bedroom house, with a large veranda in the front, a beautiful garden at the back, now neglected and over grown with weeds and a rooftop gallery, the common, basic and every day facilities were elementary, especially when compared with my luxurious flat in Bombay.

My flat was situated in one of the most desirable part of Bombay, right in front of the Juhu beach, with all the modern gadgetries that a bachelor person with a limited free time may need or desire.

But Ganga Mahal has an atmosphere of its own that could not be matched or recreated any where else in the world. Perhaps childhood memories, heroes and sweethearts are unique, once in a lifetime experience only.

No matter however hard one may try to erase them, these memories always remain buried deep down in our heart, our subconscious mind which may surface again when least expected.

There was a heavenly peace, compelling and easy to feel at ease atmosphere in this practically vast and empty house.

I took up residence in my old bedroom, the most spacious bedroom in the house. It was left untouched, time wrapped, preserved as it was some ten years ago when I last slept in this bed.

As Chital was a tiny place, there was not much to do, nor were there any young men of my age and background with whom I could mix, socialise and pass my time. Moreover the purpose of my visit was to spend as much time as possible with my ailing mother, my only living blood relative, family member.

In the morning and evening, I went for long walks, in the foothills, forests and along the tiny streams, river banks. Being a hill station, Chantal is a walker's paradise. I spent the rest of the time in the house, chatting with my mum and reading and writing.

During my college days, I had developed a taste for writing, especially for our college magazine. But after passing my law exams, I joined a prestigious law firm that put paid to my aspiration to become a fledgling, a budding author.

Now reading legal books was more my cup of a tea than reading novels. So whenever I get such an opportunity, two to three weeks of peace and tranquillity, I make the most of it, reading, writing and corresponding with college friends.

This hobby of mine also kept me indoor, that suited Maji right to the ground, as it gave us a quality time together, reminiscing the nostalgic past.

After qualifying as a solicitor, I had to move to Bombay where most lucrative practises are located, where most millionaires live and earn their livelihood and perhaps, where most crimes are committed as well? In a way Bombay is a heaven, a paradise for legal eagles like me.

There was hardly any gainful employment in Chital, except back breaking hard work in agriculture, lumbering and a couple of small shops, a priest, a barber and a school teacher but certainly no lawyers.

Whatever problems, dispute that may arise, were fairly and wisely dealt with by the village elders. There words were law and obeyed by every one, at least so far, but the time is changing very fast. It is only a question of time before the court will take over the decision making machinery.

The place could provide only a subsistence living with a motto, a maxim, "want not, earn not, waste not", an every day existence that would not be my or to that matter any one else's cup of tea, especially after spending four years at the university. So there were hardly any young men in the village that I could relate to.

When I settled down in Bombay, I invited my mum to come and live with me. Being her only son, she duly obliged. But it was a sad and a lonely life for her, as I was out most of the time, working, meeting and socialising with clients which were part of the curriculum, a prerequisite to climb the professional ladder and gain fame and success.

I soon realised that it was cruel and selfish for me to keep Maji in my tiny flat, just to ease my conscious. So when she expressed her desire, her wish to move back to Chital, I could not really oppose it.

But she would dutifully spend a month or two with me, her only child, every year, travelling all the way from Chital. But I would send some one from the office to accompany her on the train journey or even go myself.

But now Maji was approaching eighties, with declining health, poor eyesight and unsteady on her legs. So we reversed the routine and decided that I should come to Chital and spend a few weeks with my dear old mum.

Early in the morning, even before the sun came out from behind the distant hills, Rupa would knock on our door, call Maji's name to deliver fresh milk.

She was just seventeen years old. But living in this fresh, cool mountain climate accompanied by healthy diet and carefree lifestyle has brought out her full potentials, a well developed body with curves in all the right places.

She was really beautiful, with milky complexion, mischievous smile, twinkle in her eyes and a provocative heap movement. I wonder how Lord Brahma, the Creator failed to fall in love with his masterpiece.

Early morning knock and the sweet, peacock's coos type voice woke me up. It was not difficult for me to beat Maji to the door and when she realised my eagerness to collect the milk, Maji gave up her struggle to open the door.

Rupa was really pleased to see me. May be I was from Bombay and there were hardly any eligible young men in the village or was it my fertile imagination? Aren't village people supposed to be friendly and helpful?

Could there be any other reason for Rupa to be so friendly with me?

Perhaps it was my solicitor's mind, trained to view every thing with suspicion.

I used to tease Rupa that she will have to come to my Bombay flat to deliver the milk or I will refuse to go back.

"Well, if you stay here permanently, Maji would be very happy."

"What about you Rupa, would you like me to stay here for good." I said with a smile.

"Pareshbhai, I may be village lass, a milk-maid but I am not stupid. A high flying lawyer like you can never be able to settle down in a village like Chital. It is nice of you to come and spend few weeks with Maji. But that is all any one can expect from you." She said in some what sad voice, as she knew I will be gone in a couple of weeks, perhaps never to be seen again.

"Well Rupa, I will come here every year as long as Maji is alive and perhaps afterwards as well?" I gave Rupa a broad smile and watched her dancing away, swinging her well developed hips, partly hidden by her colourful costume and disappearing round the corner. I could not take my eyes of her as long as she was within sight.

Rupa's mother Sonbai was already looking after Maji, visiting the house everyday, occasionally cooking and washing her cloths. But with my arrival, she had taken a back seat. Perhaps she may not want to intrude or just give us the privacy that she thought we may want, we deserve.

But in such a tiny place, it would be difficult not to bump into each other.

Knowing that she is Rupa's mother, made me amiable to her. I could not help talking with her, albeit just to say how are you and enquiring about Rupa in a casual way.

Within few days, I was as friendly with Sonbai as I was with Rupa. So one day when I saw Sonbai at our door, I was not surprised at all. After all she was my mum's friend, her minder, her nursemaid.

She obviously looked worried, had some weight on her shoulder, making her uncomfortable.

She asked me nervously, "Beta (son) can I ask you a question?"

"Maji (mother) Ask me whatever you want. I will try my best to give you a reply and without charging my fees as well." I joked to lighten the atmosphere. For a moment I thought it could be about Rupa, as she was obviously ready for a marriage. Most girls in such villages get married by the time they are sixteen.

"Beta, do you think children who go to a big city for further studies forget their parents, their families?" The pain, sorrow and sadness were obvious in her voice. She turned her face to hide her tears.

"How can you say that Maji. Have I forgotten my mum?" I answered her question with my own question. I knew it was not the answer she wanted to hear but it was the best I could do when put on the spot.

"Beta, looking at you reminds me of my own son Ram. I have not seen him for a long time, no letters, no messages, as if he has disappeared from the face of the earth. He may not be aware whether we are alive or dead. Does he not care for his own mother, his baby sister?" Her voice was breaking down with emotion and difficult to control her anguish, her agony and her grief. She turned away her face to hide her tears.

Sonbai was a woman of strong character, self belief, a proud and dignified woman. That is why she had survived such an upheaval in her life.

When she regained her composure, she continued her obviously sad and heart-breaking story, a true life experience that is so often stranger, more gripping, and more unbelievable than fiction.

"My Ram was a very clever boy. He always gained first place and passed his metric exam with distinction. We celebrated his success by distributing penda (Indian sweet made from milk and is distributed to every one, even to strangers, to celebrate a happy event.) to every villager.

When the Mukhi (village elder) offered his fifteen year old, sweet, petit and pretty daughter Sharmi (shy one) in marriage, our happiness was complete.

Ram also willingly agreed to his engagement to Sharmi, as she was indeed a pretty little girl from a well respected family.

Ram wanted to go for further studies but we were not so keen. His head teacher persuaded us to let Ram go to Bombay so that he could qualify as a doctor. The community provided the fund, the scholarship.

So we at last agreed, thinking that our son will become a doctor one day and will be a joy and pride of the community, giving us, the villagers the medical facilities we can only dream about.

For few years, every thing was fine. Ram used to come to us during holidays, even spend some time with Sharmi, who was fast turning into a beautiful, eye catching young woman.

But when his in-laws, Sharmi's parents pressed Ram to get married and take her with him to Bombay, he rebelled and stopped visiting us. Sharmi's parents were outraged and who can blame them. There daughter was now eighteen year old, the oldest unmarried girl in the village. This was the first such incident in the village. It had now become a talking point, a topic for gossip that hurt us all very much.

It was a question of honour for them. How dare a boy from a common family challenge the authority of the village elder, the most respected and wealthy family amongst all the surrounding villages.

Village elders even met Ram in Bombay, tried to persuade him to come back and talk to Sharmi at least once before he make up his mind, decide what to do and take a decision that will ruin so many lives, including his own.

Ram made us an outcast in our own village. We could not show our faces.

Ram's father took it very badly. He was angry, hurt and shamed. Villagers turned into judge, jury and executioner, all in one. Then we heard that Ram got married not only outside our own community but outside our culture, our erudition and most of all, outside our Hindu religion.

This was the final straw that broke the camel's back. His father suffered a massive heart attack and passed away, leaving us at the mercy of the villagers. But this tragedy in a way helped us. Villagers soon realised it was not our fault. Indeed village elders were eager to send Ram to Bombay, against our wishes. So why should we alone take the blame?

After all our loss was greater than theirs. Sharmi had turned into such a fine, beautiful and sensual girl that she soon got married to a nice boy from a respectable family. In fact a better catch than our Ram.

With the death of Ram's father, we lost everything, the respect of the community, the field that gave us our livelihood but not our home or the few cows that gave us the milk. But it is difficult for me to find a good boy for my Rupa. She is such a clever, beautiful girl with charm and sensuality that is so rare in a village girl. But we have lost our good name, our honour that is most important in a village community."

Thinking that she has taken up so much of my time, she finally said, "Beta, if you see Ram in Bombay, please tell him that he is forgiven and urge him to visit us once, with his wife. It is my fervent, the last wish to see them both before I join his father, up there. Please beta, don't forget it." She could not control her anguish, her tears and cried openly, perhaps for the first time in her life.

Even I could not hide my tears, a seasoned, hardened lawyer like me who has seen it all. I took Sonbai into my arms and give her a hug that I normally give to my mum and wiping her tears with my bare hands, I said,

"Maji, if I ever see Ram in Bombay, I will personally bring him here with me. That is my solemn promise to you and to Rupa"

"Beta, you have brought a smile on my face and hope in my heart. How I wish Ram had a friend like you." With these parting words, Sonbai took my leave.

I kept watching this amazing woman, till she disappeared down the narrow lane, a woman with love, hope and forgiveness in her heart, a rarity amongst the city dwellers.

After Sonbai departed, I retreated to my room but my heart was heavy, full of sorrow. My early college life began to unfold; memory came flooding back as if I was watching an Indian movie on a large screen.

When I first entered college, my room partner was a young, handsome boy called Ram. We were as different as chalk and cheese. I was lazy, idle and workshy, while Ram was just the opposite.

Ram used to get up at the crack of down, go for a long walk. Then he would clean and tidy up the room, change the water and cook the breakfast. He was an excellent cook while I could just manage a cup of tea and coffee. So I depended on Ram a lot. That brought us closer and formed a sort of bond that is hard to explain, to put it in writing.

Ram was a shy person, having lived a sheltered life in a tiny village, keeping away from girls and also from flashy city boys who may look down on boys like us. Although I have also lived in a village, we used to travel a lot, as my father was a Collector that required him to travel to all sort of places.

His high position also gave us the financial freedom that enabled us to go on holidays frequently, as far a field as Kashmir in the north and Kanyakumari in the south and visiting such hill stations as Darjeeling, Simla, Ooti and many more.

Ram was tall, handsome, with good physique and body structure that gave him a headlong start when it came to participating in sports. Within two years, Ram now known as Raj, changed beyond reorganisation. He took to the college life like a duck to water. He played practically every sport but he was especially good at, excelled at cricket and tennis.

The shy, aloof and distant looking Ram, who kept away from everyone, was now surrounded by pretty girls. After my final year exam, I went home to my parents. When I came back, I was told that Ram had vacated our room and moved out.

But when he learnt that I have returned, he came to see me the next day. He told me in a serious, sombre voice, "Paresh, I need your advice, your help and your support. I am alone and you are the only one I can really trust."

"Ram, have I ever let you down?" I said with as much determination as I could muster.

"Paresh, this is a very serious matter. I have to make a decision that will change so many lives. There is no room for error, mistake or miscalculation.

I want your honest, unbiased and sincere opinion. Please tell me the truth, not what I would like to hear, what would please me."

Ram was clearly struggling with his conscious. This made me nervous. What could be that important that some one like Ram, a cool, calm and extremely self confident person had to rely on my opinion?

"Paresh, I would like to marry Mumtaz. You know her well, as we have been friends, going out for some time. Now it is time to tie the knot, make the union permanent. That is what we both want." Ram was serious. I have known for some time that Ram and Mumtaz were not only good friends but they used to partner each other in tennis and badminton tournament, in mix doubles. But I had no idea that they were serious about each other.

Ram and Mumtaz was a perfect couple in many ways. Like Ram, Mumtaz was tall with slim, lean but with proportional figure and curves that would put most models in shade. She was one of the most beautiful girls on the campus.

She was clever and being a daughter of a high court judge, she was never short of money. Her dress sense was immaculate, whether she wore Sari, dress or skirt. She looked particularly stunning in her short white mini skirt she used to wear while playing tennis.

She was a number one beauty amongst all the girls, one in a million, every one's dream girl, a life partner who would make all dreams come true, create a heaven on earth.

Many of us used to turn up just to watch her play. So I was not surprised that Ram was smitten, was head over hills about Mumtaz. Who wouldn't be? In a way Ram was fortunate, even blessed to get a life partner like Mumtaz.

She could have any boy from the college. Even some young professors were always hovering round Mumtaz but she was a sensible girl.

Although they were a perfect match, there was a big divide, a religious divide that could turn into a death sentence if not handle with utmost care. It put me in quandary, in a difficult situation, a dilemma that would need serious thinking.

How can I bless this union which may ruin so many lives, including that of Ram and Mumtaz? They would alienate themselves from everyone, their families, friends and the community, shunned and despised by all.

I tried to reason with Ram. Is he really in love or was it just a physical, sexual attraction that will wear off with the passage of time? Would their love stand the test of time, conquer all obstacles? There was no turning back once they get married. What about your parents?

I put forward all the arguments that I could think of but Ram had all the answers. They have already obtained the permission, the blessings of Mumtaz's father, a shrewd, wise and practical person.

He knew that Ram and Mumtaz's relationship has progressed beyond redemption. Being adults, he cannot stop them marrying even if he wanted to. Moreover Ram could be such a charming person when it is needed. He could win the heart and mind of the most obstinate person if need be.

Giving permission was a damage limitation exercise on the part of Mumtaz's father. As soon as the marriage was over, Ram and Mumtaz were flying to America. Judge Sahib had already made all the arrangement. They will continue their studies in New York.

The restrain of caste, colour, creed and religion do not normally apply to people in the high society. They already live in a multicultural society of their own where outsiders are not welcomed.

Ram and Mumtaz may even settle down in America where they could live a normal life without being in the limelight or having to choose between two conflicting cultures.

I could not really find a fault; discover a crack in Ram's armour. Some times in lives we have to make a difficult decision that may heart some. But in the end we all have to look after our own interest, make a decision that is in our best interest.

What would I have done if Mumtaz was in love with me, I was in Ram's shoes? I am sure I would have made similar decision to Ram's. I would have made any sacrifice to marry one in a million girl Mumtaz. So how could I oppose Ram?

So in the end I gave my blessings. Ram even made me his best man. No body bothered to contact his parents, as he knew they would never agree to this union. They left Bombay the day after the wedding and settled down in New York where both had enrolled in their chosen fields.

The last letter I received from Ram was over two years ago, to give me the good news that he has gained his FRCS qualifications in London where he spend a couple of years working in the world renowned Harefield hospital.

Ram has specialized in heart transplant surgery and Mumtaz was a professor of Economics, settling down in Los Angles in the state of California. They have indeed made a success of their lives.

"Beta, dinner is getting cold. Come down and help me set the table. Why don't you get married like a normal boy? It would at least relieve me from the cooking duties."

"Maji, no one can cook like you but you must write down the recipe so that I can pass it on to your bahu. (Daughter in law)" This brought a smile on Maji's wrinkled face. I knew how eager she was to see me get married and settle down. Even I wanted to oblige Maji but I was not so lucky when it came to falling in love.

In all these years, this was the first time I felt Ram could have made a terrible mistake in cutting himself off from his family, from Sonbai and above all Rupa. Like Mumtaz, they were also one in a million. He would never know what a bhagirath sacrifice he has made in order to marry Mumtaz.

Perhaps this bliss, this ignorance was a blessing in disguise. But I was determined to do all I can for Sonbai and Rupa. I could not resist thinking if only Rupa was ten years older and living in Bombay?

****

PENTHOUSE AND PAVEMENT

I believe that every cloud has a silver lining. So when the mishap I suffered in NH Hospital which made me disable and mostly confined to my home, gave me the opportunity, time, encouragement, motivation and stimulation that I needed to take up my favourite hobby of writing that I had abandoned some twenty five years back, the pretext being I was too busy, preoccupied with work and social engagements. But then who is not? If there is a will, there is certainly a way. After all we perform our daily chores, our drudgery and visit our favourite pubs, clubs and restaurants without any reservation, no matter what little time we may have to spare.

Although now a day I write everyday, I prefer to write short stories, based on true experiences on most part. But I must admit this story is based on a tiny piece of information which I extracted from one of my guests, a VIP I interviewed on behalf of a prestigious publication India Link where I have my own regular column, under the heading **"From Far and Near"**

When I asked my guest what made him enter politics, his answer to my simple question was a bit different, some what surprising. I believed his sincerity and perhaps this was the first time I had met a politician who was genuinely interested in helping people and improving their lives. Such politicians are a rare breed indeed.

But with some imagination, writer's liberty and my own life experiences, I am able to convert a simple statement into what I hope will be a long and touching story, that is what every reader would like to read and appreciate.

This is his story as narrated to me, but with the liberal use of my own imagination and journalistic licence.

"As a youngster, I was giving a voluntary service to a charity that was looking after the homeless, especially during festive seasons. I distinctly remember one incident in my life that perhaps pushed me to politics.

On one occasion, in fact it was a Christmas Eve; I had just completed a long and a tiring shift. I was in a hurry to go home, to my warm, comfortable home, to my loving family members and above all to my soft and inviting bed, as I was dead tired after working non-stop for some twelve hours, preparing and serving hot meals to the homeless, the needy and destitute.

In my hurry to leave the shelter, I inadvertently kicked a black plastic bin bag which was lying on the floor, beside a worn-out, exhausted oldish gentleman. The contents spread on the floor. I bend down to gather and put them back in the bag. It was the least I could do, as these guests, the term I would like to use to describe them, these homeless people are on most part proud people who had fallen on hard times due to variety of reasons, some not of their choosing or making.

I was shocked and surprised when I picked up a couple of half torn shirts, jeans and smelling blankets which were so dirty that it was difficult to notice the true colour.

There were also some pots and pans equally in depleted condition. This was his sole possession, his life savings? Even a destitute in a third world country would have more and better personal effects than what I saw on that eye opening incident, on the night of fate and awakening.

This sight jolted my conscious, made me realise how lucky I was to have a wonderful, loving and caring family, to support and encourage me every step of the way. Indeed life was and still is kind to me and to most of us.

When I handed the bag to its owner, I could not resist asking the gentleman his name.

"Son, every one calls me Charley, the charity nut case, as I am always first in the queue to get in the shelter during these bitterly cold and damp winter months. My old body which would not pass even the simplest of MOT does need warmth and shelter now and again to replenish my near empty reservoir of strength and stamina." He said with a dry, weary smile.

It was obvious that he was an educated person, who may have fallen on hard times. Then it is not that difficult in our super materialistic society where we have to compete and keep up appearances at all times. It is easy to lose our goal, our priorities, our aspiration and our objectives in life. We easily forget that true love and happiness come from within, can not be bought with money and possessions.

I can not say why but talking to him, I some how felt empathy, rapport and affinity that I have never experienced before with any one in this situation.

After all we were taught to be professional and not to involve personally with any one, as they are here today and literally gone tomorrow. I sat down with him and we talked and talked for well over two hours. His life story was sad, touching and in a way melancholic.

Charlie had a happy, indeed a wonderful childhood. In a way he was a spoilt child, as he was the only sibling, the only child in the family. But underneath he was a kind and a caring person. His real personality came out in his adulthood. He had a university education and got married with Amanda, his childhood sweetheart.

Both, Charlie and Amanda were professional people who enjoyed life to the full. But his happiness was short lived. He lost his wife when she was in her early thirties, after a long and painful illness. She had a breast cancer that was diagnosed a bit late. The illness, the suffering, the agony and the torment lasted three long years. She had to undergo two major operations, losing both her breasts.

She lost all her hair, the long, thick, blonde hair that gave Amanda her looks, her personality and her confidence.

By the time Amanda passed away, Charlie was a broken man, having seen his childhood sweetheart melting away in front of his eyes. She was not only his wife but a friend, his soul mate, his sole reason for living.

After her death, he sold up and went away on a long journey, visiting as many places as he could, some remote and far away places like Tibet, Bali Japan and Nepal. He tried hard to find inner peace, salvation and deliverance. But his broken heart, sagging spirit and troubled soul never healed, never mended and could not overcome the loss of his beloved Amanda.

He could not find the peace, the tranquillity and the Mox (Deliverance) he was seeking so desperately, he needed so badly, in his hour of need. He could not come to terms with his loss. He felt that the nature had dealt him bad cards and he asked the question, why me a thousand times. This is what we normally do when we find in such a position, an unexpected, unforeseen and unpredicted event that would have turned our life upside down.

When Charley came back after roaming the world for some three years, he had nothing left except huge debt on his credit cards, loans and a heap of unpaid bills that he had neglected for such a long time.

If he had received the right help, support and counselling, then perhaps he would have survived, gone back to his profession and the old routine. What he needed most was love, support and comfort of a loving, caring human being. But alas! There was no one he could turn to. It was not meant to be?

Since then he has lived rough, under the bridge, in a shop entrance after they are closed, in a park, in a cardboard city with his equally luckless companions. That was more than twenty years ago. I still find it difficult to understand how any one could survive for such a long time, in a cold, wet, damp and hostile element, unfriendly atmosphere when we find it difficult to survive even a week without running water or central heating? But now Charlie was on his last leg, ready and eager to meet his maker, reunite with his beloved Amanda. The separation was too long, too painful. It was time to bring it to an end. The doors, the gates of heaven were open and inviting him to come in.

This was unbelievably touching story, although I do not feel that I have managed to capture even half of Charlie's pain, sorrow, loneliness and sadness in my writing. Then I am not a professional writer who can twist words and make them believable, touching and sad that would bring tears in readers' eyes.

But my heart was certainly heavy. There were tears in my eyes when I bade goodbye to Charlie. Don't forget, I was myself hardly out of my teens, a very young person indeed.

Some how I had a gut feeling, perhaps you may call it a premonition that this could be our one and only meeting. But this chance meting, a brief encounter did change my priorities in life, made me think, gave me some insight in life on the other side of the divide.

By the time I left, it was midnight. My heart was in turmoil. I spent the whole night turning and twisting, some times half a sleep, confronted by demon dreams that we normally get during day time when we are just dozing off.

The next day when I came back on duty, Charlie was gone. I was told he had a mild heart attack and was taken to the local hospital where he would be kept for few days.

It is needless to say I never saw Charlie again. But this experience touched me deeply, opened my eyes and perhaps made me a humble, caring person that I feel I am today. I realised for the first time that life is not all bed of roses. It can be full of thorns as well.

It was then that I decided to become a politician. I felt, rightly or wrongly, that politicians have more power, opportunities and ability to help people and change their lives than people engaged in any other profession, perhaps with the exception of medicine.

In any case I was terrible in science subjects? That is when I joined a major political party, at the tender age of sixteen, when most boys concentrate on sports, girls and clubbing, at least that is the trend today. I hardly see any one under forty at local ward or constituency meetings.

Most of our Councillors are well past their fifties and most of us have passed our sell by date before we take interest in politics. Normally only political deed we do is to go out and vote, perhaps one or twice every four years or so.

I may be wrong, as like in any profession, there are good and bad politicians. It is the people that make politicians, good or bad, not the other way round.

Well Bhupendra, this is my reason for becoming a politician. I honestly do not know what profession I would have chosen if I had not met Charlie.

Call it a fate; call it a Kismat or a divine intervention. I am happy in my chosen profession and I should thank Charlie for guiding me to politics and judging by my post bag, I can honestly say that I am able to help people, my constituents and make a difference in their lives. That's all I ever wanted to do and I am getting a handsome financial reward and above all a job satisfaction that is beyond my wildest dream.

****

AMAR-JYOTI (Eternal Flame)

Rajpar was a small town, rather a village of no more than three thousand people. It was strategically situated on the bend of the river **Saryu,** at the foot of the **Eder** mountain range.

Rajpar was part of thirty such villages that formed the principality of **Ramper, ruled by Rana Pratapsinh Chauhan.** His loyal subjects affectionately called him **Ranaji.**

Rajpar was surrounded on three sides by river Saryu, while eight thousand feet high mountain peak of Little Eder was standing majestically on the remaining side, some twenty kilometres from the village, keeping a watchful eye on Ranaji's favourite village, a seat of his mini empire?

Although Ranaji's kingdom was small, his palace, built some three hundred years ago, at the height of the dynastic power, was indeed majestic, grand and a real beauty that would do proud to any Maharaja. The palace was surrounded by a fort, a fortified parapet with a small settlement inside, mainly for servants and guest quarters, for lesser dignitaries who may not deserve a suite in the palace.

As the palace was situated on the edge of the precipice, with a fall of some two thousand feet, it was protected by nature, very difficult to attack.

Ranaji's principality, like most Indian kingdoms, was under the protection of British Raj, part of British India, all but in name.

Although his kingdom was small in size, with fifty thousand subjects, scattered in some thirty villages, along the mountain slopes, its location, with a background of Eder mountain range, made this tiny kingdom strategically important.

The forest on the mountain slopes were the home of some of the most fascinating wildlife in this part of British Raj. The wildlife, that include sought after tigers, leopards, elephants, wild buffalos, deer, languor, gibbon monkeys and wild pigs, swine and occasional pack of wolves made this forest a favourite hunting ground for the white Sahibs.

The forests were also the home for the mountain and river birdlife, with trees such as Indian Oak, pine, silver birch, sycamore, pippal, wild almond, cedar, cypress and thorny bushes like bawad and wild berries spread widely on the slopes, from two to ten thousand feet.

These forests provided a natural habitat to hawks, fish eagle, woodpeckers, barn owls, kites, bustards, lesser floricans, long tailed broadbill and many Indian birds a natural home and a heaven for the bird watchers. Even giant Himalayan Bearded Vulture or Lammergeyers were occasionally visible in these forests.

No wonder Ranaji's palace was seldom without guests, neighbouring Maharajas and white guests that include British Officers, Royalties and occasionally politicians from England who were always visible, ever present at Ranaji's vast and tastefully furnished palace.

The patronage of these privileged white guests gave Ranaji an aura of invincibility, a higher pecking order than his tiny kingdom deserved. They came mostly to hunt and occasionally to observe, to photograph the wild life, although it was the era of machoism when camera took a poor second place to guns.

Well, cameras were not that advanced as we have today and of course there was no television that brings wonderful wildlife documentaries into our living rooms. It was a different age with different priorities and different values in life.

Then the British always knew which side of their bread was buttered. It was a marriage of convenience, a match made in heaven that suited both the Ranaji and the British authority down to earth.

Ranaji's kingdom would have been swallowed by the giant neighbours without British patronage and Ranaji was aware of it. He was indeed grateful to British Raj under whose protection, Ranaji lead a peaceful but hectic life without a care in the world.

Today Ranaji was in a happy, joyous mood. His only son Amar, heir to the throne, was returning home from London, after a long and for Ranaji, a painful separation.

Amar spent seven long years in London while qualifying, first as a doctor and then as a surgeon. In those bygone eras, the golden age, there was only one mode of travel in use between Bharat and Britain and that was by ship.

It was a romantic era for travel, mainly by train and ships. The luxurious liners like ill fated Titanic, Queen Mary, Princess Ann and Queen Victoria ruled the waves. These were indeed floating palaces. These ships would put today's cruise liners in shade with ease.

Then they were not built for the masses as today's liners are. They were only for the privileged few, with more sailors and servants than the passengers.

It would take from six to ten weeks to sail from England to Bombay, the most popular port for disembarkation in the British Raj. But there was not a dull moment on the ship. Ever busy Mediterranean Sea and the romantic Indian Ocean provided famous stopovers, port of call like Gibraltar, Malta, Port Suez and Alexandria, named after the most famous Greek Emperor Alexander the Great, Aden and Karachi before the ship dock at Bombay, the gateway to Western and Southern India.

On such voyages, life long friendships, alliances were formed and even life partners were found with occasional marriage ceremonies performed by the ship captain.

On disembarking at Bombay, Amar boarded the Toofan Mail, a fast train that would stop at only a couple of places before reaching Jaipur, famous for Hawa Mahal, the Wind Palace, a pink city, the heart of Rajasthan.

During British Raj, those who were in their good books were the privileged class. So Amar had a two room accommodation in a first class compartment, with all mods and cons at his disposal. It was like a special suite in a five star hotel. It was indeed a hotel on wheels that moved from town to town.

The train left on time. Then during British Raj, all transport ran on time, except elephant ride. Today nothing runs on time, not even in London. How the time, the people and priorities have changed, not for the better that is for sure.

Unseasonal rain or rather a drizzle accompanied the train for some twenty minutes when the train left Bombay Central station in the mid-morning.

Amar opened a bottle of cold beer from the fridge and sat down in the luxurious leather arm-chair, near the window.

Amar started reading the book **Siddhartha** by the noble literature prize winner German author Herman Hesse who was a conscientious objector during World War One and became a Swiss citizen in 1923.

The book is based on the wisdom of Lord Gautam Buddha and the eastern philosophy. But it made a heavy reading, at least for Amar.

Amar realised he should have brought books that make light reading, such as books by Sir Arthur Conan Doyle, Agatha Christie, James Hilton, Oscar Wilde and Jules Verne that require very little concentration but provided a lot of fun and light relief.

These would have been an appropriate reading on a train journey. But then again, he had already read most of these books during his student days, as he was an avid reader while studying.

It was natural that after reading so many medical books, he was experiencing a bit of a reading fatigue. After some two hours, Amar put down the book and started looking at the changing sceneries from the comfort of his chair.

The train was now entering the green and fertile land of Gujarat. On both the sides, there were rows and rows of heavily cultivated fields, as far as eyes could see.

The millet, wheat and maize were the main crops but there were also occasional fields of sugarcane, especially near a water source and fruit orchards with mangos, papayas and sweet lime, banana, berries and guava trees were visible now and then.

Looking at the villagers harvesting their crop, Amar remembered his own childhood. The events began to unfold as if he was watching them on a big screen.

As Amar was the only child, he was rarely allowed to venture out on his own. Ramudada, the palace gardener was his friend and bodyguard. Amar used to visit the neighbouring fields especially that of Ramudada's brother Shankar, to eat freshly harvested crops of maize.

The famous Indian village dish, the wheat cooked in earthenware utensils, deep in the ground known as pokh, was his favourite meal, along with fresh onions, green chillies and yogurt made from goat milk.

Chillies were hot but onions were even hotter, good for cleaning the eyes. This was the food fit for the royal banquet but mainly eaten by the poor. These were carefree, happy days for Amar, bathing in the shallow fresh water of the irrigation dam, water being drawn from the deep well, into the vast but shallow structure made of stone and cement that would irrigate the whole field. It was indeed fun to bathe in this ever changing fresh water, falling from a height of some ten feet.

The cereals were planted on a raised bed with narrow channels on both sides of the raised crop bearing lanes, water being pumped to these channels from the irrigating dam. Amar learnt how to swim in such a dam.

Amar enjoyed eating these mouth watering meals, listening to his favourite bhajans (devotional songs) in the company of these fatherly figures who would willingly give their lives to protect him.

Even Ranaji knew of these outings and willingly allowed Amar to venture to these fields without a bodyguard. Then terrorism was unknown and Satyagrah (civil disobedience) was the main weapon to fight the British with, what a romantic notion to liberate a country from the clutches of the greatest empire ever known in human history.

There were no guards or locks on the prison cell doors where political prisoners like Gandhi, Sardar, Tilak, Subhash and Nehru were kept. They could walk out at any time. But they would for once not break the law, however unjust it may be?

The harsh whistle of the train broke Amar's chain of thoughts. Now the train was entering the rugged terrain with vast patches of barren land. The barrenness was more due to the hard, non porous and stony surface of the land, devoid of fertile top soil than due to lack of water. Indeed the rainfall in these parts of Gujarat was more than average. But the imporous nature of the land allowed the water to flow away without benefiting the ground.

Where there was depression, big and wide holes or hollow indentation in the landscape, there were indeed ponds, small lakes and deep holes full of fresh water.

This landscape provided a perfect breeding ground for some type of water birds, such as Indian whiskered and common terns, herring gulls, Indian skimmer, dusky redshank and sandpipers, a few among the teaming birdlife on display.

Some of the ponds were also covered with a mass of vegetation. Amar's favourite flowers, white, blue and purple water lilies were there in abundance. It was a pity the train would not stop any where near here for Amar to buy a bunch of these pretty flowers.

As Amar had skipped lunch, he was pretty hungry and waiting for the dinning car to open its doors. After a long and six course luxurious dinner, with a bottle of his favourite Spanish red wine, vino tinto from the region of Castile La Mancha, Amar was ready to go to bed, not a bunk bed but a spacious double bed found in most prestigious hotels. Some how Amar enjoyed sleeping on a train journey. The rhythmic noise of the moving train acted as a sleep inducement, a sort of tranquilizer. Well, there is no saying for taste, habit or a hobby!

Moreover Amar was dead tired after the hustle and bustle of disembarking from the ship early in the morning and catching the Toofan Mail.

He only woke up when the peon, the footman, especially allocated to Amar knocked on the door, at 7am with a breakfast tray on a heavy wooden trolley.

Amar always enjoyed his early morning cup of coffee, although he was not a heavy eater in the morning when staying at the palace or during his college days in Bombay.

But doing medicine in London changed all that. Early morning was the only time Amar could have for a long and leisurely meal, without disturbance of the beep going off and rushing to action station for the emergency. That is part and parcel of being a doctor, especially if you are working in a busy hospital.

By the time Amar finished the breakfast and looked out of the window, from his favourite window seat, he realised that the train had left the fertile and green land of Gujarat.

It was now speeding through Rajasthan with a complete change of scenery. The sun was well above the horizon, dispersing the early morning mist and the cold that is a hallmark of desert climate. It is a fresh, dry and a healthy climate, especially good for people with lungs and breathing problems.

The sky was clear and devoid of any water bearing clouds that accompanied the train throughout Gujarat. By midday the Toofan Mail stopped at Jaipur.

It was only the third and the last stop before Delhi, the final destination, where this train journey would terminate.

As soon as the train stopped, Amar started looking for a familiar face among the crowd. It was not easy when more than a couple of thousand people are herded together in such a small place.

But Amar soon saw the familiar face of his uncle Chote Rana Mansinh, with a couple of servants and drivers. He was greeted in the traditional Rajput style. Amar touched his uncle's feet, a ritual to show respect to one's elders.

Once the greetings were over, they hurried to their cars. Rajpar was a long way from Jaipur. But fortunately the cement roads provided a comfortable drive all the way except the last forty miles, especially in Rolls Royce and Bentleys, Ranaji's favourite cars.

After some four hours drive, the Eder Mountain began to appear on the horizon. The scenery was changing by the hour ever since they left Jaipur.

The first couple of hours' journey was through the typical Rajasthan desert.

The shifting sand dunes and dry arid land was punctured with thorny desert plants like cactus, aloe, thorn bush and typical Rajasthani desert plants that do not have English names.

It was monotonous, unchanging scenery but an occasional camel caravan would provide a welcome change. Rajasthani people are famous for their colourful costumes, especially ladies.

The red, green and blue colours dominate ladies dresses; decorated with tiny pieces of shining mirror like metals, mirrors, glass beads and flowers.

It was difficult to imagine wearing so many colourful clothes in a desert heat that would routinely touch 100ºF and much worse during the hot dry summer months with 140ºF.

There were also tiny settlements around an oasis where underground water reserve is brought to the surface by deep bore wells or natural streams spouting from the ground. Where there was water in abundance, the desert bloomed. Fruit trees that include palm and pomegranate, guava and berries as well as vegetables were grown and marketed locally.

There were no cattle but goats were every where, as they can survive on any type of vegetation, providing milk and meat for the local people.

After a long hard drive, the cement road came to an abrupt end. It was a dirt track from here on which would become impassable during monsoon months of July and August.

The desert gave way to lush, green countryside, with Eder Mountain on the horizon. Amar's tired eyes became alive with the greenery and the bumpy ride. This was a virgin land, devoid of any settlement, human interference. The grass was some six feet tall where left alone, with occasional cluster of trees.

At one time these forests were teaming with wild cats but now the occupants were more gentle animals, monkeys, deer, wild goats and docile but not so gentle wild buffalos. Occasionally the desert nomads would bring their cattle here for grazing. But this practice was not encouraged by the authority.

On approaching the foot of the mountain, the scenery changed again. Here there was a human settlement, with small farms.

So often tiny fields carved out of mountain side, turned into narrow strips of land known as step fields where crops thrived under artificial top layer of soil deposited by the torrents.

It was a hard, backbreaking work to create these narrow step-farms so often washed away by water tumbling down the mountain during the rainy season or the sides caving in due to erosion.

Amar's escort arrived in Rajpar just as the sun was setting, disappearing behind the majestic Little Eder Mountain peak.

With the setting of the sun, the darkness spreads rapidly and without cloud cover, the heat loss is fast, rapid and severe. It is almost as cold here as in London during winter months.

Before entering the village, the driver stopped the car at the outskirt, near a deri (small temple) of Lord Hanuman, a loyal and devoted servant of Lord Rama. Once some one asked him how we trust that you are a devoted servant of Lord Rama. He said without hesitation, Rama and Sita are in my heart and then he opened his chest to show the images of Ram and Sita. No wonder Hanuman was the patron saint of the Chauhan dynasty and many Rajput kings who demand similar loyalty from their own followers.

No member of the royal family would enter Rajpar without first praying at the temple. No one would ever break this unwritten law that had stood the family in good stead for the last three hundred years.

In Bharat, tradition and religious belief takes precedent over any and every other belief, custom and ritual. Every one in the village knew that crown prince Amar, now a qualified surgeon, was returning to his beloved village after a long, painful but immensely successful exile.

The narrow streets were overflowing with people. Some were holding lanterns as it was getting dark. But Amar opened the soft top of the car and stood up, waving at the cheering crowd, who were no more than a couple of feet away. The motorcade had to travel at snail speed so as not to crush any one and to give the people an opportunity to see the prince.

On entering the fort, reaching the palace, Amar saw the temple priest who put a Tilak of sandalwood on his forehead and ladies did the traditional arti and garlanded the prince.

Amar was eager to see his mother Manharba, a gentle, kind and obliging lady. As soon as the welcoming ceremony was over, Amar entered the palace and bent down to touch the feet of his father, mother and his uncle, in typical Indian tradition and gave a big hug to his mother who was shedding tears by a bucketful but they were tears of joy, happiness and a reunion of mother and the son, after an absence of long seven years.

After a light dinner, Amar retreated to his luxurious apartment. It was a long and a tiring day for Amar. He fall a sleep as soon as he hit the soft, inviting bed and did not wake up until there was a knock on the door, from his mother.

It was now two month since Amar returned from London. But after spending some seven hectic but fruitful years in London, where he learnt how to look after himself, be useful, Amar found the life here some what meaningless, idle and without aim or purpose in life.

Being a crown prince, Amar's every wish was attended to. He was waited hand and foot. But for Amar, who was now a self made person, this babysitting was more of a hindrance than a help.

There was a tiny hospital in Rajpar that served the entire principality of Ramper, as most of the residents still believed in traditional ayurvedic (herbal) medicine practiced by Vaids, as well as in faith healing, performed on most part by temple priests and other Brahmins, the upper class who are mostly teachers, preachers and temple trustees.

There was no shortage of such medicine men, as it does not require any formal qualification. In fact it was a family tradition; the knowledge passed from father to son and on most part, herbal medicine was pretty effective and affordable, as most herbs were gathered free from the forest.

But it required faith and patience that we, the Westerners do not have. There were two full time qualified Indian doctors and an English consultant by the name of Mr. Knight who would come once a week to look after the royalty, British expatriate and very rich residents with royal or political connections.

After a long and sometimes not so cordial discussion with Ranaji, Amar was, at last able to join the hospital, working two days a week, replacing the English doctor, as Amar was far better qualified than Mr. Knight and moreover he was willing to look after the locals as well as the rich and the privileged class.

It was a far cry from what Amar was used to in London. This was a primitive hospital without even basic equipment, drugs or fully trained staff. It was not meant for serious illnesses, only for curing routine, every day medical necessities, minor ailments. Delhi or Jaipur were the place to go to for the privileged patients with serious health problems.

Amar's favourite pastime, before going to London was riding his best-loved horse Chatak, named after a bird that flies majestically and monopolises the sky. The appearance of the bird is also a good sign, an omen and the start of a rainy season.

Amar, in the company of his cousin Ajit, used to ride into the forest for hunting, bird-watching or just relaxation.

Now with plenty of free time on his hand, Amar resumed his hobby but he left the hunting and killing to Ajit while he concentrated on watching, observing and studying the wild life, sketching them, transferring them on to his sketch book, either in water colour or just in black and white, using only a drawing pencil, enjoying the open air life which he missed so much when he was away from his palace. Today Amar was on his own, as Ajit had gone to Delhi for a few days, riding Pavan, (wind) the son of his favourite horse Chatak. They formed an immediate close bond from day one, as if the horse knew of the affection between the prince and his father.

After an hour's ride, Amar dismounted from his horse Pavan. Today he only carried a gun for self protection which was essential at all time, although his prime weapon was his camera and a pair of binoculars.

Amar spread the straw mat under a banyan tree and started searching the sky through his powerful binoculars, watching skylarks, fish eagles and woodpeckers at work and play. On the ground, on the forest floor, Amar targeted the forest wild-life, watching deer, langoor monkeys, hogs and occasionally wild cats not much bigger than the domesticated ones but much vicious and a threat to the ground hugging birds like peacocks, guinea fowls and swans.

These wild cats were the only forest animals Amar wound not mind hunting, as he loved birds, especially peacocks, swans and guinea fowls so much. Their colourful presence and sweet coos, soft murmuring sound and love or mating calls would make the forest alive and a pleasant place to have a picnic or just to roam and pass the day.

After a couple of hours intense watching, Amar lowered binoculars, to give rest to his tiring eyes. He instantly fell a sleep until a sweet, sensuous and extremely pleasing voice woke him up.

The voice was coming from a distant but in the peace and restful atmosphere; it was carried far and wide. Amar directed his binoculars in the direction of the voice and soon found the source of his aspiration, the focal point of his curiosity.

She was a young girl, some eighteen years old. Watching from a binocular, it seemed she was right beside Amar.

She was singing a traditional song. In this mountain community, their lives were interwoven with nature. All their songs, dances, music and even traditions were based either on their religion, culture or nature.

She was singing a song that narrated the story of a rogue elephant, a lonely elephant that has been driven out of the heard.

An elephant is a social animal, like humans they live in a group. They like company and care for each other. A herd of elephants is always led by a strong and a wise bull whose reign is supreme.

Inevitably his leadership is challenged from time to time and fight ensues, the loser, if he survives, is expelled from the herd and lives a solitary life but not for long.

He turns into a rogue, raiding farms, destroying crops and attacking any one in sight. A rogue elephant is normally shot dead by a game warden or dies of wounds sustained in a battle or even kills himself by starvation. Only on rare occasion, he is allowed back into the herd.

Amar could not take his eyes off her, a rare beauty, scantly but decently dressed, at least according to the tribal way of life. Being a mountain girl, she was clear-skinned, hazel-eyed, well built with long light brown hair, milky complexion and curves in all the right places, indeed an untamed beauty struggling to hold back.

Strangely enough these mountain girls are scantly dressed compared to their village counterparts and the city girls. Their innocence and naivety is so often reflected in their dressings, in their every day activities and in their lives.

So often these mountain lassies are not averse to expose their well developed breasts with the tiniest of the cloth, albeit unconsciously and without a care in the world, but mostly their chests are covered by a lose cloth called chundadi or a shawl. It was the age of innocence in a country that gave the world the most explicit ancient book of love making, the one and only Kama Sutra.

Her voice was as sweet as she was beautiful. Amar had heard this song before, perhaps watching a tribal dance in the palace compound, as tribal entertainers were invited to perform on special occasions, such as Ranaji's birthday, Diwali and Christmas festivals or to entertain other Indian VIPs, maharajas and their likes.

It was a sweet but sad song, inappropriate for the pleasant surrounding, the love filled environment. Then who knows what a pain this village lassie may be harbouring in her inner most bosom or a wounded heart. Perhaps she was giving vent to her innermost thoughts, feelings and unfulfilled manokamna or her life's desire. The song, when translated in English, loses some of its charm, pain and heartbreak.

ROGUE

Alone alone all alone
In this wild, bewildering forest
This was a vast tropical playground
In the middle of Indian heartland
We call it Eder forest
So serene, so beautiful, so fulfilling
With flowing water and tall grass
A heaven on earth all year round
Birds and animals live in harmony
Easy to fall in love with nature
Heaven on earth, paradise revisited
Sweet home to one and all
Land of honey and milk, glory and adoration
A nature's creation, this heaven on earth
I was not so tiny a baby, even when I was born
In an elephant herd, pride of the Eder forest
Drove of loving, caring, sharing animals
Congregation of some thirty and three
Small and large, young and elder
Weak and strong, suckling and grown
Picture of health, happy and content
A real family, a contented assembly
My early life, my childhood prime
So lovingly spent on this mountain slopes
Soon I grew into a big, strong bull
My advent of youth, prime of life
Made me adventurous, challenging the pride
Herd is always led from the front
Strong and healthy, a bull impudence
His reign is supreme, a master of pride
Challenge him at your peril
Advent of youth, mating desire, no place to hide

Call of nature, difficult to deny
Soon it turns a young bull hostile
Battle primed no one can deny
A challenge is inevitable, win or die
A young bull, a pride of his generation
How when and where could he hide
Gauntlet thrown, Seconds announced
Challenge propelled, willingly accepted
Soon two mighty bulls fight for survival
The winner will be crowned a king
His reign supreme, his harem preserved
It is a fight for life, faint heart won't survive
The ground shakes, hurricane strikes
Earthquake abound, dust cloud rise
Trumpeting sound awakening the dead
Sunrise masked, sunset in sight
At last the battle is over, winner crowned
Loser retreat to live a solitary life
A young bull, a life in prime
So unceremoniously deprived
Defeated and expelled
No where to hide, making him a ROGUE
Life nearing an end, when in prime
What a sad end for such a noble pride.

****

Amar listened with attention, as some words were lost in the wind. It took a long time for her to finish the song, as she repeated some of the verses again and again.

With her skimpy dress of tiniest blouse piece, held together with a string, revealing most of her upper torso with consuming ease, she looked gorgeous, sexy and even beautiful in her simple but colourful Rajestani dress. Her shawl or dark red mantle cloak, with which these girls usually cover their upper body to look modest, as well as keep warm, was fluttering on a nearby rock, presuming drying in the sun, after a wash.

She was sitting on a stone, on the river bank, washing her long, slim line legs. She had pulled her long skirt up to her thigh, completely unaware that some one could be watching her. After all, it was a forest where privacy is more or less guaranteed at most time. Some how Amar could not help but to focus his binoculars on her private parts, on her boson, long legs and thighs. He knew it was ungentemanly, discourteous and unbecoming of some one in his position to become a peeping Tom but so often we all fall in such traps, do something we normally do not do or behave in such a manner. It is not uncommon to let our hearts to rule our heads.

The big pile of firewood she had collected was neatly tied up into a big bunch, ready to take home. Amar could not restrain his curiosity but to walk silently where the girl was taking a wash.

Amar watched her from behind the trunk of a big tree. After the wash the girl spread her mantle clock on the ground and spread her body. Obviously she must have covered a great distance to gather all these firewood.

Amar watched her for some half an hour. He could not resist taking a last, close look before mounting his horse Pavan. But the slightest noise of the footsteps startled her. After all she was a mountain girl who knew the forest like a back of her palm and capable of taking care of herself if faced with a tricky situation.

She gave a muffled cry when she saw Amar that in turn startled Amar. In his hurry to assure her, Amar clumsily stumbled over a piece of rotting wood and hit his head on a rock, with blood pouring down from his wound. For a few seconds, Amar lost consciousness.

Looking at Amar, she realised that this was not some one from the village but could be a palace guest, a Babu from Bombay, a gentleman. When Amar opened his eyes, he saw this fairy of a girl, a mermaid splashing sweet river water on his face and wiping blood from his forehead with the shawl.

Amar gave her a smile, then said, "Divya-Jyoti, (Candle light) sorry to spoil your lovely shawl with my blood."

"How do you know my name, were you watching me? Divya said in one breath" somewhat startled that he may have watched her bathing, cleaning her body with very little cloths on.

In reply Amar smiled again and pointed to her locket dangling from her neck. "Look, your name is written there and yes, I was watching you. But you are the most beautiful human being around. How could I resist such an opportunity?

But believe me, I mean no harm to you and if you are upset, I apologise."

Amar said it again with sincerity and honesty that is rare among noble, upper class, especially when talking with these so called village people who are only fit to be their servants.

Then introducing himself, he said, "My name is Amar and I am a guest of Ranaji." He could not give his true identity, as Amar feared that if Divya knew he was a Crown Prince, she would run a mile.

Divya was not an ordinary village girl. She was smart and a good judge of character. Trying to get angry but without success, She said, "Amarji, it is not nice to watch a girl secretly. I may have taken a bath in the river, without many clothes."

"Well Divya, Lord Krishna always used to watch gopies bathing in the river Jamuna. Gopies did not mind, nor did Lord Krishna. Next time I will tell you in advance if I am going to watch you. Would that be fine?" That brought a smile on her bemused face.

"Now you are making a fun of a poor village girl, aren't you?" Although shy, she was enjoying this conversation.

"Well Divya, why do you call yourself a poor village girl? You are as beautiful, as clever as any girl I know." Amar said with a mischievous smile, may be enjoying pulling her leg. He was also a good judge of character and he instantly knew that the girl was not only not mad at him but was enjoying the attention she was getting from him, some one who was educated and surely well above her normal admirers, the village idiots!

They chatted for nearly an hour, as Divya was convinced that Amar was a gentleman who will respect her and she was not in any danger, being alone with him. It was enough for Amar to know her as well as it could be possible from such a short but fruitful chance encounter.

Amar helped her to gather the scattered firewood, mount the bundle on her head and watched her with a kind of apprehension, uneasiness, nervousness and some anticipation, expectation, until the forest swallowed her as she disappeared behind the tall, dense forest trees.

On her part, Divya turned around a couple of times to make sure that Amar was watching her and her extravagant, prodigal and profligate heap movement which seemed so natural but some how Amar felt that it was for his eyes, for his attention. Amar could not help thinking that these village girls are in many ways not different from their city counterparts. Are they?

Then again all women have heart, ambition and desire to be loved, admired and treated like a princess? Why should a coincidence of birth make a girl any different?

The sun had descended a great deal from its midday high. It was beginning to get cold without the rays and heat of the midday sun. So Amar mounted his horse and rode back to the palace.

Every one in the palace was waiting for Amar on the dining table. Amar took his designated seat but was quiet throughout the dinner, making Ranaji wonder how come a chatterbox has lost his voice! But he could not bring his inner most thoughts to the dining table conversation.

When Amar woke up half way through the night, he began to wonder how come a village lassie, albeit a beautiful and sensuous one makes him so nervous who may not even be suitable for a servant's job in the palace. Could it be just sexual desire, physical attraction?

Amar remembered his life in London, his first girlfriend Rita, the daughter of his landlady.

When Amar first came to London, he was all alone, away from every one he loved and respected. It was, in many ways a strange, unfamiliar country with strange, odd and unusual custom, a completely different lifestyle. Even the food and climate were enormously different to what Amar was used to in his kingdom.

In Rita, Amar found solace, comfort and alleviation. It was not too difficult for an eighteen year old Amar to fall in love with a sweet, sensuous seventeen year old girl, with milky white complexion, curly golden hair and above all her nature, her self confidence and the way she handled herself in any company. Rita had so much self confidence, self belief that she would easily pass as a princess if she was judged on this one aspect alone.

Then it is the symbol and emblem of the Western world where women are treated as equal and encouraged to be as self sufficient, assertive and independent as men. This was in sharp contrast to the way women were brought up in the pre-independent Bharat.

Within six months Amar was deeply in love with Rita, his constant companion in this strange country with even stranger customs, tradition and climate that keep on changing like a woman's mind? Knowing that Amar was a prince; Rita did not held herself back. Soon they were living like a married couple.

In any case in the Western society, even before the World War Two, cohabitation especially in the upper circle was not a taboo, a forbidden fruit that was and still is in our ultra conservative Indian society.

Rita, like most English girls of her background and upbringing, was a free spirit. She could sit on the dining table, drink, smoke and openly discuss her personal, sexual problems with her parents, especially with her mother, without reservation, embarrassment or any sort of discomfort.

That does not mean that our culture, our way of life was in any better or superior to the Western culture or their way of life.

It was just different to suit their life style, their social environment. Every coin has two sides; every culture has their tradition, their hallmark and a stamp of approval. Some may not be to our liking or indeed conducive to our wellbeing. But that does not mean that their customs were better or worse than ours, just different to suit their lifestyle, their social environment.

Amar knew this and adopted the English tradition that he considered to be an asset and would stand him in good stead back at home. The English tradition, the way of life he admired most was the hard work, the ambition, honesty and the love for their motherland, their religion and the wellbeing of their fellow citizens. These qualities enabled this tiny nation to rule half the world.

The relationship between Amar and Rita was more of a sexual attraction on most part. While Amar was engaged in his studies, his hobbies and interest of intellectual nature, trying to build up his future, become a surgeon, Rita provided a perfect distraction, a change from his dull routine that goes with medical studies.

Rita was a practical girl from a working class family with social interest. Her world was to drink, visit pubs, go dancing and enjoy life to the full. Her motto was eat, drink and be merry. Who knows what will happen tomorrow or what fate awaits us round the corner.

Once their sexual attraction had reached the height, enjoyed each other to the limit, making love every night, Amar realised that Rita was not the girl he could marry, take her back to his kingdom and one day make her a queen.

Although Rita was beautiful and full of self confidence, she simply did not have the grace, the etiquette, the protocol or the upbringing that is obligatory to mix at his, royal, privileged level. After all these royal princes are trained, prepared from the young age to play their part, be part of the high society, royal and influential circle.

In any case when he moved to the campus, he was obliged to work long hours as a junior doctor. This brought ebb in their relationship and Rita soon moved on to the pasture new. She was not the girl who would put her life on hold until Amar qualifies, completes his studies.

Amar was so lost in his world that only the sweet sound of the temple bell broke his chain of thoughts and the realisation that he was no more in London but in his beloved Rajpar. But Amar will always remember Rita, as she was his first girlfriend, his first love and his first partner who stumbled together through their sexual adventures. They learnt a lot from each other.

As it was nearly a day break and the rhythmic sound of the bells from the Devi Ambika (Goddess) temple was calling the faithful for prayer; that Lord Suryadev (Sun God) was on his way to light up the world. In other word, it was time to get up and get going?

It was pointless for Amar to try to go back to sleep. So he put on his walking boots, overcoat and with a walking stick, went on an early morning walk.

The fort was large enough to take a long, undisturbed walk, in the palace compound. The sun was trying hard to penetrate the dense layer of mist, come out from the distant hills but without much success, at least for the time being.

It is always cold here early in the morning until the sun comes out and spreads its powerful rays all over the surrounding areas, especially on the summits of the high rising Eder Mountains, dispersing the mist and the low clouds that normally hung around in hilly places.

After half an hour's brisk walk, Amar came to the temple for rest, a hot cup of masala tea and a chat with the Pujari (priest) Premji kaka (uncle) who was more like an uncle than an employee of his father.

Since returning from England, Amar was not able to spend a quality time with this kind, caring gentleman. So before sitting down in front of the altar, the image of Devi Ambika, Amar knelt down and touched the feet of the priest, an ancient Hindu custom that even members of the royal family observe and respect.

But to a humble Pujari, it was a kind gesture for a Crown Prince, a gesture beyond call of duty, to kneel down and touch his feet. No wonder he loved Amar like his own flesh and blood.

Pujari was not married nor did he had any relatives, at least not in the village. He had devoted his life to the temple, serving the royal family and the Devi Ambika.

But according to Hindu tradition, all temples have images of various Hindu Gods and Goddesses, deities, in particular that of Lord Rama, Krishna, Ganesh, Shankar and many more. So this temple was no different, no exception from that liberal Hindu tradition, Hindu thinking and Hindu way of life.

So often it is difficult for Westerners to understand this Hindu unity, the solidarity that exist between Hindus who worship different Gods, different deities but without any conflict, any misapprehension when Catholics and Protestants are at each other's throats and so are Sunnis and Shias in Islam, although they worship the same God, the same prophet, Lord Jesus Christ and Prophet Mohamed.

As the arti was over, Pujari was alone in the temple. In any case only a few foolhardy, impulsive and perhaps suffering from insomnia usually attend the early morning prayers, from some three hundred people residing in the fort. Hindus have never been regular temple goers, unlike Christians, most of whom would never miss a Sunday service. In any case, all Hindus have a small temple in their home where they light a divo.

The eldest member of the family, usually the grandmother will get up early in the morning, take a shower, light a divo (candle) and say a prayer, lasting no more than ten minutes at the most.

The rest of the family members may bow their heads and say a few words before leaving home early in the morning. But no one would go near this tiny temple without first taking a shower. That is the Hindu tradition, the Hindu culture going back ten thousand years.

But in most part it is the duty of the elders to light the divo which is willingly taken over by the next person in line when the eldest person fell sick or depart.

Pujari was the custodian of this ancient temple, the scripts and various, ancient holy Hindu books housed in the adjacent room, a sort of reference library. Pujari was completely in charge. His authority in the temple was supreme. Even Ranaji would not dare to interfere in temple affairs.

While drinking a cup of hot masala tea, prepared entirely from goat milk, without adding any water, Amar had a long, heart to heart chat with Pujari, an elderly person who was held so high, respected by every member of the royal family.

After an hour, when the tea was almost drunk, Amar bade farewell, to take a short cut through the garden before returning to his royal duties.

Somehow Amar could not help but to observe the temple with love, respect and admiration. It was constructed of stones mined from the surrounding hills. These stones were used more for their durability and strength than appearance or beauty.

The temple was of a simple design with traditional dome at the top. The interior pillars were carved with Sanskrit Sloaks (scripts) from the Hindu holy books of Gita, Ramayana and Vedas.

The temple was incorporated within the fort boundary when Ranaji's ancestors built the fort. After all, no Hindu king will demolish any place of worship, especially a temple.

Now the temple belonged to Ranaji and his family. It was out of bound for the people of Rajpar except during the nine days of Navratri, a holy occasion Hindus celebrate when they bring in the harvest before the onset of winter.

So Navratri is also known as a Harvest Festival and is celebrated with panache, dash, style and flamboyance. It is a jolly occasion, especially for the young at heart when they dance away the night, so often in the company of their loved ones, their intended life partners. They could only mix so freely during Navratri festival when all taboos are confined to dustbin but only for nine short days?

The older generation come here to watch, listen and renew the friendship, the acquaintance that may have been neglected, lapsed during the year. There is an interesting story, an ancient history behind the popularity of Goddess Ambaji. Temples dedicated to her are found all over India but the ones on Arasura and Abu mountains are most famous and well known not only in India but wherever Hindus live, throughout the western world. According to ancient history, it is believed that Ambaji was the favourite Goddess of Anaryan or the Dravidians, the people who occupied the southern most part of Bharat, dating back some 7000BC. After all India is the cradle of ancient civilization.

The Aryans who were the indigenous people of Northern Bharat, readily adopted Ambaji as their Goddess when they moved south, conquering every thing that lay in their path. Since then Ambaji has been the favourite Goddess of all Hindus, all Indians, especially the ruling class, the Rajput kings and Maharanas.

Even today the Goddess is as popular as ever. From Lord Krishna's wife Rukhmani to Maha Rana Pratap and warrior Maratha king Shivaji, who was the thorn in the flesh of Mogul emperor Aurangzeb; were all devotees of Devi Ambaji.

Like Amar, Ranaji had spent few years in England where he acquired a few good habits, the etiquette that is associated with royal culture and protocol.

These conduct, culture include playing polo, cricket and appreciating good wine, Scottish Highland whisky and bagpipes and having a rose garden where the weather permits.

After all who does not love an English Rose? They come in all shape, size and configuration. If one is not careful, it could become addictive? Rita was such an English rose for Amar!

Ranaji had created a beautiful garden behind his palace, designed and constructed by a famous English architecture Sir Christopher Humber who was a regular guest at the palace when Ranaji was a crown prince.

Now this garden, with flowing water in the form of a natural stream, flowing in a zigzag course with occasional water falls, lovely clear water ponds with teaming rainbow colour fish and beautiful water lilies, a favourite flower of the Goddess Laxmi, the Goddess of wealth and wisdom, was the jewel in the crown, the most admired beauty spot in this vast fort that also attracted attention from English visitors, the servants of the Raj.

In Bhimji, Ranaji had an expert gardener. With the help and encouragement of Ranaji, he had created several rose beds, each devoted to a particular rose colour, that include white, red, yellow, pink, blue and many light shades in between. The various arches, some made from marbles and covered with climbing rose trees were breathtaking and every one's favourite.

Beside roses, the garden was blooming with all sorts of flowers, bushes and climbers. The prominent among them were sweet smelling ratrani (night queen) gardenia, jasmine, champo (Indian magnolia) and karan. (pink rose)

These were all sweet smelling flowers that would turn any garden into a perfumery, a royal garden fit for a king. No wonder Amar would take a stroll in this paradise whenever he went out for a walk. The trees and bushes attracted a lot of wild life, especially birds, squirrels and not so welcomed guests, snakes. Fortunately these mountain snakes were not poisonous on most parts and there were definitely no King Cobra snakes, the scourge of the village people.

For the next three days Amar came back where he first saw Divya but could not see her any where. He searched the forest with his binoculars, in anticipation, hope and expectation but there was no sign of her.

Then he realised that gathering wood may be only an occasional task. But one day he will see her again. Then again he was afraid that this chance meeting, unexpected encounter may become his last, his only encounter, what they say in Hindi, a chotisi mulakat, a brief encounter.

Amar wanted to tell her so much. Perhaps in time, come clean and tell her every thing about him, who he was and learn about her, her family and their way of life, which were in a way as remote and distant as those of the Red Indians of North and South America?

After spending a week in Jaipur, Amar came back, revisited what has now become his favourite place, the scene of their chance meeting.

After an hour or so, he sat down, under the same tree and dozed of to relive his beautiful dreams. Once again he was woken up by a sweet but now a familiar sound.

Amar was curious. Where did she learn this song? It was not a traditional mountain tribal song they sing on special occasions. It was well composed and touching, more of a Western verse than a traditional tribal song.

But it was even more romantic, touching than the first one. Even this song was about wild life but a sea life rather than a mountain, forest life.

A CRY FOR HELP

I saw a shoal of whales
Small and large, happy and content
Swimming in the vast open ocean
As free and happy as could be
One of them, a leader of the shoal
Swam out to me and said
Hai! My friend, can I speak to thee
Please lend me thy ear, for I may not be here
You humans are supposed to be kind and clever
That is why God made you supreme
To be our guardian angel
Then why, oh why you act like mindless butchers
And make us suffer a living hell!
Please look at my family, some twenty and three
Young and small, suckling and strong
A picture of health, happy and content
Playing with Mother Nature
Without a care or a worry in the world
The lifestyle we appreciate and enjoy
I am afraid, I will be caught one day
A big harpoon, all steal, sharp and solid
Fired from a Japanese whaler
Will pierce my body, my heart
A river of blood will pollute thy ocean
My life span, one hundred years of joy and fun
Humans have reduced to no more than twenty and five
Ducking and diving, having no respite
Having fun, you must be joking
What have we done to offend thee humans
That you want to hunt us to obliteration
Rubbing salt in our wounds, calling it science
I have only one message for you, the mindless thugs
The destroyer of Mother Nature
Please leave us alone to play with Mother Nature
So that we could also have some fun
A family, some respite and hopefully a long life
If we become extinct, it will be a human tragedy
A loss to man kind, for your children will never see

A spouting spectacle, on the vast ocean stage
This beautiful green, green planet
Will no more be your mother earth.

****

By the time the song was over, Divya had gathered enough firewood. She sat down near the edge of the fast flowing but shallow water.

She opened a small metal container and took out roti, a kind of Nan bread, made from half ground coarse millet flour, fresh green chillies, spring onion and a piece of traditional goat cheese. She filled a cup from the sweet natural water of the spring which half the population drink and the other half had water from deep wells that would never dry up, even in worse draught and hot summer months.

This time Amar approached her with extreme care, making sure not to make any noise or to step, stumble on any dry wood. When near enough, Amar put his vast hand on her eyes and waited for a reaction.

"Let me go Amar. How can you harass an innocent village lassie in such a way. You should be ashamed? This is not Delhi or Jaipur." Said Divya coolly and calmly.

"How did you know it was me?" Amar was taken back by her reaction.

Divya pointed a finger at Amar's reflection in the clear water and said.

"This is jungle. If I had not seen your reflection, I would have died of shock or may have thrown you in the river. Then I would have to look after you again and spoil another of my shawl.

After a long pause she said, "Would you like to join me, share my humble lunch? It is rude for us to eat alone. It is nothing special, no more than a roti but I have cooked it myself."

Amar thought she was a very clever girl. Never answers in a hurry and knows all the right words. She knew Amar would never be able to resist this challenge, to taste food cooked by her." Why not. I am hungry and I have eaten such a delicious food many times when I was a child. Amar remembered his frequent visits to Shankarbhai's farm, with his guardian, bodyguard Ramudada.

While eating the meal, they talked and talked. Some how Divya trusted Amar completely. She told him some of her inner most thoughts.

Her father, Shambhu Bhai was a fisherman and mother was Shantuben.

While Shambhu caught fish from the river, down the foothills where the river widens, her mother tilled the land. These cold waters of the river were well stocked with various types of fish.

They had a small stall in the local market where they sold fish and home grown vegetables.

Divya was their only child, having lost three children even before their first birthday. That is why Divya-Jyoti was so special, an apple of their eyes.

They had a small farm or rather a few steps carved out of the mountain slope. But the land was fertile and with plenty of water available, it was a productive land, producing potatoes, onions, carrots, cabbage, tomatoes , muli (radish) and such vegetables in abundance. They also kept few goats, a mountain tradition so that no children go without milk.

Divya helped them on the farm and at the stall. She occasionally went in the forest to gather firewood. The income from these combined enterprise kept the family in relative comfort that is according to the tribal living standard.

Divya's father was a liberal, forward looking person with views that were out of step with the rest of the community.

He enrolled Divya to the local school when she was just five and let her study all the way, that is as far as the local school would teach, which was up to standard tenth, just two years short of metric, the hallmark for calling one self an educated person, in those distant days when science was still in the infant state and university education was reserved for the privileged few.

Naturally she was the highest educated girl in her tribe. But that was more of a hindrance than an advantage. In a small community, one has to be a part of a herd, to be led, to fit in. In a town where every one has one leg, two legs are a hindrance, makes you an outcast. Divya, being young, well built, beautiful and smart, besides being well educated, soon got engaged at the age of twelve, a normal age for the village girls. The boy, like her was smart and came from a respected family.

Unfortunately, her fiancée died in a drowning accident a year after engagement. From time to time, the river gets flooded after a heavy rain.

Those living on the river bank and the low laying areas are in danger of their lives. But as these people have lived all their lives in the vicinity of the river, they were well versed in the danger of flooding. It was rare for some one to drown, to lose a life in such an incident as people would move to higher areas which were not only plentiful but well prepared for such an emergency, such an eventuality.

In a small village, any death is tragic. People are superstitious. Such an incident will inevitable brand the girl as unlucky at the best or cursed at worst.

Although Divya was a good catch for any boy, no one would accept her hand in marriage after such an accident, except widowers thrice her age with half a dozen children.

Divya would rather be left on the shelf than be a step mother to such children, a free baby minder and a nursemaid. She did not mind being single, especially looking at her school mates who were already lumbered with a couple of children and looked at least ten years older than their age.

She enjoyed her freedom, her independence and above all avoiding the burden of becoming a mother every other year.

Village girls were in way sex slaves of their husbands, always ready and available to satisfy the sexual desire of their men folk, so often under the influence of drinks and drugs, one of the gifts from the British Raj to these tribal people.

Divya was indeed lucky that she had the support and tacit approval of her family, especially her father. Now Amar knew why Divya was single at the ripe old age of 18 and why she was so clever, full of confidence.

Before departing, bidding her farewell, Amar gave Divya a beautiful red shawl and said, "Divya, this is a present from me, to replace the one I spoiled when you wiped the blood from my forehead. I have borrowed it from my sister Madhuri." Amar made up the story of her sister to put her mind at rest, not to alarm her unnecessarily. Divya looked at the shawl, felt it and realised that it was pure silk, indeed a very expensive present.

"Amar, you should give this to a princess, some one who can appreciate it better than me. Moreover how would I explain it to my Bapu?" (Father)

Divya said it in a soft, eager voice. But she was in two minds, whether to accept the gift or hand it back to Amar.

"Well, tell your father that it is a birthday present to a charming Pari (Angel) from the Prince of the Mountain God?"

This brought a smile on her deceptively innocent looking, pale but beautiful face. "Well Amar, shukria (thank you) for comparing me to a Pari. But neither I nor my Bapu knows my exact birthday.

We mountain people do not have papers to prove our identity." But she did not try to give back the shawl to Amar. She knew she would never be able to compete with Amar if it comes to an argument or stubbornness. Then again she was in a win win situation and she certainly deserved this present. After all she did spoil her shawl.

She was beginning to admire, trust and appreciate his company, as she did not have any contact with a young and educated person like Amar. After all she was a young, intelligent, beautiful and attractive person, full of armans, ambitions. A coincident of birth does not negate these dreams which are universal to each and every human being, no matter what your background may be.

So now Amar knew why Divya was single at the age of 18, the oldest unmarried virgin girl in the village.

Day by day, this innocent, strange and even odd and some what bizarre friendship between a prince and a pauper grew stronger. It was beauty and not so much of a beast and the beauty friendship. But perhaps Professor Higgins trying to convert an Eastender lassie, a cockney girl into a high society success, a princess that would grace any table, Amar's fair lady and why not!

While Amar tried to teach Divya how to ride a horse, shoot a riffle and to read and write English, as she was already prolific in her Rajestani dialect and Hindi, even better than Amar, Divya tried unsuccessfully to teach Amar how to survive in jungle, how to identify edible roots, how to fish with just a long stick, with a sharp, long and narrow metal tip.

Divya would stand still in the freezing fast flowing river water, often on one leg, spear ready and pointed to pierce any fish that would venture within the range of the spear.

Although it looked easy when Divya did the fishing, it is an art difficult to master. It has to be perfected by many hours of practice, especially in the young age, during childhood. She can prepare a barbeque with trout, game birds and root vegetables, a dinner fit for a prince.

Amar knew that there was a heaven and earth distance, difference between his friendship with Rita and Divya. That is why he was trying his best to keep this stranger than fiction friendship innocent and free of physical attraction. But he knew that he was fighting a losing battle. How long he will be able to keep his emotion, his sexual and physical desire in check when in the presence of such a young, beautiful and sexy girl who had all the curves and so often they were not that well hidden either. As she was not flaunting her assets deliberately, it became even more tempting, more desirable than when Amar met Rita who, more or less gave every thing Amar ever wanted in a relationship on a plate. After all hard earned money, fruits of labour goes a long way, much more appreciated than a birthday gift.

But Amar knew he could not touch her, especially against her will, without her making the first move. Even then it may not be appropriate to take advantage of Divya who by now had really captivated Amar.

Soon it was a festival time, the nine days of Harvest Festival when the people of the village were allowed to enter the fort to celebrate the festival in the temple compound.

Ranaji even obliged the villagers by erecting a huge tent in the open ground by the side of the temple, as it is usually very cold in the night, as the festival coincides with the arrival of winter which is pretty cold on the mountain slopes, at the height of four thousand feet.

Navratri means a happy time, a festive time of the year, especially for the young at heart. It is the only time of the year when youngsters were allowed to roam freely, stay out until late, although on most part, under the supervision of an elderly member of the family or a friend.

Divya would come to the temple with few friends. Amar would join them, occasionally participating in the stick dance, dancing until late without a care in the world. For Amar, it was a strange experience, to mix with people who would normally be barred from even entering the palace. But he soon realised that they were no different then the rest of the mankind. They have ambition, aspiration, arman, zeal and goal in life that is no different than his own, any member of the royal family.

It is usual practise for boys and girls to play together, some hiding their true identity by wearing fancy dress, costumes. So it was not difficult for Amar to hide himself under the face mask of a lion, a bull or even dressed as a Maharaja, the king or covering his face, his true identity as best as he could under the circumstances.

Soon Amar and Divya would leave the crowd and meet in the bush for an hour or so, enjoying each other's company and occasional cuddle and a close proximity that would raise the blood pressure.

Today it was Sharad Poonam, (full moon) the last day of the celebration for the villagers to enter the fort without permission, without hindrance. After playing stick dance for an hour, Amar and Divya left the tent and disappeared in the palace garden, out of bound to every one, where complete privacy was guaranteed.

Amar knew no one would disturb them here, in the Garden of Eden where he can enjoy his forbidden fruit, Adam can have his Eve. The full moon was lighting up the sky. Rays of the moon passing through tall trees and bushes and the sweet smell from the rose garden, gardenia and the night queen (ratrani) provided a romantic atmosphere that was difficult to imagine.

For the first time Amar could not control his feelings, suppressed for so long so as not to distress Divya. Holding her tight to his vast chest, he gave her a passionate kiss, without any protest from Divya.

Their kissing, cuddling and embrace, gentle and restrained love making lasted some half an hour before Divya broke lose and moved away.

With tears in her eyes, she said, "Amar, you know I love you and you love me. But you are a prince and I am a pauper, an uneducated village lassie. Within days you will go away, disappear from my life, never to be seen again.

What would happen if we are unable to control our feelings, our love making, our desire, our divani youvani? (Mad, youthful desire) You will go away but I have to live here. I would bring shame not only on myself but on my family, my Bapu as well. My Bapu trusts me so much and has given me freedom that is the envy of every village girl. I do not want to betray him, betray his trust and spoil his reputation." Divya's eyes were wet with tears and the emotion breaking up her voice.

"Divya, do you trust me? Do you think I am an honest, sincere and a good person, a kind and caring human being? I know what will happen if I leave you, abandon you in your hour of need." Amar sounded sincere.

Yes Amar, you know I trust you with my life. Otherwise I would not be here alone with you. But you know our closeness, our physical attraction and our youthful desire will one day make us lose control; lose restrain that we have displayed so far. I would rather die than face the consequences." Divya could hardly speak but continued.

"You know my background. I was dealt the wrong cards, a bad hand. I am still a virgin but I have all the desire that any well educated, city girl may have. Amar, I am confused, happy yet angry. What should I do?" Now the tears were freely flowing from her eyes.

"Divya, I am here to stay and if I leave, you will be coming with me. I will never abandon you or cross the line, the Laxman Rekha that would bring shame on you. It would be as much my shame, my guilt as yours. That is my promise on this holy night, in the presence of Devi Ambika." Amar tried to be as convincing as he could but could not bring himself up to telling the truth. He knew it would cause Divya more pain than joy.

Amar and Divya came back to the temple. Divya joined her friends and Amar came back to the palace wondering where his life is going and where and how will it end. But he was too deep in love to retreat. Moreover he is a Rajput, a descendent of Maha Rana Pratap, the most respected Rajput king in the history of Bharat. For Amar the saying, "Pran Jaya magar vachan na jaya" (I would rather give my life than break a promise) was as true today as at any time in history.

How could he break his promise to Divya, break her heart and condemn her to life of misery and loneliness? Amar went to sleep with a million questions in his heart but not a single answer except that he was madly in love with Divya and life without her was unthinkable.

It did not take long for Shambhu Bhai, Divya's father to learn about her friendship with a stranger from the palace. It was Chagan, a middle-aged man who had fancied Divya for a long time, as he knew no young and unattached man would be willing to accept her hand in marriage, a woman who may bring bad luck to her husband and his family.

Chagan was single and had lived in Jaipur for a couple of years. So he considered himself a bit superior to these villagers who had not set foot outside the village.

But he was twice Divya's age and moreover he was married to a bottle and drugs. So often he was found drunk on the village streets. But when sober he was pleasant to talk to.

Normally no one would pay any attention to what Chagan had to say. Buy him a bottle of whiskey and he will sing like a canary. But Shambhu Bhai had noticed radical changes in Divya, in her life style which were hard to explain. These are the normal changes that a girl undergoes when she is in love head over heels.

Divya, once a carefree girl who paid scant attention to her appearance, her clothes, was now a changed girl. She regularly washed herself, sometimes twice a day. Gone were her loose, shapeless clothes and oily, tightly knit hair style which made her look ten years older than her true age?

Her clothes were now of matching colour, tight fitting and body hugging that showed her shapely body and well-formed curves, all in the right places.

She regularly washed her long, dark brown hair with a shampoo that gave it a shine and a silky touch, kept loose and flowing freely in the mountain air that enhanced her beauty a million times.

She had started wearing Chappals (loose footwear) and massaged her long, shapely legs with cream. The transformation was so complete, so striking that it would be difficult to miss.

Her appearance must have been a topic of conversation and envy among girls of her age, among the village gossipmongers, as she looked indeed stunning and beautiful.

One day when Divya was returning after meeting Amar, her father called her on one side and told her what he had heard from Chagan. Divya readily confessed, told her Bapu the truth, about meeting Amar, being in love with him, some one high about their stature.

Listening to Divya, Shambhu Bhai was serious, pensive and in reflective mood. He remained silent and thoughtful for a while before he responded.

"Beti, (daughter) I have no objection with your friendship with Amar. You are a good judge of character. If you say he is good, sincere young man of unimpeachable character, then I believe you.

But remember Beta, he comes from a royal stock, a product of high society. We are low caste in their eyes, only fit to be servants in their household.

People from palaces are like honey bees. They are normally after one thing and when they had their honey, their fun, they inevitably return to their own honeycomb, leaving behind a weathered and trampled flower that no one would want.

Oil can never mix with water. It can only float on the surface, remain aloof, be a superficial component of the mixture.

I know I have failed you. Kismat has conspired against us. You are in the prime of your life, so beautiful, clever, and full of hope and expectation. Your arman (ambition, desire) has been buried deep, your dream unfulfilled.

I do not want to be a thorn in your happiness, how can I? But Beti, please take care. Do not take any step that you may regret later, ruin your and our lives." There were tears in his eyes. He could hardly contain his anguish, his pain, his sorrow and his failure to provide a life partner for his wonderful daughter.

"Bapu, please trust me. I am your daughter and proud of you. I know our position, our rank and our place in society. I would rather jump in a deep well or take a poison than bring shame on me and my family." Said Divya, as she grabbed her Bapu and hugged him with tears flowing freely from her eyes and her heart in turmoil.

Whatever doubts Shambhu Bhai had about his daughter, about Divya, evaporated and their mutual love, trust, respect and admiration for each other grew by leaps and bounds. Now Bapu will never question Divya about Amar.

Divya was now living in a dream world. She had faith in Amar and confidence in her own ability and judgement. Some how she felt she is not heading for a nasty fall but her life may change beyond belief, beyond reality. Her dream is about to become a reality, her happiness will multiply a million times.

Today Amar was going to Jaipur, to meet Roopmati (beautiful one) the daughter of Maharaja Digvijaysinh. Amar was to accompany her back to Ranaji's palace.

Amar had known her since childhood, as she used to accompany her father Maharaja Digvijaysinh whenever he visited Ranaji for a hunting trip. All her friends called her Rani (queen) as she was the daughter of the most powerful Rajput king, the Rathod dynasty in Rajasthan.

Maharaja's kingdom covered a vast area of some eighty thousand square miles with three thousand villages and the major towns of Jodhpur, besides the capital city of Ajmer. The total population of his kingdom exceeded twenty million.

No wonder Maharaja was one of the favourite Royals of the British Raj. Not only he had an excellent polo and cricket team with British players, but he also maintained a string of palaces in his vast kingdoms which were all available, at the disposal of the high ranking officials of the Raj and British Royalty.

There were two game reserves within the boundary of his kingdom, one on the banks of river Luni and other on river Sukri. Being a desert kingdom, wildlife was not that much in evidence but with tigers plentiful, who were nurtured with care and these game reserves were popular with the visitors. Occasional hunting was allowed to the most senior members of the British Raj.

With Rani as a guest, Amar had to change his routine, his timetable. So when Amar met Divya at their usual place, at the bank of the river, he took Divya on one side and said, "Divya I have to tell you some thing important. So listen carefully."

Looking at Amar's serious face, without his usual innocent smile and playful, mischievous behaviour, Divya was worried, became apprehensive, and feared a bad premonition. Could it be true, what Bapu had told her, warned her against? Could Amar be leaving the palace for good?

A thousand questions suddenly filled her mind, her heart and could not control her tears. She could not imagine a life without Amar any more. Amar realised what is going on in Divya's mind. Drawing her near and wiping her tears Amar said, "Don't be silly. I have not come to bade farewell. Didn't I tell you I am here to stay, no matter what!

But listen to what I have to say. There are some guests at the palace. I will have to look after them and take them on the hunt. So I will not be able to see you every day. But I will leave a note in the Bunyan tree. Meet me at the time I suggest and don't be alarmed if I am late. This is only for a week or so."

"Amar, why you have to look after Ranaji's guests? Surely that is the duty of Ranaji and his Crown Prince?"

"Divya, you are naive beyond belief or are you pretending to be one, making a fool out of me, a prince? The smile and the mischief were back on Amar's face.

"Divya, what is the name of Ranaji's son, the Crown Prince?"

Divya was happy and relieved to see Amar back to his innocent best? "Amarsinhji." She tried to look as innocent as possible under the circumstances. But now she was full of mischievous smile.

"I am the same Amar." And he squeezed her hard, fearing she might dart away never to be seen again. In any case it was so difficult to let her go at any time. So how could Amar let her slip out when she was at her best, full of innocent lust, an Eve in the Amar's heart, his garden, his Vrindavan?

In the comfort of Amar's arms, Divya felt safe, unruffled, calm and composed, then asked Amar, "Why did you hide the truth from me?"

"Divya, when we first met, I thought it was unimportant, unnecessary to tell you who I am. I never thought we will meet again, let alone fell in love. But when I fell in love, head over heels, I was afraid I may never see you again if I tell you the truth. But now I am sure that you love me as much as I love you. Nothing and nobody could come between us, not even Ranaji. Am I right or am I right?" Amar was back to his usual self.

Although Divya had suspected all along that Amar was hiding some thing, was not telling her the truth, she never suspected that Amar may be the Crown Prince, Ranaji's son and heir to the throne.

Divya was happy that Amar was a doctor but worried that he was a Crown Prince and heir to the throne.

Although by now Amar had won Divya over, she was still apprehensive.

During the last three months, Divya had gained tremendous self confidence. She was completely reformed, a new person indeed. She was beautiful beyond imagination, smart and witty but above all she was kind and caring. She had all the qualities that Amar wanted in a woman, in her wife.

She knew that it would be a completely different ball game, she would be out of her depth when and if she ever enters palace. Amar will not be always around to hold her hand. Yet somehow she was not that apprehensive, that nervous. Perhaps being in love makes a person strong, installs self belief beyond one's wildest dream.

But she was too deep in love. Amar had given her all she ever wanted. It was sink or swim and it has to be with Amar. There was no turning back. There was too much at stake, too much to lose. Without Amar, life will not be worth living.

Amar knew that Divya was worried and who would not be? After all she was only 18 and until now had never met any important person, let alone a crown prince!

Divya remembered the incident, the storyline in the Hindu epic book of Ramayana when Shabri, a low caste manual worker was privileged to welcome Lord Rama in her hut. She was petrified. It would be a similar experience for Divya if and when she enters the palace and is greeted by Ranaji himself?

"Divya, I know what is going on in your mind, in your heart. Even I am thinking how to tell Ranaji about us. But leave it to me. I will sort out every thing, resolve all our problems. Just tell your Bapu that we would like to get married as soon as possible."

Divya could not believe her ears. "Amar, please repeat what you said just now?" I am not sure I heard you right.

"Divya, would you marry me!" Amar said it with a sweet smile that would melt any heart, any iceberg, even the iceberg that sank Titanic!

Divya bit her lip to make sure that she was not dreaming and the cry of pain with blood pouring down soon convinced her that she was wide awake and in the company of Amar.

Amar accompanied Rani daily, to a picnic or on a hunt. But Amar was no longer interested in killing innocent, harmless wild animals just for fun. He accompanied them on the shoot but shooting was done by Rani and his cousin Ajit.

Ajit liked Rani or rather her position on royal pecking order. He was eager to please her, willing to catch her every word. Her command was his wish.

After all Rani was a princess of one of the most powerful kingdom in Rajasthan.

But in comparison to Amar, Ajit always took a distant second place. He was neither a doctor nor a Crown Prince. But Ajit had his admirers. He was a number one polo player, playing at the highest level, with Maharaja of Jaipur and British Royalties. He was not bad at cricket either and above all he loved hunting, a crack shot who could be an asset in a tight situation, when facing a wounded tiger or an elephant, especially a rogue elephant.

Amar tried to bring Rani and Ajit together. Amar would spend most of the day with them but at night, he would either retire to his room or go to the temple where he would read, write, putting his innermost thoughts on paper, or just listen to the bhajans and hymns so sweetly sung by the Pujari who loved Amar's company.

Like Amar, Rani had also stayed in London for four years. She had adopted many English customs and traditions but unlike Amar, she was there not to learn, to study but to enjoy herself, move in the high society and perhaps find a husband that would please the Maharaja.

Amar met Rani in London when he was doing medicine. He had just separated from Rita. So he was elated to meet a childhood friend, a familiar face, little realising what mischief Rani was up.

One day Amar found Rani waiting outside his front door. Soon they were in each other's pocket and went on a week's holiday to Switzerland. It was more like a honeymoon than a holiday.

Rita may be forward but beside Rani she was an armature. Rani would not do any thing by half, whether it was binge drinking, binge sex or drugs. She was a classic example of a rich spoilt child out of control. For Rani there was no tomorrow. Why postpone some action, some fun for tomorrow if you could have it today. They spend most of the week, partying at night and remaining in bed during the day, not sleeping much but making love.

Even Amar, a strong and healthy man could not cope with her demand in bed. To satisfy her or rather her wild and almost unnatural, unhealthy obsession with sex, Amar treated her with scant respect, making love as passionately, as unnaturally and as brutally as he could, hurting her and giving her painful bites on her most private parts, on her breasts, high on her thighs and all over the body. In fact Amar felt guilty that he was treating Rani so brutally as if he was having a sex with a paid girl.

Amar was hoping against all hopes that such a brutal love making will put her off and will leave him alone. But on the contrary she enjoyed it, asking for more and treating Amar in the same brutal manner, having sex in each and every position. Perhaps she was the author of the famous Indian sex book Kamasutra. Rani was enjoying every minute even though she was not able to wear her revealing, see through dresses for a while.

Amar had hard time ditching her when they returned to London. Amar had his work; his studies came in as a perfect excuse. Rani soon got tired of waiting for Amar and moved on to new boyfriends, to pasture new. She was never short of boyfriends, both Indian and English, as she did not particularly mind the social status of her suitors, admirers and bed hoppers.

Today Amar was a mature person. He could no longer be tempted, bought off, mesmerized or bewitched by power, influence and especially sexual adventures and fantasies. He already had fulfilled his every pervert desire with Rita and Rani. He was more simulated by the gentle, restrained, dignified and emotional love making of Divya than any wild parties. Amar soon realised that Rani was here to rekindle their short but stormy relationship she enjoyed so much in London.

She was in the market for a suitable suitor, to get married. There was no way Amar could marry Rani even if he may not be involved with any one else, such as Divya.

Her overdeveloped bosom, loose and hanging as if she has raised a brood of children were in need of a plastic surgery. Her waistline was covered with flab and her hair was dry, coarse and receding. She was only 26 years old but looked at least a decade older.

She only made herself presentable with heavy makeup and loose, concealing clothes. Gone were her body hugging, all revealing clothes that she once wore to show off her beautiful and sexy figure, her big, over developed breasts, her long thin proportional legs, prime asset, a figure fit for a princess?

Perhaps that is why Maharaja Digvijaysinh was looking; willing to climb down, accept a suitor from a small kingdom like that of Ranaji.

After spending a week in the palace, Rani went back to Jaipur. Although she guessed that Amar was not keen on her, she was not yet willing to give him up. She could not forget the wonderful love making she enjoyed with Amar in Switzerland. Amar was strong, young and healthy who could give her every thing she want in bed.

Amar knew in a way there was no comparison between Divya and Rani.

He may be madly in love with Divya; but it would bring him nothing but heartache and misery.

Ranaji would never accept Divya, a daughter of a lowly fisherman as his daughter in law. He will have to give up his right to the throne. Perhaps leave Rajpar for good. But some how this sacrifice did not deter or discouraged him in any way. He was fully capable of earning a living as a doctor, if need arise. He also knew that no other girl would make him as happy as Divya, who was in her own right a very beautiful and charming girl, but without the baggage of expectation. Perhaps even Ranaji may accept her given time and opportunity.

Ranaji did not see much of Amar for the last few months. So often he was away for a day or two but Ranaji had no idea where he was going or how he was spending his time. But Amar looked happy and that was reassuring for Ranaji.

Today when Amar came back to the palace after meeting Divya, Ranaji was eagerly waiting for him. He looked pleased. Without waiting for a response from Amar, Ranaji said, "Amar, there is a very good news for you and me.

Maharaja Digvijaysinh has invited us at Rani's birthday party and if you agree, he would like to announce your engagement to Rani.

Beta, this is a wonderful opportunity to further your career, to climb a ladder and reach for the sky. We all know how important he is."

Ranaji had already made up his mind. He knew about their friendship and their close relationship when they were both in London.

After a long time Amar had a dinner with Ranaji who was determined to have a dinner and a chat with Amar. He even missed his usual dinner time.

But when he saw no smile, eagerness or anticipation on Amar's face, Ranaji was disappointed.

"Why Amar, are you not interested in Rani? Have you fallen out?" Ranaji was eager for Amar's response.

"Pitaji (father) I know the importance of this match-making. I also know that to hurt Maharaja's feelings, to go against his wishes is like inviting a conflict, like throwing sand against the sun, to enter in a no win situation.

But Pitaji, we are completely two different people, with different interest, different friends, different aim in life and definitely different goals.

As you may have noticed Pitaji, I am no longer interested in hunting, playing polo, drinking or partying the night away, unlike Rani and Ajit. Our thoughts, actions and priorities are different. There is no common ground where our thoughts meet, have a home for our aspiration and share our ideals."

"Beta, you are making a mountain out of a molehill. You were once so close. It is not impossible to change her in some ways. She loves you and willingly meet you half way. You know what would happen if we reject this invitation, make Maharaja an enemy. Our kingdom is like occupying one room in his palace." Ranaji was serious and worried as well.

Amar knew it would not be easy to placate Ranaji, make him understand why he would like to keep away from Rani.

So as a last resort, when every argument failed to convince Ranaji, Amar had to tell his father about the week they spend in Switzerland, Rani's life style, her sexual habit, her drink and drug problem, as well as string of boyfriends and lovers she had in London. Amar also expressed his doubt about her health and the toll this lifestyle had taken on her, physically and mentally.

Amar would not like to assassinate some one's character, especially that of a princess. But he had no choice if he was to convenience Ranaji that Rani was not a right person to be his life partner.

Ranaji had to believe Amar, as he had himself seen the physical changes in Rani. He could imagine what Rani would look like early in the morning, without her makeup. That was one of the reasons Maharaja was willing to seek a suitor from some one far his junior, much lower in the pecking order than himself.

Amar also seized this opportunity to tell Ranaji about his involvement in politics, the reason why he was away from the palace for days. He confessed of his interest in the Quit India Movement and his admiration for Gandhiji, Loke Manya Tilak, Sardar Patel, Subashchandra Bose and other politicians who were involved in the political movement, Rabindranath Tagore, the first Asian to receive Noble prize for literature. Amar admired these leaders who have devoted their lives, gone to prison to liberate Bharat from the clutches of British Raj.

Amar knew this was like a death sentence for Ranaji. His influence, friendship with the British and other kings, rulers and noblemen will come to an end if it ever became a public knowledge that Amar was involved in Quit India Movement. That is why Amar was secretive and promised Ranaji that he would not rock the boat. He would take a back seat; serve the masses as a doctor.

Even British could not object to this humanitarian work. But Amar could not tell Ranaji about Divya. He had given Ranaji enough pain, anguish and heartache to last a lifetime.

Although Ranaji used to read in papers every day how young, talented, and educated men from rich and famous families were leaving the life of comfort, privilege and security, in order to join Gandhiji, to participate in his political struggle and to adopt a lifestyle that was a million miles apart, living in Ashrams (communes, kibbutz) , sleep on the floor, walk hundreds of miles in order to visit villages and spread the message, he never thought for a moment that this idealism, madness and sacrifice, whatever one may call, will one day come home to roost.

Ranaji was lost in thoughts. Is this real? Where had he gone wrong in raising his only son? Was it a mistake to send him to England? It was said that the thoughts for Quit India Movement were first discussed, surfaced in London, among the Indian students who were there to study law. Their aspiration came from Irish politicians, patriots who were also involved in such a movement to liberate their own country from British rule.

Before Amar retreated, he reassured his father that he will not get directly involved in politics. He loved Ranaji too much to jeopardize his position, his way of life, make him an enemy of the British.

In a way Ranaji was proud of Amar. He was willing to give up his life of luxury and was so different from Ajit and Rani who would like to squeeze every ounce of happiness, in any way they can, regardless of consequence.

Ranaji was now convinced that it would not be too difficult for him to say no to the invitation he had received to attend Rani's birthday party. But he had to handle the story carefully. After all who would want a son in law with such liberal ideas, idealism that would ruin a kingdom?

Amar was pleased that at last he was able to tell Ranaji part of the truth. Now he could live a free, less complicated life and spend more time with his sweetheart Divya.

Amar's life was like swift flowing river water. On one bank may be tall buildings, offices and homes overflowing with humanity, a lifestyle that would turn the night into day, people with power, living in the lap of luxury, while others had to struggle to find a simple meal or a roof over their heads.

On the other bank, just across, separated by no more than a mile or two of water, one may find frost, trees and birds, wild animals. Forest dwellers living a simple but happy life with few possessions but no one would go hungry or sleep rough. There was love, care and brotherhood. Every thing was shared; every asset was a communal property. It was in a way share and share alike.

Amar was glad that he would soon be leaving behind his aimless life where he was more like a prisoner of circumstances, a bird living in a golden cage rather than a free man leading a useful life.

He knew where he belonged, on which river bank he would like to settle, plant his roots and build his home, raise his children.

The next day when Amar met Divya, he was in a happy, contented mood.

His heart was beating with joy. He tried to explain to Divya what his future plans, his ambition were and his aim in life.

Divya was not into politics, nor did she read newspapers. She did not understand much about Satyagrah (civil disobedience) or the Quit India Movement but she was happy that whatever plan Amar made, it included her. They were going to work, participate and fight together, as husband and wife.

Divya at last realised that this is not a dream but a reality. She would soon be Amar's wife and living together as husband and wife, without fear or recrimination. She could not control her emotion, her tears and cried like a baby, without trying to hold back her emotion which she had done for so long. When Divya regained her composure, they both came to her hut, to tell Shambhu Bhai the good news.

It was impossible for him to understand or grasp the situation but by now they all had blind faith in Amar.

Within few days Amar and Divya got married, in the palace temple, according to Hindu tradition, in the presence of Divya's parents, the temple priest and a couple of palace employees who were close and loyal to Amar.

But Amar could not invite Ranaji, as he knew he would never give his blessing or approve Divya, although by now she was a different girl, beautiful, charming and full of confidence. She would definitely pass as a princess without any difficulty. In fact Rani would look pale, unattractive and old compared to Divya. What Rani was at the age of 14 or 15, Divya was today.

Bending to touch the feet of Pujari, both Amar and this grand old holy man were shedding tears by a bucketful. Both knew that this may be their final meeting, the last encounter, the final farewell.

Amar requested Pujari to perform, to carry out his last wish, to hand over a letter to Ranaji after twenty four hours.

When Ranaji was reading Amar's letter in total disbelief, Amar and Divya were touching Gandhiji's feet at his residence, Sabarmati Ashram and asking for his blessings.

Giving them his ashirvad, (special blessings) and helping them to stand up, Gandhiji said, "Beta, if people like you support my zumbesh, (struggle) then no one, I mean no one could stop us from gaining independence," then added with a smile, "Beta all those who live in this ashram with me, has to take three vows, make resolution. I have decided not to eat meat or drink and to stay away from women. What are your resolutions?"

Looking at Divya, Amar said without hesitation, "Bapu I promise not to eat meat, drink or seek the company of any women except my wife Divya." And all three had a hearty laugh.

****

DISAPPEARING DREAMS (Chandni)

Chirag was sitting on the soft, silvery sand of the Oyster Bay sandy beach, his favourite place, his favourite beach to pass the evening time, enjoying the beautiful scenery, watching the sun setting in the distant over the shiny waters of the vast and magnificent Ocean, on the far, far horizon, slowly but surely sinking in the athul blue waters of the romantic Indian Ocean which was on our doorstep, part of our every day life.

The shining rays of the setting sun, like a diamond in the sky, were appearing and disappearing in the surging and ebbing waters, multiplying the golden rays of the disappearing sun a million times. It gave the evening, the end of the day, the setting, departing sun a romantic atmosphere, idealistic dream and starry eyed optimism that would melt even the most stubborn, obstinate heart. This was the pace or rather lack of it in the British East African colonies just before and after the brutal Second World War that destroyed the peace, tranquillity and above all the innocence of life, the one ingredient that made our lives so happy, fulfilling and worth living.

The whole coast of East Africa is fortunate enough to be blessed with the presence of this mighty, majestic Indian Ocean on their door-step that most of us took for granted until we were forced to move away to a desolate place, a cold, damp and soulless place far away from any mass of water, any romantic ocean which suddenly became so important part of our lives that we travel thousands of miles, spending our life savings to visit, to enjoy beautiful beaches of Goa and Kerala, the warm climate and the friendliness of the Indian people. One has to understand the Indian (Hindu) culture to comprehend why we, the Westerners get so much respect, love and attention from these people of India. According to Hindu culture, guests are Deva; special people "Atithi Deva Bhava" Guests are welcomed in the form of God. The word God is used not as an Almighty, divine power but some one who deserves their respect, attention, love and care. Parents are Gods to children, so are elderly and wise people who are in an authoritative position who serve the community, people like teachers, doctors and temple priests.

Within half an hour the sun completely disappeared on the distant horizon, giving stars and the tiny new moon the opportunity to penetrate the rising tide of darkness but without much success. How can a candle light bathe a mighty palace in the bright light of a midday sun?

The darkness, slowly but surely was gaining an upper hand. By now the beach was nearly deserted. The stall holders and the hawkers, having closed their shops, that is their tiny cane baskets full of mouth watering delicacies, fried mogo (cassava) liberally covered with salt, chilly powder, lemon and ambli sauce, roasted peanuts, cashew nuts and corn on the cob similarly immersed in various spices and sauces but not the tomato catch-up, as it was considered to be too mild, too timid that would dent the taste buds?

But Chirag's favourite was not food but drink, not the popular Tusker beer that many youngsters would prefer but the green coconut water that would keep cool even in a 100°F heat, as the husk cover acts like a natural cooling box, protecting it from the heat of the scorching midday sun.

With the demise of the sun and the delicate state of the moon, the stars were the master of the sky, the dominant force in the universe, even if for a short while only. Their mischievous twinkle, sweet smile and romantic gestures were bright, encouraging and appreciative enough to feel one's heart with hope, anticipation and love, the one ingredient that keeps the wheels of our turbulent lives oiled, smooth and on track. But when it breaks down, some times on a flimsy excuse, the life so often becomes a living hell, not worth living.

The few, lonely hearts still remaining on the beach were preparing to leave before the darkness completely engulfs the beach and the surrounding area and makes this beach, a heaven of peace and tranquillity at most times into a dangerous place to be in, a muggers' paradise and the dense coconut grove a dangerous place to walk, to pass through.

But Chirag was still sitting or rather laying on the sand, watching stars, trying to understand the signals emitting from the distance of a million light years. Naturally they were oblivious to Chirag's pain, dilemma and heartache. Chirag had no urge to leave the beach, not even before it becomes dangerous in the dark, for a single, lonely person, an easy prey to a wandering gang of thugs and vagabonds who are always on the lookout for an easy target, so that they can feed their habit, the drug fuelled life, the sole reason for their miserable existence.

How could Chirag go back to his lonely flat? Without his beloved Chandni (Sweet, cool moonlight) there was no soul, no love and certainly no happiness in his tiny but well decorated flat with all modes and cons of life that make it a pleasant living, in the company of his charming, caring and loving wife.

It was Chandni's flat, decorated, furnished and arranged by her. No wonder her presence was every where, in every corner, in every item, in every minute detail. There was no escape from her in this flat.

Chirag's mind was in turmoil. Was he at fault behind Chandni's decision to leave him? She may have tested his thoughts, his idealism, his superfluous thinking but so often our idealism never matches our action in real life, when it is put to test.

In fact our idealism, our thoughts, our high principles, our seat on the pedestal and holier than thou attitude evaporates at the first sign of reality. It is not worth the paper it is written on. Our need, our wellbeing always comes first.

Chandni may have tested Chirag's idealism but certainly not his practical attitude, his undying love and devotion for her. Chandni badly failed to understand Chirag but perhaps her past experiences have made her weary of human beings, made her weary of human frailty. Who can blame her for the loss of faith in people surrounding her, no matter how loving and caring they may be? Once beaten twice shy, that is but natural.

Chirag and Chandni used to come here, on this beach practically every day. They would sit here, on the warm, soft sand or on the wooden bench just off the sandy beach, for hours, watching the setting sun, listening to the murmur of the sea and the squabbling of the sea birds, dominated by the large and incredibly aggressive sea gulls. On rare occasion albatross, one of the largest birds in flight with an eight feet wing span would grace the sky, making it a rare but a majestic spectacle. How human wished they could have the freedom of the sky just like albatross who can wonder all over the world on wings, without a care or even a second thought. Well, that is bird freedom; albatross freedom, humans are tied to the ground in more ways than one.

When the tide had ebb, the water would retreat a long distance, enabling the beach combers to walk mile after mile on the soft and wet sand, with occasional pools of sea water where young children would swim or just laze around. The trapped sea life, mainly tiny fish provide a feast for the sea birds. This was nature at its best, serine, peaceful, majestic and entertaining in a way that would be difficult for the city dwellers to understand or appreciate.

The luckiest day in the life of Chirag arrived when Chandni accepted his marriage proposal. Chandni, a sweet name which means cool, romantic moonlight, was indeed a very charming and sweet person who would melt any heart, no wonder she melted, captured Chirag's heart.

Chandni was tiny, petit but a beautiful girl in many ways, at least for Chirag, as beauty is in beholder's eyes. She was just five feet tall, weighing less than seven stone. Although Chandni was 26 years old, she looked no more than sweet sixteen, with schoolgirl appearance and innocence, pale complexion which was a rarity in this tropical climate where people spend most of their time outdoor, in the sun that would give a dark, mature complexion with some what rough skin, as neither sun cream nor skin softener were in use in those distant days.

Her loving, trusting nature and giggling smile, accompanied by her silky smooth, knee long hair, always kept loose with a hair band, gave her a unique personality. She may not be every one's cup of tea but for Chirag she was a girl one in a million. These solitary characters made her some what different, perhaps with a touch of eccentricity that would make her stand out in a crowd.

These qualities, her pleasant, accommodating nature along with her unique appearance made Chirag fell in love with her at the first sight.

Some men like tall, slim and well developed girls with all the curves and body projection in the right places, especially the bulging chest. But for Chirag small was beautiful, tiny body but bright, sharp mind that was stimulating and sexy for him. It was mind over matter, not body but personality that attracted him, made him take notice of Chandni. The saying "One man's food is another man's poison" was true in Chirag's case. Well, some may say there is no saying for test? How right it is in this case?

Some men may prefer not to be seen in the company of such a tiny, young looking girl, with flat chest, under developed body and no sexual attraction. But for Chirag that did not matter. He was love mad, not sex mad.

In a way Chirag and Chandni were made for each other, a perfect couple, a rare couple, a couple with different priorities than what one may consider a norm in a society that so often goes by the book, the mass opinion, the set standard.

When Chirag proposed to Chandni, on this beach, holding her tight in his arms, she was in a way a prisoner. She was so light and delicate that it would have been difficult if not impossible for Chandni to escape from Chirag's grip, his hold. But there was no need. She said yes straight away, as if she was just waiting for Chirag to prop up the question.

Chirag was over the moon. He lifted her and covered her with kisses and love bites that would make her blush for days. Chandni did not even try to resist, knowing that it would be futile to holt, to control Chirag who had been waiting for this moment for a long time. After all Chirag was the love of her life. She would be proud to be his wife. She wanted to be with Chirag, together until the death do them part!

After the whirlwind romance, they got married, the union of body and soul. The marriage certificate, a piece of paper gave them the permission, the blessings, the stamp of approval to be seen together in the public, live together and have fun, family and future.

But the course of true love never runs smooth. After the marriage, Chandni changed dramatically. She looked worried, depressed and anxious. Gone was the sweet innocent smile, schoolgirl type giggle, a carefree nature and happy go lucky attitude that had captivated Chirag and made him proud of his tiny, pretty and mesmerising wife he thought was one in a million, a very special person in his life whom he adored, loved to bitts, without exception, without any reservation.

Today it was Sunday. As usual Chirag and Chandni were on their favourite patch. She looked stunning in her black and white dotted sari with broad silvery border, wore with elegance, a tiny sleeveless black blouse with sexy overture, even without protruding, bulging breasts, as if to captivate Chirag and make him grant all and every wish of her.

Her slim body reminded Chirag of the tiny new moon that was trying hard to come out of the silvery cloud, even before the sun was ready to call it a day, to retreat to his fort like abode, beyond the realm of reality.

Chandni insisted that they should walk to the far end of the beach which was normally devoid of hawkers, peddlers and beach hut traders but graced with the occasional young couples who may be madly in love, who did not want to share their passion, their cuddle with the rest of the world. After all it was a primitive and not permissive society where even a tiniest of familiarity with the opposite sex instantly becomes a topic of conversation, a curiosity that would fuel a thousand minds.

The lone hearts, lonely young men always made their presence felt, especially on Sundays which were in a way a ritual for finding a life partner, attracting attention or even declaring one self to be in the marriage market, like a male peacock that would spread his beautiful plumage to attract the attention of a peahen, under the shade of a mighty pippal tree, a gathering place for love birds?

There were no clubs, top restaurants or dinner and dance programmes or such avenues open to young at heart, to meet, to socialise and find a life partner in those distant and in some ways primitive days.

On finding a near perfect, deserted spot on the beach, Chirag and Chandni sat down in the dry, hot and pure white sand that would not leave a mark or a stain even on a snow white sari or a cloth.

In one sudden move, catching Chandni by surprise, Chirag grabbed her and kissed her passionately, long and hard, leaving love bites, without reservation or restricting his hand movement. It slightly embarrassed Chandni but she knew it would serve no useful purpose if she resisted in any way.

She let Chirag had his wish, his desire fulfilled but it was obvious that her heart was not in harmony with that of Chirag. She was not enjoying this precious moment, this romantic overture, unique atmosphere or appreciating her own stunning looks, beauty and sexuality.

She was just letting Chirag to have his wish, his desire fulfilled. After all she was his wife and Chirag was entitled to have her. If any thing, Chirag was too patient, too understanding and a thorough gentleman to impose himself on his petit wife who was too tiny to fight him off, even if she wanted to?

After few moments, when his passion subsided, Chirag realised that Chandni's heart, her love, her desire were not on the same wavelength. She was simply trying to satisfy Chirag's desire without being a willing partner. It was a one way traffic although it was not a one way street.

This was all too much for Chirag. She has been behaving, ignoring Chirag for the last few days but he had absolutely no idea why she was behaving like that, what was troubling her or had he offended her in any way?

Today Chirag could not keep his cool or control his frustration. He wanted some answers and fast. After all they were married only for three months. It was still a honeymoon period. How could romance, love, glamour and sexual attraction disappear, dry up so soon?

"Chandni, what is wrong? Have I offended you in any way? Why are you so cold and indifferent to me?" Chirag was serious but restrained. He did not want to upset Chandni any more than she already was.

In reply, Chandni leaned her face on his chest, tears pouring out of her large, almond shaped eyes, running down her pale cheeks and ruining her makeup. Chirag slowly lifted her face, wiped her tears with his bare hands and kissed her gently on her forehead, her cheeks and her neck.

"Chirag, whenever I come here, I remember Reshma who was my classmate." Chandni said in a sad, some what shivering voice.

"Are you referring to the girl who committed suicide? I remember reading some thing about her in the local paper."

"Yes, the same girl. She killed herself because she could not get the support of her husband in her hour of need." Chandni could hardly control her emotion, her voice breaking down.

"But why does it worry you so much?" Chirag was not sure why it was upsetting Chandni to such an extent.

"Chirag, if you listen to her story, the way she was treated by the society, you will also feel for her. Moreover we were very close friends once, before we met." Chandni was regaining her self control, her composure.

"So why don't you tell me her story? If it could give you some relief, some respite, peace of mind, takes you out of this gloom and doom, back to your normal self, a happy, smiling girl I fell in love with, then I am prepared to do any thing." Chirag was serious but hopeful that this could be the end of his miseries.

"Let me start from the beginning. But you have to listen with care and attention and at the end answer few questions that I may ask you. In reply Chirag nodded his approval.

Reshma and Ranvir were childhood friends. They were neighbours and went to school together. As they grew older, shed the innocence of childhood, entered the age of desire, love and expectation, they naturally fell in love."

"Just like us?" Said Chirag to lighten the atmosphere.

"Please do not interrupt me." Pleaded Chandni.

"Sorry. Please continue."

"Like us, they used to meet on the beach. But they preferred Kunduchi beach, as it is more isolated and gave more privacy. There is hardly any one on the beach during week days. It provides a perfect isolation, a perfect hiding place from the preying eyes.

One day, as they met after a long break, they lost all track of time. It is not so unusual when people are in love.

When they realised that it was already dark, gloomy with cloudy sky and a hint of rain in the atmosphere, they took a short cut through the coconut grove to reach their parked car. But before they could reach the safety of their car, they were attacked by four thugs, gundas and vagabonds.

Without even thinking of Reshma, the coward Ranvir ran as fast as he could, leaving pretty Reshma at the mercy of these four half drunk, sex mad criminals high on drugs.

Reshma was brutalised, raped and badly assaulted. She lost every thing, her virginity, her innocence and above all her trust in their fellow human being, that also on a paradise beach, with cool breeze sailing past, accompanied by the sweet murmur of the sea waves and the call of the wild birds returning to their loved ones, to their nests. A romantic atmosphere turned into a nightmare by the cowardice of Ranvir."

"Poor Reshma." Chirag could not help but to feel sorry for her.

Chandni continued. "After this tragedy, Reshma had nothing but hatred for Ranvir who did not even said sorry to her or offered her any help, comfort or opulence. How could he face Reshma? That was the end of their lifelong friendship.

Reshma was tiny like me. She was so badly brutalised that she had to stay in hospital for a month, her vagina had to be stitched up, as it was torn and badly savaged, followed by not months but years of therapy with a psychologist. Although her physical wounds healed after few months, her mental wounds, in a way never healed. She tried to commit suicide several times but when one is down on luck, even the God is not with them.

Reshma concentrated on her studies, made new friends in the college and the pain was beginning to ease, to ebb a little.

As the saying goes, passage of time blunts the pain; the new dawn brings hope and a ray of sunshine, however tiny it may be. After few years, Reshma met Parimal. They fell in love. It was one occurrence Reshma thought would never grace her life. She thought she could never let any man touch her, let alone sleep with him. But love does strange things, changes priorities and make us do, behave in a way we may never think possible."

"Then why she had to commit suicide?" Chirag was eager to hear the end of the story and move on.

"Have some patience. I am going to tell you every detail, every thing. Just bear with me. Slowly but surely their love blossomed. Soon they got married. Reshma wanted to tell Parimal every thing but it happened so fast. Before Reshma could realise, she was madly in love with Parimal. Even the thought of losing him was too much to bear, to contemplate.

Reshma struggled with her conscious. She was sad, upset and thought she was a fraud, a liar for not telling Parimal the truth.

Reshma knew she would never be happy until she tells Parimal her dark secret. She had to choose between the devil and the deep blue sea. She was in no win situation. But in the end she could not live a life of lie. She had to tell the truth even at the risk of losing Parimal, her love, her life, her sole reason for living.

Deep inside she felt Parimal will forgive her, will not reject her, as he loves her so much. What happened was not her fault. But what if he rejects her?

.... No. He is not like others. He will forgive her and Reshma told Parimal every thing.

That was the end of her dream, her marriage, and her life with Parimal. Parimal had married her against the wishes of his family. When they came to know about her ordeal, they were quick to tell Parimal "We told you so?"

Reshma could not take this second blow. She was angry, upset and depressed and sought the comfort, the salvation and deliverance in death. She ended her life, committed suicide. What an end of a young and aspiring life!" Tears were flowing down Chandni's white, pale face, spoiling her already fading make-up.

In apprehensive mood and thinking that the story was over, Chirag tried to stand up, to walk back to the main beach and to the safety of their car.

But dragging Chirag back, Chandni said, "Do you consider Reshma innocent? Should Parimal have forgiven Reshma for not confiding in him?"

"Well, it is not impossible to forgive Reshma, especially if she had told Parimal the truth before the marriage. But I must admit she can not be a good judge of character. She badly misjudged Ranvir and then kept Parimal in the dark well until after the marriage. She should have confided in Parimal before the marriage. I am sure he would have forgiven her and they could have got married without the burden of a dark secret hanging around her neck. But by concealing the truth, she played a game with Parimal and how could any one trust her after that? Did she really loved Parimal or he was just a scapegoat, a replacement for Ranvir?

Well, we shall never know the answer!" Chirag was now getting a bit agitated, as this conversation had dragged on for nearly two hours. Moreover Chirag was not sure why Chandni was making his life so miserable over some event that had nothing to do with them. Chirag had not managed to make love to Chandni for a while. After all they were a newly married couple, still on honeymoon, who should be making love at every available opportunity and they had plenty in their own home, not worrying about some one else's love life. Charity begins at home and it was Chandni's duty to look after him, satisfy his wish, his desire and his every expectation.

That was a typical male response prevailing at the time. Unfortunately such incidents and tragedies happen in our society all the time. Yes, we do feel for them but the life goes on, especially if they are strangers or not part of our immediate friend circle.

Even when they returned home, Chandni was sad, could hardly contain her tears. She retreated to the spare bedroom without even touching her dinner. On Chirag's part, he thought it would be prudent to leave Chandni alone, allow her time to come to terms with the tragic death of her old friend Reshma. Chandni was a sensitive and a loyal person. No wonder she felt bad at the suicide of her friend.

Next day when Chirag got up early to go to work, Chandni was still in her room, in her bed. Thinking she might had a restless night, Chirag did not disturb her before leaving for work.

In the evening when Chirag returned home from the office, he found the flat empty, all lights switched off with ghostly silence echoing throughout the flat. Some how Chirag felt un at ease, as if the roof was about to come down on him, on his arman, his ambition, his future plans.

On the dinning table, there was a sealed envelop, addressed to Chirag. He opened it with shivering hands, as if he knew the contents of the letter.

"Dear Chirag

After a long deliberation, heartache and soul searching, I was at last able to gather the courage to open my heart to you. I do not know any Reshma whose suicide made headlines in the local paper. In fact I told you my own life story, my history in the name of Reshma. I was hoping, perhaps against all hopes that you will understand my pain, my heartache and my sufferings, that as you love me so much, you will be able to forgive me, give me a second chance, consol me for my sufferings rather than condemn me.

But hearing your views, your opinion that Reshma was not worthy of forgiveness, that she lied to Parimal, got married under false pretext, I lost the ground I was standing on. I felt I was violated again, punished for the second time, left to fend for myself in this cruel and selfish world.

Knowing your views, that I am not worthy of your forgiveness, how can I pretend to be your loving wife, live under the same roof, live a life of sham and deceit?

Chirag, it is easy to say that Reshma or for that matter I should have told you the truth before marriage. Perhaps you might have forgiven me and we could still have got married.

But Chirag, I was not only afraid of losing you but I was living in a make belief world, as if that brutal rape on a dark night was a bad dream, not a reality. It is impossible for any one to imagine the pain, the shame and the humiliation I felt on that fateful night. I wished I had died there and then. The death certainly would have come as a blessing in disguise.

You know how tiny, petite, fragile and delicate I am. Can you imagine what pain, injury and humiliation four sex mad, half drunk yobs can inflict on me? It is not easy for me to talk about it, even after five long years. In fact the only way for me to cope, to survive was to block the incident out of my mind, as if it was a bad dream, not a reality. So how can I talk about it, to tell you about the incident that I find it difficult to accept, to believe that it ever happened before our marriage?

As you know, our Indian girls do not have sex before marriage. Practically every girl is a virgin on her honeymoon night. I also pretended to be such a bride. But the sex, although in a loving relationship, brought back the gruelling pain of that fateful night. No matter how hard I tried, I could not cope with it without your understanding and support and how could I get your understanding, your support and the gentleness in love making, in sex without telling you the truth?

In fact it is impossible for any one to imagine what I went through, even for my family members or the medical staffs. I tried to kill myself several times but I was too weak, too coward to do it properly. How I wish I had succeeded in bringing my miserable life to an end. It would have been much easier, certainly less painful to end it all than to go on living in a hell. Perhaps every one, including my beloved Lord Krishna had abandoned me in my hour of need?

Perhaps you came in my life at the right time, as a God send gift, a messiah to save me, to take me to a promised land. You were my knight in shining armour; at least that is what I thought at the time.

This letter is my goodbye, my final farewell. I am trying to make amend what you consider was my big mistake in not telling you the truth. But I am confused, not sure what really the truth is. Was I ever raped or was it a bad dream which will disappear with the passing of the night?

Please forgive me, forgive my mistake. I will always love you and wherever I go, I will remember you. You are now free to do what you wish, pursue your dream in any way you like. Please do not worry about me or try to find me. Leaving you is the most difficult decision of my life. Please do not make it any harder. Perhaps we may unite in the next world.

Alvida .... Goodbye.

Yours Unfortunate Chandni"

Chirag was stunned. How come he never thought what Chandni was going through! Not even an inclination! It must have been a hell for her but she bravely tried to cope with her pain alone and I was trying to make fun of her sexual pain, telling her it was her inexperience, her virginity. I let her down badly.

For the first time in his life, since he became an adult, Chirag cried uncontrollably. How he wished Chandni was there so that he could hold her, wipe her tears and assure her that no matter what, he will always be there for her. But it was all too late.

Chandni spread the cool, sweet moonlight in Chirag's life for a few days but left behind darkness for ever. Chandni tested Chirag's superfluous views but not his love for her, the reality of their lives. Chirag could have forgiven her without any hesitation. In fact there was nothing to forgive. The society, Chirag and others should seek her forgiveness, not the other way round. Chirag even hated himself for letting Chandni down, although unintentionally. As a husband, it was his duty to understand her and gauge her sufferings.

After all people so often think one way but act completely differently. Chirag could not help but wonder where Chandni is today, how is she coping with life or whether he would ever meet her again on this earth? Only the time will tell.

****

KISMET (FATE)

Rakesh has just completed six months in his new job as a manager of the Everest Tea Estate. It was one of the biggest tea estates in the area with a workforce and dependent people numbering some one thousand people, mostly Assami but few Bengalis as well, especially refugees thrown out of East Bengal, a part of Pakistan but now a poverish independent nation of Bangladesh, after a violent separation from Pakistan.

The estate was some three hundred kilometres from Cherrapunji, the nearest town in this green wilderness of Assam. The hills around Cherrapunji are world famous as the place that receives the highest rainfall, some six hundred inches of rain every year.

Charapunji is one of the most interesting, fascinating places on earth. Many books have been written about the Indian monsoons but **Alexander Frater's** book **"Chasing the Monsoon"** is a fitting tribute to India's annual love affair with the monsoon which arrives in the month of June, to give the people some relief from the scorching heat of the summer.

Charapunji is perhaps the only place in the Indian subcontinent where there is only one season and that is monsoon. The rain varies from heavy to light showers, even an occasional dry month but during heavy rainy season, which stretches from the month of May to June, it literally rains cats and dogs, so often up to thirty inches of rain falling within twenty four hours, transforming the land into a vast inland sea with tiny gushing rivulets. This area is also the home of one of the most spectacular waterfalls, the Mawsmai Halls where the water descends, cascades from the height of 1035 feet, the third highest waterfall in the world.

Naturally such an unique weather pattern will give rise to an unique flora and fauns with a variety of rare orchids, ferns, creepers and moss as well as unique fruits and vegetables found only in very few places on earth. Although Rakesh was a highly educated young man, he was not aware about the peculiarities of this unique but mostly unknown place, especially that of Charapunji.

Rakesh has a BSc in agriculture from the famous Wadia College in Pune and a master's degree from Durham University, England, where he had spend two years studying agriculture and Estate Management, just after Bharat gained independence in 1947.

Since returning from England, Rakesh had worked at various tea estates, mainly in Kerala, on the slopes of Western Ghats, the green, fertile and most beautiful land in Southern India.

The tea estates on the slopes of these mountain range were much smaller in size and less productive than those in Assam, at the foot of the mighty Himalayas where climatic condition for growing tea are most favourable in the world, producing the best type of tea in the world that include Darjeeling and Dehra Dun tea, widely consumed amongst the aristocrats in India and England.

The last tea estate where Rakesh worked as a deputy manager was a Rani Tea Estate, near the beautiful hill station of Munar in Kerala. Today Munar is a world renowned place, a centre of tourist trade, due to local beauty spots like beautiful village of Thakadi on the shores of Lake Periyar and the nature reserve, the wild game, the safari park where lions from the forest of Gir in Gujarat are introduced and allowed to roam in relative freedom in this vast and well managed natural cum safari park that has become a focal point for wild life in the south.

This place is a favourite holiday destination for the people of Indian origin now residing in the West, especially in America, Canada, Britain and Europe as well as most Commonwealth countries, all ex-British colonies with significant Indian expatriates population, that include Singapore, Hong Kong, Fiji, Guyana, Surinam and Mauritius.

But during early fifties it was an unknown place outside Kerala. All big tea estates were concentrated in Assam and Ceylon, now known under its new name of Sri Lanka.

When Mr. John Smith who was managing **"Everest Tea Estate"** took an early retirement, perhaps due to the changing political climate that many colonial minded British expatriates found it difficult to adjust to, the holding company in Britain "The Windsor India Company" found it prudent, wise to appoint an Indian as a manager to replace a retiring British expatriate.

Rakesh had all the qualification to manage such a tea estate. In fact he was more qualified than the retiring Mr John Smith who was purely appointed for his Englishness, his colonial background.

Rakesh had a degree in Agriculture and Estate Management from a famous British University. He had also lived in England as well. So he was familiar with the English etiquette, code of behaviour, the all important British protocol to deal with the directors who sit in London but may occasionally visit the estate to make sure that the estate was run smoothly and profitably.

Profitability and the aptitude to be part of emerging Bharat was their sole concern but the knowledge of English social life was a distinct advantage when entertaining the Managing Director and his associates who may visit Bharat from time to time.

Rakesh, being a Punjabi, was a tall, well built and adventurous person with a taste for hunting which would be an asset on such a lonely posting, far removed from civilization.

Rakesh had also worked as a Forest Officer, as a Chief Game Warden and involved in tracking down and killing men eating tigers and rogue bull elephants that would go berserk when ousted from a herd, after losing a leadership challenge. Such wild animals are the most dangerous preys and it takes the nerves of steel to go after these animals once they have tasted human blood, human frailties and the human weaknesses.

Assam was at the time Garden of Eden, the most fertile land outside the Ganges river basin and attracted more foreign agricultural investment than any other sector and other states in the Indian Union.

These were still early days for industrialization for an agricultural country like Bharat, although the Communist countries, especially Soviet Union was trying to help India to lay the foundation for the heavy industry, such as steel making. Unfortunately India made the mistake of choosing Soviet Union as a role model on the economic front, a system now being discarded by every country, including Russia, in favour of free market economy once described as a capitalist imperialism. How times have changed?

In a way Assam was neglected, a far flung province, corner of British Raj where people were kept poor, uneducated and ill-informed so as to provide a cheap, so often a bonded labour on such vast, profitable tea estates which required an enormous number of farm workers, cheap farm labourers to pluck the tea leafs as soon as they open, before these leaves mature, lose flavour and produce lower quality of tea.

It was not luck or coincidence for such a tiny country like Britain to establish the greatest empire in the history of the world, far bigger and more prosperous than the one established by Alexander the Great, The Roman, Greek or the Mongol Emperor Kublai Khan, the greatest warrior king ever to rule the world. It was said that the sun never sets on the British Empire which stretched from Hong Kong in the East to British Guyana in the West, from Ireland in the North to Falkland islands in the South, a distance of some twenty thousand miles, covering one third of the land mass, with countries like Canada, India, South Africa, Central and East Africa and Australia being the mainstay of the Empire in its hay days. Even USA was a British colony once? It was like a dog keeping an elephant as a servant.

Missionaries were very active in this part of the Raj but they were more interested in converting the locals, who as Christians would be more loyal to the Raj than to their own kith and kin, to their motherland. They were trying to create a privileged class based on their religion and political thinking, political affiliation and not on their ability, their achievement. It was a caste system within a caste system.

But missionaries did provide education, health clinics and tried hard to break down the caste system based on Indian tradition that had divided the people of India for centuries. Even Gandhiji, the saintly figure and father of the nation failed in his attempt to eradicate the caste system because it was and still is so deep rooted.

Even after independence, the people of Assam were underprivileged class, the majority tea estates remaining in the hands of British Companies and expatriates holding the high post but doing little work.

It was beginning to change, slowly but surely. That was the trend, the survival game, change or perish atmosphere in the aftermath of the independence hysteria throughout the British colonies in Asia and Africa.

The owners of the Everest Tea Estate were a few English aristocrats, through a private limited company. MD may visit the estate, a kind of social visit, to show the face if not the flag but they would leave the day to day running to the staffs, especially the manager. They were satisfied as long as the estate makes a good profit for their share holders, a good return on their investment, their capital, in true British tradition.

Rakesh was as capable as any Englishman. He had some twenty people working directly under him in the office, to administer the estate. That included office secretary, office junior, accounts clerks, a welfare officer and financial overseer to run such a vast state efficiently, with some one thousand labourers, tea leaves pickers and general maintenance men employed on the estate.

These were mainly Assami and Bangladeshis who all lived on the land owned by the estate, most with their families. Half the workforce was made up of women who were more efficient pickers than their male counterparts. Besides picking leaves, they would keep the estate tidy, clear the undergrowth and work in the factory where leaves were dried, graded and packed in wooden boxes.

The accommodations provided by the company were basic but most were given a piece of land, an allotment where hardworking families would grow their own vegetables and keep few goats or an occasional cow to keep them supplied with milk.

There was a school and a health clinic run by a couple of English nuns in association with the local Church, with the help of local Indian converts. An Indian doctor would visit the clinic a couple of times a month or whenever he was badly needed in an emergency.

There were two Englishmen working directly under Rakesh, an accountant and an engineer who was also responsible for other tea estates. So his presence on the estate was intermittent but the accountant, financial expert was ever present, to keep an eye if nothing else!

They were there as a token presence, the legacy of the Raj. They were no match to Rakesh when it came to management skill, hard work and dedication. They knew it and respected Rakesh's overall authority and management skill.

Rakesh had a large, well furnished office in a building which was situated in the middle of the estate, making it easy and quick to reach any part of the estate. Today before entering his office, Rakesh stopped for a moment, looking proudly at the board on his office door,"**Rakesh Sharma MSc. Estate Manager.**"

He could not help thinking how proud his late father would be if he was alive today. Rakesh lost his father when he was barely in his teens. His mother Motibai brought him up, working all God send hours with peanuts of a pay. Then it was the sign of the time when a single woman, a widow was exploited on most parts by the wealthy.

Rakesh was her only son, her sole reason for living after her husband died of a heart attack at a relatively young age of forty. Rakesh, in return worked hard, gaining scholarship and was now at the height of his career.

His first action, his first good deed for the family when he was financially independent was to buy a small but comfortable and well furnished flat for her mother in their village, with a live-in girl, what we call au pair to look after her aging mother, as he could not be with her all the time.

For Rakesh, charity certainly begins at home and no one was more important to him than his mother. He would visit her three to five times a year, even if some of these visits may be just a flying visit for a day or two, during public holidays on Dipawali and Christmas.

Rakesh was a conscious and energetic worker who would prefer to perform as much work and carry out his duty, his responsibility personally as humanly possible. But on such a large estate, delegation of work, duty was the name of the game. This is where management skill would come in, be helpful in running the estate smoothly and efficiently. His learning curve was never ending, even when he was at the height of his career. He believed in learning not from his own mistakes but from the mistakes of others, as one can not live long enough to make them all by one self.

His constant presence on the estate, among the workers, his readiness to get his hand dirty and mix and mingle with the workers made him not only popular but easily accessible as well. The previous managers, especially the English ones, hardly used to leave their comfortable, air conditioned offices, rarely seen by the workers on the ground, at the bottom of the ladder who produced the goods, are responsible for success or failure of the company, its profitability.

No wonder the production was on the increase, absenteeism due to illness, drunkenness and laziness was also down. The disputes among the workers were settled fairly and quickly before they get out of hand and the production could be affected.

Although Rakesh was well acquainted with managing an estate, this one was a large estate, even among Assam standard where most tea estates were large, even enormous.

This Everest Tea Estate was also one of the most modern tea estates in the country. Except picking tea leaves, the young and tender foliage, most other tasks involved use of some machinery.

The tea bushes were restricted in height, allowed to grow up to a height of six to ten feet, depending on the age of the plant but allowed to spread, thus making it easy to pick leaves. The undergrowth was kept clear of weeds and long grass with the use of straws, gravels and ground hugging plants, so as to keep the snakes, the main danger to workers, out of the estate. Snake bites, mainly from the most poisonous King Cobra snakes were the main cause of deaths in the past, with one in fifty workers regularly bitten by these snakes. It was now a rare cause of death since Rakesh took up the management and introduced these measures, to remove the habitat where snakes can live, breed and multiply.

Now pickers could work in peace without the fear of snake bites thus raising the productivity and the quality, as more and younger, tender leaves were picked as soon as they open, grows to the right size.

These leaves were left in hot and damp air for twenty four hours, in a specially constructed storage places. Then the leaves were moved on a conveyer belt, to a drying place.

When dried to the right standard, they would come under a light roller, then sheaved, graded and packed with most work done with minimum human involvement, a rarity in those early days of mechanization.

In a short time, Rakesh came to know the estate well. Using his powerful, spacious and well equipped 4 by 4 military Jeep, the vehicle he demanded as part of his employment package, he would tour all four corners of this vast estate, working long hours. But this was as much a labour of love as his duty, his obligation and his desire to prove his worth. Rakesh would also send a detailed regular three monthly reports to the head office in England, a vast improvement on the previous management when an annual report was the norm.

But now, with the beginning of the rainy season, the estate roads became impassable, some areas impenetrable, even for a four wheel drive vehicles. Most of the work on tea estates in Assam come to an abrupt holt for two to three months during a monsoon season when up to 500" of rain fell in a short period, often washing away part of the estate, especially on the steep mountain sides where steps were created by hard work, digging the mountain sides and creating a narrow field where tea shrubs thrive and produce the best tea.

The land management was as important as the estate management, to make sure that the land does not lose its fertility, do not lose the fertile layer of top soil, as without top soil the land would become unfertile scrub land. It was important to plant trees, create a forest to avoid land erosion. This is where Rakesh's experience as a forest officer and his education in England became his great asset, gave him the edge over other managers in the region. He put the theory he learnt in college in Durham into practice and came up with a winning formula, a winning solution.

As a manager, Rakesh had the best accommodation, a three bedroom bungalow, built in the colonial style, but on an artificially raised land, with a raised veranda and an open, large patio in the front. The bungalow was fitted with all the modern facilities that an English expatriate would expect and demand when living and working such a long way from home.

Besides being well furnished, all doors and windows had mosquito proof wire-nets, iron grills, ceiling fans in all rooms and primitive but effective air-conditioning in the main lounge, the best available at the time.

The location of the bungalow gave it a panoramic view, being on an elevated land, overlooking the estate and the surrounding area, the distant hills adding to the beauty and charm of the location.

Rakesh had a perfect view of the ruins of the castle from his main bedroom as well as from the veranda, as the ruins were on a hill some three miles away. He was eager to visit this place but until now he was too occupied with his work so that such personal interest, activities not connected directly with his work took a back seat for the time being.

Today it was Saturday, the beginning of the weekend for rest and recuperation for all estate workers. The rain had also failed to materialize, a break of three days, a dry spell that occasionally punctures the rainy season.

It was a perfect day for walking. So after early lunch, Rakesh put on his knee high rubber and lather walking shoes, put a loaded revolver in his holster, a must for Rakesh, along with a strong sesame walking stick embodied with cast-iron beadings and knobs. The stick was a formidable weapon in itself, especially if attacked by fellow human beings, capable of doing serious harm if used as a weapon, used in anger.

After walking for a couple of hours at a leisurely pace, observing the surrounding area which was more of an open ground then a dense forest, Rakesh was some three quarters way to the ruins which he wanted to visit.

But as usual in this part of Assam, during rainy season, it suddenly got dark with lightening and thunder on the distant horizon.

Rakesh knew that in less than an hour, the rain would be upon this area, with dark, heavy clouds that would turn the day into the night, making it dangerous to walk, to be out and about in the forest.

So Rakesh decided to turn back, to put on hold his desire to view the ruins and with brisk walking, he just managed to reach his bungalow before the sky opened up, the nature went berserk and the thunder and lightening had a field day. From the safety of his living room window, Rakesh was looking outside, at the distant hill with the castle ruins which soon disappeared behind the mist, clouds and the lashing rain, in the doom and gloom of the rain soaked day.

Breaking his chain of thoughts, Rakesh heard the worried voice of his servant Motilal but every one including Rakesh called him Dada (grand father) as he was considerably older than every one on the estate, with silver- grey hair but remarkably fit for his age.

Dada and his wife Jamuna who was considerably younger than him, perhaps his second or third wife, took care of Rakesh's every need. It was unfortunate but common occurrence to lose a wife, especially in child-birth and subsequent wives may be much younger. It was a common practice among the hill tribe girls to get married as soon as they reach the age of puberty, that is at the young age of fourteen and even younger.

As these hill tribe girls were well built, even at the tender age of fourteen they look strong, mature and more of a woman than a child, unlike their city counterparts.

Jamuna, who was in her late twenties or perhaps early thirties, was not only a kind and a caring person but a wonderful cook who treated Rakesh as a kind of a younger brother, called him Bhaiya (brother) rather than a Sahib (boss) and she loved taking care of him. Although it was unusual for lowly servants to call their boss a beta (son) or bhaiya (brother) it did not matter to Rakesh, as both Dada and Jamuna took good care of him. They called him these names, beta and bhaiya out of love and respect, not to gain familiarity or any advantage. But they were careful to address Rakesh as Sahib, Sir or the boss in the presence of guests and other estate employees.

Rakesh himself was not a bad cook either. Having lived a bachelor life, so often in far flung, remote places, away from cities and civilization, he had no choice but to learn cooking which he took to like a duck to water, as most Punjabis love their food.

Jamuna soon picked up all the tips, mastered cooking Rakesh's favourite dishes and with fresh vegetables and spices widely grown on the allotments, Rakesh lived a life of luxury, at least as far as food, gourmet dishes were concerned.

Rakesh's favourite dishes, cooked with enthusiasm and expertise, were chicken tikka masala, chicken corma, vindaloo and Madras curry, lamb special, bhuna and balti lamb, Karai dishes (dry) and some Chinese dishes such as aromatic crispy duck, chow mein and noodles along with vegetable curries of potatoes, peas, bhindi bhaji marinated in vinegar and stuffed with mixed curry powder, spinach, aubergine sliced and grilled with cheese, green peppers, crushed garlic and fresh tomato slices were indeed appetizing and mouth watering.

These dishes went well with egg; mushroom and jeera fried rice and freshly baked tandori chilli or garlic naan over an open fire. Jamuna was good at making pickles, from lemon, mango and ginger, along with yogurt mix and green salad using garden grown fresh ingredients. No wonder Rakesh thought she was a better cook then her mother? Then again his mother had to do without half the ingredients, spices and fresh vegetables, as money was tight and whatever she earned was used on educating Rakesh, not on food or clothes.

Breaking Rakesh's concentration, his chain of thoughts, Dada said in a soft, kind but concerned voice, "Beta, did you visit the ruins on the Anupama hill?" This was the first time for a while Dada had addressed Rakesh as beta rather than Sahib. Normally Dada would address Rakesh as Sahib in presence of other estate workers but when alone, he may call him beta.

"Yes Dada, it was my intention to visit the ruins. But the sudden darkness and the rain made me turn back before I could reach the ruins." Rakesh said it in a calm, calculated voice.

"Beta, thank God for his mercy, his timely intervention. Any young man who visits these ruins a few times normally dies within a month or two. Please beta, promise me that you will not go any where near that fateful ruins." There were virtually tears in Dada's eyes.

Rakesh could only smile as he has heard such stories about ghosts, witches and even angles on most of his postings, especially among the hill tribesmen.

But as dada was like a grandfather for Rakesh, a kind and caring person, Rakesh could only oblige.

"Well Dada, I would not go there but please tell me how any one can die after visiting these ruins?"

"Beta, what can I say to an intelligent and educated person like you! I am sure you would not believe me but this is my own personal and true experience with two young men of this estate.

There is a witch who lives there, among the ruins. She is indeed very beautiful and young men like you are easily attracted to her, like a bee to a honey, a fish to an angler's bait and dance to her tune, like a snake to a snake charmer's flute.

Life here for a single man is indeed lonely, isolated and unfulfilled in many ways. But Sahib, can I give you one good advice! Why don't you get married? I understand she does not trap, snare or lure married men. She leaves them alone." Dada was suddenly relived, with a smile on his wrinkled face which was only a few minutes ago, full of fear and apprehension.

"Well Dada, I will have to meet this angel of death one day but not before I get married." Rakesh said it with a smile, half expecting Dada to say that he had already selected a girl, a bride for him!

Dada said nothing but retreated to go back to his hut not too far away. Perhaps dada felt he may have gone too far, crossed the line, spoken out of turn to a Sahib. But Rakesh knew there was nothing but love and concern for his wellbeing in Dada's heart. He was not offended in any way but amused certainly he was and perhaps his curiosity, his interest and inquisitiveness made him determined to meet this girl that is if she really exist, was not a fabrication or an extension of fertile imagination on the part of dada and other estate workers.

Next day being Sunday, a bright and beautiful day, Rakesh could not resist but go out for a walk to the ruins. Today he was in a hurry to reach the ruins. Dada had whetted his appetite rather than put him off visiting these ruins, with the tale of a beautiful, charming young witch, a princess or perhaps a local village beauty. Such local beauties were not rare among the hill tribesmen. Rakesh may not admit but he would not be averse to meeting this mysterious beauty.

Rakesh remembered the history he had learnt as a child, the love triangle, the love story between Siddhraj Jaisinh, the emperor of Gujarat and Ranakdevi, a low caste woman who was working as a labourer on the fort he was building on the slopes of mount Girnar.

The king was so obsessed with this tiny but very beautiful girl, who looked stunning even when covered with dust and mud, who was in fact a married woman that the king kidnapped the girl and kept her a prisoner, tried to add her to his harem. But the girl killed herself rather than live a dishonourable life but not before she cursed the king and ultimately brought his downfall and death. This was a tragic story that made Ranakdevi a Goddess, a patron saint of married women and the king a villain and a dishonourable king. According to Hindu custom and tradition, a married woman is honoured and respected, not abducted and turned into a slave sex.

Today Rakesh was even better equipped, adding a powerful torch and a light raincoat with a plastic hood to his normal accessories of a walking stick and a revolver, to give him a complete protection against the rain, in case he is caught in a storm.

Avoiding Dada and Jamuna, Rakesh slipped out unnoticed. Yesterday he had spent some time in observing the surrounding area but today he took the short cut, the direct route to the ruins, passing through some long grass, a passage made by occasional human activity but almost hidden under the weight of long, tall grass. Perhaps Rakesh was eager to keep an appointment with his destiny!

Rakesh was walking at a brisk pace, whistling his favourite tune from the Swan Lake Opera and keeping a watchful eye on the surrounding area, the long grass and thick bushes through which he was passing.

Although there were no dangerous wild animals like tigers and elephants in this part of Assam, there were wild pigs, large monkeys and occasional sighting of leopards but the most danger was poised by huge king cobra snakes whose bite would kill a man in minutes. Moreover these snakes can spit the poison, the venom at human beings from a distance of twenty feet, aiming at eyes that would render a man blind if not treated quickly.

The best protection against spitting cobra is to wear tight fitting glasses to protect eyes and long boots to protect against snake bites. Rakesh would never go out without this simple but effective protection, always ready for any eventualities. This is the name of the survival game, learnt over a long apprenticeship, first as a Game Warden and later as a Forest Officer.

His first aid training and the generous use of his own money provided such essential items to many estate workers who may be too poor to take such precautions themselves.

The footpath was made by the constant use of the track by the local villagers who used it to visit far flung and isolated settlements. Rakesh was enjoying the walk. He was an avid walker. He loved walking on the soft soil, changing pace, running, jumping or just loitering, drinking water from a spring that may be just spouting, water being as fresh as rainwater, picking wild berries and fruits, stopping at every vantage point to observe the scenery, be part of nature.

It would be difficult for a city dweller even to imagine the forest life until one has tasted it, although to be honest, it is not every one's cup of tea, especially with snakes and other wildlife in abundance.

Rakesh loved hunting but not just for the sake of thrills. He would only kill wild animals if they become a danger to villagers. He would shoot wild pigs, deer and antelope so as to provide fresh meat to plantation workers who are on most part under nourished. Game meat is a luxury they appreciate.

This was the life Rakesh loved and yearned for, rather than living in a city with pollution, traffic and overflowing with humanity. Some city dwellers are super rich living in the lap of luxury while others live on the street who may not get even a single square meal a day, reducing their lifespan to less than forty years.

One may never find such disparity in villages or on plantations, tea estates and remote settlements where every one has a roof over his head and no one goes completely hungry. They believe that God may wake you up hungry but would not let you go to sleep on empty stomach.

As Rakesh neared the ruins, he found a lovely mixture of nature and human endurance, with bamboo bushes, occasional hardwood trees and even some rogue tea bushes hidden among the long grass, huge boulders and rolling hills.

The trees and occasional tiny patches of forests were hidden in the valleys and lower ground at the foot of the hills, like a neglected Garden of Eden. The whole area was sparsely populated, almost devoid of human presence, human activities. As a result, it was immersed in peace, calm and beauty that gave the place a unique atmosphere difficult to describe, to put pen to paper.

It was like a glass of nectar, an expensive wine that we would not like to stop drinking once put to lips but difficult to get hold of in the first place. Rakesh was so engrossed in his thoughts that he arrived at the ruins without even realising it.

Rakesh started viewing, examining these ruins of an ancient castle. The building may not be artistic from the outside but was well built, with security uppermost in mind. The fort was in ruins, a sleeping beauty castle, covered with wild vegetation, thick stone walls crumbling with age, neglect and some vandalism.

The interior was well planned with all the necessities taken care of. Janankhana or ladies quarters were isolated. There were plenty of storage space for water and grain and stables for horses. Bedrooms must have been spacious and well decorated, bathing areas tiled with marble and granite.

This was Rakesh's impression, accompanied by his experience, as he had seen, visited and studied many such ruins in various places, forests and hills, including many castles in Wales and Scotland. Rakesh also had a vivid imagination that went hand in hand with his experience, familiarity and reality.

After browsing through the courtyard for half an hour, soaking the silent atmosphere, akin to Shah Jahan's tomb, spirit wondering in search of one of the most beautiful women, Noor Jehan, the Aphrodite of Indian history, sad silent yet some how fulfilling, the atmosphere that would completely drain the admirer of his emotion, sentiment and ardour.

The whole of Bharat is an ancient museum, every state, city and forest is littered with thousands of years of history with monuments, castles, battle grounds, mausoleums, tombs and palaces fit for kings and emperors, not forgetting the places of worships, such as temples, mosques, gurudwar and churches. Bharat is the crossroad and cradle of civilization of Asia, if not the world.

There was an outer wall, a perimeter fortification some thirty feet high, still standing intermittently, with occasional soaring watch towers, deep moat now all but filled with mud, rubbles and vegetation and stone parapet but these outer ruins were plundered by the locals for their stones and building material value but no one would touch the palace ruins as they were supposed to be cursed. In a way such a superstition helps to preserve the ruins and historical buildings in many parts of Bharat.

The roof was missing from all the rooms and most of the walls were covered with vegetation, with wide cracks and the floor was covered with rubbles and overgrown with weeds, a perfect place for snakes to monopolize. So Rakesh was extra careful, avoiding all places where snakes may hide, make a nest to mate, using his long and sturdy stick to make a way, to study the place before venturing in, putting a foot in a lion's den.

Within an hour Rakesh inspected the ruins from top to bottom, from room to room, having a very good idea of how it would have looked when it was first built, in its heydays or how it could be restored. He would have become an architect if he was not so much interested in outdoor life, living away from cities.

He sat down at a vantage point, on a big boulder or some sort of structure, clear of all debris and weeds. The sun, a ball of red fire, was fast sinking behind the distant hills, covering these ruins in perpetual darkness.

Suddenly Rakesh felt unusual loneliness. Perhaps he was sitting on a tomb, not a boulder, realized he was all alone in this wilderness which may be dangerous if it becomes dark.

He remembered the lines he read on a tombstone when visiting a castle in the far flung corner of Scotland.

> "I rest here, in a sombre isolated place
> Put to rest, well over thousand years ago
> Now covered with pest, overgrown with weeds
> Yet I lived a life, full of zest and valour
> But it all came to an abrupt end
> As suddenly as I came and went
> Remember me as you pass by my grave

> I was once what you are today
> A healthy, wealthy, wise and cheery
> A soul respected, in essence a pillar of society
> A VIP in making, a bud about to blossom
> A man of substance and influence
> But do not forget, you will be one day
> What I am today, a soul lost in a maze
> Entombed in a coffin, forgotten by all
> For this is the way of nature
> Here today, gone tomorrow
> Sunk like a Titanic, without a trace
> So make the hay while the sun shines
> Good deeds never go unrewarded
> Before the sky laden with dark clouds
> Gloom and doom, all too familiar
> Descent upon you from the thundering grey sky
> To reunite in death, with Mother Nature.

****

Rakesh started going down the hill, an easy descent, a pleasing, effortless walk, hoping to reach the safety of his comfortable and inviting bungalow before the sun completely disappears behind the distant hills and plunges these hills in perpetual darkness.

Somehow Rakesh felt nervous, as if he was watched, being followed but he knew that it was just his fertile imagination. Moreover he was well armed with a lethal walking stick and a revolver, more than enough to deal with any small wild animals that inhibit this part of Assam.

Rakesh was glad that no wild animals like tigers and elephants were seen here for well over thirty years. But somehow Rakesh started remembering his encounter with a man eater, a tiger known as Devi's tiger, the one he had to track down and shot dead when he was a forest office in the state of Madhya Pradesh, a vast state in central India, with world renowned game reserves and forests especially reserved for hunting during the British Raj.

The tiger had already killed, devoured well over two hundred villagers before Rakesh was called upon to track down and shoot the tiger.

One of tiger's preys was a white forest officer by the name of Peter Kenyon who was a well known hunter. Having shot dead, hunted some fifty such tigers, he took the challenge lightly and paid with his life.

Normally a tiger becomes a man eater due to old age or injury sustained in a fight with another tiger or loses a paw due to thorn penetration, becomes lame when caught in a trap laid by poachers. Such injuries prevent tigers from going after their natural preys. Humans are easy preys as they could neither run nor fight back.

Once a tiger tastes a human blood, he would rarely go back to his normal preys, even after recovering from such injuries. With each killing, the tiger becomes more dangerous, more difficult to track down and to shoot.

The tiger soon learns how human mind works and would never return to the kill, even if he may have eaten only half the kill, that he normally does in the forest where no kill is allowed to go to waste.

The tiger, an experienced man eater would also not fall in the trap of attacking a goat, tied to a tree. He almost senses human presence that may be detrimental to his survival and would stay one step ahead of their pursuers. It is not an easy task to kill such a tiger and before they lose their lives, they normally devour a few dozen helpless villagers.

Perhaps one has to be an eccentric, a foolhardy with a heart and nerve of steel and of course a very brave person indeed to go after such a wild and dangerous animal. Then all forest officers, game wardens are a different breed of people, not our every day city dwellers, office workers. They live dangerously, enjoy flirting with death. It was the thrill and not the money that attracted such breed of men to become Game Rangers, Forest Officers.

This young, strong and fierce man eater tiger had an interesting history, an unusual tale. The reason behind his injury was that it foolishly tried to provoke a porcupine with its sharp, defensive spines and quills. The tiger ended up with its sharp quills being lodged in the tiger's paw. This made him lame and unable to chase deer, pigs and other wild, hoofed, grazing animals, natural preys of tigers, lions and leopards.

This man eater, known as Devi's tiger had already killed well over two hundred villagers. The superstitious mountain tribesmen were unwilling to help Rakesh in tracking down this man eater and to provide drum beaters to force the tiger into a corner. They believed that the tiger was protected by the Goddess. So no human, no hunter can kill it. Those who assist the game ranger will be cursed and killed by the tiger.

Rakesh had to enlist the help of the trackers and drum beaters, torch bearers from other areas, other tribes to pin down and kill the tiger. Rakes nearly lost his life, became another victim of this cunning animal. But he did lose two of his trackers and drum beaters before the tiger finally succumbed, became the victim of Rakesh's super determination to kill any and every man eater.

Thinking about this encounter, his worst nightmare, brought fear and sweating even on this cold and damp evening, with sun fast disappearing on the horizon.

When Rakesh negotiated a sharp bend on this narrow track, he suddenly observed a person some hundred feet in front of him. This startled Rakesh for a moment, as he was lost in his thoughts, least expecting to see another human being.

Rakesh had no inclination that any one else could be so near, let alone just in front of him. He was even more astonished when he realized that the person in front of him was a girl.

She was tall, at least five feet eight, a really good height for an Indian girl, although mountain girls are normally much taller than city girls. She was wearing a long leather jacket with a fox tail fur scarf round her neck. Her long, thick jet black hair were artistically arranged, so that it covered most of her back from the neck to her hips which were moving rhythmically and artistically. Her slow walk and easy going manner were more akin to walking in a park rather than in a wilderness where a danger could be lurking at any corner.

Rakesh could not take his eyes off her. The path or just a narrow trail was so narrow that there was no way Rakesh could pass her.

Within few minutes Rakesh was right behind her and to draw her attention, he said, "Excuse me. Can I pass?"

The girl looked back and gave Rakesh a broad smile, a smile that would melt any heart. For a second, Rakesh was speechless. He had never seen such a beautiful face, a perfect match for her equally gorgeous figure, a lean, slim line body but well developed features. Rakesh could see, imagine all the curves, although most of her body was covered with her black, knee length leather jacket.

"Sorry for blocking your path. I did not know you were walking behind me." She said apolitically, in a sweet, sensuous voice, to go with her equally good manner, a sign of good upbringing.

"Thank you" and after a long pause Rakesh continued. "Are you alone?" Thinking how could any girl risk her safety wandering in such a desolate and lonely place?

"Not any more! I am in good company." Said the girl with a mischievous smile. She seemed to have a permanent smile, a feature on her pretty, smooth and radiant face, with pale complexion that is normally the result of lack of sunshine but very much appreciated by Indian girls. Scandinavian people in Europe have such pale complexion as they more or less live in perpetual darkness for six months in a year.

Not knowing what to say, Rakesh restricted his response to a mere smile. Then smile is the best weapon, both defensive and offensive. But the young lassie was not ready to give up or let Rakesh walk away.

"Your face does not look familiar. Have you moved here recently?" She said without letting the smile dwindle in any way.

"Yes, I moved here some six months ago. I am the new manager of the Everest Tea Estate." Rakesh said, putting emphasis on the word manager.

"Oh. So Mr. Smith has retired. Has he gone back to England?"

"Yes. He retired a month before I came here. So I have not met him." Rakesh was surprised. How did she know Mr. Smith? Rakesh had never seen this girl before.

As the footpath was narrow, walking side by side obviously involved physical contact. So often Rakesh had to fall behind when it was impossible to walk side by side. But it seemed she was not averse to physical contact. She was dignified, accepting that such a contact was impossible to avoid if they were to walk together, appreciating Rakesh's willingness to fall back when it was unavoidable.

"May I know your name?"

"Why not? I am Rakesh and as you know, I work on the estate."

It seemed she was more forward, friendly than Rakesh had expected. But it was too early to read anything from such a short conversation.

"My name is Rajshree but all my friends call me Raju, short and sweet." The customary smile accompanied her all the way. Then she continued.

"I come here for a walk whenever the weather is nice. So I expect we will meet again." Raju said it casually.

Half a mile from the estate bungalow, the footpath divided. One was leading to the bungalow while the other was going downhill towards the settlement where there were few bungalows.

"Would you like to come to my place for a cup of tea?" It was now Rakesh's turn to be forward, not to miss a golden opportunity to know a girl that may be a God send gift in this wilderness.

"Not today Rakesh. It is getting late. I would better reach the safety of my abode before it is too late." With these words, they parted company.

Rakesh wondered why she said abode and not home? Her language, some of the words she spoke were, how to put it, Shakespearian but very sweet and polite, civilized and refreshingly assuring.

"Good night, sleep well and hope we will meet again soon." Said Raju before she disappeared down the tall grass and the bending, twisting footpath, making sure that Rakesh was watching her elegance, her natural but captivating hip movement.

While serving dinner, Dada was quiet, in apprehensive and anxious mood with almost tears in his sad, old eyes and wrinkled face, looking even older than normal.

Rakesh realized that Dada, some how knew about his visit to ruins and perhaps his chance meeting with Raju. But Rakesh was in such a happy, jolly mood that it would have been obvious to Dada that the reason for this euphoria, elation and exhilaration must be a girl, a beautiful and charming girl that could elevate Rakesh. Dada was an old, wise man from whom one can not hide any thing, difficult to keep any secret. He can read the face and the mind like an open book.

Rakesh did not bring up the subject, although he was tempted to tell Dada about Raju. If any one knew Raju, Dada would. But he thought it prudent to keep quiet.

After their fifth meeting in the ruins and around, Raju at last agreed to come for a late lunch, afternoon tea. On Saturday, Rakesh was eagerly waiting to greet Raju. The clock struck three and at the same time Rakesh heard the bell.

Rakesh rushed to the door. There she was, in a stunning pale blue sari, the traditional Indian dress, with slightly darker blue, sleeveless blouse that showed her long, pale arms right up her armpits with glimpse of her under garments. She was teasingly dressed, as if to attract Rakesh's attention and to raise his blood pressure.

During all these meetings, she wore a kind of Punjabi, Rajasthani dress; that is a top, a loose trouser with a dupatta or scarf like long, thin and silky piece thrown across her well developed bosom. But in the windy condition, on a hillside it was always difficult to keep the dupatta in place.

So often she would just wrap it around her neck, leaving her low cut top to revel her beautiful bosom, her upper chest with consuming ease and without embarrassment. Well, if you have got them, why not flaunt them? That is the motto, the norm in so called higher society, the fashion world. That surprised Rakesh but he was not in a position to comment or judge and why should he?

She hardly used any makeup but then she was so beautiful she hardly needed any makeup. However she never forgets to put a bindi, normally a red spot on the forehead. But her bindi always matched the colour of her dress. She also had some very beautiful pattern on her hand, her palm made up, painted with henna or what we call mehendi, normally used by the bride and the bridesmaids during a wedding. This was a permanent fixture on her soft hands that Rakesh had examined whenever they set down at a lonely place. Today she was wearing beautiful and very expensive gold bangles, eight in each hand. In her neck a long gold chain with an oblong diamond pendant with at least a dozen good-sized diamonds. She looked even more beautiful than usual in this traditional Indian Sari and very expensive gold jewellery. In a way Rakesh was stunned and a bit nervous. She indeed looked like a princess, a very desirable young lady.

She had a full head of jet dark but smooth hair that constantly covered her face in the wind, enabling Rakesh to sweep them back with dignity.

Rakesh had fallen head over heels in love with Raju, although he was careful not to make his feelings too obvious or be too forward, in case he may startle her, driving her away.

Today was again a bright and sunny day. It seemed whenever Rakesh met Raju, they always enjoyed a perfect day, as if Raju knew what the weather would be like and come prepared for the eventuality that is lightly dressed, never carrying an umbrella as if she knew it was not going to rain, even in the middle of a rainy season?

As it was warm, they sat down in the front veranda, right in front of the sitting room and the front entrance. It was thatched for comfort and coolness in this hot and humid climate. But so often such a roof also attracts snakes. So one has to be careful, be vigilant when one had a thatched roof.

When they sat down, Dada brought the teapot, milk, sugar and some biting, followed by China cups and plates, the ones Mr. Smith had specially brought all the way from England but left behind for the new manager. It was clear from Dada's manner and his face that he was worried but could not speak out of term, insult a guest, a special guest that his boss had invited.

Rakesh preferred biscuits, goat cheese and scones. But today it was supplemented by traditional Indian savoury, Bombay mix and methi bhaji specially prepared by Jamuna. She was more amiable and less worried about these stories associated with a beautiful girl, the ghost of a young, beautiful princess who was some how responsible for the death of two young estate employees.

When the tea was over and table cleared, Rakesh excused Dada and Jamuna, as Rakesh was aware that Raju was not at ease with Dada around. How could Rakesh blame her? Dada's manner made it clear that she was not a welcome guest in this bungalow.

They listened to the Indian and English music, as Rakesh had a vast collection of records, the only entertainment available in such an isolated place.

Rakesh had now known Raju for well over two months but knew next to nothing about her, except that her father was Diliprai and mother Sitaradevi. They lived in one of the bungalows scattered on the slopes, a couple of miles from the estate. From their names, Rakesh gathered they may be Rajputs, once a ruling class.

After enjoying each other's company for few hours, it was time for Raju to leave. Raju would always leave before the sun went down. Perhaps it was a sensible, a wise precaution for a single girl walking alone.

Today, as she was wearing such expensive jewellery, Rakesh insisted that he should accompany her to her front door. She was looking so beautiful, sexy and desirable; it was difficult for Rakesh to take his eyes of her, let her go. But how could he detain her against her will? Rakesh was too much of a gentleman to behave in any improper way, especially with such a charming and sophisticated young woman.

Today, instead of separating at their usual junction, Raju let Rakesh walk with her for another half an hour, until they were some two hundred meters away from those bungalows.

"Rakesh, my home is just over there. You will have to let me go alone, as my parents do not know about us, at least not yet." Raju pleaded.

Rakesh had held her hand all the way and was reluctant to let her go. In one swift move, he grabbed Raju and gave her a passionate kiss, a long lingering, full blooded kiss. Raju did not oppose or showed any sign of resistance but let Rakesh feel at ease; let his emotions flow for a while before gently sliding away from his grip and said,

"Rakesh please let me go" and she disappeared among those bungalows.

Rakesh always came second best in front of her charm, beauty and persistence.

When Rakesh came home, the evening was young but it was a beginning to get dark and a bit late to sit in the veranda, as mosquitoes were a major health hazard, especially during a rainy season. So Rakesh moved to the lounge but kept the mosquito proof door leading to the veranda open, letting in the fresh air and the rays of the setting sun without being troubled by mosquitoes.

He stood at the window, with double peg of single mart whisky, poured over crushed ice, shaken but not stirred. This was his favourite drink, a habit he picked up in Scotland when he used to visit Scottish highlands while in Durham.

Today he even lighted a Havana cigar to go with his drink. He rarely smoked, on special occasion and that also Havana cigars only. He was looking at the setting sun, fast disappearing behind the hills.

He could not help but murmur his favourite song from the film Kismat, starring his and every one else's favourite actor Ashok Kumar.

"Dhira dhira, badal dhira dhira ja
Mera bulbul soo ra ha hai
Shore tu na macha!"

In the film, Ashok Kumar sings the song, standing on the balcony, adjourning the bedroom of his sweetheart, looking at the sky, the clouds and the moon, pleading with the clouds.

"Slowly slowly, the clouds go slowly
Without a noise or a murmur
For my sweetheart is sleeping soundly
Do not disturb her, wake her up
With the sound of your movement
Your wondering habit."

It was difficult for Rakesh to go to sleep after seeing Rajshree today. She was looking so stunning and beautiful that Rakesh was bowled over. It was a dream, not a reality. He would not have believed it if Dada and Jamuna were not the witness.

Slowly but surely their friendship blossomed in the ruins of the castle where they would meet once or twice a week. Raju had a mesmerizing effect on Rakesh. But then who could resist her charm, her permanent smile and her near perfect figure, well developed body, almond shaped innocent eyes and her long silky free flowing hair, along her sense of humour, her intelligence and her ability to converse on almost any subject. She was Rakesh's equal on intelligence and intellectual level. She was beyond human endurance, too good to be true.

For the last few days, Rakesh was having a strange experience at night. For some one who would go to sleep as soon as he hits the pillow, he was finding it difficult to go to sleep. So often he would wake up in the middle of the night, perspiring so much that he wound need a change of clothing. Windows of his bedroom would fly open even when there was no wind. His mind would wonder, thinking unthinkable, having a strange feeling that some one, Raju was sleeping next to him, urging him to make love to her. He was feeling nervous, irritated, disgruntled and enraged, without reason, without justification or cause.

Even Dada, Jamuna and those who work closely with him noticed these mood change and deviation from his normal behaviour. But even though Rakesh was aware of this change of personality, he could not put a finger on the cause, the reason for his irritation except that he was not getting enough sleep. There was no change in his lifestyle, diet or work pattern except his closeness, his involvement with Raju. Some how he felt Raju may be the cause of his problems?

Rakesh could not help but wonder Dada's warning and occasional comments by those who work closely with Rakesh. But how could an intelligent, England return person with modern outlook, who could compete on equal terms with any Westerner, could believe in such superstitious nonsense. He even refused to entertain such a thought, lower his intelligence threshold.

Rakesh was head over hill in love with Raju, although he was too proud to admit it. Then who wouldn't be in love with her, a princess, a beauty queen and a nice, articulate, well bred person with immaculate manner and ever increasing charm. She was almost a perfect girl, a perfect life partner, too good to be true.

Rakesh could not help comparing Raju with his first girlfriend. When he went to England, he met a lovely girl at the University, with an unusual name of **Gaurita.**

There was an interesting story behind her name. Her parents were posted to India before the Second World War. They were stationed at Simla, a very beautiful hill station, not too far from Himalayas. In fact on a clear summer day, Mount Everest could be visible on the horizon.

Simla was more like English or rather a Scottish town with similar weather, fauna and flora. Simla was the summer capital of British Raj where all high ranking British officers retreated during the height of oppressive Indian summer months of May to September.

Gaurita's father was an administrative officer in charge of looking after the high flyers and VIPs when they come to Simla. Her parents, Graham and Genevieve had an Indian couple who looked after all their needs.

This couple had a lovely, cute four year old daughter called Gauri, the name of a Hindu Goddess Parvati, consort of Lord Shiva. Graham and Genevieve were so fond of this tiny little girl that that treated her like their own daughter, as they had no children of their own, even after ten years of marriage. When they had to return to England after India gained independence, they wanted to adopt Gauri and bring her to England with them.

But Gauri was their parent's only child and an apple of their eyes. How could they allow her daughter to be whisked away to an unknown land, so far away that they would never be able to visit her, see her again, although they knew that Gauri would be treated like a princess in England? Poverty does not mean lack of devotion, dedication and diminishing of parental love for their children. It was a very difficult decision for them not to oblige, to let Graham and Genevieve take Gauri to England.

So when Graham and Genevieve had their own child, a lovely daughter, Graham wanted to name her Gauri while Genevieve preferred the name Rita, after her baby sister who died so tragically, at the age of twelve, from a brain tumour.

In the end they compromised and named their daughter Gaurita, a sweet name, although a bit unusual name for an English girl, with a milky white complexion and blonde, golden hair, accompanied by well built and fully developed body, a hallmark of the European race.

Gaurita had all these essential statistics in addition to being tall, slim and lovely shoulder length hair with natural curves, which she let grow to waist length, to please Rakesh who liked long hair in true Indian, traditional style.

Rakesh and Gaurita were a perfect match physically with many common interests, including mountaineering, walking and tracking for which Scotland and Wales are an ideal part of Britain.

In those days racism in England was widespread. Many houses, establishments that lent out rooms used to have a sign "NO dogs, black and Irishmen need apply." But mercifully the word Paki was not yet invented.

Even in this harsh racial environment, Gaurita's parents were willing to bless her only daughter's marriage to Rakesh, as they were fond of him. They found Rakesh as clever, charming and with good manner and would treat their daughter with love, respect and will definitely make her happy. What more parents could wish for their children?

But there was one serious obstacle. Rakesh found the English weather, especially long and dark English winters damp, cold and some what depressing, especially in the North.

Rakesh loved sunshine, warmth and vast open spaces of India. He could never settle down in England, even for the love of Gaurita, who loved this climate, where she was born and brought up.

Gaurita was not willing to leave her native Durham where her parents and most of her friends were, not even for the love of Rakesh, the sunshine and wide open spaces of the distant land of Bharat. India was only a name, a distant place that held no attraction for her. It was not the age of mass travel, package holidays or even adventure travel. People were happy and content to remain where they were born. They preferred familiarity of their country and their loved ones.

So after a close and a loving friendship, Rakesh and Gaurita parted company, much to the sadness and regret of her parents who were even willing to let their only daughter settle down in India, the country they loved, where they had spend some ten happy years.

They still regard India as their second home, a country where they learnt a great deal, about love, human brotherhood, sacrifice, the richness of Hindu culture and religion. They admired enormously the way India fought and won independence, under the leadership of Mahatma Gandhi, who single handedly brought the British Empire to its knees, without firing a single bullet.

They love Bharat as a land of Mox, deliverance and enlightenment, the land that gave the world Lord Rama, Krishna, Buddha, Guru Nanak and Gandhi, a few among many noble citizens of the world, the contribution unmatched by any other country, singularly or united.

They knew that their daughter will be treated like a royalty by every one, including Rakesh's family. The day they split up, albeit on a friendly term, was a sad day for every one, especially for Gaurita's parents. Their dream of visiting their only child in Bharat was shattered.

Rakesh believed in fate, Kismat, destiny. Although he was heart broken at losing Gaurita, a charming and beautiful girl, he consoled himself that every cloud has a silver lining. Some good may yet come out of this tragedy, the heartbreak. At least he met an English couple who were more Indian, Hindu at heart than most indigenous Indians. It was indeed a rarity at the time when every thing British was the best, including the Christian religion.

The uneasiness with his friendship with Raju brought back Gaurita's memory. He wondered what she would be doing, whether she was alone or got married, as he had lost all contact with her. But first love never goes away. It is always there in our subconscious mind and will surface from time to time when least expected. It was indeed his good fortune that he met a girl like Gaurita and still wonders whether he made a right decision in not marrying and staying in England. But he could never leave his mother alone in India. Perhaps she was the deciding factor in coming back to India.

It was Sunday. As Rakesh had not met Raju for nearly a week, he some how knew that she would call, pay him a visit and he was not disappointed.

Sharp at three in the afternoon, Raju knocked on his door. She was wearing her usual walking cloths with knee high leather boots, a must when visiting the ruins.

Raju was an expert in martial art, quite capable of defending herself if ever attacked by another human being. But it was an age of chivalry when women were accorded respect they deserve. No one wound insult them in any way, let alone attack them physically. Moreover Raju had a divine personality. She looked every inch a royal princess.

Soon Rakesh and Raju were at the top of the hill, among the ruins, Raju's favourite place, perhaps her abode in her previous life or could it be this life?

Rakesh was determined to solve the mystery of Raju, the reason behind his sleepless nights, his strange, nervous and sensuous feelings that was draining his strength, damaging his health and above all interfering with his work routine.

Rakesh was not the person, the manager who would sit in an office, behind a desk and delegate the work. He was a man of action who would like to be in the thick of things, where action is.

The estate was so large that it would take some four hours to travel from one end to another, requiring Rakesh to put an occasional twelve hour shift. He could only do such an arduous task with a good night sleep.

Rakesh and Raju had by now known each other for four months. They were meeting, on average twice a week, enjoying each other's company and occasional picnic. But Rakesh was none the wiser about Raju's background, her family members whom he had not met so far. Raju was very clever at avoiding such a talk, using her considerable charm that would be difficult to resist for any one, let alone lonely Rakesh.

Rakesh and Raju sat on a large boulder, their favourite seat, hand in hand, watching the red hot sun casting a long shadow.

Raju was looking even more beautiful, in a sleeveless, almost transparent top but modestly covered with a dupatta and her dark, soft and silky hair, flowing gently over her face obliging Raju to flick them back when they covered her eyes, the action, the coordinated movement of the face and hand Rakesh found so delicate, pretty and sexy!

Without the cover of dupatta and her hair, Raju looked really sexy with her breast half revealed. Rakesh could not help but gently grabbing her, holding her tight in his arms, barely able to restrain his feelings.

Looking in her eyes and playing with her hair, kissing her gently on her forehead, Rakesh said, "Raju, you know that I love you very much and I would like to marry you. But can I ask you one question?"

Raju was startled. She could not believe her ears. She kept quiet for a long time and then said in a soft and shivering voice. "Rakesh, I love you too, more than you will ever know. I had an inclination that you are eager to ask me a question, in fact more than one question. Go ahead; ask me any question you wish to put your mind, your anxiety at rest. But answers may not be to your liking, what you want to hear."

Rakesh told her what he had heard from Dada and a few other estate employees.

Hiding her face in the broad chest of Rakesh, Raju kept quiet for a long time. Getting no response, Rakesh gently lifted her face by her chin. Seeing tears in her wide, almond shaped eyes, Rakesh said, "Sorry Raju. I did not mean to upset you or hurt your feelings in any way. But there are a lot of questions that need answers" and to lighten the atmosphere, he added, "before we get married and go on our honeymoon. But right now, I am in a quandary, predicament and perplexity. I have never met your parents. I do not know where you live, that is after we have gone out more than thirty times, while you know every details about me, even about my first girlfriend, Gaurita.

But if my questions upset you so much, then please forgive me. You do not have to answer them. I love you unconditionally, regardless of what or who you are, your family background.

"Rakesh I want to tell you every thing, to come clean, even if that mean losing you." Raju was equally determined to answer Rakesh's questions.

Freeing herself from the grip of Rakesh, standing up and moving away from him, Raju said, "Rakesh, I do not know how to begin. I guess the best way is to tell you the truth. But as you know, truth is so often stranger than fiction, more unbelievable than a made up story. Be prepared to get the shock of your life. But please believe me when I say I love you and that you are absolutely safe with me. No harm will come to you."

Rakesh was confused, puzzled but he realized that Raju's answer would not be what he wants to hear. Raju was preparing him for the worse, fattening him up before sending him to a slaughter house, giving him a kiss of Dracula. Is he in for another Gaurita type experience or even worse? But Raju soon put his anxiety, his mind to rest, in a sort of way.

"Rakesh, what Dada told you is the truth. I am not an ordinary girl but I am indeed a lost soul, what you may call a ghost but that is not a right word to describe me, not a proper definition."

"R A J U .... This is not the time or the occasion to make jokes." Screamed Rakesh. There was a shiver in his voice and in spite of the cold wind going through his spine; his forehead was covered with perspiration.

"Rakesh, I know how serious you are. Believe me I could never joke with you when it comes to a matter of life and death and this is as serious as that for me but especially for you."

After a long pause, Raju continued, "Rakesh, you must have heard that ghost, angel and god do not cast a shadow. Look at your long and clear shadow. Every tree, every object casts a shadow in the setting sun. Now look at me. Could you see my shadow at all?"

Raju was absolutely right. She had no shadow at all, as if she was transparent like a glass, the light going through her without any resistance."

She continued, "Do you remember you took a couple of my photos, against my wish, ignoring my protest? The film was spoilt. You could not capture me on the film. That is why I gave you my drawing which you keep near your bedside table."

Rakesh was dumb struck. Raju was absolutely right. She cast no shadow. Rakesh remembered dada's words, his warning but looking at Raju's kind and smiling face, her light make up spoiled by her tears, Rakesh knew that he was not in any sort of danger, not from her. Raju could never harm him, as she loved him so much and he was absolutely right.

Sitting beside Rakesh, she continued. "So now you know that I am not an ordinary girl. I am a wondering, a free spirit with no home, no parents that I could introduce you to. But my love for you is real and I will never let any one harm you. In fact I will always keep an eye on you, become your guardian angel so that no one can harm you. I owe you that much."

Then with a smile, the innocent smile that had captivated Rakesh, she continued. "My life story goes back a very long time in history. My father, as you know was Diliprai and mother Sitaradevi. We were Suryavansi, the descendent from Sun dynasty, originally from Rajputana or Rajasthan.

My father was a ruler of a small kingdom, with Suryapur (Sun City) as the capital. It was some one hundred miles from these ruins. The city is now buried under hundreds of feet of earth, after a severe earthquake.

I was the only child. As you know my name was Rajshree." Then she added with a mischievous smile. "I was considered the most beautiful princess and an object of desire for many a prince and kings."

"Well Raju, I can certainly vouch for that. You are definitely the object of my desire and now I know why I am unable to sleep soundly at night." Rakesh could not resist this opportunity to lighten the atmosphere, to grab Raju, hold her in his arms. But some how he could not kiss a princess, not without her permission!

"Rakesh, remember I am a princess, not an ordinary girl." Joked Raju and then continued.

"Just west of Calcutta, there was another small kingdom, ruled by Arjansinh. My father and Arjansinh were great friends. His son, crown prince Pratapsinh used to visit us, along with his father. We were brought up together. We knew sooner or later we will get married and bind the two families, cement the friendship for ever.

It was the happiest day of my life when our engagement and then marriage were confirmed. I was over the moon. He was indeed a handsome, charming, dashing and a caring person, a rare quality among princes in those days.

At the time there was a tradition among Rajput kings to have many wives. But both our families believed in the tradition set by Lord Rama, one man, one wife.

My father even had the famous quote from our holy book framed and hung in his bedroom.

"Paranu hu eak, age manave ta no tek
Ghani Rani no shu cha cam
Eak Sita a santoshya Ram."
Translated in English, it means:
"I marry but once, that should be the tradition
The custom, the belief, the conviction and the ritual
Why do I need so many queens, concubines
When one queen Sita was all that Lord Rama needed
To satisfy all his wishes, his desire."

As my beauty was well known and as I was the only child, naturally many princes were eager to request my hand in marriage, with the hope that one day they will inherit the kingdom on the death of my father. But most of these suitors were already married with a wife or two and many more concubines.

After our marriage, we came here, to these ruins for our honeymoon. It was a beautiful, comfortable and above all a safe place to relax and enjoy, to start our married life.

This fort was in the middle of no where, in joint ownership of our two families. It had high walls all round, with watch towers at the interval of five hundred feet, with a clear view stretching on all sides. It was impossible to attack without being seen.

Moreover with a deep well, we had our own water supply and huge silos were full of grains. The palace was lavishly decorated with sandalwood furniture, Kashmiri silk furnishings and every kind of tropical flowers growing within the fort.

Every inch of our honeymoon suit, floor space was covered with petals, mainly marigold, sunflower, periwinkle, Champo or Indian magnolia, sweet smelling gardenia, jasmine and ratrani (night queen) Fresh petals were spread daily early in the morning before sunrise.

We arrived on the day of our honeymoon. As soon as our guests who were mainly family members left, we retreated to our honeymoon suite. We talked, kissed and cuddled until midnight.

It was time for us to retreat to our four poster bed, covered with rose petals and smelling like perfumery. This could have and should have been the happiest day in our life, a day or rather a night to remember. Instead it turned into a nightmare.

Before we could consummate our marriage, become one, lost in each other for ever, there was a knock on our door. A messenger from my father had delivered a message that shattered our lives that would make me a widow even before we could have our honeymoon, spend a night together and consume our union of body and soul.

Some where near our present day Calcutta, there was a town called Kanakpur, the capital city of the Mayur (peacock) kingdom, a powerful kingdom ten times the size of our two kingdoms put together.

Mayur Naresh (king) Virendra had a son, his crown prince Vanraj, a real playboy but a good general and an apple of his father's eye.

Vanraj was not only married with two beautiful wives who would be future queens but he also had a harem of young, beautiful and innocent girls with an addition of one or two every month.

Naresh Virendra had frequently expressed his wish, asked my hand in marriage for his Crown Prince Vanraj, as his third wife. He was bewitched by my beauty, charm and personality. Like a spoilt child, he would not rest until he gets what he wants.

But my father knew that I would never be happy or be treated with respect and dignity I deserve. I will be no more than a trophy to be hung on his bedroom wall, for every one to see and admire. Moreover my father knew that I was in love with Pratapsinh who was like a son to my father.

So he tactfully turned down the marriage proposals of Prince Vanraj. But when I got married to Youvraj Pratapsinh, all hell broke lose. Both Naresh Virendra and Prince Vanraj took it as a personal affront, a snub and provocation.

There was no reason to hold back their anger or not to take this opportunity to conquer our tiny domain and merge with his vast kingdom. Vanraj himself led an army of 20,000 soldiers to attack Suryapur, the capital of our kingdom known as Devital. My father had an army of some five thousand soldiers, mostly part-timers.

My father was a kind, trusting and caring person who considered Naresh Virendra as a friend. He did not imagined, even entertained the thought that my marriage will result in a war. As far as he was concerned, he had done nothing wrong. It was his big mistake.

My father had emptied his treasury of money and his silos of grain by distributing these commodities to the poor people of his kingdom. Our marriage was the most important occasion in his life since he himself got married to my mother Sitaradevi over thirty years ago.

He was caught unprepared, caught napping. He only had few weeks before he had to surrender or die. The message from my father was that we should leave at once and take shelter with Samrat (Emperor) Ranjitsinh, the ruler of the kingdom of Mahapradesh and a family friend. His kingdom was vast that include the present day Orissa and most of Madhya Pradesh. He would not be intimidated by Naresh Virendra and his cronies.

But on hearing this tragic news, my husband, my life partner, my soul mate was eager to join my father and his family to fight the tyrant Vanraj. I was tempted to urge him, even beg him to heed the advice of my father and seek shelter with Samrat Ranjitsinh.

But my husband was a born warrior, a full blooded Rajput. How could I try to stop him from doing his duty, rushing to help his and my families. Vanraj surrounded the castle. My husband was not able to enter the castle. But he camped some thirty miles away with his just five hundred soldiers and harassed Vanraj every night.

After six weeks, food and water ran out forcing my father to attack Vanraj one day at midnight. It was a sudden and a coordinated attack in true Rajput tradition, known as kesaria or do or die attack. In the ensuing battle both my father and my husband died a heroic death. But not before they destroyed more than half of Vanraj's army.

After destroying, ransacking Suryapur, Vanraj came for me. We had some four hundred loyal and well trained soldiers guarding this place, this castle which was like a fort Knox that we could defend with minimum soldiers. At the interval of just five hundred feet, there was a tall watch tower which can be manned, defended by just two soldiers.

We held Vanraj back for long four months. As you know, these hills are so often immersed, hidden in thick mist. During such a time, we would lower, send a team of five to ten soldiers, with bows and arrows and can of kerosene to attack his camp and set fire tents housing his soldiers. These soldiers would then disappear in the nearby forest if not killed or captured. At one time Vanraj even thought of abandoning the siege and go home. But my attraction, making me his queen, the temptation, the greed was too great for him. In the end we ran out of food and water.

I led the suicide attack with just three hundred soldiers. It is needless to say that we all died a heroic death. During the six months siege, Vanraj again lost half of his army. By the time he went back to his capital Kanakpur, he had just four thousand soldiers left. He was so weakened that he could not dare attack my husband's kingdom. Moreover he was a figure of hatred, loathed by all the small kingdoms.

But I lost every thing that was dear to me, all my family members and above all my husband even before we had an opportunity to consummate our marriage. I died a virgin bridge.

There may be honour among thieves but certainly not among Rajput kings. I hate to say that we are our own worse enemies. It is sadly true. Rajputs are responsible for keeping Bharat desh a slave nation for the last three thousand years, if not more. Our kings hate each other more than they hate our real enemies who invade our motherland, rape and plunder the rich and holy land of Bharat. They were responsible for Bharat being occupied by Alexander the Great, Moguls, French, Portuguese and the British.

Although my father in law Rana Arjansinh survived, he lost his son Pratapsinh, his crown prince and the apple of his eyes, not forgetting his best friend, my father and our entire family. He was determined to get rid of tin pot Naresh Virendra and his playboy prince Vanraj.

Arjansinh send an envoy to Emperor Ranjitsinh, inviting him to attack Naresh Virendra, promising him to provide a well trained army of at least ten thousand soldiers, raised by various small kingdoms who were enraged with Vanraj, his attack on our tiny kingdom and my death, as I was a popular princess.

Ranjitsinh accepted this invitation, sent a huge army, led by his popular and battle hardened commander Mansinh. Within two years of our deaths, kingdom of Mayur was conquered and all the members of the Naresh Virendra's family were killed. Rana Arjansinh took a leading part in the downfall of the Naresh. It was the happiest day throughout small kingdoms. At last our deaths were avenged, justice delivered and the tyrant removed for good.

Soon afterward Rana Arjansinh died of a broken heart, as if he was just hanging on to take revenge for the loss of his Crown Prince, his only son Pratapsinh. No one was the winner in this tragedy of Herculean proportion. This is my tragic story, the kahani (life history) of my unfilled life, so brutally ended before it even began; the end of my arman, ambition and attainment.

This unfulfilled lechery, lust and the desire of the flesh denied on the verge of consummating the marriage made my soul a gypsy, a wonderer and an outcast, denying me the salvation, the Mox, the ultimate release from the cycle of birth, death and punishment, turned me into a ghost, what I am today.

Raju's voice was cracking up; choked with emotion and her eyes were shedding tears by a bucketful. She was hanging on to Rakesh tightly, as if afraid of losing him?

"But Raju, what is the difference between you and a real human being like me? I know you will remain young and beautiful for ever and you can not die, as you are already dead. Aren't you? So in a way I am lucky. I will always have a young and a beautiful wife, even when I may be using a Zimmer frame?" Rakesh tried to introduce some humour to lighten the atmosphere. That joke certainly brought a smile on the face of Raju, covered with tears that Rakesh was trying hard to wipe with his bare hands.

"Well Rakesh, I can never give you children nor can I mix with your society. I am not human. I am not real." Then added with a mischievous smile, "I can't cook either but I do love you."

Rakesh tightened his grip on Raju and kissing her on the forehead said, "Raju, I love you and I would like to marry you and by the way, I am a good cook. So it does not matter whether you can cook or not"

"I know this does not sound right. I may be crazy but I have been a sane, mature and sensible person too long. I do not want to lose you. I lost a wonderful girl Gaurita once but not again. It is time to misbehave, be an idiot?" There was a smile on Rakesh's face.

"Raju, I love you so much. You are one in a million, Please marry me." Repeated Rakesh.

Raju stood up, moved away from Rakesh and said, "Rakesh, you have liberated me from this hell. Now my wandering spirit will attain Mox, nirvana. I will be able to join my husband, my soul mate in heaven.

We have been apart for too long.

My burning desire to spend my honeymoon, to enjoy the fruits of marriage, to satisfy my sexual fantasies which remained unfulfilled when my husband was so brutally taken away from me on our honeymoon night make my spirit wonder, turned it into a ghost.

My liberation, my escape from this hell, my curse would only end, lifted if a human being, knowing that I am a ghost, a wandering spirit and not human, is willing to marry me, proposes marriage, then and then only my curse will come to an end and I will be a free, a liberated spirit.

I can not explain why, how or for what reason I was burdened with this curse but I know that you, your selfless love for me have liberated me from this hell.

Dear Rakesh, you are a carbon copy of my husband. I fell in love the day I saw you, set my eyes on you. In fact it was so difficult for me to keep away from you that I was sleeping with you in your bed, in my invisible, suspended state.

My regret is that now I have to leave you. We will never meet again. Please forgive me for playing with your emotion, your love and your kind and caring nature. Forget your beloved Rajshree, your Raju. Consider it as a dream and not a reality.

Please believe me when I say that you are not destined to be alone for long. You will soon find a wonderful girl by the name of Amisha, who will be your wife, give you wonderful children and you will have a long and a happy married life.

I have left a leather pouch where I was sitting. It contains a gold chain with a diamond Pendant. On one side there is our Coat of Arms and on the other side an image of our Kuldevi. (Family deity) This piece of jewellery is thousands of years old and priceless. Wear it round your neck and you will be protected, no one can harm you. I know you will not sell or misuse my parting gift. That is why I am giving it to you. That is my final, ultimate present to you, my liberator, my hero and my darling as well.

The figure of Raju started melting away in the evening mist of the setting sun, rising high in the sky. The ground where Raju was standing was soon covered with white rose petals, falling from the sky. Soon there was no more Raju.

Rakesh could not believe either his eyes or his ears.

"R A J U .... R A J U ....please do not leave me alone. I love you." Shouted Rakesh but his voice was lost in the wilderness.

Rakesh could not control his anguish, his pain and his extreme distress. For the first time since he was a little boy, he cried uncontrollably. But there was no one to consol him, wipe his tears or say a few kind words.

At last he got up, put the chain that Raju had left behind, round his neck, gathered some rose petals in his handkerchief and started the long, dangerous and lonely descent to his bungalow, a few miles down.

Rakesh could understand, comprehend losing Gaurita but not losing Raju. It was bizarre to say the least. He remembered an Urdu ghazal he liked so much when he was at the college.

"Muze ye baat ka gum nahi
Ke meri kesti, naya dub gai
Magar gum ya baat ka hay
Ke jaha meri kesti dubi
Waha pani bhe both com tha!"

Translated into English, it comes out like this.

"I am not perturbed
That my boat has sunk
But my misfortune is that,
Where my boat sank
There was hardly any water
Even to immerse my tiny boa

To justify the sinking
In such a shallow water
That is my misfortune, my bad luck.

How true the situation was for Rakesh. No one would believe this story if he is mad enough to tell any one, perhaps with the exception of Dada who always suspected that Raju was not real. She was too good to be true, to be a human being!

The sun had already gone down some time ago. It was getting darker by the minute, making the descent dangerous. It was lunacy, insane to be out at this time of the evening.

But today Rakesh was not worried about any danger, any wild animal, not even the man-eater Devi's tiger or a spitting cobra.

In a way Rakesh was glad that the God gave him this opportunity to be an instrument in liberating Rajshree, her wondering spirit and send her back to her husband whom she loved so much.

The few months he spent with Raju were wonderful time. Raju was indeed a very beautiful, charming and sensuous girl, one in a million. Could it be Kismat, nasib, destination that he got this manager's job against all odds, in order to meet Rajshree, help her and liberate her spirit?

At last he felt a little relief. His pain, his sacrifice was not in vain. When Rakesh reached his bungalow, he was already calm and reconciled with the evening's event which was stranger than fiction, unbelievable in the extreme. He never believed in ghosts, in supernatural happenings. But he had the gold chain and the diamond studded locket that would worth a fortune to prove that it was not a dream. But Rakesh could not help wondering about Raju's prophecy of meeting a wonderful girl by the name of Amisha and his future happiness. Well, only the time will tell whether Raju's prophesy will come true or not!

****

CASA BLANCA (White House)

When Dr. Pathak received the notification that he had been transferred to Songadh, he felt not only happy but also relieved and elevated. He was tired of living out of a suitcase in Chotila.

Although Songadh was not a big town, with a population under 30,000, it had at least a good school, a well equipped hospital and above all it had running water and sanitation.

His best friend Naimesh was also living in Songadh. Chotila had none of the modern day infrastructure that makes life bearable. But with a population of just one thousand people, made up of mainly small farmers, what infrastructure one could expect?

As there was no surgery, no medical doctor in or around the village of Chotila, the government was obliged to post a doctor in Chotila who was responsible not only for Chotila but also five surrounding villages and various isolated settlements with a combined population of between 8 to 10 thousand residents.

Although Dr. Pathak was based in Chotila, he had to visit the surrounding villages on a rota basis. Fortunately the Doctor was provided with a transport, very comfortable four wheel drive combie with a driver called Shantu, an appropriate name which means a quiet one. Indeed his nature well justified his name. He was a middle aged gentleman, familiar with the area, as he had lived in Chotila all his life.

The combie was fitted with all the basic necessities, a comfortable bed, small kitchen and even a fridge, to keep the medicine fresh in the sweltering heat. Shantu was not only a driver but doctor's friend, companion, cook and dispenser.

In fact Shantu was doctor's Man Friday, an all round handyman that made doctor's life stress free, leaving Doctor free to concentrate on the medical side and in such a vast area, medical needs were vast and varied. That is why a doctor of high calibre was needed for this area.

So on receiving the transfer notice, Doctor was naturally elevated but his one regret was parting company with Shantu whom he had come to love and respect as an elder brother. It was Government's policy not to keep any doctor in Chotila longer than one year but Dr. Pathak had to spend just nine months. On rare occasion some doctors had to spend up to two years, as good, experienced doctors were always in short supply during the early days of independent Bharat.

So Dr. Pathak was indeed lucky to get away from this desolate place within such a short time.

On arrival of Dr Trivedi, his replacement, Dr Pathak caught the first available train for Bombay (Mumbai) where his family was based while he was in Chotila. He was given a three weeks leave to spend some time with his family before reporting for duty in Songadh.

In a way Songadh was a familiar place for Dr. Pathak, as he had spent three months there, some five years ago when the local hospital doctor had a heart attack.

Songadh was indeed an attractive place. Having situated at the height of 2000 feet, it was half way to gaining a reputation as a hill station. Pavagadh Mountain Range was only a stone throw away, at a distance of some forty miles. Dr. Parekh was a keen naturalist and unlike most Gujaratis, he was not averse to occasional hunting.

With his childhood friend Naimesh in Songadh, Dr. Pathak was assured of a good company. Moreover with a good school, he could bring his wife and two children to Songadh. Indeed he was lost without his wife Avni. She was not only his wife and mother of his two beautiful children but she was his friend, his partner, his soul mate and a companion.

They met when both were in high school. They managed, against all odds, to keep in touch throughout ups and downs and various period of separation, especially during University time, as Anu (Dr. Pathak) chose medicine while Avni, in common with most girls, did her masters degree in social science, specializing in vegetarian culinary dishes and interior decoration, a combination that would win any one's appreciation, heart and soul. After all the quickest way to a man's heart is through his stomach?

This different career choice kept them apart for well over five years. But as the saying goes, distance, separation makes heart grow fonder and cements true love while the shallow love and sexual attraction will wither away with time and distance. So it was indeed a true love between Anu and Avni that has and always will survive separation and upheaval in their lives.

After graduation, while Anu was still doing his training, Avni gained a reputation as a top order chef. She had her own business, supplying and taking care of the dinner parties for the rich and the famous, while at the same time running, demonstrating her skill at various colleges. It was her father's influence which moulded her career, as he had one of the most prestigious restaurants in Bombay, appropriately named "Mumtaz's Culinary" with a client base that would be an envy of the rest of the profession. So it was not that difficult for Avni to get a foothold in this envious business, dealing with celebrities.

She was the first person to introduce curd cheese dishes, as a starter with barbequed vegetables, especially mushrooms, tomatoes, green papers and onions. She also made aubergine, a rarely used vegetable popular, using it as a mashed, grilled or oven baked dish, mixing it with peas and potatoes to make a curry or as a starter with aubergine slices, lightly cooked under the grill, slightly garnished with olive oil and with a topping of Cheddar cheese, spring onion, tinned corn, fresh mushrooms, a touch of garlic and green chillies. It is a Greek dish which Avni had adopted with ease for Indian taste. Italian pasta dishes also figured prominently in her menu along with Chinese fried rice and various fresh vegetables cooked rare in Chinese style with Soya, mushroom and garlic sauce that gives Chinese food a distinct favour. Avni preferred vegetarian food, although she was not averse to fish and chicken when the occasion demanded.

It was indeed a profitable and prestigious business. But with the marriage and two young children, lovely Priya and adorable Prem to look after, her career took a back seat to that of her husband Anu. However a couple of her cookery books were and still are in great demand with low budget and dishes for a single person popular and well received, under the catching phrase, "**Prepare Your Meal In Under 20 Minutes**"

She regularly writes her own column on food, hygiene and beauty in a couple of leading fashion magazines read at the highest level, among film stars, high flying ladies and career minded girls. In fact her face was and still is more familiar and her maiden name she uses in her writings better known than that of her husband, as she wisely kept her married identity separate from her work.

But now her husband Anu and her two lovely children Prem and Priya took precedent above her work, her career and her social and business commitment.

Today it was nearly a month since Dr. Pathak arrived in Songadh. In a way he was already at ease here. Naimesh and his wife Neha were taking good care of him. But he had failed to find a good house to rent and without suitable accommodation, he could not bring his family to Songadh.

Every day in the evening, Anu and Naimesh would go flat hunting but in Songadh there were hardly any accommodation worth renting, although being a summer retreat for the town's wealthy expatriates, there were many beautiful bungalows but all locked up at this time of the year. Moreover these expatriates, who were affluent on most part, were not interested in letting out their well decorated and expensively furnished properties.

At around ten o'clock at night, Naimesh's phone rang. Sheth (successful businessman) Pramodlal was on the line. His wife had a sudden and severe stomach pain. Being a good friend of Naimesh's family and an influential resident, Anu was obliged to go on a home visit.

In a small town like Songadh, it was common to ask for such a favour. It is in fact a custom, a tradition to help each other in their hour of need, even without asking!

It was a suspected case of appendicitis and the patient had to be transferred to a hospital. While she was being x-rayed and prepared for an emergency operation, that is as soon as she can be anaesthetized. In such a small hospital, it was difficult to find a specialist doctor who could perform such a duty, otherwise

Anu would have to do both the duty, to anaesthetize as well as perform the operation.

While they were waiting for the x-ray results, Anu and Sheth started talking. Sheth knew about Anu's search for a good accommodation and how desperate the doctor was to bring his family to Songadh. In a small town every one knows about one's problems and are willing to help out, extend their hands in friendship, even to a stranger.

Anu could not help but mention about his search and his need to find a house as soon as possible.

After a long silence and some hesitancy, Sheth said, "Doctor, I have the keys of a beautiful bungalow or rather a town house, as it has two floors that belong to my brother Milan who lives in Bombay. Here in Songadh, all isolated buildings with a garden are known as bungalows, no matter how many floors it may have!

It is some five miles outside the town. It has four bedrooms, a big garden and all the modern facilities that people like you are accustomed to, that include fitted kitchen and English type shower, washroom. But I am not sure whether I should offer it to you or not."

Anu was surprised. How come no one had mentioned it? It sounded like a perfect accommodation and having his own car with a driver, a distance of five miles should be more of a blessing than a hindrance.

"Please Seth; let me have a look at the bungalow. Rent is no problem, as I will be reimbursed whatever rent I pay by the government." Anu was more than eager to see the bungalow.

"Doctor, I am not worried about the rent. In fact I do not want any rent. But some town folks say that the place is haunted. Although I do not believe in such nonsense, I am not a superstitious person but I do not want to put your life at risk." Sheth tried to explain why he was reluctant to offer the bungalow to Anu, although it may sound like a lame excuse!

"Sheth, I am an educated person. I do not believe in such gossips, old wives tales. These talks are on most part vivid imagination, a topic of conversation for idle minds. Let me worry about the ghost. I promise you I will take every precaution, as my wife and children will be living there." Anu tried to reassure Sheth.

"OK doctor. The bungalow is yours, rent free for the first six months. But doctor, if you are at all worried about the safety of your family or feel unhappy in any way, please do not hesitate to return the keys." There was slight apprehension, some anxiety in his voice.

"Thank you Seth Pramodlal. I promise you that I will not put the safety of my family in jeopardy. Please trust me." Anu replied in a reassuring voice.

Anu realised that Naimesh was not at all pleased with his decision to move in the bungalow appropriately named "Shive Sadan" after the most famous Hindu God Lord Shiva, a fearless warrior and a God of destruction.

According to Hindu mythology, there is one Supreme Power, the Permashvar or Ishvar. Then there are three Gods, Brahma, the creator who created the world, the universe, Vishnu the administrator who looks after every day running of the world and Mahesh or Lord Shive, the destroyer who will one day destroy the world when we are living in a sin bin, sunk so low that there is no hope of salvation. Looking at the world today, with terrorism, suicide bombing and unprovoked attack on even Hindu pilgrims trying to visit Amarnath, it will soon be a time for Lord Shiva to act, to raise his Trishul, the weapon of mass destruction, in anger.

It was obvious that Naimesh had known about this place all along but he was not eager for Anu to move in this haunted place. But now it was out of his hand.

Next day Anu and Naimesh collected the keys and went to inspect Shive Sadan. It was indeed a very beautiful place, a bungalow that had every comfort. Obviously it was built by some one who must have lived in the rich suburb of a city like Bombay or Madras. Perhaps he could be an architect familiar with such project, planning and construction.

It was built for comfort, privacy and security. The bungalow had four double bedrooms, two with en suite facilities. All four bedrooms had built-in wall to wall, walk in cupboards, with matching dressing table and concealed lightings.

All bedrooms had wooden floorings which was tastefully varnished or left with natural wood colouring. The authentic wood provides a cooling effect in summer and is warm to walk on in winter.

The lounge and the rest of the ground floor had a white marble floor, with occasional black tint. The lounge had a big piece of Kashmiri carpet covering the centre.

Besides the lounge, there was a vast kitchen, incorporating the dining room, with a ten feet rosewood dining table and twelve matching chairs. There was a utility room with a large American type fridge-freezer and plumbing for washing machine, although such utility items were a novelty rather a norm that is today.

There was a large play room for children with a folding table-tennis and a proper size billiard table. The garage could easily take three cars. The rooftop was the most charming part of the house.

It could be turned into a beautiful entertainment place, if handled by an expert; that is by Avni who is always full of ideas, with pot plants of varying shape and size, small shaded places, beach type thatched huts and barbeque area, a rooftop garden fit for a five star hotel. It seemed Anu was running away with his imagination.

All the windows were fitted with iron grills and mosquito proof wire nets. The bungalow was surrounded by an eight feet high wall with sharp, broken glass imbedded at the top of the wall. There were security gates with a small cabin beside the gates for Chokidar, a security person.

The bungalow or rather the house was perfect in every way, needed no more than a coat of paint here and there, although the garden was overgrown with weeds and tall grass.

It took just one week for Anu and Naimesh to restore Shive Sadan to its former glory. As it was fully furnished and tastefully decorated, with running cold and hot water, Anu was able to move in after a week and within a month Anu was reunited with Avni and his two children. It was like a dream come true. If Anu and Avni had to build their own bungalow, they could not do better.

The bungalow was built over a two acre of plot, thus providing a four hundred feet back garden with a seventy feet frontage and plenty of open space on the sides which were mostly paved with granite slabs mined from the nearby quarry, at the foot of the Banaras Hills, except for flower borders which were now covered with weeds.

The back garden had several matured fruit trees, such as guava, mango and tiny black plum (Jambu) which had stood intact, even when neglected. It also had a deep well with motorised pump to water the garden during the hot, dry season, a real blessing as Songadh routinely ran out of water during the worse months of summer. The garden poised a challenge to Avni which would keep her occupied for a while. But it would be a labour of love rather than a hard, tedious work.

The place was isolated except for one bungalow that was some one thousand yards away from Shive Sadan. As the place was isolated, Anu tried to visit this place, to get acquainted with his neighbour but without much success.

One Sunday when Anu saw a car enter this bungalow, he thought it was a right opportunity to go and knock on the door.

The bungalow was called **"Casa Blanca"** a Spanish word meaning **The White House."** Anu could not understand why the place was given such a foreign name. The name plate stated **Dr. K. M. Sadashive M Sc, PhD.**

No one in the town knew Dr. Sadashive nor had any one seen him. It was assumed that he was a recluse, a sort of research scientist, perhaps discovering new drugs. The huge outbuilding was his laboratory. Only God knew what sort of research was going on behind the always drawn curtain of the mystifying lab.

Anu pressed the bell several times before a servant came and opened the door. He was a big man, more like a bouncer than an ordinary servant. With his unshaven face, long, untidy hair and abrupt manner, Anu felt as if he was an intruder, an unwelcome visitor, uninvited guest. The servant introduced himself as Lodi.

When Anu pressed his card with the word Doctor in front of his name, it impressed Lodi and led Anu to a lounge, closely watched by a huge Alsatian dog aptly called Ravan, the name of a demon in the most revered Hindu epic of Ramayana.

"Don't worry Sir, the dog will not harm you as long as I am with you but do not enter the house on your own." Said Lodi in a polite but firm tone. It was more like a warning than a friendly advice.

In few minutes Mr. Sadashive entered the room and shook Anu's hands. It was a firm, strong grip. They spend less than fifteen minutes together before he departed, saying he has a meeting to attend, leaving Anu to finish his cup of tea, poured from a silver teapot to the most expensive teacup, a part of his expensive collection.

Dr. Sadashive had an impressive personality. He was over fix feet tall, well built, with small trimmed beard and wearing an expensive rimless spectacle. He looked every inch of a professor or a scientist. But there was an absence of the traditional Indian hospitality in his manner.

It was clear from his manner, his attitude and body language that he did not like or encourage visitors. He was too busy with his work to socialize, even with a medical doctor like Anu, the medical profession so highly thought and well respected in our Indian community.

Anu was very much impressed with the décor, furnishing and the colour scheme. The paintings on the wall, the antique furniture, some made from fragrant sandalwood or black hard sesame wood while others imported from Europe, mainly from Spain, with Inca influence clearly visible in most Spanish art effects. The most impressive pieces were the two life-size marble statues of Goddess Venus, goddess of love and beauty that welcomed the visitors in the wide entrance hall.

It was obvious that Dr. Sadashive had spent some time in Spain. He even spoke in fluent Spanish with his so called servant. That may be the reason why he named his bungalow **"Casa Blanca" (White House)** the name which is fashionable in Spain and Latin America, as the president of the most powerful nation on earth lives in White House, in Washington DC.

Anu enjoyed his brief visit and a short but useful talk with his elusive neighbour. But he knew this was his first and perhaps the last visit to Casa Blanca, that he was unlikely to have dinner invitation or even the opportunity to meet Dr. Sadashive again.

Within two weeks Anu was well settled in his new home, one of the most luxurious, comfortable and enjoyable home he had ever lived in. The bungalow was alive with the laughter and chuckling of his two adoring children. The presence of his beautiful and loving wife Avni, whom he missed so much when Anu was posted to Chotila, was a great bonus, considering her immense cooking skill.

It was not long before Avni came to know the history of their beautiful but haunted bungalow. Avni was a well educated person with a modern outlook on life. She would not be worried about such idle gossips or old wives' tales. But with two little children and the fact that the bungalow was completely isolated made her a bit apprehensive. She could not even depend on the neighbour, who normally would be the first call of port, to ask for help, one to come to the rescue in our hour of need, riding a white horse, a knight in shining armour.

Although Anu was calm and confident, he was not willing to take any risk. Fortunately for Anu, he found a Ghurkha couple, Bahadursinh and his wife Rukhiba to come and live in the annex to the bungalow, a one bed room self contained extension, especially built for a live-in servant or an au pair girl, a tradition common in Europe but fast catching up in India, among the rich families.

Bahadursinh whom every one called Chacha (uncle) was a retired army personal, a perfect bodyguard for the family. Rukhiba helped Avni in the home. They were more like elderly relatives than an employee. Anu and Avni accorded them the respect their age, wisdom, devotion and loyalty deserved.

Anu was indeed lucky to find such a couple to take care of his family. Ghurkhas are world renowned for their bravery, loyalty and dedication to their masters, their employers and friends.

Hardly a month had passed before Anu and Avni had their first bad experience, the beginning of their problems, their harassments. Anu used to drop the children to school early in the morning, before starting his morning shift at the local hospital.

As the school was only a short walking distance from Naimesh's home, his wife Neha would collect the children in the afternoon, as their own two children were studying at the same school. Anu would collect them at the end of the day, at 5pm when his shift was over. Anu had not managed to employ a driver yet.

Today Avni left home early with Anu, as she wanted to attend the ladies show to watch the film "Sangam" the most talked Indian film for a decade. It was a smash hit with Raj Kapoor, Vijayantimala and Rajendra Kumar, the three superstars of Bollywood starring together for the first time.

When Anu returned home at 7pm, he saw Avni with a long, sad face, hardly able to control her tears or anger?

Anu knew straight away that some unpleasant, a terrible incident has happened to upset Avni. As his two children were safe with Avni, it was a relief. He did not have to wait long before he came to know that the lounge curtains were set on fire, completely ruined.

It happened at around 3pm. Fortunately Bahadursinh was in the house and he put down the fire before it could do any damage to the furniture but curtains were ruined beyond repair.

As Avni had personally chosen the material and sewn them on her tiny sewing machine, she was naturally upset.

Moreover half an hour before Anu came home, the telephone rang. Avni, thinking Anu was on the line, rushed in to answer the phone. But what she heard was a terrifying, blood chilling laughter that one could associate with a horror movie. Avni put down the phone as fast as she could. But the damage was already done. She was shaking like an autumn leaf in a pre winter storm, until Rukhiba gave her a glass of water and then made her a cup of masala tea.

Although Anu could not work out how the fire was started, he thought it would be wise and prudent to cover this and every other window with fireproof plastic blinds rather than cotton or nylon curtains. He also installed a fire extinguisher in every room Anu was glad that this loyal Ghurkha couple were taking care of his family, as without them, it would be impossible for Anu to leave Avni alone in the house during the day time when he was at the hospital.

Anu had a permit to keep a firearm, a revolver, which he cleaned and made ready for use in an emergency. Anu knew that he was fighting an unknown, unseen enemy that could not be stopped by a gun or force of any kind. It was a mind game, a game of chess that would require a great deal of patience, cool head and a detective work to get to the bottom of the problem. But there was definitely no ghost.

Anu was given the licence to carry a firearm when he was posted in the forest of Gir, to use against wild animals, not against his fellow human being, in an emergency, if the car breaks down in the middle of nowhere.

Today it was Saturday. As nothing unusual or worrying incident had occurred for two weeks, except a few telephone calls which were all answered by Bahadursinh and losing the electricity for a brief period, Anu and Avni had arranged to go out for a meal with Naimesh and Neha, to take their mind of living in Shive Sadan, a haunted house?

But by six in the evening, it started raining, a light rain to begin with, which soon turned into a mini storm that now and then hit this part of Pavagadh Mountains.

With lightening and thunder thrown in, it was wise to stay indoor. Anu rang Naimesh and cancelled the programme.

Anu thought the best way to pass the time was to retreat to their bedroom, to their king size, soft, warm and comfortable bed, in the company of his beautiful, charming and sensuous wife, albeit after an early dinner.

After a long, heart to heart chat and kissing and cuddling that Anu had missed so much when he was alone in Chotila, they fell a sleep.

At around midnight, the phone rang. Thinking it could be an emergency at the hospital, Anu grudgingly answered the phone.

It was the familiar, spine chilling laughter of a devil or may be Dracula that lasted longer than normal. It sounded even more evil, scaring as the storm had still not died down. Moreover it was accompanied by a warning, "Vacate my abode or else ....!

Anu put down the phone before the sentence was complete. A thought just passed his mind. What if Avni had answered the phone? Even on this cold night, Anu was covered with perspiration.

When Anu returned to bed, Avni realised what the phone call was about, although Anu tried to make out that it was a wrong number. But his face could not hide the fear, anguish or the anger. Anu and Avni knew each other too well, can read each other's mind, thoughts and feelings.

Anu knew ghosts do not make phone calls. So there is some reason behind this harassment, some human angle. It was now impossible to go back to sleep. They took the phone off the hook to prevent any more disturbances.

The storm had subsided and the sky was getting clear, with few stars twinkling intermittently, as if smiling at their predicament, their plight, their quandary.

Suddenly Anu's attention was drawn by a small fire at the far end of the garden. Anu jumped out of the bed, put on the gown, took the revolver out of the locked drawer, loaded the gun and equipped himself with the torch to go out and investigate.

All these commotions had also woken up Bahadursinh and his wife who had now moved into the fourth bedroom from the annex, so as to be near to Avni and the children, after the curtains were set on fire.

Avni bagged Anu not to go out, as the fire which was confined to a small area, was already dying out, unable to set alight the wet grass and the vegetation.

This was the last straw that broke the camel's back. Avni could not take it any more. She gave the final ultimatum to Anu, solve this mystery, stop these harassment within two weeks or she would go back to Bombay with the children, but only after Anu had moved back with Naimesh and Neha. She would stay in Bombay until Anu could find an alternative accommodation.

Although Anu did not show his concern, his worry to Avni, he was clearly troubled with all these going on, about the safety of his family. Clearly there was a sinister motive behind this harassment. Some one wanted to see that the bungalow remain empty, unoccupied.

Anu had made inquiry about the telephone calls. But they were not registered at the local exchange. All the harassment was done so expertly that not only there was no proof but it was difficult for any one, including police to get involved.

They would not have even believed Anu but for the fact that Anu was a doctor and the bungalow had a chequered history of unusual occurrences that were already well documented and every one knew. Police could only advise Anu to move out.

In the morning while having breakfast, Avni smiled and said, "Anu, how come we do not remember Vinod. If any one can help, can solve this mystery, Vinod can."

Avni was spot on. Anu and Vinod had been good friends since their childhood. While Anu qualified as a doctor, Vinod, who was not only a brilliant student but a very good all round sportsman and an athlete, became lawyer and a barrister.

He was one of the best known barristers in Bombay, popularly known as Vinod Vakil. (Lawyer) His surname was Mehta but every one called him Vakilsahib.

Not only Anu and Vinod were best friends but Avni and Vinod's wife Vimi were soul mates as well. Vinod was a real life Perry Mason. His working style was based on this fictional character.

Vinod never had any of his clients convicted so far. But he would only take on cases if he believed that his client was innocent. But to be honest, it does not always work out that way.

Vinod was a practical person. On rare occasions he had to defend youngsters of well-known politicians, super rich clients and even underworld figures on whom Vinod had to depend occasionally for information.

But the enormous fees he charged them would help Vinod to take on cases where he would hardly make any money, where the defendants were honest and decent person, victims of the circumstances or framed.

Vinod's friend Kulvir was his partner and right hand man. While Vinod would attend to the legal matter, Kulvir was an expert detective. As a Sikh, he was tall, well built and a fearless person. Then most Sikhs are brave and daring unlike Gujaratis, although Gujaratis are now becoming militants and patriotic under the leadership of the most gifted politician Shri Narendra Modi, the Chote Sardar, who carries the mantle of Sardar Patel, the torch bearer of the freedom struggle, the Quit India Movement, alongside Mahatma Gandhi and Subash Chandra Bose.

Vinod and Kulvir were not only well respected but feared as well. No one would like to take them on, faced them in a courtroom.

Avni and children had spent many months at Vinod's luxurious home on the Juhu beach, whenever Anu was posted to a tiny place where he could not take his family. That is until Anu was able to buy his small flat in Juhu, not too far from Vinod's flat and with his considerable help.

The friendship between these two families was like the unshakable bond that existed between Lord Krishna and the shepherd Sudama, one a prince and the other a pauper.

Vinod was already a multimillionaire with a lifestyle and a friend circle that included most well-known, super rich and influential people of Bombay. But his fame, lifestyle or friend circle never came between them, their friendship.

Anu was a couple of years elder than Vinod. He was a kind of an elder brother, a calming, restraining influence on Vinod. Both Vinod and Vimi would do any thing, help in any way. So how come Anu and Avni forgot them in their hour of need?

On the next day which was Sunday, Anu went to hospital, just to use the public telephone, as he was suspicious that his home phone may be tapped. He did not want to involve his friend Naimesh by using his home phone.

Anu had Vinod's unlisted private number that only a handful of his privileged friends were allowed to use. It was also under Vimi's maiden name, so that no one could connect it with Vinod.

Being Sunday, Vinod was, as usual in bed but Vimi answered the phone. On hearing Anu was on the line, it did not take long for Vinod to come to the phone. They talked for an hour. Vinod wanted to know every detail, every minute incident. In the end Vinod promised to be in Songadh on Tuesday but he requested Anu to keep his visit secret, not to tall a soul, otherwise it would not only be a wasted journey for him but it may also endanger the lives of Anu and his family. Both Anu and Avni knew how Vinod work. So they took his advice very seriously indeed.

As soon as Anu put the phone down, Vinod was on the line, talking to his partner Kulvir, asking him to find out all he can about DR. K.P. Sadashive. Kulvir was an expert investigator with the underworld connection and friends in the police, playing golf with judges and Police Inspectors. Nothing could be safe from his prying eyes, not even a birth mark in the most inappropriate part of the body! In fact Kulvir was a real life Paul Drake, a fictional detective, Perry Mason's right-hand man.

Anu was at the station on Tuesday to receive Vinod. As soon as Vinod disembarked, they drove to Shive Sadan, Anu's troubled abode. Knowing Vinod, Anu had prepared the spare bedroom for him.

On seeing Avni, Vinod gave her a big hug and said, "Bhabhi, (sister in law) what has happened? Look at you! You look as if you have just recovered from a long illness."

Vinod was right. In just over two months, Avni had lost over a stone in weight. As she was normally tall, slim and underweight, this loss of weight, worries and sleepless nights did not help her a bit. Avni looked some ten years older than normal which worried and upset Vinod who was very fond of her indeed.

"Bhabhi, you know very well that solving such cases is my profession, my speciality, just as Anu looks after his patients and makes them physically well. Why did you wait for so long before contacting me? Oh Bhabhi ……….. You know Anu is my elder brother and you, children are all I have got, my only family."

Vinod could not continue. He was chocked with emotion. He could hardly contain his tears. Vinod was a big, strong and well built person who would hardly flinch an eye lid when notorious criminals were hanged. But he had a soft spot; he was a pushover when it came to Anu and his family.

Vinod had lost his parents in a car accident when he was in the college. He had no brothers or sisters. In fact he was the only child. When this tragedy happened in the life of Vinod, he was all alone, confused and even lost the will, the desire to live.

Anu was his friend and room partner who looked after him, nurtured him and helped him not only to overcome this tragedy but came out strong and full of self-belief. Anu used to take Vinod to his home during college holidays, helping him financially. In fact they were inseparable during their college days.

Vinod, in return never forgot this help, this kindness shown by Anu and his family in his hour of need. For him, Anu was his elder brother and he would willingly give his life for Anu and his family.

Vinod had no children, so Prem and Priya were like his and his wife Vimi's children, his elder brother's children. For Vinod and Vimi these children, Anu and Avni were all the family they had, they needed.

Avni could not contain her tears, the tears she had held back for so long, so as not to upset Anu but today she could not remain strong, contain her pain, anguish and tears. She cried like a baby. They were not only tears of relief but that of joy as well. She knew Vinod will bring their nightmare to an end in no time at all. Vinod's sheer personality normally gives so much relief, confidence and self-belief to every one who knows him well.

Vinod and Avni were glad that Anu and children were not in the lounge, to see them cry, shed tears, even if they may be tears of joy and relief. Vinod soon settled down and went to work. He opened his specially made lather case full of accessories that included a range of equipment including various firearms.

As Anu had a Second World War Beretta revolver with six chambers, he was naturally interested in Vinod's collection. Vinod reciprocated his interest and showed Anu his favourite firearms.

Picking up one tiny handgun, Vinod said, "This is Japanese M14 handgun. It weighs only one pound when fully loaded. It is easy to use and even easier to conceal, being so tiny. It has an effective range of 200 feet and fires bullets rapidly. It is also very effective in a close range or hand to hand fight."

Vinod picked another firearm and said, "This is Smith and Smith PPK 75 revolver, used by the British Secret Service Agents. It does not fire bullets as rapidly as Japanese M14 but it is more powerful with a range of up to 4oo feet. It takes 45 calibre bullets widely available throughout the world. So it is the favourite weapon of most secret service personals throughout the Western world.

The latest handgun was the American US111 which weighed just twelve ounces and takes 30 calibre tiny but powerful bullets which explode on impact. It may be illegal to use this type of firearms in some countries, as it is meant to kill rather than wound. But it was most effective when it is a matter of life and death, as it kills rather than wounds a person. It is still on a secret list and very difficult to get hold of. Kulvir had one and Vinod was waiting for his. Only Kulvir can get these guns as he had connections at the highest level.

Beside guns, bullets and silencers, Vinod had powerful binoculars, including night vision ones, magnifying glasses, cameras of various size and shape, listening devices, finger print kit, gloves and various types of disguises.

Although Anu knew that Vinod was not a conventional, stereotype lawyer, he did not know that Vinod was so deeply involved on the detective, detection side of his practise.

Once he had settled down, Vinod locked the door with his own lock and key, covered the door knob and the floor just outside the door with a practically invisible layer of powder or dust and asked every one not to go any where near that room.

His next step was to inspect the ground where there was fire. He collected some soil sample and ashes in small plastic bags and sealed them. He took some photographs of the animal footprints clearly visible in the muddy soil. All the time he was careful that no one was watching, observing them, especially from the balcony and the rooftop of the "Casa Blanca", the only building overlooking Anu's bungalow.

Vinod even wore an overall, with a wheel barrow full of soil, pots and gardening equipment, so that if any one watching, would presume they were digging, planting and doing a normal garden work.

Anu and Vinod also removed all the dry grass, the undergrowth, dead wood, thus reducing the risk of fire.

The mobile phones we use today were not invented then but Vinod had a cordless phone that used radio waves to transmit, mostly used by the police and the army. It was the most vital equipment, as phone calls made from this device could not be traced.

Vinod rang Chief Inspector Mr Agarval who was in charge of half a dozen police stations in and around Songadh. Vinod knew Mr Nari Agarval when he was an Inspector in Bombay. Vinod had helped him in solving a couple of difficult cases, putting behind bars some of the most notorious criminals in Bombay's famous underworld which resulted in Nari being promoted to the post of Chief Inspector.

It was in Vinod's nature to let other people take credit for the cases he had solved. That was why he was so popular with his fellow barristers, judges and especially with the police.

Vinod would treat every one, even the most unimportant person, such as a peon or a cleaner with respect. The tragedy in his life had made him strong, determined but also just and a humble human being. No wonder he had so much love, feelings and respect for Anu and his family.

They met Agarval in a small restaurant, outside the town, rarely visited by any one from the town but patronized by passing motorists and tradesmen. So three unfamiliar faces would hardly attract any attention in such a place.

Vinod introduced Anu to Mr Agarval. Both asked Anu to keep a low profile and to make sure that Anu was not seen in the company of either Vinod or Nari in public and not connected with the police in any way.

Although most of the police officers working for Mr Agarval were loyal and trustworthy, it was not beyond realm of imagination, realism to find a couple of low ranked officers to be corrupt, dishonest, in the pocket, in the pay of the crooks, smugglers and the underworld. That is the norm throughout the world, even in Western countries where police officers are so well trained and well rewarded financially.

It seems both Vinod and Nari knew exactly what they were up against, who was the enemy and why Anu was being targeted and harassed so mercilessly. They were pitching their talent, strength and expertise against a ruthless gang who would not hesitate to murder any one who may be a threat to their organization.

By now Anu was familiar with Mr Agarval to call him Nari who was a very efficient and caring Parsi gentleman. Nari also insisted that one of his most trusted and armed CID officer should accompany Anu and his family 24 hours a day, until the case was over, culprits apprehended, put behind bars.

Next day Vinod came out very late from his bedroom which he had converted into an office and a lab.

At around mid-day he went to the rooftop to observe Casa Blanca, the White House which he was sure was behind these incidents to drive Anu out of Shive Sadan. But why? The answer was obvious to Vinod and Nari. They only needed proof; apprehend the culprit red handed in order to put them behind bars. Even a tiny mistake, a lose word or action will alert the enemy who will disperse and melt away like a bar of ice in the desert midday heat.

Vinod observed the surrounding area which was barren and desolate, with thorny bushes, shrubs and small trees covering the landscape. There were no buildings within a mile except Casa Blanca bungalow. Vinod noted the big room which was practically made of glass except the roof. He noted the direction of the sun, the wind and tried to penetrate the rooftop room which was heavily covered with thick curtains and plastic blinds, as if to stop any one from looking into the room.

Vinod did all these observations from behind a big water tank that gave him a perfect cover, to observe without being observed, seen by any one from White House. He took numerous photographs of the buildings from every angle and the garden from different angle and height.

It took Vinod some two hours to complete the observation and take photographs. Then he borrowed Anu's car and went to meet Agarval. He came back late at night.

Next morning Vinod left early in the morning and did not return until late in the afternoon. He had borrowed some equipment from Nari, including a heavy double tent that would keep out not only cold but also light. He pitched it on the roof garden, behind a huge water tank, not visible from the opposite bungalow Casa Blanca.

Nari joined them at around 7pm and they all had a delicious dinner that Avni, the master chef had cooked with delight, appreciation and love. With Vinod around, Avni was a changed person, all her worries, fear and apprehension confined to a dustbin. She was once again a happy and contended person, her normal self.

Observing photographs through a powerful magnifying glass, Vinod explained to Anu what he had discovered, why he was targeted and how close Anu came to being murdered. They were dealing with a ruthless Bombay mafia. Dr. Sadashive was one of the main culprits. Kulvir had prepared a thick file, with some one hundred pages, giving a detailed profile of his life and career. Vinod also promised Anu that they will solve the case within the next twenty four hours.

Nari and Vinod were going to keep watch all night. Kulvir had passed on some information to Nari that suggested that tonight may be an important night, a busy night.

The tent was well equipped with a paraffin heater to keep them warm. Hot drinks, tea, coffee and occasional peg of brandy or whisky were good enough to keep them warm and active.

The tent was so well insulated that no light was visible from outside, not even a tiny spark. There was nothing unusual, out of ordinary for any one to suspect.

It was a cold and dark night and without moon and stars in the sky, it was pitched dark, almost sinister, wicked and villainous atmosphere to be out and about in this wilderness.

The ghost like silence was occasionally broken by the flight of owls and the howling of wolves and other nocturnal wild animals that abound in the foothills, forest and open savannah grassland of the Pavagadh Mountain Range.

This part of Gujarat Rajasthan border was lightly inhabited, some what barren and unproductive with patches of green fertile land near the slopes and the source of underground water where green, fertile fields and orchards give this barren land a helping hand to produce the much needed food, vegetables and fruits for local consumption.

Vinod was lost in his world, smoking cigarette one after another and drinking strong, black coffee to keep awake and alert in this dark, cold and unfriendly atmosphere. Vinod rarely smoke except when he was in a tight corner, an unenviable situation, on the verge of striking a blow for the justice.

At around midnight, Vinod saw some activities in the White House. There were a couple of people on the rooftop, in the glass room which was always covered with thick curtains and plastic blinds.

Suddenly a powerful red and green light signals were exchanged, perhaps with a big van parked some distance away. These exchange of signals lasted no more than a minute. Both Agarval and Vinod knew what it exactly meant. It was an all clear signal to the parked vehicles. It was an invitation for the van to proceed to the bungalow. These exchanges at least brightened the gloomy atmosphere.

At around 1am, a dark van entered Casa Blanca, the White House and went straight in the big garage. The garage doors were shut. The garage was so well insulated that not even a beam of light was visible from a distance.

The bungalow suddenly became a hive of activities but with minimum light and disturbance, even though the surrounding area was as desolate as a Sahara desert, with the exception of Shive Sadan.

At this time Vinod and Nari left on foot, to join the police team that was waiting some distance away from these two bungalows. They advised Anu to go to sleep and not to switch any light until early in the morning, leaving a CID officer on the premises.

As Anu was dog tired, he fell a sleep as soon as he hit the pillow, a welcome relief for a hard working doctor. At around 5am, there was a commotion, police sirens and mobile search lights that turned the early morning darkness, the haze into midday sun brightness all over Casa Blanca, every inch of the place bathing in the floodlight.

Within half an hour, Dr. Sadashive and his servant were led away in handcuffs to a waiting police van, with armed CID officers, brought especially for this operation all the way from Punjab who were patrolling the area in case Sadashive may have alerted his associates. These well connected and super rich Mafia had their own private army with modern weapons capable of engaging a small police force. They even had leading politicians, judges and high ranking police officers in their pay. Secrecy was the best weapon, the only weapon.

Soon the culprits were handed over to the Special Force, to be taken to a safe house until the trial. These special force officers were the best trained, well paid and patriotic officers beyond approach, even for Bombay Mafia. They had never lost a prisoner once in their custody. No one would dare to interfere, not even a Minister or a High Court Judge once a prisoner is in their hands, in their custody.

Vinod came in at 7am, tired but elated. Anu did not have to wait long before Vinod narrated the event, the early morning drama to Anu and Avni, over a cup of coffee and Avni's special breakfast.

After leaving at around 2am, Vinod and Nari joined their fellow officers who were stationed a few miles down the road, away from the White House. A couple of Jeeps and an army coach were parked, hidden in the dense shrubs with some fifty, well armed officers on duty, wearing bullet-proof vest and carrying pepper spray, batons and teargas.

It was not difficult to stop the van once it was well away from the bungalow. Police laid down a trap, a two feet wide metal strip fully covered with nails, hidden under the layer of soft sand. It is known in the trade as bed of nails for the crooks.

The van soon came to an abrupt halt, as all four wheels were punctured. When the two men came out to find out what had happened, they were quickly apprehended, taken into custody without a protest. The surprise was utter and complete. They were taken back, seeing so many armed police. They soon realised it was a well laid trap. They were only hired hands, paid peanuts to drive the van.

The van had a load of forty pure gold bars, each weighing a kilo, some 500 bottles of high quality alcohol, brewed illegally by the hill tribesmen and some narcotic drugs such as cocaine and marijuana which would fetch a fortune if smuggled to America or Europe. The illicit cargo was worth a small fortune, a king's ransom even in those days.

Within fifteen minutes of the capture of the van, some twenty well armed police officers battered their way into the Casa Blanca, shooting dead the dangerous dog Ravan while the two occupants were still in their beds, thinking that the night's work was done, gone as planned, without a hitch. The whole operation took just ten minutes, as it was so well planned and brilliantly executed.

The police recovered another one hundred gold bars and a thousand bottles of Scotch whisky they use to blend with the local brew.

Turning to Anu and Avni, Vinod said, "Now let us look at your problems. Shive Sadan was unoccupied for a long time. Dr. Sadashive tried to buy this bungalow but unfortunately it was not for sale. So he spread the rumour that it is haunted.

His plan worked well, that is until Anu came to live here. If some one occupies Shive Sadan, then sooner or later they will realize that White House is not what it looks, a residence of a well respected professor, a scientist engaged in a life saving research.

He could not afford any one to notice the night time activities, to watch the vans come and go. It was too dangerous, too risky for the whole operation. It was of utmost importance to drive you out of this place. But Sadashive knew that you are a medical doctor who would not be deterred by rumours alone. He was well prepared for such an eventuality. First he would try all the tricks of the trade and if that fails, a fatal car accident, kidnapping and even murder would be the ultimate solution. Anu, you were so close to the final solution. Thank God that you remembered me in the nick of time.

As soon as you rang me, I asked my partner Kulvir to prepare a complete file on the so called Dr. Sadashive. It was clear from the information he gathered that we were dealing with a very dangerous organization. One may even be killed just for asking questions about people like Sadashive. But Kulvir is an expert with influence in the right circle. Even some one like Dr. Sadashive will respect him, would not make an enemy of him. Dr. Sadashive is a science graduate of Bombay University and has studied in Spain. In fact he is half Spanish but his PhD is a bogus degree so freely available in Spain from South American Universities. But it does give him respect, especially as he speaks fluent Spanish. He was one of the top brains behind this criminal organization.

As these are very dangerous people, we have tried to keep Anu out of this sting operation. In fact only a couple of CID officers know Anu. They will keep an eye on you all until the trial is over and culprits are behind bars.

Now let me explain how your curtains were set on fire. The sunlight falling on his rooftop room were expertly passed through a powerful magnifying glass and targeted on your cotton curtains which would catch fire within minutes. You were lucky that Bahadursinh, your brave and loyal Ghurkha was on the premises who extinguished the fire before it could spread. Otherwise it would have burned the whole bungalow down. Then you wisely replaced the curtains with fireproof blinds.

The fire in your garden was a simple, elementary process. Do you remember Anu, we used to have phosphorous in our science laboratory when we were at the Uni? Phosphorous has to be kept submerged in kerosene. If exposed to air, it catches fire. It is also found in human bones. That is why we sometimes see a fire in our crematoriums where human bodies are openly burnt with ashes and bones so often not collected and submerged in water.

Dr. Sadashive used a well trained circus cat to deliver, to deposit a piece of this material in your garden. He used a bag that kerosene would melt in ten minutes. Once the bag is ruptured and kerosene spread all over the grass, it is easy to start a fire. Again you were lucky that it was a rainy night and the grass was wet.

Perhaps it was just a warning, not a serious attempt to harm you physically. You were also wise to cut down the undergrowth and remove the dead grass but that would have ultimately infuriated Sadashive and forced him to take more drastic action, employ a professional killer to solve the problem. He could have tempered with your car breaks, arranged an accident with an oncoming lorry. We deal with such cases every day. Human life is cheap, worth no more than five thousand rupees?"

"What about the frightening telephone calls and the lights?" Anu wanted to know every thing.

"It is also simple. Both the telephone lines and the electricity wires were taped from the supply polls. Underground wires were taken to the White House from where he can switch off the lights and make telephone calls. That is why they were not registered at the exchange. Sadashive was clever. He would only switch it off or make calls lasting less than a minute. So there is absolutely no chance of discovering it unless you know where to look. After all such breakdowns are common throughout India. Who would listen to you even if you complain?

The work was done expertly, perhaps by the engineers employed by these utility organizations. After all money can buy every thing and every favour in our beloved Bharat. It sounds so simple but to a layman, it is frightening. The terrifying laughter was taped from the film, the horror movie "Dracula and the Virgin Vicki."

Every one was relieved that Vinod had solved the problem but Vinod was apprehensive about the safety of Anu and his family. But with the reassurances from Chief Inspector Agarval, the family will be safe, especially as none of them will be called upon to give evidence in the court, as all were caught red-handed and many will sing to escape a life imprisonment.

This was only a tip of the iceberg. The main headquarter was in Bombay. This operation, code named "Where Eagle Dare" was meticulously planned by Mr Agarval and the Commander of the Bombay CID Avtarsingh Kapoor. Only a handful of officers were aware of this sting.

Raids on suspected warehouses and homes of some prominent members of the society netted millions of rupees' worth of illicit goods, not forgetting the capture of some top criminals and prominent members who were leading a double life. This success means another promotion for Mr. Agarval, again thanks to Vinod and Kulvir and perhaps a posting back to Bombay where Vinod would like him to be.

Vinod stayed a couple of more days before returning to Bombay, as it was a long time before Anu and Vinod, two brothers were able to spend some quality time together.

When Vinod left, boarded the train, he was not alone. He had persuaded Anu to let Avni and children to accompany him to Bombay for a couple of weeks. How could Anu refuse? He knew when Avni returns, she will have regained her weight, her health and her joyful nature. Vinod and Vimi would look after them even better than Anu could. Moreover it was impossible for Anu to say no to Vinod. This was the price he extracted, his fees to help Anu and Avni in their hour of need.

Nari and a couple of his most trusted officers were there to bid farewell, with a CID officer to accompany them on the train, all the way to Bombay.

****

PREET NA JANA REET
(Love Knows No Constraint)

Sheth (successful businessman) Biharilal's Mercedes, an expensive, latest model with all mod cons, especially all important air condition but now, in modern technical jargon, a climate control, which is a must in this hot, humid, dirty and polluted air of the modern metropolitan city of Mumbai; (Bombay) was gliding smoothly, effortlessly and silently on Marine Drive, one of the most famous roads in Asia, the abode of the rich, the famous, superstars and of course the Bombay Mafia who finances the film industry and reap the harvest. Any one, who is some one, has a flat, an office or a house in this prestigious part of Mumbai.

The control of Mumbai Mafia on Indian film industry is so complete that they virtually choose actors and actresses for most films. Then again, why shouldn't they if they are to invest in what is basically a very risky business, as just one is a box office success out of every ten films produced? No one would invest their hard earned money, a product of sweat and labour. It has to be easy come, easy go, a black market riches that has to be converted into a legal tender. This is what used to happen in America during prohibition era when Italian mafia had a virtual monopoly on drink and drug trade.

The road, hugging the beautiful sea front, is always clogged with vehicles, the famous black and yellow cabs, a trademark of this bustling city, rickshaws, motorbikes and occasional horse drawn carriages, mostly for advertising stunts but occasionally for filming, as this snail speed mode of transport has long been confined to a museum.

Mercifully the days of human Rickshawalas, a tiny human being weighing no more than seven or eight stone, pulling a vehicle overloaded with bulging bodies are well and truly over. It was cruel, inhuman and degrading. Western tourists never felt at ease using such a mode of transport which many felt were akin to a slave labour, degrading trade, human beings turned into animals and worse.

Mumbai, affectionately known as the Bollywood of the East, is in a way an ultimate dream city, a mega money making machine, where film stars are idealized and worshiped as Gods, industrialists, financial experts, entrepreneurs, politicians and legal eagles, all have their luxurious properties, abodes, love nests, mostly vast, spacious villas and detached bungalows with huge gardens and army of servants, where all these dignitaries get together, congregate to give this city a unique place, exclusivity and romantic notion that makes Mumbai a paradise in the world, at least for the super rich, powerful, healthy, young, ambitious and romantic at heart. This is one of the cities that is alive twenty four hours a day, seven days a week. There is no difference between the day and night activities except at night the traffic is a bit lighter.

Then again one man's food is another man's poison. Many would not set a foot in this smoggy, polluted, dirty city where some half a million people sleep on footpaths, slums are a common sight and where one has to watch one's back constantly, where pickpocket thieves, tricksters and swindlers thrive and flourish on the innocent and the newly arrived villagers.

This is a city where money can buy anything and everything, from a ten year old boy or a girl for sex to a government minister and a Supreme Court judge to get the judgement one may want, where the right or the wrong do not come into question? Money and influence speak, can buy police and judiciary. In short money is God, the root of success.

Ambition is a wonderful quality. No wonder millions flood into the city not only from the surrounding villages but as far a field as Delhi, Kolkata (Calcutta) and Chennai (Madras) every year, although most return to their villages disappointed and some in poor health, broken men, infected with AIDS, the scourge of major cities in India where prostitution is a major profession, employing millions, serving the needs of the people who reside on their own, leaving their families in villages.

Mumbai is not a city for the faint-hearted, weak, timid or an idealist. One has to be streetwise, clever, determined and not afraid to break laws, bribe a few in high places and grab an opportunity when it falls in one's lap, which in any case is as rare an occurrence as a snowfall in Sidney or a flash flood in the Saharan desert.

No wonder only a handful of the new arrivals make to the top, the vast majority ended up earning a subsistence living at best. But for those who make to the top, sky is the limit, the world is at their feet and Mumbai is a heaven on earth. There is no other city on earth with the glamour, allure and fascination that Bombay inevitable provide.

In the front seat of his Mercedes saloon car, a luxury on wheels, besides the driver, a Ghurkha by the name of Sharpa Taj Bahadursinh, Sheth Biharilal was sitting silently, lost in his own world, as if he was in a trance.

What could worry such a powerful man who had not only climbed the ladder and reached the summit but was blessed with a wonderful family, that included his beautiful, gorgeous, cuddly, sexy, young looking wife, one of his pride possession and the envy of his friend circle, three wonderful, gifted children and every luxury one could imagine, one may desire, money can buy.

Sheth's friend circle included every one who is some one, from police inspectors, judges, barristers, politicians, actors and actresses to super rich and the influential people and personalities, in the field of medicine, law, commerce and education.

Wife Minal Devi was seated at the back, with her daughter Nita, looking at the ever changing scenery, from the comfort of her temporary abode. The car was so specious, comfortable and well equipped that one can spend hours without getting uncomfortable, bored or tired. There was a drink cabinet with a dispenser, a small fridge, a music system and a TV to entertain the passengers if one get stuck in the city traffic, get tired of observing the human crowd or the scenery they pass by most days. Then there was telephone to keep in touch with what is going on in the business world.

Minal Devi was touching her early fifties but the skilful makeup covering her occasional grey hairs, plastic surgery in all the right places, healthy diet and regular visit to a fully equipped gym, albeit in the basement of her own bungalow, under the watchful eyes of her fitness Guru for the rich and famous, the one and only Lena Fernandez, kept her not only young looking and healthy, not a day over thirty but sexually as attractive as a sixteen year old well developed beauty.

No wonder Nita and Minal were mistaken as sisters, rather than mother and daughter. She was Mumbai's answer to Joan Collins who at seventy is still a sex goddess and object of desire for most men in Hollywood.

On reaching the Nariman Point, the car stopped at a designated point, parking the car at the especially reserved slot for the Sheth. The three went to five star Youvraj hotel roof gardens, some thirty storeys high. This was one of the most luxurious places to have a lunch, an afternoon tea or an evening dinner.

It was an exclusive place reserved for members only, with a waiting list of twenty years and the entrance fee that would buy a small new car. Obviously it was not for the shallow pockets or faint hearts. A party of four could easily spend a month's salary just to have a simple dinner.

Then in Mumbai exclusivity is expensive and money is no object for the privileged few. This is the place where one can meet one's heroes and heroines, may they be cricket superstars like Sachin Tendulkar, Rahul Dravid or mega film stars like Amitabh and Ashwaria Rai.

But as every one is some one, no one bothers or asks the autographs of these guests. This may be the only place where there was anonymity in being famous and rich? That was the beauty of this place, this wonderland, the Garden of Eden, Ravan's Ashok Vadika where Devi Sita was kept prisoner by the demon Ravan.

The view from the top was breathtaking, out of this world. The distant islands with the famous Elephant caves dating back two thousand years were clearly visible today, as the sky was clear and the smog, the scourge of the city was less in evidence than usual, due to a couple of hour's heavy rainfall the previous night that has cleansed the air and made it fresh and breathable.

The spacious roof garden with a sitting capacity for some two hundred guests, over two elevated floors, tables being artistically hidden amongst the curtain, barrier of luxurious tropical plants and shrubs with hidden lights that would turn the night into a day and the midday sun into a hazy evening, with extractor fans and state of the art air-conditioning, was a luxury one can only believe when experienced. It was a garden, an art gallery, a flower shop and a luxury club, all rolled into one.

Minal Devi was more interested in watching people, especially what other ladies, her fellow diners were wearing, the latest fashion in saris, blouses and of course gold and diamond jewelleries. Perhaps this is the standard behaviour of the super rich and the famous, those who have nothing better to do except look glamorous and mix with the people from the so called high society, with empty, shallow talk, the latest gossips and exchanging invitations or perhaps finding a life partner for their spoilt rotten off springs, even a partner for the night if one may not be in the right company or have arrived alone?

In comparison to her mum who was immaculately dressed for the occasion, with milky, skin colour matching sari, so expertly adhered that it almost became part of her slim and tiny body, showing all the contours so much appreciated by men folk, sleeveless tiny blouse that gave ample scope to flaunt her surgically enlarged, perfect shaped bosom, visible from every angle, expertly uplifted by new moon shaped wonder bra or may be a G string for most conservative ladies, making it difficult for the male guests to look else where, was mixing with ease with all the people present at this early hour of the evening. Then Minal Devi had attended the finest school for etiquette and personally knew most of the guests who were present at this prestigious venue.

In contrast, Nita was quiet, shy; retreating and she distantly felt at unease in the company of spoilt, rich kids or rather young people who were similarly inclined in taste and attitude as their parents.

Nita was attired in an elegant but simple Punjabi suit in ocean green colour, her favourite, with matching accessories and a minimum of makeup, more to please her mother than to impress any one else. She was definitely not interested in spoilt rich kids that her background would attract in dozens, like bees to sweet nectar bearing flowers like roses and honeysuckle.

Then Nita was not in need of expensive cloths or a makeup to make her look artificially beautiful. The God had given her all the vital statistics to look beautiful, gorgeous but perhaps not glamorous without the aid of artificial means and definitely not even half as sexy looking as her mother who had made her business, her life ambition to look glamorous and extremely sexy looking.

She would never flaunt her some what under developed breast or expose her underwear, her under garments to get attention. Despite her tender age and natural beauty, most men would opt for her mother Minal Devi, at least as far as sexual attraction or choosing a bed partner was the main purpose but definitely not as a wife, as Minal Devi would be too expensive to keep, to maintain in the manner she was accustomed to and too sexy to keep away male predators without the wealth, power and the influence of the Sheth whom no one would dare to cross or to be in his bad book.

It would be like inviting a social exclusion at best and death sentence at worse to cross swords with the Sheth, especially when his wife Minal Devi was concerned who he guarded like a lion looking after his pride or a Sheikh guarding his harem. In a way Sheth had a dual personality. He was like Dr Jekyll and Mr Hyde, a tower of strength to his friends and admirers and a scourge to his enemies and all those who cross his path, give him a reason to be in his bad book. So it was not surprising that even after flouting all her sexual assets at her male admirers, she never had an affair which was the norm in this high society where even wife swapping was common in many circles. But it was absolutely out of question for Minal Devi. But no one had any inclination, knowledge whether Sheth had any affairs or was he averse to young and beautiful virgins that people in his position would have at regular interval?

At five and a half feet in height, Nita was a tall girl according to Indian standard and with smooth skin, milky complexion and long, silky, light brown hair reaching her knees, expertly allowed to float in the gentle breeze, unusual to have such a hair style in so hot a climate, she was indeed pleasing to look at, an alternate attraction and perhaps for some a real beauty, in true Indian tradition, without much Western influence.

Nita's pleasant, mixing nature and modesty added to her charm. But her modesty and lack of bulge in all the right places made her stand out in the crowd, in a different sort of way where most young men were interested in girls wearing scanty dresses, mini skirts, see through garments revealing with ease their upper thighs and even the tips of their boobs, their bulging vital parts, a gift from a plastic surgeon rather than a God, Nita has never visited, that is plastic surgeon and not God? Her attribute, both physical and mental were a gift from God, who in a way was certainly kind to Nita in more ways than one.

The three sat down in an isolated corner table that would normally be allocated to a larger group, with jasmine, night queen (ratrani) and gardenia plant screen that would not only give privacy but would also perfume the atmosphere. With such dense vegetation, the air circulation was most vital; to disperse the carbon dioxide that plants normally breathe out at night.

The silence was deafening. Nita knew that her father was upset with her as she had not yet said yes to her proposed engagement to Naimesh, a match made by the Sheth while playing golf with his partner Nandkumar, a Supreme Court judge with immense influence.

This could be a match made in heaven, the ultimate marriage of convenience that would unite not only two prominent families, one super rich, the other influential beyond imagination but it will open all sorts of doors and opportunities for both the families.

Nita had met Naimesh several times, on social occasion. He was tall, handsome and a good catch except like most spoilt kids, he was rotten to the core. Drinking, womanising and ruining the lives of many innocent girls; was a routine, a pastime for him. With father a Supreme Court judge and money no hindrance, who would dare to cross his path, lodge complain against him!

Meera, one of Nita's college friends was his latest victim. She fell for his charm, when she was introduced, innocently by none other than Nita herself. He made her pregnant with a promise of marriage and then abandoned her in her hour of need, forcing her to get rid of the unwanted baby.

While having a back street abortion, she nearly died. Only Nita's help and money saved her but her health was more or less ruined for ever. She was not the only victim of Naimesh either. Nita had told her mother what type of boy Naimesh was but as usual she would not take the sides of her children against her husband, even though Nita had pleaded with her, told her she would have nothing do to with Naimesh, a monster, a wolf in human clothing.

At last the Sheth looked at Nita and said in a soft and emotionally charged voice, "Beti, (daughter) what have you decided about getting engage to Naimesh. You will soon be completing your Masters degree in economics, business studies and information technology. It is time for you to get married and settle down before it is too late."

Sheth knew that Nita was not keen on Naimesh and the reasons behind her disapproval, her dislike of Naimesh. Sheth was a clever, well informed person. Nothing would escape his attention but he was more interested in acquiring wealth, power and influence than to worry about the happiness of his children. Perhaps children were no more than chattels, the means to extend his dynasty, his power and his wealth, even though he had enough wealth to last several life times, many a generation.

Although Nita loved her parents, she was not willing to sacrifice her life, her arman and ambition, her future happiness, just to be a daddy's girl, to please her parents who were selfish beyond imagination.

"Daddy, please give me some more time to think. Did Mummy tell you what Naimesh did to my friend Meera? She is not alone but only a tip of the iceberg. How could some one like him make me happy? Could I ever trust him? Daddy, this is a question of my life, my happiness and your happiness as well, that is if you love me?"

Nita could hardly hide her emotion, her anger, her anguish or her tears. But she was too clever to offend, openly defy her father. She knew it was a mind game, a game of Chess where a cool head wins the battle and she was determined to win this battle at any cost. All she has to do is to create a false sense of security and play a part of an obedient daughter.

Although Sheth was a hard man, he did love Nita. She was the best, most clever and sensible child out of his three brooding. So he was willing to give Nita as much time as she may need, as long as the final answer was affirmative, just like in the old Soviet Union where one can buy a car in any colour as long as it was in the shade of red!

"Beti, I know and share your misgivings. But as you know most young men in his position are no different, especially as so many young and beautiful girls throw themselves at his feet. More over the Judge Sahib has promised me that Naimesh is ready and willing to settle down, mend his ways and be a good husband. He knows what price he and his family would have to pay if he ever double crosses me, mistreats my favourite child. So I am confident he would not dare to take you for granted. Moreover beti, you are strong and clever enough to handle him, tame him and make him a good, caring husband. After all he is good looking, educated, clever young man who could marry any young and beautiful girl. You should be proud that he has chosen you." Sheth tried to reassure Nita as best as he could but without much conviction.

Nita looked at her mum for support but as usual there was a blank expression on her face. Her attitude was seeing no evil, speak no evil and certainly hear no evil. That way one could not offend, antagonize or alienate any one. That is how she had acquired such a vast and influential friend circle, more admired than Sheth himself.

Although Minal Devi looked glamorous and sexy like a dumb blonde, with long, curly, smooth, silky hair and a dress sense which made her curves all that much bigger, better and sexier with ease and minimum cover up, she was a clever person indeed, with charm and ever present delicate smile, etiquette of a princess to go with her immensely pleasant personality.

In fact the Sheth owed most of his success on the social front to his wife, who was always in demand at parties and glamorous occasions. So it would be inconceivable to imagine that she could not be aware of her daughter's dilemma, her fear and her misgivings in accepting Naimesh as her life partner. Moreover Nita had a heart to heart talk with her mother. That in itself was a rarity? But Minal Devi did not believe in rocking the boat, going against the wishes of her husband, not even for her charming and favourite daughter.

Perhaps Minal Devi was unwilling or unable to go against her husband's wishes who had always controlled her through his wealth and overbearing personality. This had made her obedient and some what timid when confronted by her husband; otherwise which mother would not feel for her daughter and care for her happiness?

Sheth was not too displeased with Nita's answer. He knew that as long as she had not said no, he could wear her down and ultimately no one could say no to him, not even his own children. So the atmosphere was warm and pleasant, if not jubilant. The three were soon joined by other friends and they all had a wonderful time, a pleasant evening drinking and eating, until they returned to their bungalow by midnight, a bit tipsy and giggly after consuming Champaign, wine and appetizer.

While in bed, Nita could not go to sleep. Although she gave the impression that she was undecided, still trying to make up her mind, she was determined not to go any where near Naimesh. How could she be the bride of a person who had ruined the life of her best friend? Who knows how many girls he may have even raped or what sexual disease he may be carrying? He was a monster through and through. She would rather starve; live in a hut, become a nun than share her life with Naimesh. Her heart was in turmoil; at the thought of how little her parents loved her or cared for her happiness. They had every thing one may remotely desire. They needed nothing nor any one to fulfil their dream. In fact they should concentrate on their children and their happiness, play with their grandchildren and enjoy the advancing age, consider retiring, handing over their empire to their children to run. But they were like a spoilt child, possessive and overbearing.

Like her dad, Nita was cool, calm and almost tranquil but never a push over. She would give her enemies a false sense of security. No one would ever be able to judge or guess what was going through her active and imaginative mind, how would Nita react when confronted with a problem.

What she was not, unlike her father and mother, ruthless, extremely ambitious, assertive and pushy or a social climber which was her mother's speciality and to be fair, Minal Devi was extremely successful as a hostess and a glamorous wife.

Then she had all the assets, curves, contours and she knew how to use them or rather flaunt them, albeit discreetly and selectively that would not attract the wrath of her husband who always kept a discreet eye on her, on her activities and the company she kept.

Nita had a brother Rohit who was seven years older than her and a baby sister Rita who was just twenty and in her second year at the college. Rohit was obliged to marry the daughter of a well known politician, in power at the time but in wilderness today, as usual under pressure from his father.

After two stormy years of marriage, they separated and Rohit was now living in London, married to a lovely Irish girl called Siobhan, a simple, uncomplicated but stunningly beautiful girl with two lovely baby daughters, Shamma and Shyama.

Rohit would occasionally come to Mumbai to meet the family but he only had a superficial relation with his father and mother, although he was very close to his two sisters and in return Nita and Rita loved him and his family, especially two little girls who were so sweet, so cuddly, almost like little angles.

Sheth tried discreetly to persuade Rohit to move back to Mumbai with his family, his beautiful and charming wife and two gorgeous daughters who would enhance his fame and reputation and perhaps make Rohit take interest in his business empire. Bur Rohit was determined to remain in London, as far away from his father's influence as possible, although he was aware that one day he may have to take over his father's empire, if not for his sake, then in the interest of his two lovely sisters. But not just yet, not until Sheth was amicable and willing to give up his control and retire from the business. In a way this was a game of Chess father and son were playing with each other with checkmate the obvious result.

Both Nita and Rita were well liked in the college. Despite their father's billions, both looked like and behaved like ordinary college girls, travelling by bus although both had their own upmarket sports cars, wearing jeans, trainers and white tops, a standard dress for the collegians.

They ate with their friends, in the college canteen, in the café just round the corner or Chinese, Indian and pizza take away. They went to local cinema, to watch Hollywood and Indian movies. In short they were no different than the rest of the crowd.

Their friends were all from middle class families whose parents had made great sacrifice in order to send their children to college and give them a head start in life.

In India, nothing is free or subsided. One has to pay for education, health care and there were no social security benefits that people enjoy in the West that consume half the national budget. One gets what one pays, what you sow, so you reap in our beloved Bharat. There was indeed no such thing as free lunch.

It was difficult for any one to imagine that these two sisters were the daughters of a billionaire father, Sheth Biharilal and their mother was a famous socialite and a beauty queen Minal Devi.

When Rita came to knew that their father was trying to force her elder sister Nita to marry the vagabond Naimesh, she was horrified. It was not difficult for Nita to get her support, for the two sisters to unite in an effort to teach their parents a lesson they would never forget. It seemed they had learnt nothing from the break-up of their brother's marriage.

They lost Rohit, their only brother, due to intransient and relentless demand their parents made on him. He even scarified his love and married a girl who was only after their wealth and wanted an easy, lazy life with partying all night and sleeping all day.

They soon broke-up and the turmoil sent Rohit as far away from Mumbai and their parents as he possibly could. Surely Nita could not follow in their brother's footstep and sacrifice her life just to please her daddy.

Rita knew that her sister Nita was in love with Nihit, although she was not willing to admit it. Nihit was her fellow student, in her class, taking his masters degree in IT, both in software and hardware. Nihit was a kind, caring person, from a middleclass family with a physic that would make Nita and Nihit a perfect couple. They were ideally suited with similar interest and caring nature. Moreover Nihit was not after her money.

Both knew they like each other but neither was able to make the first move, first approach, fearing of upsetting the other and perhaps losing their friendship, although they were spending so much time together, studying, gossiping and going out and simply enjoying each other's company.

Simple things in life gave them most pleasure, may it be going to a cinema, taking a walk on the soft sand of the Juhu beach or spending an evening in a park, watching the sun setting in the distant horizon.

Whenever they went out in a group that consisted of beside two sisters, Meera, a very close friend of Nita and a stunningly beautiful and sincere girl who fell for the charm and cunningness of Naimesh, was betrayed by him and ruined her life, Rakhi, Rakesh and Nihit, a group of four girls and two boys. Rakesh and Rakhi were brothers and sisters.

It was a close-knit group of varying age and interest. Rita, at 20, was the youngest and Nihit, at 24 was few months older than Nita. In many ways it was an unusual group, a Laurel and Hardy combination, as rarely two sisters or brother and a sister go out together in such a way, not in Mumbai any way.

It did not take long for Rita and Meera to bring Nita and Nihit together, to admit that they were madly in love with each other. Once the ice was broken, when each knew that the other was deeply in love, it was impossible to separate them, although they had to take great care that their love remained hidden, their feelings in check and no one should suspect any thing, especially the Sheth, not until both Nita and Nihit were out of the country.

Although Nihit was over the moon, at the thought of marrying his dream girl, he was worried what Sheth may do to his family if he comes to know that Nita had eloped with him. While Nita was a princess, Nihit was a pauper, an odd couple as far as social standing and wealth. Call it Krishna and Sudama type friendship, one a prince, the other a pauper.

No one would like to be in the bad book of Sheth Biharilal. But Nita and Rita promised that not only his name will never come out but Rita would handle Sheth and protect his family if the truth ever came out before the dust had settled and Sheth wanted to take revenge, punish Nihit's family. Surely Sheth and Minal Devi could not risk losing Rita, their third child, the only one living with them by then.

Rita, like her elder sister was a clever, charming girl who was expert at manipulating their parents and getting her way, by any means, fair or foul by hooks or crooks. She had a mature head on her young shoulders. Her motto was not to get angry but to get even. Even Sheth knew how strong willed Rita was. He would never take Rita for granted or put such a pressure on her as he would on Rohit and Nita.

Rita, although the youngest child was much more streetwise than Nita, knew the strength and weaknesses of her parents, their social standing and how to use her charm and immense talent, wealth and power. She also loved her elder sister so much that she would do any thing to protect her, protect her happiness and let Nita fulfil her heart's desire and her dream come true. After all that is what sisters do for each other. Nita was indeed lucky to have a sister like Rita who could manipulate her parents to her advantage.

Under pressure from her father, Nita agreed to let Sheth announce her engagement to Naimesh and his demand to set a date for the marriage, four weeks after their exam was over. But her one condition was that she would have only superfluous contact with Naimesh and that also in presence of her mother Minal Devi, until her exam was over.

Although Naimesh was not pleased with this arrangement, he could not make demands or cross swords with Sheth Biharilal. He knew how powerful his in-laws were and what he was getting in return, a charming, beautiful bride, an angel in disguise with immense wealth. He would never have to do a day's work from the day he gets married.

Naimesh was marrying into the richest and one of the most powerful families in the city. In fact he was prepared to accept any condition as long as he could get Nita and her billions.

The time soon passed, exams were over and the date was approaching, the marriage was just round the corner. It was time to put their planning, their plot and their wishes into practice. It was time to act. Nita received her passport a week before her marriage. They were flying to the beautiful island of Mauritius for their honeymoon, two days after their marriage. This is the new, recent, popular trend, replacing Switzerland that was once the honeymoon capital for newly married Indian couples. Any one who had visited Mauritius would realize why this tiny island, just off the coast of South Africa, in the clear blue waters of the romantic Indian Ocean, with a majority Hindu population has become such a favourite tourist destination, where even Hindi films are shot, bypassing Goa, once the heart and soul of bustling Bollywood.

Sheth had hired for two days, at an enormous expense, the entire seven star Shalimar hotel with 200 luxurious rooms, mainly for their overseas guests. The luxuriously decorated reception, conference hall that would accommodate well over two thousand guests was the best available in the city.

The marriage ceremony was at three in the afternoon, an auspicious time given by the family priest, albeit with a little persuasion and a bundle of Rs100 notes from Rita, to give Nita and Nihit enough time to be London bound before the marriage ceremony start. The reception, an all night partying would start at 10pm. It was the social event of the year and those who were invited were the lucky ones, as any one who was some one, would be there. It was an occasion to meet old friends that one might have not seen for decades, make new friends and even broker business deals and find life partners for their sons and daughters if not for themselves?

Sheth had a luxurious five bedroom apartment on the Juhu beach they used occasionally but was mainly reserved for the guests who come from Europe and America, many of them business partners, relatives and fellow industrialists.

It was not difficult for Nita to persuade her parents to let her stay at this flat and to travel to the marriage venue, the Conference Hall, as it was just half an hour away by car from the flat but more conveniently, it was very near to the airport, for a quick get away if their plan develop a hitch.

So Nita, Rita and Minal Devi, along with their friends Meera, Rakhi and Kalpna moved in a couple of days in advance. The charade, pretence and the act was so convincing that Minal Devi suspected nothing. In fact she was relieved that Nita had at last realized that this was after all a good match and Naimesh would be a good husband to her.

On the long awaited and anticipated and perhaps a fateful day, the bridal procession left the Juhu flat in two luxurious cars, one a Rolls Royce and the other a Bentley, an hour before scheduled time. In one car was Minal Devi with her hair stylist and make-up artist and Seth's two sisters while in the other one, more spacious and luxurious one was occupied by the bride, covered from toe to head with an expensive sari and in true Hindu tradition, the face was hidden underneath the veil of sweet smelling and traditional flowers of Jasmine and gardenia.

In fact Nita's place was taken up by Meera. As they were both similarly built and surrounded by none other than Rita and their close friends, no one would suspect any thing until the veil was lifted and the face seen by the close family members. By then it would be too late and the mission accomplished. They would be officially declared husband and wife, legally married in the eyes of the law and in front of all these important guests. The newspapers and some enemies of the Sheth will have a field day, a rare occasion to crucify the Sheth who had many enemies as well as influential friends.

If any thing Meera was not only a wonderful person but was much more beautiful, articulate and desirable bride than Nita, except that she was not the daughter of a billionaire like Sheth Biharilal. In a way, Naimesh would be fulfilling his promise to Meera when he made her pregnant. So perhaps, all's well that ends well, the end justified the means.

By 4pm, the marriage ceremony was in full swing, the vows were exchanged and it was nearly time to lift the veil, to introduce the bride and the bridegroom to each other and then to the gathered guests, the dignitaries, the VIPs and high ranking officials like Chief Minister, the Police Superintendent and the Attorney General Satpal Singh who was a close friend of the family.

By this time Nita and Nihit were on their way to London. The Air India flight, having left Mumbai airport at 10am, was already nearing London. Even the Sheth with his billions and all the influence was in no position to do any thing, alter the course of the event which was unfolding in front of him like a bad dream, a nightmare which was of his own making. As per our Indian saying, those who are beyond law, beyond justice, untouchable by all, will succumb; be punished by their own children.

Rohit was waiting patiently at the Heathrow airport to welcome his sister. He only knew that Nita was running away from an arranged marriage that would ruin her life. So he was more than happy to help her sister to avoid the pain, the heartache and the upheaval that he had to endure just to please his parents, not to go against their wishes. He would not wish any of his sisters to go through this nightmare that he had to endure.

Enough was enough. He had vowed not to let his parents ruin the lives of his two beautiful sisters whom he loved to bits, would do any thing to help them settle down in London where even his domineering father would have no influence to impose his will on his children.

As far as Sheth and Minal Devi were concerned, when the charade was ultimately unmasked, Nita had flown to London, on her own to be with her brother and his family. Nita and Rita were determined not to tell their parents the truth, that Nita would soon be marrying Nihit, perhaps at least not until they become grand parents for the third time which may soften the blow!

One act of kindness the Sheth had performed was to give his son a generous allowance, had bought him a five bedroom, upmarket and very expensive house in the most prestigious street in London, on the Bishop Avenue where even a one bedroom flat may cost half a million pound. This generosity was perhaps to atone, to make amends for his mistake of forcing him to marry a girl who was clearly a gold digger and never a right life partner for his son.

The marriage between Sheth Biharilal and Minal Devi was an arranged marriage, a marriage of convenience in more ways than one but in a way both got exactly what they wanted from the marriage. However today's young persons want more out of marriage than to please their parents and be a perfect couple outwardly, a marriage of sham and pretence.

They want love, partnership, equality and above all happiness. Every thing else come second, especially the approval of the society and the fringe benefits that were valued so much in the past but not any more. So in a way, our society has made progress and for once moved in the right direction. Let us hope that this progress will continue and like in the West, all our children will be allowed to choose their partners, as long as they realise that their chosen partner come from our culture, religion, background and tradition but not necessarily from the same caste, creed and social standing.

****

RADHIKA

It was Good Friday, beginning of the long weekend. After having a lunch and a bit of rest, Shyam was ready to leave for Pune, with his beautiful and charming wife Sharmila whom he would lovingly and teasingly call Sharmili, the shy one; although she was far from being shy.

Having been born, brought up and educated in Los Angles in California, she was forward, full of self confidence, self belief and a very capable girl indeed, at least according to Indian standard, Indian tradition. She could ride a horse and drive any vehicle with ease and confidence. This was a great asset on such a lonely place, especially if Shyam was away visiting Mumbai on business. Both Shyam and Sharmila are urbane, articulate and capable of managing the estate with dignity and efficiency.

Shyam was living some seventy miles from the city of Pune, on a remote farm, just off the main road, a well built cement motorway linking the city of Pune, the second biggest city in the state of Maharastra, with an important provincial town of Kolhapur, right at the southern most state boundary with Karnataka.

It was not a traditional Indian farm that normally grows cereals like wheat, rice, maize and millet or cash crops like cotton and sugarcane. This was in fact a vineyard, some one thousand acres of prime site situated in one of the most beautiful areas in the state of Maharastra, with the ever popular hill station of Mahabaleshwar lurking on the horizon.

The surrounding area is littered with mountain peaks, lakes, valleys and plateau that provide the region with a variety of climate, with varying degree of rainfall, coolness and extreme heat, at least in summer months. So in a way it was a perfect site for a vineyard, to grow premium wine grapes, the variety that include popular and fast growing Airen White with large, tightly packed bunches and alcohol content of between 12% to16%, Bobal Black, rich in colour, the grapes that produces Rose Wine, ever popular Cabernet Sauvignon that grows in most part of the wine growing areas in the world and last but not least Chardonnay and Riesling, popular American variety, widely grown in California that produces high quality wine that would grace any dinning table.

All these varieties were modified to suit the local climate and the soil structure but more or less retaining their original taste, flavour and alcohol content of between 8% and 15% producing from cheap table wine to more expensive and exclusive classic wine, allowed to mature in traditional wooden caskets.

The abundant sunshine, relatively cool temperature for six months in a year and rainfall in short, sharp burst with hot, dry ripening and picking season, made this place a prime site for establishing a vineyard with different variety of grapevines.

India is not famous for her wine production. But that is not due to lack of suitable climatic condition. It is more due to Indian custom and tradition where alcoholic drinks are not that common or fashionable.

This is about to change, with fast developing tourist trade and India becoming a hub, a centre for White Collar jobs, mainly in call centres but also a magnet for train, air and other transport networks in the West, printing and issuing timetables, air tickets, books and even monthly magazines being printed and distributed from India.

The multinationals are attracted by India's ability to supply a cheap but highly qualified and disciplined workforce, easy and cheap to build and maintain, to establish work places, as land is cheap and easily available. With each State fighting hard to attract inward investment, acquisition of land and planning permission is easily available, cutting through red tape like a hot knife going through butter with ease.

With influx of Westerners and rising living standard of these Indian workers, wine, beer and spirit are fast becoming popular. The Kingfisher, Taj and Cobra beer are already household names in the West, as they go hand in hand with popular Indian cuisine of starter Chicken Meat Samosa, Chicken Tikka, Tandori Chicken Wings, Muskaki and the main dishes of Chicken Tikka Masala, Chicken Jalfrezi, Chicken Bhuna, Madras and Vindaloo curry, Khima (minced) meat curry and various dry Karai meat dishes that has almost replaced traditional English cuisine with the exception of ever popular Fish and Chips.

But as the seas are fast running out of Cod, Plaice and other such edible and popular fish, it is only a question of time before the fish will disappear from Western menu or become too expensive for ordinary consumers to buy, to enjoy their popular take away, that is unless these varieties of fishes are farmed on land or enclosed seas, in line with the salmon fish so successfully farmed in Scotland and Norway.

It is only a question of time before Kohinoor, Himalaya and Maharani Wines would go the same way as Indian beer and become household names, first in India and then in the West. Shyam would like to be there, be a pioneer when Indian drinking habits change.

Shyam was the youngest and the brightest son of Sheth (businessman) Ramdayal who owned a chain of supermarkets in the major cities of Maharastra, Rajasthan and Gujarat. Sheth sent Shyam, his most astute son to America for further studies, when Shyam completed his studies in Mumbai and obtained his Masters Degree in Business Studies. The Sheth would like his favourite son to obtain MBA and PhD in Financial Management and Information Technology from a prestigious American University.

While doing his MBA, Shyam met Sharmila who was also doing her MBA but in Estate Management and International Finance, as her family had a vineyard in the most beautiful part of the Californian Valley, famous for wine production of the highest quality.

So after finishing his MBA, Shyam joined Sharmila to work on the Ranvir Vineyard, instead of doing his PhD, as his father would have preferred. But Sheth was not averse to Shyam working on a vineyard, as he knew how hard working and ambitious he was. Shyam would never take any decision on the spur of the moment, without thinking it over, weighing pros and cons of every situation that he may find himself in. He had mature head on young shoulders.

Moreover Sharmila sounded like a sensible girl who would be a good addition to the family, especially as they were equal in status. It would be an advantage to have in-laws in the West, in case he has to spread out, to expand, to diversify their financial empire overseas, as the Indian market was getting saturated on the supermarket front, with the arrival of the famous British and American names, the multinationals with immense purchasing power and financial muscle that no one in India could compete against. It seems multinationals are as powerful and influential as any super power?

After spending two years on the vineyard, starting at the bottom but soon reaching the top, albeit with hard work and the help and enormous encouragement from Sharmila and her family, Shyam was ready to return home, to his family and start his own business.

He had learnt practically every thing about wine making. He made himself familiar with the Californian climate, the soil structure, the grapes which were widely cultivated and how the wine was made, allowed to mature and how to blend various types, various varieties of wine to produce a marketable quality and quantity.

Sharmila was expert at the marketing, financial management and the administration. So between them they knew every thing, had expert knowledge to make such a project success. All they needed was financial assistance and logical support that was readily made available from both the families.

The grapes that grew widely in California were Chardonnay, Pinot, Riesling, Sylvaner, Muscat and many more. The areas of California that produced really good wine has winter rainfall and long, dry summer, that include Chablis, Loire, Nahe and Puget Sound, Willamette Valley, a few among many places where grapes are grown widely and some of the best American vineyards are situated.

Shyam and Sharmila got married before they came to India. There marriage was a grand occasion, as money was no obstacle. Sharmila was the only daughter, with three big brothers who all wanted to give her a wedding that will be the talk of the town, with VIPs from both the country on the guest list. The civil ceremony was first held in Los Angles, followed by a traditional Indian, Hindu marriage ceremony in Mumbai and a grand party in Los Angles and Mumbai.

It was not difficult for Shyam to persuade his father that he would like to buy a vineyard and go into growing grapes, making wine that his father in law would market in America; that is until they establish themselves and have an outlet in Europe, their ultimate goal.

Shyam purchased a depleted, neglected vineyard of some five hundred acres. Within two years they added another five hundred acres, purchasing the neighbouring farms, as money was no object and the value of land rarely goes down. So the purchase of land is a wise investment, provided it if financed from one's own resources and not on a huge bank loan, that will burden the business with interest payment.

It is now five years since they first bought the vineyard. It was hard work, replacing old and unproductive vines, planting the new variety that would not only grow well in this climate but most importantly are disease resistance, would not succumb to pests and flies. The first two years were spent on developing the vineyard. They also built new buildings to press grapes, using the latest but easy to maintain machinery that would press the grapes and squeeze every drop of the juice, the job once done by human feet?

A huge cellar underneath, the basement was built with rows and rows of shelving ten feet high, that could easily hold one million bottles and special platforms for huge wooden kegs and casks to store the wine until maturity. Wherever possible local building material, mainly stones and wood were used in preference to iron and steel. They also built three very comfortable bungalows and some accommodation for the key workers they would like to stay on the farm.

At first the wine was exported to California in wooden kegs and bottled there on Ranvir vineyard but now there is a facility to bottle the wine on the site, especially for the local market and widely sold in his father's chain of supermarkets, as well as in special wine and beer shops that were beginning to occupy the prime sights on the high streets. Holiday hotspots of Goa and Kerala were the main Indian outlet for the local wine.

In five years, with an investment of one hundred million rupees, an enormous sum in rupees but not in terms of US dollar or pound sterling, Shyam and Sharmila had transformed the neglected vineyard into a modern one, with hard work and all the help they could get from both the families.

Indeed Sharmila's eldest brother Ranvir, who is an expert at managing such a vineyard, spent a year on the site to organize and help his only sister to settle down and build a future in India, a country some ten thousand miles away from his home in California but the country they regard as their motherland and loved being there. It seems an Indian, like Irish, never forgets his roots no matter where he moves. They always maintain their culture, religion and tradition as well as remain in touch with their motherland Bharat.

It was a huge undertaking, removing dead and unproductive vines, planting new ones, staking and positioning, employing a labour force, building three bungalows to recreate their Californian home comfort, obtaining all the planning permission, buying machinery, vehicles and to put into place the production and financial management.

But Ranvir, Shyam, Sharmila and John, their operational manager on Ranvir Vineyard were more than a match for such a task. Not only they managed to built and make the vineyard operational but also bought a further five hundred acres of prime land for future expansion. They have already utilized half the land to plant high quality grapes, capable of producing Champaign or Cava type high quality wine.

The rest of the land they put on one side, not yet sure how to utilize it. Perhaps to develop it as a fruit orchard or to build holiday homes to rent out to a Western Package Holiday Company, as this type of farm holidays, wine tasting themed holidays were fast becoming popular. It would be prudent to have an income from two or even three different source in case vines are affected by disease, their only source of income.

Now, after five years, the Maharani Vineyard was not only up and running but was producing more than a million bottles and some ten thousand kegs, mostly for export to America and Europe. All the workforce, including an American Operational Manager, were in place, leaving Shyam and Sharmila a bit of spare time to spend in Pune and in California, on the Ranvir vineyard, with her family who loved her to bits, being the only daughter and the apple of her dad's eyes! Like all parents, they were eager to welcome a grandchild in the family and after five years of marriage, they all thought it was the right time, especially as the vineyard was running, managed well and above all, making a handsome profit.

While Shyam was patiently waiting for Sharmila who always take such a long time to dress up, especially when she has to wear sari, as being an American girl, she was naturally not used to wearing such a traditional Indian dress, preferring to wear jeans and blouse, a loose top, except on rare occasions when attending special events, such as engagement and marriage parties or religious celebrations like Holi, Diwali and Navratri festivals.

So Shyam had to be calm and patient if he wanted Sharmila to look at her best, wear a Sari and look gorgeous, beautiful and sexy, especially when visiting his folks in Pune who loved Sharmila more than even Shyam? She was such a lovely, sensible and polite girl without an ounce of pride, ego or aloofness that is mostly associated with rich young girls, a daughter of a millionaire father.

Her favourite colour was pink with a sleeveless matching blouse in a bit darker shade, with matching accessories. If any thing, Sharmila was clever at make up and knew how to maximise her charm, her beauty and limited curves, as she was a tall, slim girl with very little bulge or excess fat. After all she was a hard working girl with little time to cook and indulge in leisure that enables girls to put on weight. But Shyam preferred her the way she was, as they made a perfect couple in every sense, especially in physical likeness. After all beauty is in beholder's eyes!

Her main assets are not her sexiness but her charming nature, slim figure, her ethics of hard work and above all her all round knowledge of vineyard and the wine industry. It would be impossible for Shyam to run, to manage such a vast vineyard without her active input, her knowledge and her tireless hard work. So often it is the tendency among the children of the rich, not to grow up, remain Peter Pan well into their adulthood. So Shyam and Sharmila are certainly different in that way. If any thing, they are mature for their age and upbringing.

After all she was born on such a farm, lived all her life among vines, grapes, wine kegs and wine bottles but surprisingly she was a teetotaller but not averse to a glass of low alcohol wine on special occasion. She knew more about the vineyard and the business than Shyam, at least to begin with. They were such a perfect couple in every sense.

Shyam was about to go up, to the bedroom to find out how long he would have to wait, at what stage of dressing Sharmila was when some one knocked on the door.

It was a frantic knock with a muffle sound. Wondering who could be knocking at his door at this time, on a long weekend holiday, Shyam grudgingly opened the door and saw a young man slumped in the porch, in the door entrance.

His clothes were covered in mud and blood and his face was swollen with cuts and bruises. It was obvious that he was involved in some sort of fight or attacked by thugs.

On hearing the commotion, Sharmila came down, quickly putting her dressing gown on, as she was not yet fully dressed, only half way to wearing the sari. She helped Shyam to bring the young man inside, spread a bed sheet on the wooden floor before gently lowering the young man on it.

Although his face and clothes were covered with blood, he was not badly hurt. His wounds were superficial. He collapsed out of sheer exhaustion than any things else, as he must have walked or even run a long distance, from the main road to reach the safety of this bungalow.

Both Shyam and Sharmila were expert at administering first aid, as living in such a remote place far removed from the medical facilities, first aid course is a must, as essential as driving a car or a tractor.

They knew that their plan to go to Pune, to visit Shyam's family will have to put on hold, at least for the time being. So while Sharmila went up to change and ring the family and give them the bad news, Shyam loosened the young man's clothes, administered the first aid, cleaning his wounds with disinfection and sticking on the plaster where needed.

As soon as he applied the ice pack on the swelling, the young man regained full consciousness, woke up, brought him out of slumber, back to real world.

Within half an hour and with the aid of a hot mug of chocolate, the young man was more or less normal, swelling having subsided considerably.

His name was Abhishek but all his friends and colleagues call him Abhi, a short and sweet name. He was a journalist based in Mumbai. He was travelling from Pune to Kolhapur to cover a Parliamentary by-election. The seat became vacant when a prominent, high flying, young and very rich Cabinet Minister was killed in a road accident.

The seat was now contested by his young and beautiful widow who was a famous film star before she got married to a young and a dashing politician, a future party leader and a Prime Minister in waiting.

His death was surrounded with rumours, mystery and intrigue. As his young widow Mansi was contesting the safe seat, against an experienced politician, a compromise candidate put forward by the combined opposition, no wonder there was such a high pitch campaign and unlimited media interest.

The result was by no means a foregone conclusion, as rumours, character assassination and saucy stories, allegation were floating freely in the polluted political atmosphere. No one can say Indian elections are dull. There are as many twists and turns in such an election as there are in a three hour long Indian movie. Both sides can present a persuasive case, put down the opponent with ease.

Abhi was forced to take a side road, no more than a dirt track when he was stuck in the traffic and heard on the radio that a serious road accident would keep the motorway closed for several hours, advising motorists to seek alternate route.

Abhi became a victim of a classic ambush that fooled even a seasoned traveller like Abhi, as the fallen tree blocking the track looked so real, with dense forest on both the side, full of trees of various size and shape. It was but natural for a small tree to fall on such a track.

When Abhi came out to see how to negotiate the obstacle, he was set upon by two men. The third one took his four by four wheel drive Toyota Frontera, a much sought after vehicle.

Abhi tried to fight back but the two men who attacked him ran away as soon as the vehicle was secured, climbing in the vehicle and drove off at high speed. They were after his vehicle and not particularly interested in attacking or beating him up.

Abhi was not badly hurt, just winded and shocked at the unexpected attack and the loss of his much valued vehicle. He knew that he is unlikely to see the vehicle again. But as it was a company car and fully insured, Abhi would soon get a new one, a replacement car. This was one of the hazards of being a mobile journalist, some one on the move all the time. But fortunately such incidents were not that common.

Yet Shyam was worried that such a serious incident, an attack, a car jacking happened near his vineyard but on a public road, as Sharmila so often drives alone but mostly within the vineyard border.

Once the formalities of reporting to the police in Pune and ringing the head office in Mumbai were over, they sat down to enjoy the rest of the evening, the beginning of the long weekend.

Although Shyam and Sharmila were a bit disappointed at the cancellation of their long awaited weekend plan, to go to Pune, see a couple of Indian movies and spend the time with his family, they soon came to terms with the situation.

According to Indian custom, tradition and practice, a guest is always welcomed and looked after, even an uninvited guest. In Abhi's case, he was forced to seek help, seek a shelter in the most unusual circumstances, robbed and attacked.

Shyam and Sharmila were more than willing to oblige, to give him shelter and help him in any way they can. As Abhi was a journalist, he had the knowledge, education and the understanding, the grasp on any subject. He could converse with any one, on any subject, without hesitation or feeling inadequate in any way, although he had to admit that to talk about wine and vineyard with this couple was like talking about honeymoon night when some one may not even had a proper date?

As Abhi was amicable, easy going with friendly disposition, it was not long before they were cracking jokes and enjoying each other's company. Now that the programme was cancelled, all three set down over a bottle of Maharani Wine and started conversation that was to last half the night.

Abhi was intrigued as he had never visited a vineyard, at least not in Bharat, although he had bought a bottle of wine, Kohinoor, Himalaya and Maharani Wines now and then from a supermarket near his office in Mumbai.

Abhi has been a journalist for a few years, working for a prestigious English language daily. But his aim in life was to write novels, plays and TV scripts and become famous like Selman Rushdie, Arundhati Roy and Sir V. S. Naipaul, one of his favourite authors, since he first read his novel "A House of Mr Biswas and A Bend in the River."

Abhi's first novel, based on his own life experience and titled **"Radhika"** was nearly complete. Only the ending was missing, as he was hoping, perhaps against all hopes to have a happy ending. Abhi had also submitted the manuscript to a couple of publishers who were willing to take him on, publish his first novel.

So Abhi was eager to plan his second novel, as publishers prefer authors who have written more than one novel, as so many authors, even promising ones find writing the hard work and perhaps not that glamorous or financially that rewarding. Only one in ten thousand manuscripts submitted gets published and only one in hundred published authors go on to be famous and make a reasonably good living out of writing. In a way it is a graveyard for many aspiring writers.

One has to be a very good novelist, a dedicated writer and a bit of luck and influence to succeed in this very competitive field. Abhi had all these qualities and more. The super successful novel, **Gone with the wind** is a classic example. Although the novel was such a success, a real hit, even as a movie, it was a one off, the author never wrote another novel.

When Abhi learnt that Sharmila was an American girl, born and brought up in California and her family owned a vineyard in Pine Valley, not too far away from the city of San Diego, Abhi was intrigued and determined to learn every thing, every minute detail he could about her life on a vineyard, how they met, fell in love and managed to established such a vineyard in Bharat, not famous for wine making or drinking. This was a God sent opportunity for Abhi to lay the foundation, to chart the plot for his second novel.

After a couple of hours' talking and consuming a couple of bottles of wine with usual biting of crisps, cheese and olives, a much healthier choice than Bombay Mix, the three of them felt as if they had known each other for a long time. That is the beauty of being an Indian. They are such a friendly people, easy to get along and even easier to make friends.

Shyam and Sharmila told Abhi every detail of their personal life. The materials they provided were enough not for one but two novels and with a bit of imagination and stretching, it could also be adapted for a beautiful mini TV serial, if not as a plot for an Indian movie.

Then again Indian movies, although they mostly have happy endings, tragedy is a must in between while Shyam and Sharmila had a happy going all the way, a more of a Hollywood plot than an Indian movie material. But with a bit of imagination, sky is the limit. As a writer, Abhi was not short of fertile imagination either.

It was his speciality to provide a sting in the tale, for his readers to expect the unexpected. Perhaps Abhi has mastered this technique by reading too many detective novels where a murderer turns out to be a person, a character least expected.

By the time Shyam and Sharmila finished telling their life story, their family background; it was time for a dinner a la carte.

Abhi, being a bachelor and used to living away from his family, was a good cook indeed. So he joined Sharmila in the kitchen while Shyam set the table and opened yet another bottle of wine.

Although Shyam was not a regular drinker, almost a teetotaller, he can drink, enjoy a bottle of wine or a pint of lager in a right company, a pleasant atmosphere and a good environment. Today he had all three. Some how he found Abhi's company stimulating, interesting and energizing. Then it is a normal feeling in the company of most journalists who are trained to communicate with any one, on any subject, with ease and charm. But on this occasion, Abhi was sincere, polite and indeed grateful to the couple for their hospitality.

Abhi managed to gain their trust, with Sharmila treating him as a brother, as he was very similar in look and nature to her youngest brother Mihir whom she loved to bits and missed him most when she moved to Pune, a million miles away from their Ranch in Pine Valley, one of the most beautiful and desirable part of the Californian State.

The area is like a rolling hills and shallow valleys, up to 200 meters below sea level, with Granite Mountain, Agua Caliente Springs (Hot water springs) and Slaton Sea, Imperial Valley, all within travelling distance for a long weekend break. Even Palm Spring with 8000 feet high Toro Peak is not too far away from Pine Valley.

Indian tradition and Hindu religion are unique when it comes to brother sister relationship, unselfish love between a boy and a girl, even though they may not be blood relatives!

The tradition of Rakhi, a special day in Hindu calendar, when a sister invites her brothers for a dinner and ties a sacred thread on the right wrist of her brother is unique in cementing this special relationship. In return a brother promises to protect and look after her till death do part them.

After the ceremony, she is allowed to make one wish that a brother has to fulfil to the best of his ability. It goes without saying that the only wish she makes is to be able to tie the Rakhi every year and the health and happiness of her brothers who are and always will be her Nights in Shining Armour. This is indeed one of the better traditions that bind Hindu community, the family together in good as well as bad times.

So often a girl who has no blood brother, adopts a son of a relation, a friend, even a complete stranger but it makes no difference. On the contrary such brother sister relations are more intense and longer lasting than between blood brothers and sisters.

Unfortunately such traditions, although still widely practiced, are being taken over, the true meaning, love and obligations are being eroded under the weight of commercialism. This is in common with most liberal and progressive religions like Christianity, Buddhism and Hinduism.

Within half an hour Abhi and Sharmila managed to put on the dining table garlic bread, hot Mexican pizza, Tikka Paneer Shashlik and two bowls of salad, a green salad with red and white cabbage, Chinese lettuce, reddish, celery and similar seasonal vegetables, with olive oil and seasonings and an onion and tomato salad with a dressing of mint and lemon juice, a special American recipe, the tradition Sharmila had brought with her to India.

This was a typical American dinner, with pizza coming out of a deep freezer, quick and easy to prepare, every one's favourite, adult and children, a good and healthy dinner indeed with big portions of salad. In America it is followed by ice cream, full of fatty milk but here it was followed by fresh fruits in season.

When dinner was over, the task of washing up fell on the shoulder of Shyam and Abhi. It was so refreshing for Abhi that they had brought back American tradition of sharing all household tasks that are normally left to women in our ultra conservative Bharat.

Now it was time, the turn of Abhi to tell his life story, his life experience, especially the one that enabled him to write a book, a novel that may soon get published.

Although Abhi was not that keen to open up his old wounds, he could not deny Shyam, especially Sharmila to learn more about him, his background and his family.

So it was now Shyam and Sharmila's turn to listen to Abhi, his life experiences. He started with a warning, "I am ready to tell you every thing, even my sweet bitter experiences but let me warn you that my story will not be that interesting to listen to, nor the ending is as happy as yours. But I am not going to hide the truth, my pain beneath the clock of privacy or my pain and discomfort. I feel I owe you the truth. That is why I am struggling to find a happy ending to my book.

You will also have to get used to my style, the way I tell a story, as I am a writer, a journalist, so I have the journalistic freedom to add, to spice my story in a way that makes it interesting. You can discard the unbelievable part, the one that may not match my personality! But we all know that so often the truth is more unbelievable, more intricate than fiction. I must also admit that I feel at ease, at home even on a bed of nail when it comes to journalism, story telling!

In many ways it is a strange story and certain parts may sound unreal, unbelievable, but what I am going to tell you is more or less the truth and I would not change any of my life experiences for any thing else. After the hospitality you have bestowed upon me, I feel I am already part of your family, with Sharmila like my sister, as we are only two brothers. A family is never complete without a girl, a sister and today I feel I have found the missing link. After all can a sister come in better shape and size than Sharmila?

According to Hindu tradition, Hindu belief, our fate and fortunes are written on the sixth day after birth when the Goddess of love, faith and fortune visit the new born child. I don't know who wrote my fortunes but I am sure it can't be this Goddess who has denied me a happy ending?

As you already know, my father Ramanujan was a well known, well respected Professor of English at a prestigious University College in the upmarket Fort area of Mumbai. He has written several educational books that are still used by the University in their English course for a Masters degree in English language and literature.

So it was natural that English was and still is my favourite subject, having read so many books by famous English writers, past and present that include Shakespeare, Sir Arthur Conan Doyle, Bronte sisters Charlotte, Emily and Anne, Ernest Hemmingway, James Hilton, Oscar Wilde, Nevil Shute and my favourite writer Ernest Hemmingway, the most prolific writer of modern times with such classic novels like A Farewell to Arms, For Whom the Bell Tolls and Old Man and the Sea. He had a deceptively simple writing style that many tried to copy but without success. He was awarded a thoroughly deserved Noble

Prize of Literature in 1954. I also feel that my style is simple, lacking bombastic description or over blowing the character actors in my book. But it certainly is very pleasant to read.

I also enjoy reading popular writings of Earl Stanley Gardner, Agatha Christie and West Indian writer of Indian origin Sir V. S. Naipaul whose novels A House of Mr. Biswas, The Mimic Man and A Bend in the River, Finding the Centre, a few among many of my favourite authors and books, novels and plays.

We had our own library, as my father was a keen collector of books. He had and we still have well over 5000 books that include all the above named titles, as well as The Hound of Baskerville, The Sign of Four, The Valley of Fear and the scientific romance The Lost World by Sir A. C. Doyle. Most were bought by my father but many were given to him as gifts by his successful and grateful students who knew about his love for books. Many of them went on to become professors, journalists, politicians and diplomats who still remembers my father with respect and affection.

All these books are in hard cover, many in luxurious leather bindings that would cost a fortune to buy today. If I try to list, to tell you the names of all the books that I have read, those that are in our library, then we will be here until dawn. But I must mention three of my favourite novels which you must read; that is if you have not read them already. They are, A Town like Alice, Lost Horizon and Snows of Kilimanjaro.

When I was a student, I used to read, on average, one book a week. That is what inspired me to become a journalist and to write books, become as famous and perhaps as rich as our Indian writers like Salman Rushdie and Sir V. S. Naipaul, a few among many who have reached the top. I promise you, Shyam and sister Sharmila that one day I will be there, among the best.

I just need a bit of luck and a push from you all? Perhaps your story, your success on all fronts will inspire me to climb the podium, to conquer the dizzy height and let the world know that I have arrived." Sharmila admired, took this young man to her heart, as he was so full of confidence. Indeed he was on his way up, going to make a name for himself. His assiduity is rewarding and created a feel good factor among his readers and listeners alike.

After a pause, Abhi continued. "Now let me concentrate on the incident in my life that has changed my perspective, my priorities and my attitude towards life, towards every thing. It has certainly made me a humble, caring and considerate person, made me realise how lucky I am.

The lifestyle I enjoy is unique and no more than 2% of the people of Bharat have a similar or a better lifestyle than me. The vast majority of the people live from hand to mouth, a subsistence existence, plodding along undaunted in face of adversity. People seek comfort, joy, happiness and salvation in the make belief world of Indian movies and have such unflappable faith in their religion.

When I was at the university, reading English, I opted out for one year to obtain work experience, what you in the West call a Gap Year. With my father's reputation and the fact that so many of his students now occupy high posts in all walks of life, it was not too difficult for me to find a suitable work experience post.

Like any collegian, any first time work experience trainee, I was eager and conscious to make a good impression. I knew that it will stand me in good stead to find a top job when I finally leave the college. This was the foundation laying exercise, a good, firm and solid base on which I can build my future. We have to make our suitability more than tangible if we would like to succeed, climb the ladder and reach the podium.

My father bought me a scooter, the most powerful one in its class, as he was not eager to give me a powerful motor bike that could be dangerous on the busy roads of the city. Still we both had to convince my mother, as she was dead against me driving any two wheel vehicle.

I can not blame her, as thousands of young men and women die or get badly hurt on Mumbai roads every year. In fact it is the most common cause of death for youths aged between 18 and 25. So we did understand her concern. In the end I was able to convince her, with some input from my father, as she knew how responsible, level headed I was and still am. It was the only way to reach the trouble spot on time, before any one else. After all, exclusive news and stories are like gold dust in journalism. We have to strike the iron while it is still hot. Today's news sell papers, tomorrow's news make the paper bankrupt.

One day, I was travelling through one of the poor, neglected and depleted area of the city when my scooter slipped on an oily patch. Although I was not badly hurt, my scooter was badly damaged.

Before I could get up, a woman who may be in her early fifties; came out from a roadside building and helped me to get up and took me in her one room accommodation. The Maji (mother) whom I later came to know as Gangamaiya, mother Ganges, the holiest river in Indian mythology, made me sit down on a neat, clean mattress spread on the equally clean floor.

There was hardly any furniture in the room. The room was large, spacious and of good size but it was also the kitchen, the sitting room and the bedroom with communal bathing facilities in the corridor. It was a classic example of a poor family struggling to make the ends meet, a far cry from our own four bedroom house in a leafy suburb of Mumbai, with our own large garden. Then both my father and grandfather were professors and the house was bought a long time ago. Not many could afford to buy such a place in this day and age.

I always carry a First Aid box under the back seat of the scooter. I gave Maji the key and within five minutes Maji came back with the medicine box and a young girl Maji introduced to me as her daughter Radha, a sweet name, the name of Lord Krishna's consort, his constant companion since childhood, one of the most famous name in Indian mythology. Maji and Radha cleansed my superficial wounds with warm water and antiseptic liquid, disinfection, bandaged a couple of shallow wounds. In no time, I was as good as gold.

We sat down and talked over a cup of tea, the milk borrowed from a neighbour. In such a settlement, a communal living, people are, on most part, compassionate and kind hearted. They all came to Maji's help, took my scooter indoor, in the locked compound, as it would be dangerous to leave it outside, even for half an hour. This is the stark reality of modern day Bharat where no one used to lock their doors not so long ago. Then this is the trend, the stark reality throughout the world. No one is able to elude the embrace of the chaotic world, where dogs eat dogs, victims of the same fatal attraction. Even churches are not safe from theft and vandalism and have to lock their doors, thus depriving the people, the believers' one comfort that was easily available to them in the past.

It pains me to say that people in a city like Mumbai are crooks and most dishonest, although it would be wrong to generalize, as I have come across many thoroughly honest and decent people and Maji and Radha were the prime example. Poverty does not mean lack of culture, lack of compassion and lack of honesty, even when they find it difficult to have a one square meal a day.

This was a typical Indian family who live from one day to another, from hand to mouth and go hungry on a regular basis. Maji had lost her husband after only five years of married life, exactly when and how I could not get it out of Maji. Perhaps it was too painful a subject for Maji to discuss with a complete stranger. Perhaps I do not have the fatal charm of the Kennedy clan?

The girl Maji introduced to me as Radha was her daughter, her only child. She was eighteen, one year younger than me but hardly looked her age, with extremely slim body and weighing no more than six stone. It was the sign of poverty, extreme under nourishment where two meals a day were a luxury. So often they had to go to bed, go to sleep on a glass of water, on an empty stomach. It seems vicious and virtuous circles are more than self-fulfilling than is commonly supposed to be.

The saying that God may wake you up hungry but will never let you go to sleep hungry must have been coined by some one born with a silver spoon in his mouth, some one who never had less than three square meals a day. This reminded me of the famous sentence uttered by the French king during the French revolution, when addressing the peasants he said, "If you don't have bread, then eat cakes?" This is what ignorant aristocrats think of poverty, hunger and homelessness. This was a sharp lesson for me that I will never forget in a hurry.

As I had a nasty fall and a shock, I thought it prudent not to go home on my own, not in a rickshaw, which would give me a cheap but bumpy ride, although it will be easily available, from any part of the city.

I gave Radha some change, my home telephone number, the registration number of my scooter and asked her to phone my home and tell my mum or dad, whoever answers the phone, to come and pick me up, send a taxi at her address. But please stress that I am fine, I am not hurt, just shocked. I knew my mother. She would get a heart attack if Radha could not reassure her about my safety, that I am not hurt, not in any danger and not in need of hospital treatment.

As we were a long way away from my home, I knew that it is going to be a long wait. The taxi will take at least three hours from my home to this place, as it will have to negotiate some heavy traffic on the way. But it will be a comfortable ride, as official taxis are spacious and drivers know all the roads, the side streets and short cuts.

Radha came back after some twenty minutes, having talked to my mum who was a bit shaken on hearing that I had fallen from my scooter, an accident she knew, she predicted will happen any day. She was against me using a scooter, as we can easily afford a second-hand car, even a new one. The question was not of money but that of traffic, as some roads in the city were impossible to negotiate, especially during rush hours. That is why my father had got rid of his car and he now uses taxis and rickshaws whenever he had to go out, travel a long distance.

Radha, in her sweet, innocent and sincere voice, managed to convince my mum that I was not hurt and enjoying a cup of tea at her place. But that the scooter was damaged, not in working condition.

As it was going to be a long wait, we sat down on the mattress that was spread on the floor, used as a sofa, as a sitting place during day and as a bed at night. We started talking. Despite her looks, age and poverty, I found Maji a very intelligent person with good general knowledge.

Maji was indeed an educated woman, having studied up to inter science but had to drop out of the college when she got married at the age of nineteen, the same age as I was now.

Radha, her only child was born when she was twenty four but lost her husband soon afterward when she was relatively young. Naturally Radha did not even remember her father, so he must have passed away when she was very young, in fact an infant.

As Maji did not want to talk about her past, I had to respect her wishes and not to ask too many questions about her past, her husband or the circumstances of her loss. But she had taken an instant liking for me and the fact that I was a journalist and coming from such a distinguished family did impress her. She wanted to know all about me and my family as I wanted to know about her and Radha, whom I started calling **RADHIKA,** the little Radha, as she was so slim, tiny and innocent looking, physically under developed for her age but with a sharp and inquisitive brain. Her appearance was deceptive, would give a false impression, as she was indeed very clever, charming and highly intelligent and inquisitive person.

She had a charm, a hidden beauty and physical attraction that would be difficult to put into words, intermittently visible through her thin, worn out clothes. She was conscious of it and tried to cover them with her hands, in the absence of shawl, a lose material that Indian ladies use to cover their chest and breast when wearing such revelling cloths.

It defies logic that on one hand these ladies, especially from the upper, middle class, would like to wear such revealing, eloquent cloths, tight, skin hugging blouses that would highlight rather than hide, cover their breasts, raising heart beats, heart pressure among admirers and then they would like to hide them under a shawl to look decent! Then a woman's mind is deeper than the deepest sea. No wonder even their creator, Lord Brahma could not understand these ladies!

Maji had wrapped the shawl round my shoulders so Radhika was helpless. Whenever our eyes met, she tried to look down, look away, tried to avoid eye contact, feeling conscious that I may be watching her, her breast, her bosom visible through her torn blouse, as she was not wearing a bra, an expensive piece of cloth for her, when every rupee goes to life essentials like food and drink. Actually there was nothing much to look at, as her tiny breasts were hardly creating any bulge but her long hair, although unwashed were attractive.

I felt uncomfortable. It was not fair to put Radhika in such a compromising position. I was a strong, well built and a healthy young man indeed. I did not need the shawl. So I stood up and wrapped it round Radhika, covering her entire upper torso, making her look respectable and comfortable. This put a soothing smile on her face. It bought as much relief to me as to her.

Even Maji's face lit up, as she had noticed how uncomfortable Radhika was feeling in my company, a male company that they may not have entertained for a long time. This was also a sign of modesty, a good upbringing on my part. Maji was a shrewd, an astute judge of character who knew that I was a trustworthy, kind and caring person with impeccable character.

It was well past lunch time and as I had left early in the morning with only a cup of tea, I was feeling hungry. So I requested Maji to send Radhika to a nearby shop and made a list of items that I would like her to buy, bread, butter, a tin of Kraft cheese, Bombay Mix, some biscuits and a pint of milk and a jar of coffee. I gave her the list, along with Rs.50 note that would go a long way in those days as it was a day's earning for most of them.

Maji was reluctant to accept money but then she didn't have much to offer to me as a lunch. She soon relented. Perhaps my smiling face and easy going manner put Maji at ease. In the end she asked Radhika to accept the money and get whatever she can.

She was back in fifteen minutes, as the shop was just round the corner, where I had slipped. She had brought all the items on my list and a couple more, yet she gave me back a change of Rs.30, what a wonderful time to live in when money would go a long way.

As soon as Maji had made tea, we all set down to have a snack lunch, bread with tinned butter and cheese, a bottle of marmalade, some salty biscuits and every one's favourite Bombay mix. It seems any food would taste good in a right company.

Just a couple of hundred yards away, beside the railway track, there was a vast open ground where an open market was held three times a week. The residence of the block had three stalls, selling household goods, cloths, pots and pens and any sundry items they could get hold of. It was a subsistence, hand to mouth living, earning between Rs.100 to nothing a week. Fortunately there was a unity, solidarity between all the residents who would come to each other's aid in time of difficulty, lending each other money if they had failed to earn any thing and sharing their food. Suitability of communal living and the culture of sharing were more than tangible among these people.

By the time we finished lunch and had a long, heart to heart chat, my taxi arrived. As I feared, my mother was with the driver, a familiar person called Raju bhaiya (brother) as we used to call his taxi all the time. My mother was relived to see me in one piece, no bones broken, alert and active and my usual self, chatting, laughing, cracking jokes and teasing Radhika. I introduced my mother to Maji and Radhika who were by now at ease with me, after spending some five hours in their tiny home.

There may be a shortage of worldly goods in her home but love, kindness and friendship were in abundance. Maji would not let us go until my mum had a cup of tea and how could my mum refuse realising what a wonderful care they had taken of me; came to my aid in my hour of need. Moreover she also took an instant shine to Radhika?

Before leaving I touched Maji's feet, a respect we show to our parents, our elders and people of distinction who serve the community selflessly, like priests, guru and even doctors, teachers and professors. That is why my father was so highly respected in the community, even after retiring from his teaching post some time ago.

Maji help me to stand up and gave me a hug that my mother always gives me. There were tears in her eyes, as if she was never going to see me again, some one she always wanted as a son.

Reassuring Maji, I said, "This is not a goodbye or a final farewell. I will have to come and collect my scooter." I gave her my card, with my home and office address and telephone numbers.

Radhika showed similar respect to my mother, touching her feet. When she tried to touch my feet, I stopped her, as we were more or less of the same age and I did not deserve such a respect. Instead I gave her a hug, a tight embrace lasting several minutes.

Although it is not that common, a hug between a young girl and a boy, neither Maji nor Radhika was surprised or taken back. Some how it looked so normal, so natural, although I could not say how my mother took it. Whatever her thoughts may be, she did not express them to me or let them show on her face. It was a relief for me.

I felt that she was impressed by the respect Radhika showed to her and to me, the way she took care of me and helped me in my hour of need. Moreover Radhika had such an innocent looking baby face, a permanent smile and a unique, grudging shyness that it was difficult not to like her, take to her, even give her a big hug.

I found it difficult to let her go. But I knew it would only be counter productive if I cross the Laxman Rekha or show my feelings in any way. This was not the time or the place to show any interest in her except paternal or patriarchal. But I could not call, address Radhika as sister. Perhaps Maji and my mother may have noticed that or I was just being sensitive, over imaginative!

As there was no way I could get in touch with them by phone, I gave Maji exact time and day I would be back to collect my scooter. It was three days from today. Some how I was looking forward to see them again, although I was finding it difficult to justify my interest in them. Could it be that I was grateful to Maji for looking after me or there could be more than meet the eye, some hidden agenda on my part? Perhaps I was unduly cynical to my own feelings?

Before leaving, I put the change of Rs.30 in Radhika's hand. She knew I would not take no for an answer and with a nod from Maji, she at last relented. I was glad to see a smile on her innocent face, the smile that gave her face a glimmer of hope, an uplift that is usually a norm on the face of such a young girl.

When we returned home, mum called a doctor who gave me a clean bill of health but removed the bandages, as they were not only unnecessary but would hinder the healing process in such a hot climate. Instead he sprayed them with antiseptic cream and put a thin, porous plaster, advised me to take a couple of days rest.

At night when I hit the pillows, I could not sleep, could not put behind today's event. Some how Maji and especially Radhika's face kept on starring at me. It was strange, as I had met many girls during my first two years at the college, the girls who were beautiful, smart and socially my equals as well. But the phrase that there is no saying for taste was spot on in my case. Perhaps no one would look at Radhika twice, not until she had put on some weight and develop her figure, her curves in all the right places. But like food, everyone's taste is different when it comes to define beauty. Some love voluptuous, full bodied, men eating women while others like slim, tiny, shy and retreating, homely women. There is no hard and fast rule when it comes to admiring women.

May be in Radhika I saw a challenge or an opportunity to be Professor Higgins and tame an East End girl, a wild Cockney girl and turned her into a socialite beauty. After all George Bernard Shaw was one of my favourite author and the book Pygmalion on which the film My Fair Lady is based is one of the wittiest, ingenious and humorous books I have read.

From my long chat with Radhika, I learnt that she had passed her matric examination with flying colours. So she had a minimum requirement, minimum education to go to college, to do her intermediate and then go on to do a degree course. As education up to matric level was free, Radhika managed to complete it, one year ahead, earlier than normal, as she was such a brilliant student.

I could not help but wonder whether I can help Maji so that they can come out of that depressing slum and enjoy a reasonable living standard with two square meals a day.

When I went back to collect my scooter, in a borrowed station wagon car, at the designated time, Maji and Radhika were waiting for me. I had collected several bags of used cloths, pots and pans, toys and other household goods that Maji can sell in their communal stalls, not forgetting a couple of good dresses and saris for Radhika to cover herself, her thin but attractive body, her underdeveloped, child like chest which embarrassed her when not covered with shawl. Moreover I was eager to see her in a beautiful sari, just to satisfy my curiosity as to how beautiful she would look in a beautiful sari with matching accessories?

As my mother was a social worker, collecting such goods for SEWA charity shops, my house was always full of such stuffs, so often more than she could handle. So it was not difficult for me to pinch some stuffs from her, stored in our garage.

Maji appreciated the six bags I dumped on her doorstep, as she had always lag behind in providing the goods for the stalls but this will redress the balance in Maji's favour. Moreover she knew that people like us always have such clothes that we want to get rid off.

Today both Maji and Radhika were smartly dressed, that is compared to what they were wearing on my last, unplanned, unannounced visit, perhaps clothes borrowed from their neighbours. As I was on a sick leave, I was not in a hurry to go back, I spent some three hours with Maji and especially with Radhika, having lunch but this time shopping was done by Maji, perhaps to give me some precious time alone with Radhika or could it be my fertile imagination?

I told Maji that perhaps I may be able to find a good job for Radhika, as an apprentice that will also pay her a good wage but I had to talk with my father and make few inquiries.

What I had in mind for Radhika was to train her as a nurse that will take just three years to qualify while working and at the end she will get the qualification of SRN or State Registered Nurse, a qualification much valued indeed. It is a tough course, especially to complete it in just three years while working, getting work experience but if any one can do it, Radhika can.

After spending some three happy hours with them I returned home and told my mother the plan I had for Radhika. She was curious about my motives, my ultimate aim but she trusted me, trusted my judgement and we trusted each other, as we were very close, as I was now her only son"

At this point we had a short break, to give me time to recover, to have a drink, as I was talking for nearly two hours. But as Shyam and Sharmila found my story, my life history so fascinating; they were willing to stay up whole night if necessary. They felt I had a natural talent at story telling, reciting my life experiences. Then I would need this talent if I would like to be a successful writer, a novelist.

After the break, I continued. "Now let me tell you about my family. We are two brothers, the only children. I am the young one. There is a gap of ten years between me and my elder brother Ajay. He was a brilliant student and wanted to follow in the footsteps of my father and grandfather, to become a Professor of English.

So when he gained his Masters degree, my father sent him to England to do his PhD, especially as he managed to obtain scholarship from the Oxford University, as he was such a brilliant student. With a doctorate from such a world renowned university, he would one day become not only a professor but a Chancellor of our University, a feather in my father's cap.

So they willingly let him go to Oxford where Ajay made a name for himself, passing all his exams with flying colours. He was offered a teaching post, followed by Professorship in English which he gladly accepted, especially as he had found a wonderful girl, his fellow student by the name Georgina whom he married and made Oxford his home.

Although my father was heart broken, he was proud of his achievement. Ajay came to Mumbai once for six weeks, to introduce his charming and beautiful wife to the family. It was obvious that he will never come back to Mumbai to settle down. His place, his home, his future was in Oxford.

So in our four bedroom detached house with a big garden, there were only three of us. We use one bedroom as a guest room and the fourth was empty. Moreover there was a lot of space on the ground floor, with a lounge, a kitchen and a separate dinning room, a library room with a large double garage we mostly use as a storage room for my mother, for her charitable activities, to store goods collected for SEWA shops.

After my mother had softened up my father, we had a heart to heart talk, a father and a son talk. I requested my father to use his influence and find a place for Radhika at the Tata hospital, so that she can train as a nurse. My father, in his usual jolly manner asked me straight whether I was interested in Radhika in a personal way.

I also gave him a straight answer, to ask me that question in three to six months time, as it was too early to commit one way or the other. That brought a smile on his face. He knew it was like father, like son, as he had a very interesting background, how he met my mum and got married. But I will have to keep this story on hold when we have more time.

Our doctor, our consultant and a good family friend Mr. Sharma was a heart specialist at Tata hospital. So I thought it would not be too difficult to arrange an interview for Radhika.

After a long wait of six weeks Radha attended the interview. But as she was educated in Marathi, her English was not up to the standard, as all the teaching was done in English. So she will have to pass an entrance exam in English and that also in three months, just before the new intake of student nurses take place, otherwise she would have to wait one more year.

By now Maji and especially Radhika had been to our house a few times and their stall was doing a roaring business with our support, especially that of my mum who gave her all the second hand cloths Maji could sell.

With two nutritious square meals a day and decent cloths to wear, Radhika was fast regaining her weight, developing into a beautiful girl. But only way Radhika could pass her entrance exam in English, within three months was to have a full time tuition, eight hours a day, six days a week. For such a commitment, Radhika had to come and stay at our place, in the guest room. Maji had no objection and my mum was eager to have her. She was practically eating out of Radhika's hands, as she was so polite, always touched my mum's feet and gave her respect she never had from any one else. As for my father, it was a challenge he could not resist.

So I had no problem inviting Radhika to our home who would be a great help to all of us. The three months that Radhika spent with us were some of the happiest time in our lives. My father enjoyed teaching his favourite subject to such a receptive, smart, young and beautiful student.

My mother was proud to take her out and introduce her as a daughter of our friend, as by now Radhika had put on some weight. She was indeed looking stunningly beautiful, as she had learnt all the tricks of the trade from my mother who always wanted a daughter, to pass on her expertise and now she had one in Radhika, the best daughter any mother could have.

Her tall slim body but now much developed, with her long, light brown hair, kept loose with a hair bend and wearing smart cloths that looked so beautiful on her milky, smooth skin and the mum's make-up box at her disposal, she indeed looked beautiful, charming, gorgeous and capable of stealing any one's heart, especially as she was a hard worker, industrious with obliging nature and a permanent smile. I so often wonder why God bestows all such wonderful qualities on just one person rather than distributing them equally. But any one's loss was mine, Radhika's gain?

Radhika would get up early in the morning to prepare my breakfast, a job she took over from my mum. Then she would take tea, toast and omelette for my mum and dad, so that they could have a breakfast in bed, the luxury they had never enjoyed before in their married life.

By the time they got up, Radhika would have showered, light a divo (candle) in our spacious temple with images of most Gods and Goddesses, especially Radhika's and my favourite Lord Krishna, with her favourite consort Radha standing next to Krishna, changed, had her breakfast and at her study, working hard, studying a minimum of eight hours a day, half the time spending with my father who was as much smitten by lovely Radhika, his star pupil, as my mother was with her sincerity and extremely good and polite manner. Radhika was in a win, win situation. She could not put a foot wrong. This was the time when Radhika came of age.

Radhika covered the course within eight weeks but had to wait another five weeks before she could take the test, the five weeks she used wisely to learn as much English as she could from my father, reading on average three books a week, discussing the characters, such as that of Miss Havisham, Julius Caesar,

Brutus, Mark Anthony, Cleopatra, Professor Higgins, Captain Nemo, Sherlock Holmes and Dr. Watson with ease and intelligence, giving my father a run for his money, a thought to ponder on? No wonder he was taken to Radhika like a duck to water.

It started as my father Lord Rama and Radhika a poor Shabri but now the tables were turned. My father was eating out of her hand and my mum enjoying this from a sideline. A lamb had tamed a lion and that also without trying?

Every day, at six in the evening Radhika would ring Maji, who would go and stand outside the public telephone booth, picking up the phone as soon as it rang, so as to reassure her that her little daughter was well and taken good care of, although Maji had absolute trust in me and my family. She was indeed glad that we were taking such a good care of her, giving her the opportunity to build a career for her self.

I spent a lot of time with Radhika, in the evening after I came back from work and we had our dinner. We watched TV, listened to music or just chatted as she was so inquisitive about my work, about journalism, before she would retire to her own bedroom, a well furnished room with en suit shower room, indeed an unimagined luxury for Radhika, with her own TV, video, music centre and phone!

Half the time, Radhika thought she was dreaming, pinching herself now and again to make sure that it was not a dream but a reality?

I must admit that I was smitten by her charm, beauty and above all her considerate, helpful and happy go lucky nature. Perhaps it was too obvious on my face how much I liked her, enjoyed her company.

We would hold hands and occasionally give a hug when saying good night and retreating to our bedrooms. But I was careful not to make her feel that I was taking advantage in any way as she was living under our roof.

Radhika and to that matter Maji as well thought of me as a kind, caring and a thoroughly decent person, some one they can trust with their lives, their honour, a knight in shining armour. I wanted to live up to their expectation, worthy of their trust.

When it was time to take the exam, Radhika was fully prepared, more than ready. It is needless to say that she passed with flying colours. She was offered the place as a student, a trainee nurse and moved in the nurses' quarters that go with the job, as nurses are paid so little.

My parents were as sad, as upset as me, at the thought of losing Radhika, that she will no longer be living with us, will not be able to see her smiling face first thing in the morning. Perhaps the biggest blow may be "No breakfast in bed?"

She had practically taken over the running of the home during her four month stay. She looked so smart, modest, beautiful and charming that my mum was proud to show her off, to introduce her to her friends and fellow charity workers, at the slightest opportunity and Radhika, to her credit, never let her down in any way, trying to be as polite to my mum's friends as she would be to my mum and dad. Indeed my mum was walking on the moon when accompanied by Radhika.

My father wanted to teach her the intelligent game of Chess, as he knew she would give him a good game, be a worthy opponent, as I was mentally too lazy to play chess. It was just not my cup of tea and as for my mother, charity does not begin at home, it begins at the charity events?

On the day Radhika moved out, I said to my father, "Do you remember when Radhika came to stay with us; you asked me what my intentions were and I told you to ask me that question in three to four months time when I will be able to give you an honest answer.

Now I do not mind saying that I love Radhika and I feel she loves me as well. I know she has a long way to go before she becomes worthy to be a member of our house. But I do not doubt that she is extremely clever and capable girl who can climb the ladder, be what she wants. With our help, encouragement and guidance, sky is the limit for her ambitions. Although it is too early to say that we will get married, I sincerely hope that it will happen and we would like to tie the knot with your blessings." My voice was chocked with emotion.

"Beta, I am glad to hear you say that. We all love Radhika. She will be more than welcomed in this house, in our hearts. I am sure you will be very happy with her, as she is such a kind, caring and sensible girl, not to mention how beautiful she is. She has such a mature head on her young shoulders. Beta, your mum is already dreaming of calling Radhika her bahu. (Daughter in law) You know it is not that easy to win her over. So Radhika must be very special girl.

I was glad that my hunch, my judgement and my first impression about Radhika were spot on. I can not explain or even justify why I fell in love with her the moment I sat my eyes on her. Call it a destiny, call it kismet, call what you like but it was love at first sight.

She was indeed an ugly duckling, an extremely thin little girl without any sex appeal but there was no doubt in my mind that this ugly duckling will one day turn into a beautiful swan. The permanent smile on her face, her natural shyness and her elusive, hidden beauty bewitched me. I knew even then that with a bit of encouragement, support and love, she can climb any ladder, sit on any podium, and grace any home. How right I was! I feel all good things in life come when least expected. Perhaps it was the second coming of the Messiah for me!

So when I took her last suitcase in the nurses' quarters, the lodgings where she was allocated an en suit bed-sit, a bit cramped but with all the modern facilities, including TV, fridge and the fitted bedroom cupboards, I was relieved. The well fitted communal kitchen and the lounge with a pay phone were just down the corridor.

Radhika was more than happy to move in such a luxurious accommodation, especially compared with her shabby one room devoid of any facility, more appropriate as a cow shed than for human habitation.

For the first time since I met Radhika, I noticed the absence of smile on her face and she was in some what sombre mood. When I put down the last bag, Radhika shut the door, came to me and gave me a hug, a tight embrace, resting her head on my broad shoulders. I knew it was very difficult for her to move out of our home, to leave us, as she had grown fond of all three of us, become an integral part of our family.

I gently patted, played with her long, silky, beautiful hair for a while. When I lifted her head, to look at her mesmerising face, I saw tears and when I tried to comfort her, hold her tight, give her a kiss on her forehead, she burst into tears, crying uncontrollably, a bit like a little lost child.

I let her emotion flow. At last when she was calm after pouring her heart out, I gently whispered in her ear, "Radhika, I love you so much. Even my mum and dad are smitten, are crazy about you. You have won the hearts and minds of all of us. They even want me to marry you."

This brought a smile on her face, covered with tears, spoiling her light makeup, expertly applied, learnt this precious art under the guidance of my mother who was a beautician, hair stylist and beauty product adviser to rich and famous in her young and glamorous working days. Can you imagine at one time she was earning more than my dad who was a professor of English? So Radhika had an expert teacher.

She jokingly said, "Abhi, you said they want you to marry me. What about you. Do you want to marry me? Abhi, I have known for a long time that you love me but our feelings are mutual. I love you ten times more but I was afraid even to think about it, let alone express my feelings, as I was a pauper and you are a prince.

Our friendship was like that of Prince Lord Krishna and his pauper, cowherd friend Sudama. But so often such unselfish love, friendship without constraint, without expectation is real, stronger and longer lasting than a friendship between two equals.

Just five months ago, I was nobody, a hopeless case. I vividly remember when we first met, after your accident; you looked at me, perhaps stared at my chest, at my tiny under developed breasts which were visible through the half torn blouse made of almost transparent material. We were so poor that we could not afford decent cloths.

I felt so embarrassed that I tried to cover my chest with my tiny hands. But like a gentleman, you took off the shawl my mother had put round your shoulders and wrapped it round me, thus covering my chest, my breast, giving me my dignity and making me feel at ease.

Abhi, you may not believe me but I realized then what a wonderful person, a kind and caring human being you are and I was determined to marry you one day!. I know it sounds crazy and you may laugh at me but that is what I felt then and I have supreme confidence in my ability. All I needed was a bit of good luck, a break and Lord Krishna certainly gave me that break."

I did not realise Radhika loved me so much, that it was love at first sight, not only for me but on her part as well.

Now there was no need to be modest, to pretend, to check my feelings or to have any reservation on my part but I should not cross the ultimate boundary, the all important sacred Laxman Rekha, the hallmark of our Hindu culture, tradition and a sign of good upbringing.

So, for the first time I kissed Radhika on her lips. It was a long, lingering kiss that we both enjoyed so much. I slowly lifted her and put her down on the bed, kissing her gently again.

After a few minutes, I sat down, leaning on the headboard and took her in my arms, holding her tight, looking at her now smiling face and playing with her tiny hand, lovely hair and cuddling her but taking care not to touch her breast, thighs or her most private parts that may make us lose control in any way and spoil our so far loving but controlled friendship. After all, we were only 18 and 19 years old. It is easy to lose self control at that age, especially when we are alone in a bedroom.

We spent three long hours chatting, talking and simply enjoying each other's company. It was the happiest day of our young lives. We made plans that include marriage as soon as we both complete our studies, in three to four year's time, when I get my Masters degree and Radhika had her SRN, the Nursing diploma. Our jobs were more or less guaranteed and my parents were more than financially comfortable, if not super rich.

When one is in love, enjoying the work and have a loving, caring family behind them, times passes quickly, it flies.

In three years' time, When Radha was 21 and myself just 22, we finished our studies. We both passed with distinction, with flying colours. It was the happiest day in our professional, educational life when we received out diploma, degree certificates at the presentation ceremony, at the hands of the Chancellor of the University and our photographs taken, wearing the ceremonial robes.

Now we can settle down, get married and have a wonderful life together. But life is not a permanent bed of roses, ups and downs, happiness and sorrows, disappointments and setbacks follow as surely as the day is followed by night, a dawn by midday and an evening with sunset.

Before we could honour our promises to each other, tie the knot and make our union, our togetherness permanent, the most bizarre event happened that could ruin our lives, mine, Radhika's and perhaps the lives of my parents as well for ever.

As I did not receive a telephone call from Radhika for a couple of days, I was worried. It was most unusual, as we used to keep in touch, talk to each other at least twice a day, say goodnight before retiring to bed, no matter how busy, how occupied we may be.

So I went to nurses' quarters and knocked on her door. When there was no reply, I went to see the Ward Nurse under whom Radhika was working, being trained. As I was a frequent visitor, she knew me well and respected me, knowing that we will be getting married soon.

She told me, with a sad and heavy voice that Radhika had suddenly resigned and left, even without giving a forwarding address. She was really worried as Radhika was indeed sad and crying. It was most unusual for some one like Radhika who always has a smile on her tender face. Some thing was terribly wrong but she had absolutely no idea what that could be.

This indeed made me worried. I rushed to where Maji was living, where I first set my eyes on shy, slim and scantly dressed Radhika, the sight that stirred my conscious, raised my blood pressure.

There was a lock on Maji's door. On seeing me knocking on the door, the neighbour invited me in, as by now all of Maji's neighbour knew me well, trusted and respected me well.

Chandra, the friend and neighbour handed me the letter, rather a large envelop with at least ten pages inside. Even she was sad and worried about Maji and Radhika, as they had known each other for nearly twenty years. She knew why Maji had left but wanted me to read the letter before I ask her any questions.

I have read that letter word by word, line by line, at least a thousand times and I can recite it by heart but I still find it difficult to understand, difficult to digest, to come to term with this life shattering event."

As Abhi was talking for a long time and was emotionally drained, holding his tears back with difficulty, Sharmila wisely stopped him and said, "Bhaiya, let us have another short break, have a cup of tea so that you can have a bit of respite. I am sure now we are entering into the most interesting but most sad and emotionally draining part of your life, your story. It may also be painful and tormenting as well.

Abhi, although we are eager to hear the rest of the story, but if it is too painful, too difficult to continue, then Abhi, we won't press you to continue. Perhaps, you may tell us the rest tomorrow, after a good night's rest.

But after half an hour's rest and recuperation, Abhi was ready to go on but he promised to keep it short, although he will have to recite the letter in full to understand what had happened and why.

No wonder Abhi had managed to write some six hundred pages of his novel, titled **RADHIKA** and the end was yet to come! The novel was entirely based on his own experiences but using literary, journalistic licence, he had spiced it up, as any novel without sex, bitchiness, hero and villain, twist and turn, romance and good ending has no chance of success, even finding a publisher would be very difficult if not impossible.

That is why Abhi wanted to change the title from Radhika to perhaps Lost and Found or Gang Maya, the name of Maji, Radhika's mother. But my literary agent and the publisher wanted me to keep the title Radhika.

In the privacy of my bedroom, I opened the envelop. The letter began with:

"My son Abhi

I know reading this letter will break your heart, as it has broken my heart and more importantly that of my lovely child Radha. You two are the most important people in my life.

I hate myself and if there was any other way, any other solution, I would have willingly taken it. So beta please read this letter carefully before you decide to blame me, hate me or worse disown me.

The area, the slum where we live are always controlled by some one, some racketeers, a gang of gundas, vagabonds. Our area, what they call their territory, was controlled by a very nasty character by the name of Ganu, the vagabond, the bone crusher, as breaking some one's legs and hands was his speciality.

He was working with his equally nasty brother nicknamed Razor, as he was expert at slashing some one's face, especially that of a beautiful girl like Radha, if they do not obey them. They would not hesitate to throw acid in some one's face if the end justifies the means. No one would cross their paths or challenge their authority.

When we were poor, living from hand to mouth, he left us alone. But as soon as we started making some money, thanks to your help, your mother's generosity, Ganu was upon us like a vulture.

He would collect his weekly cut, what he called "Protection Money" some Rs. 50 a week from our three stalls. But he was flexible. If the trade was poor, he would relent. He knew exactly what was going on in our area, our shops, stalls and our lives.

We did not mind paying him, as long as we had enough to survive, to live on. But his activities were not restricted to just collecting money. He was involved in drugs, prostitution and petty crimes as well. Even shopkeepers were paying him protection money.

One day he saw Radha visiting me, even though I had told Radha not to visit me any more. Ganu could not believe his eyes. A tiny, shy and skinny girl without much physical attraction had turned into a most beautiful, clever and charming girl any one would like to have, fell in love with, an ugly duckling turned into a beautiful swan.

Ganu demanded that I should persuade Radha to marry him, which means sooner or later he would drag her into prostitution. To prove his point, he beat me up and even broke my arm. But worse, he knew all about you and your family and threatened to break your both legs if I do not cooperate. He gave me two weeks to make up my mind before he would act. Even local police are under his thumb, on his payroll.

Beta, how can I put your life, the life of my little girl in danger? I already have one such tragedy in my life. I do not want another. My only escape was to disappear without a trace, go where Ganu can not find us. So beta, we had no choice but to leave Mumbai.

We do not know where we will end up but as soon as we are settled, we will get in touch with you. In the mean time take care and always watch your back. You are the son I never had. I would rather give my life than let any one harm you.

Now that I have opened my heart to you and you love Radha so much, I feel it is my duty to come clean, to tell you my life history. If you are ever going to marry my little girl, your little Radhika, then you deserve to know the truth.

You are under the impression that Radha's father, my husband has passed away long time ago but that is what I wanted every one to think. It is much easier than to tell the truth.

My husband, whose name is Raghuram, is in jail, serving a life sentence for manslaughter, the crime he did not commit. He was framed for being too honest, too caring and too loyal to his union members.

He was the union leader, Chairman of the Factory Workers' Union, elected by a huge majority by the ordinary members. He was working at a **Bargain Garment and Clothing factory.** In those days most union leaders were in the pocket of the Sheth, the mill owners. Even today nothing has changed. If any thing, people are more dishonest.

Raghuram was an exception to the rule. He would not accept any bribe or any privileges. But worse, he would not allow any one else, other officials to be in the pockets of the owners. That made him unpopular, not only with the employer but also with his own officials as well, as their side income dried up; making it difficult for them to maintain their life style they had got accustomed to.

It was getting difficult to pay the cost of sending their children to private school, the memberships of health clubs, golf courses and visiting expensive restaurants with their families and friends.

The last labour dispute was a long drawn out and a bitter affair. The latest offer put forward by the management was no better than the one rejected by the Executive Committee. (E.C) that is until their private and personal demands were met, the wheels of their private finances were oiled.

The offer was disguised in a mountain of paper work, double talk and a jargon, a patois of hidden clauses that would be interpreted in any way one may want, depending upon the lawyers who may have drafted it in the first place.

Due to the pressure from the NEC members, who were all corrupt, Raghuram had to put the offer to the union members. He was alone in opposing them while the entire NEC members canvassed, made speeches in favour of accepting the offer, thinking that the union members were tired of the long drawn dispute with loss of income.

My husband was a highly educated person, in fact a lawyer specialising in such disputes. His sincerity won the day and the offer was rejected by a massive vote, the proposals were rejected outright.

The dispute was soon settled, based on the recommendation made by my husband but it cost a great deal to the mill owners and the NEC members lost the bonuses promised by the owner. From then on, Raghuram was a marked man. He knew it, so did most ordinary union members. He took great care but he had made too many enemies.

One day there was a fire in the warehouse, the depot where cotton was stored. The safe in the nearby office broken into and one lakh rupees were stolen. Worse still, a union official, a loyal and right hand man of my husband was killed in the fire.

My husband was blamed for the theft and the fire, as some of the stolen money was deposited in his private account. It was a stitch-up job involving NEC members, mill owners and the police. Even Raghuram's own lawyers were bought, working against him, pleading with him to confess, in return for a lighter sentence.

In the end he sacked his legal team and conducted his own defence. It was a hopeless task from the beginning, as even the judge was a crook. He put up a creditable defence that would have convinced any decent, honest judge but not a corrupt one.

He was found guilty and sentenced to life imprisonment for theft and man slaughter. Not a single union member believed that verdict but they had no say, no input.

When my husband went to jail, I was six months pregnant. Union members looked after me until Radha was born. The mill owners wanted to give me a life pension, 25% of my husband's salary but how could I accept blood money?

In a strange way, justice was done. One year after my husband was jailed, a massive fire broke out that not only destroyed the mill but several union officials who were having a wild party, a drink, drug and sex bonanza, were killed, including the eldest son of the mill owner. All together, fifteen people lost their lives. Sheth was heart broken at the death of his eldest son, his heir to his vast industrial empire.

The mill never opened again for business and some two thousand people, employed directly and indirectly lost their jobs, their livelihood. Today there is a housing estate where once the mill stood. It is now twenty years since my husband was sent to jail, for being too honest, too stubborn and too arrogant to listen to me or to any one else. He used to say we live in the land of Gandhi, Sardar and Bose. We have to maintain their tradition, their faith and their legacy. But one can not fight fire with kerosene. It takes a thief to catch a thief.

I did not want to commit the same mistake, be stubborn and take on Ganu that may hurt Radha, you or your family. Please believe me Abhi; we will get in touch with you as soon as possible, when the dust has settled down. I do not want to be the cause of your unhappiness, your separation from my little Radha who worships the ground you walk on.

Please take care, look after your self and your parents and above all watch your back. Please don't think too badly of me. I have stumbled from one disaster to another since that fateful day when my husband was jailed for life. But I am determined to unite you too, even if that is my last act on this earth. This is not a goodbye, just an interval, half time, lunch break.

Take care my son and see you soon.

Yours unfortunate Maji.

Although I understand Maji's concern, I feel she should have confided in me, come straight to my home with Radhika and we could have sorted out Ganu and his likes.

My father got in touch with a Chief Inspector Balbir Singh who was his student. He pulled in Ganu and interrogated him and his brother, threatening them with kidnapping but we all knew they were not involved in the disappearance of Maji and Radhika. Now I will have to wait until they get in touch with me. It is now seven months and my hopes are fading fast." Abhi left the room to hide his tears which were now flowing freely from his tired eyes and shattered hopes.

When he regained his composure, Abhi came back and said, "Well Shyam, this is my life story. I am losing hope. There may not be a happy ending for me after all. Perhaps I will have to invent it for my book.

Sharmila gave Abhi a big hug and said,"Bhaiya, I promise you that there will be a happy ending. Sisters usually have an inclination about such things. Your separation, your heartache, your loneliness is about to end. You will find your Radhika, get married and live a long and happy life. But don't lose hope and above all don't give up. If there is any thing we can do, please don't hesitate. This is a sister's promise to a brother."

Looking at Sharmila's innocent, smiling but confident face, Abhi some how believed her.

It was nearly midnight and every one was exhausted, mentally, emotionally and physically. As soon as Abhi hit the pillow, he fell fast a sleep, but Sharmila's words, prophesy ringing in his ears. Perhaps consuming half a bottle of wine may have help?

Next morning they all got up late, at around 10am and by the time they had breakfast and got ready, it was nearly midday.

Shyam and Sharmila insisted to take Abhi to Pune from where he could take a train for Mumbai. It would be a comfortable journey in a first class, air conditioned coach. A press card is a great help, a weapon of influence. It can open many doors, buy many favours, especially if some one is with Mumbai Daily News with a daily circulation of five million copies.

But as Abhi had a bit of a swelling on his left hand, they decided to take Abhi to a private hospital first, on the outskirts of Pune before catching a train.

Abhi was soon given a clean bill of health, after a couple of x-rays which showed no facture, only a minor bruising. But his hand was put in a sling so as not to lift any heavy article with that hand. It was just a precaution.

While they were walking to their car, Abhi saw some one walking in front of them, a girl wearing nursing uniform. She looked so elegant even though Abhi was looking at her back, with her starched, snow white uniform and long hair neatly arranged under a cap, nursing head gear that is the trade mark of her profession.

Some how, without thinking, Abhi shouted, Radhika. The girl stopped and turned her head. Abhi could not believe his eyes. There she was, Radhika looking at Abhi, looking at each other in sheer disbelief. Surely it can't be true! Abhi had to bite his tongue to make sure he was awake and not having a beautiful dream.

Abhi ran, forgetting his injury, the slightly limping leg and one hand in the sling? But it was only some one hundred feet which Abhi covered like a champion sprinter. He wanted to grab Radhika and give her a big hug but he hesitated, but only for a while, as it was now seven months that they had not seen each other.

Looking at various bandages on Abhi, Radha could not hold back her tears. Resting her head on Abhi's chest, she could only murmur, "Abhi, please forgive me. I do not deserve you."

In reply, Abhi held her tight for a long time without any resistance from her. In fact she was crying her heart out. In the end Abhi said, "Radhika, I am not going to let you out of my sight, not even for an hour. The past seven months had been a hell, the worst period in my life. Why did you not trust me, told me about Ganu? You know how influential my father is. We could have sorted him out without any problem. You must learn to trust me.

After a long pause, Radha said, "Abhi I have not slept soundly since we left Mumbai. I do not want to be away from you even for a day. Let us get married so that no one can ever separate us." Radhika had unlimited adulation for her hero Abhi.

But realizing that she may be putting Abhi on spot, she said, "I know you have to talk to your parents first, get their permission. I hope they are not angry with me, disappointed in me. I do need their love, their understanding more than ever.

"Don't be silly. No one is angry with you. We know you acted in our best interest. But we were worried thinking that we may never see you again.

While Abhi and Radha were in embrace, Shyam and Sharmila stayed away; maintained their distance to give them some privacy. It was a union of two mind, two souls, two bodies, after a long and painful separation. At last Krishna had found her long lost Radha, Rama her Sita.

After some ten minutes, Abhi and Radhika walked to Shyam and Sharmila and Abhi introduced Radhika, although by now they had heard so much about Radhika that they felt as if they have known her for a long time. She was as beautiful, as charming and as pleasant as Abhi had described her last night, although her long, beautiful, silky hair was hidden under her head gear, her nursing cap. She had not applied any make up.

Even her ever present smile and her easy going nature were a bit restricted; some what missing but only for a while. The seven month break, the upheaval, painful separation from Abhi whom she loved so much had taken its toll, affected her far more than Abhi.

As Radhika's shift was over and she lived just ten minute's walk from the hospital, all four of them got in Shyam's spacious four wheel drive. When Maji opened the door, she was surprised but very pleased indeed, to see Abhi with Radhika. But she could not hide her perceived guilt, the fact that she may have been responsible for separating Laila and Majnu, Anarkali and Prince Salim, Romeo and Juliet, two people who loved each other so much, who should never have been parted, not for even a day. But Maji and Radha found themselves beleaguered by Ganu. So it was impossible for Abhi not to forgive Maji and Radhika for not trusting him.

When Abhi bent down to touch Maji's feet, although he was injured and uncomfortable, Radhika stepped in and stopped Abhi from bending and hurting himself. Maji, a tough lady who had gone through hell, coped well under most difficult circumstances, even during her darkest days when her husband was stitched up and sent to prison for life, could not held back her tears. So, being a proud lady who had never shed tears in front of her tiny, delicate daughter Radha, Maji retreated to the kitchen until she could regain her composure, her poise and her self-control.

As soon as they entered the flat, Radhika excused herself to go and take a shower. It is the duty, the obligation of every nurse to take a shower as soon as they come off duty. It is the first rule of hygiene and most nurses take shower in the hospital itself where such facilities are provided for.

After half an hour, when Radhika emerged, having showered, washed her hair and regain her composure, her smile, her self confidence, her self belief, she indeed looked beautiful, even stunning, with long free flowing hair, smooth skin and wonderful figure, lean but curvy.

She went to Sharmila and gave her a hug, thanking her for taking care of Abhi. They looked at ease in each other's company. Then she went to Shyam but before she could touch his feet, Shyam hold her upright and said, "Radhika, we are all friends, all equals and no one deserves a special seat on a podium. What we want, we need, we desire and indeed we deserve is love, understanding, friendship and our ability to come to each other's help in our hour of need. I am sure we can depend on you both if we ever need your help, your assistance."

Shyam and Sharmila were down to earth people. Although they were children of a millionaire father, came from a dynastic background, there was not an ounce of pride, ego or self-importance in either of them. Indeed Abhi and Radhika were fortunate to have met them, made acquaintances and consider them as friends.

After half an hour's stay, having some tea and biting, Sharmila and Shyam bade farewell but not before Sharmila took Abhi to one side and said, "Abhi, didn't I tell you that all will be well and there is a happy ending waiting for you just round the corner?"

"Yes Sharmila, I know that a sister's blessings, her heartfelt best wishes never go unrewarded. Thank you for all your help, understanding and hospitality. I will always remember these couple of days. It seems whenever I get involved in an accident, I find love, happiness and good friends! Take care and get ready to come to Mumbai for our wedding"

"Abhi bhaiya, no one can keep us away from your wedding. But be quick before you lose Radhika again."

"Sharmila, there is no chance of me losing Radhika again. Titanic can not sink twice. I am going to put an electronic tagging on her, similar to one they put on prisoners when they are released early. I would know exactly where she is, every minute of the day." Abhi was joking but sounded so sincere?

They could not help but have a good, hearty laugh at Abhi and Radhika's expense. They gave each other a long hug before bidding farewell. It seems in such a short time, less than two days; they have managed to become life long friends.

When Shyam and Sharmila were gone, Maji, Radhika and Abhi had a long, heart to heart talk. Abhi could not help but scold Maji for leaving Mumbai in such a hurry, without confiding in him. But the beating Ganu had administered on her, breaking her left hand and his threat to kidnap Radhika, harm, break Abhi's both legs rattled Maji. She acted in a hurry and in a way it was not too difficult to understand Maji or the action she took. Her mind was clouded by love, duty and obligation.

To compound, to complicate the matter, Abhi had just changed his telephone number as he was getting too many crank calls and in a hurry to leave, Radhika lost her diary with all the addresses and telephone numbers.

So she could not even ring Abhi at his home. But now that she had settled down, she was ready to return to Mumbai and tell Abhi every thing, ask for his forgiveness. But before she could do it, Abhi found her first.

Addressing Abhi, Maji said in a sombre voice, "Beta, take care of Radha, take her with you, as I would like to spend the rest of my life, a short period, few years left, on the banks of river Ganges. Beta, it is time for me to gather some credit, some goodwill for the next life, so that I do not have such a hard time. I have seen; endure nothing but pain, sorrow, sadness, misery and heartache for the last twenty years or so. I must have done some thing terrible, be a really bad person to suffer such an agony." Maji's voice was breaking down and tears were freely flowing from her eyes. This time she did not even tried to hide her pain.

Abhi and Radhika took Maji in their arms and let her cry, shed tears and pour her heart out. At last when Maji had shed all the tears, her tear tank was empty, when she was calm, Abhi said in a soft but reassuring voice, "Maji, trust me. Won't you trust your son? Every thing is going to be all right. Every cloud has a silver lining. The happiest days of your life are just round the corner. You do not know how much power a newspaper has, especially the one I work for, with a circulation of over five million. No amount of money can buy a judge, lawyers or police when they face the might of media. Pen is not only mightier than sword but in this case no one would dare to double cross a pen!" Although Abhi did not elaborate, both Maji and Radhika knew what he was trying to say and above all now they knew that Abhi would keep his promise.

Abhi stayed in Pune for a week, for Radhika to give a week's notice, settling her financial affairs before leaving for Mumbai, along with Maji and Radhika.

Abhi's mum and dad were over the moon when they welcome Radhika back in their home but Maji would not stay at Abhi's place. They had to find a room near by, just a five minute walk.

Shyam and Sharmila take it easy at weekends, staying in bed up to 10am compared to their weekday routine of getting up at 7am.

Today, even though it was Saturday, Sharmila got up early, at 8am. Some how she could not sleep or relax. Her left eye was flickering and that normally means, at least to Sharmila and some may call it superstition, that she will get some good news, some thing nice is about to happen.

She told Shyam but he just laughed and said, "Sharmili, I have not purchased a lottery ticket, so there is no chance of winning a fat, big prize. As for finding a beautiful girl, a Sita for Ram, I have already been lucky in that department. Please come back to bed and let me cuddle you. That is some thing nice about to happen to me, to us." Shyam could not help but pull her leg.

While they were talking, cuddling and kissing, there was a knock on the door. Sharmila went down and opened the door, half expecting to see Abhi and Radhika, but it was a postman, who handed Sharmila a big envelope, too big to put through a letterbox. She signed for it and came back to bed with a pot of tea, to keep Shyam occupied!

Well, didn't I tell you that we are about to receive some good new! This envelope is from Abhi and you know what that means. They both opened it together. There was a hard cover book, the first edition of Abhi's six hundred pages novel **"RADHIKA"** signed, autographed by Abhi with an inscription, "To Shyam and Sharmila, a couple in a million. We cherish your love, affection and friendship. With best wishes from your loving brother Abhi and Bhabhi Radhika."

PS: Keep this copy safe, as this may become a collector's item!

That was not all. There was a wedding invitation. Abhi and Radhika were getting married in six weeks time. There was a long letter, reciting every event that occurred in the last six months since they bid goodbye at Radhika's flat in Pune.

"Dear Shyam and Sharmila

I must admit that every prophesy Sharmila made, every blessings she bestowed upon me and Radhika, her every wish about my happiness, our future has come true. It seems she is in the wrong profession! She is as good as French physician and astrologer Michel Nostradamus who made some two thousand predictions, prophecies in rhyme in his famous book **Centuries** published in 1555.

The last six months had not only been the happiest period in our lives but most profitable as well, in financial term. We have made more money in just six months than in the rest of our lives put together. But money never had and never will be a prime consideration in our lives.

We value friendship more than any material wealth. How lucky we are in that department with friends like you and all the students who still keep in touch with my father and honour him as a Guru. Some even call him Dronacharya, the guru of Pandav, an ultimate honour for a teacher, for a professor in our culture.

When I came back to Mumbai, Maji and Radha accompanied me. Radhika moved back in her old room, the guest room. Although there was plenty of space for Maji in our home, she would not agree to move in with us. It is an old Indian tradition, custom that a mother should not accept any form of long term hospitality from her married daughter or her in-laws. Among Indians, old traditions die hard, although you Indian Americans have moved on with the time!

It was not too difficult for Radhika to get her old job back when they were told why she had to resign, leave in such a hurry. In any case her Ward Sister was eager to welcome her back on the team, as Radhika is such a conscientious, conscious and sentient worker with an ever present smile on her face.

Every patient loves her. Now she is specializing as a theatre nurse, an ICU (Intensive Care Unit) nurse which is the most responsible as well as the best paid job in the nursing profession.

But the best news is that Radha's father Raghuram has been freed. His appeal, backed by my newspaper who investigated the case under their special column **"Miscarriage of Justice"** was upheld and the judge made it clear that he was wrongly convicted, on the flimsiest, unsubstantiated evidence. The cover up was too obvious to miss. He was found not guilty, with his honour intact and was awarded substantial damages, a seven figure sum, more than enough to live in comfort for the rest of his life.

As Raghuram is himself a lawyer, he had kept an up to date file, in triplicate, with his trusted and loyal friends. The investigative journalists found one of the file that provided all the information to reopen the case, including names and addresses of many witnesses he wanted to call but was unable to do so, due to police cover-up.

It came out in the examination, from the prosecution file that the handwriting on the paying in slip which was used to deposit money in Raghuram's account were not his, not even remotely similar.

Despite Raghuram's repeated request to find out whose handwriting it was, to trace the person responsible for framing him, police did nothing. Moreover

Raghuram had a perfect alibi. He was at home with his wife and a neighbour, working on a case.

This neighbour mysteriously disappeared for three months during the trial. So Raghuram was unable to call him. Apparently police made no effort to trace him. There were half a dozen forensic mismatches, inadequacies which in it self were more than enough to find him not guilty.

But with a corrupt judge, corrupt prosecutor and police working against him, he had no chance. Even his own defence team wanted him to plead guilty, in return for a lighter sentence. In the end he had to sack his team and conduct his own defence.

This time, it took just three days for the judge to free him with his name, his honour intact and ordered the prosecution to pay a huge compensation. Perhaps you may have read about the trial in the paper. It was a cause celebre that attracted headlines in all the national newspapers and on local radio and TV.

As the original judge and the Public Prosecutor who brought the charges were already dead, the judge could not bring charges of corruption, bribery and extortion against any one. I was chosen, as a part of a three reporter team, to write about this case. It is needless to say I thoroughly enjoyed this assignment. Above all it gave me enormous satisfaction. The smile on Maji's face was worth all the effort.

The success story does not end here. As you have not been to my house, you may not know the area, what a prime location it is, just half a mile from the famous Juhu beach, with all the prestigious five star hotels, top of the range restaurants, health clubs, boutiques and many more.

There are ten spacious bungalows with vast gardens and plenty of space. The first one with the most land was purchased by a developer over two years ago. He built sixty luxurious flats of one, two and three bedrooms, in a fifteen story high tower blocks, named Shalimar Tower.

These are upmarket flats, mainly aimed at the NRIs who live in Europe and America but need a holiday home for winter months. These luxurious flats have marble floor, granite work tops with fitted kitchen, en suit bath or shower rooms, real wood floors, air condition and concealed lightings, a few among so many special features.

The Shalimar Tower has an underground car park for up to one hundred cars and state of the art leisure and sport centre, with swimming pool, sauna, steam bath and every equipment that is a standard in such an establishment in the West.

This business venture was such a success that the developer wanted to buy our bungalow. My father was ready to sell, as the money on offer was mind boggling. Our condition was that he should offer three flats, one a three bedroom one for me and Radhika and other two with two bedrooms, for my mum and dad and for Maji and Raghuram, in the Shalimar Tower, on the highest floor possible, so that we can enjoy fantastic views of the city and the beach.

We all have now moved in our flats, on the tenth and twelfth floor with unbelievable views of the countryside, the city and the Indian Ocean. It is like dream come true, a step nearer to heaven. Maji is still stunned. She can not believe the change in her fortune when she had to go to sleep with a glass of water as dinner. No wonder she sees me in the form of Lord Krishna but then she gave me my Radha, little Radhika, a perfect partner for any one. The sale of our bungalow has made my father a very rich man, even after paying for the two flats.

As you will see from the enclosed book, my first novel **RADHIKA** which was published just a month ago, I am indeed on the way up. The first edition of fifty thousand copies is almost sold out and the next edition will be of not less than two hundred thousand copies.

Raghuram has also written a book, based on his bitter experiences, entitled **"A Long Road to Freedom"** In a way it is more interesting, with twist and turn that would keep readers in suspense until the end. But he does not want to publish it in his name, so it has to go under my name.

Raghuram's comment that to have a daughter like Radha and to gain a son in law like Abhi is worth spending twenty years in jail moved my heart, moved me to tears. Reunion of Maji with Raghuram is the best reward, the most satisfying outcome for us.

I have already submitted this second novel to my agent. He is thrilled to bits and says TV and Film deal will soon follow for the two novels. Both my agent and publisher wants me to give up my job as a journalist and concentrate full time on writing, as the financial reward is so enormous. But I am not sure, as I love my work and they have already reduced my workload by half. I couldn't ask for more. Moreover I like to carry my press card that is so prestigious.

I am the luckiest man alive. I am marrying the most beautiful, charming, kind and caring girl, a one in a million. By the way Radhika now plays Chess and gives a tough time to my dad! But he loves it. At last he has found a worthy opponent!

Our parents are financially secured. They have bank balances beyond their wildest dream. They can now enjoy their retirement in peace, without a worry. They are thinking of going on a mini world cruse, to Japan and the Far East, Australia and New Zealand. They deserve it. I would like Sharmila to come a week early that is if you could spare her. My mum and Radhika need an extra hand. By the way I would like Shyam to be my best man, as my brother could not make it.

With lots of love from me and Radhika.
Your loving brother Abhi.

Sharmila's joy knew no bounds. Winking at Shyam, she said, "Now do you believe me! I did tell you that very good news are just round the corner but I did not know that they will come by a bucket full. I also have some of my own good news, especially for you."

"Really, when did you know? Am I going to be a father?"

"Yes Shyam. I am two months pregnant but I only came to know yesterday"

Shyam jumped out of the bed, lifted Sharmila gently and put her on the bed and said, "From now on, I am going to take care of every thing. Just look after yourself. **This was the height of their happiness, their married life.**

****

SPRING TIME IS A HAPPY TIME

Krishna, no relations to Lord, the favourite God of Hindus, was quiet, lost in his own thoughts, wandering, rambling, meandering and circuitous in his own world, in pensive mood. It was unnatural, out of character for him not to be heart and soul of any party, not to be centre of attraction at any gathering, especially when college friends and colleagues are involved.

Krishna was simply a happy go lucky character who looked at the world through Rose tinted glasses, even though he had gone through some very difficult and tricky times indeed. Perhaps that has installed steely determination, built his character as well as made his street wise.

He was certainly not born with a silver spoon in his mouth. It was more like a poisoned dummy. So often people who had been dealt bad cards, had to face difficulties at every stage in one's life, out of luck on most part, are more kind, considerate, obliging, accommodating, good and model citizens on most part. Krishna was a perfect example of a ripe, sweet mango that has come out of an oasis of deprivation.

Perhaps the unexpected absence of Mamta, his wife of only few months may be the cause of his pensive, thoughtful mood, his discomfort and a bit of bewilderment, the state of his obfuscation.

It was not easy to hire this fantastic, luxurious, upmarket vessel **Jalpari. (Mermaid)** Krishna and his friends, some of them children of rich and influential parents, had to pull out all plugs, spend a lot of money to hire this yacht, a floating palace, well equipped for ocean cursing, so that they could sail to the offshore island of **Mahuva,** an isolated place with beautiful beaches, a tiny fishing community and much more. Mahuva was situated some forty miles from the Maharastra shoreline, in an ideal setting, a paradise island.

This was their annual gathering, an outing that they undertake every year without fail, to different places like hill stations Simla, Dehra Dun and Madurai, famous historic cities like Jaipur, Ajmer, Delhi, Agra and Amritsar, the Golden City for Sikhs, as the holiest shrine of the Sikh, the Golden Temple is located in Amritsar, beautiful picnic spots, game reserves or a boat trip. This tradition was set in motion when they were all at the college and single. Now all were married and well settled.

But marriage did not change the pattern, the feelings and the closeness of their special relation, friendship. In fact most of the girls they married to were with them in the college, some having love marriage and mixed with them like a lump of sugar that dissolves in a glass of milk and makes milkshake, a wonderful, cool, tasty drink. It was the time, the era and social environment that encouraged such comradeship, one for all and all for one, a friendship, a marriage until death do us part.

It was their way to keep their college friendship going, the candle, the flame of love, brotherhood and comradeship flickering and to keep in touch. So ten couples had planned this fantastic trip a long time ago. But there were only nine couples and Krishna were on the boat, besides the Captain and his first mate, Mamta being the only but notable absentee.

Mamta had to drop out at the last minute, due to diarrhoea and some vomiting, perhaps as a result of mild food poisoning. This is a hazard people residing in cities like Bombay and Calcutta had to endure, the price they had to pay for this dubious honour of being Bombayvasis. (Residence of Bombay)

As the programme was arranged long time ago and Krishna being the architect of this sea adventure, it was difficult for him to drop out at the last moment. Moreover Mamta herself insisted that he should go, especially as she was being looked after by the parents of her best friend Kalpna, who were both doctors.

She was in as safe a hand as could be possible. Their diagnosis was that it could be a mild attack of food poisoning which required drinking plenty of fluid, supplemented with dioralyte sachets to replace the lost minerals. She would be as good as gold by the time they return from their cruising adventure.

In those early days of independence, people were patriotic, nationalistic but content, kind and above all considerate and loyal. The country was tranquil and peaceful in many ways that is difficult to imagine in today's topsy turvy world, with terrorism and religious fanaticism raising its ugly head throughout the world.

This was in spite of much hyped cold war between East and West, between Capitalism and Communism. We had two superpowers, America and the Soviet Union. At least it kept each other in check, prevented them from committing atrocities which is a norm today, with America being the only superpower, a self appointed policemen of the world, guardian of democracy, albeit on a selective basis. It differentiates friends and foes, friends being allowed to get away with murder while foes like Iraq being punished severely for shoplifting?

On Saturday evening, at 4pm to be precise, the party of nineteen and two crew members left Ballard Pier, from a private jetty. The yacht was soon on its way, sailing smoothly, cutting through the water like a hot knife making its way through soft butter, producing tiny waves and a foaming, frothing lane that would disappear within few minutes, merging with Mother Sea, the vast mass of water in the mystic, romantic Indian Ocean, with warm waters and majestic islands that would steal any one's heart.

Soon the yacht was leaving behind the harbour traffic. Within half an hour, the dirty, tea coloured sea water was beginning to turn blue, the small islands littered in this part of the sea were fading away and within an hour they were so far away that nothing was visible except sea water below and the clear blue sky above, except a row after row of sea and marsh birds, sea gulls, pelican, heron, egret, bittern, stork and ibis were filling the sky, returning to their nests on number of tiny islands that have sprung out of the sea in this part of the Maharastra shoreline, too small for human habitation but large enough for these birds to colonize them, in the absence of destructive and overbearing human habitation, the only species that is unable to live in peace and harmony with mother nature.

On the distant horizon, the sun was fast sinking in the sea. The last, slanting golden rays of the setting sun were turning the sea surface into a kind of shining, reflecting surface, a giant mirror that would reflect and enlarge the object a million times over.

The sight of a setting sun in the middle of a mighty Indian Ocean is a luxury, a miracle for city dwellers who rarely venture beyond few feet from the shore, when bathing in sea. Some how it was not and still is not an Indian tradition to learn swimming, be adventurous with water. The water sport, such as diving, skiing or parachuting, speedboat adventures were unheard of at the time and still a taboo with most Indians in this day and age.

The moon was out even before the sun completely disappeared, swallowed by the mighty ocean. With the demise of the sun, the half moon was the master of the sky, king of the universe, bright enough not to plunge the sky into perpetual darkness but not too bright to rob the romance out of semi dark, mesmerising atmosphere.

Then there were stars, lots and lots of them that would be difficult to spot in the polluted sky of Bombay, made worse by the ever present neon lights. They were twinkling at us and at each other, perhaps reminding us how insignificant we were in the universe. It is beyond human imagination to contemplate the might and mystery of the Universe, the ultimate creation, the ultimate puzzle for the scientists to solve.

Some of the stars that we could see now may have died, exploded or swallowed by black hole whose gravity is so great that nothing can escape from it, not even the light. A black hole which is an inward collapsing star sucks in every thing, including other stars as large as our sun, forming a solid mass a million times more dense than diamonds, the most solid object on earth. It defies logic and even the most fertile imagination is not capable of drawing a picture, understanding the mystery of the ever expanding universe. One may wonder whether even the creator understands his own creation!

But as it takes millions of light years for the light to travel to earth, we will be able to watch these dead stars, twinkling for millions of years before they finally disappear from our sky, laid to rest.

Once the sun had gone down, it was chilly enough for us to take shelter in the vast, covered deck lounge, fully equipped with bar and music to have a wonderful party.

Now the real party started. Even Krishna had regained his composure, mixing with every one, offering drinks, the favourite being light wine for the ladies and lager beer for the boys. There is nothing like alcohol to raise the spirit and keep the party going but mercifully binge drinking was not even on the drawing board.

Every one felt a relief looking at the smiling face of Krishna; as such an outing would not be an unqualified success without the participation of a happy and smiling our own Lord Krishna!

The music was dominated by two favourite singers of the time, the King Elvis Presley and the Crown Prince Cliff Richard, with hits like Rock Around the Clock, Jail House Rock, Don't Knock the Rock, Love Me Tender, Are You Lonesome Tonight, Put on Your Dancing Shoes, Young Ones, Summer Holidays, Puppet on a string (Sandy Shaw), Sex Machine (James Brown) and many more, backed by their musical groups like Shadows and Bill Haley and his Comets who were the first country musicians to turn to rhythm-and-blues music thyme and took America by storm!

The time passed so quickly that no one realized when our luxury cruse liner, nick named the Tiny Titanic, reached its destination, at around 10pm. It was a leisurely sail, as we were not in a hurry to reach our outpost of Mahuva Island.

Now it was time for dinner, prepared by ship's first officer who was Man Friday, expert at every task, especially cooking. His starter of meat samosa, dal bhaji and shammi kebab and the main dish of garlic and rocket Nan (hot!) vegetable and chicken biryani, bhindi bhaji, tarka dal, Chicken tikka masala and Kashmiri mix kept us at the dinning table until midnight.

From the windows of the dining room, the island was hardly visible, as only the lighting, mostly kerosene filled lantern and open wood fire was in use, as there was no electricity or any kind of generator, except one in the temple complex.

This primitive way of fighting the darkness gave us the clue that the land was there, less than a mile from where the boat was anchored but far removed from our Bombay lifestyle.

There were twenty cabins, each with four bunk beds or two double beds, a bathroom and shower facilities. So there was plenty of room for every couple, as some treated this excursion as their second honeymoon and why not? In those distant days, travel was the privilege of the few; honeymoon was a hotel bedroom at best or just a room in one's own home at worse.

The cool sea breeze and lack of any noise made it a strange night for most of us. Every one was fast a sleep in their own cabin in no time at all, as it was a long and tiring but extremely enjoyable day. No doubt the drinks help us as well. These cabins were probably more luxurious than their own flats, mostly shared with other family members. But it was not a honeymoon night, at least in sexual sense.

Early in the morning, when the Jalpari let out its battle cry to wake us up, we some how managed to get out of the bed and to the breakfast room. But after last night's heavy dinner lasting until midnight, no one was particularly hungry enough to take up the offer of a cooked breakfast, the full breakfast of masala omelette, mushrooms, chips and baked beans.

Instead most of us had a cup of tea or coffee with some Chapatti or Nan, a pale imitation of bread, which was not yet fashionable or desirable. Indians, having just gained independence, were proud of every thing that was of Indian origin.

Mercifully Western and Abrahamic culture and morality was still at an arm's length. The attraction of Western goods, culture and corruption came a bit later, although not the music which was an instant hit with the film industry, albeit side by side with the Indian classical music that maestro Naushad, Shankar Jaikishan and singer Saigal, Mukesh and Lata Mangaskar so expertly exploited, provided to the Indian film industry.

As we gathered in the dinning room, the sun was just coming out from behind the island. The sea was calm with clear blue water and there were already some fishing boats near our yacht. Perhaps that may be the sole occupation for the people of the island. The sea water was teaming with fishes of all shape, size and colour but most were greyish in colour and too tiny to be of any use as a food but not to sea birds that would eat any fish, as long as it can hold the prey in its beak.

It was like a giant aquarium. We were in a kind of sea world. For most of us it was unreal, too good to be true, as if we were part of the crew of Nautilus, the famous submarine with captain Nemo, in the novel "Twenty Thousand League under the Sea" our Captain, on our yacht Jalpari, being compared to Nautilus, the novel was written by my favourite author, the Frenchman Jules Verne. I do not know why the author described Captain Nemo as of Indian origin! It seems mystic India and her past glory is understood, admired and appreciated much more in the West than we would like to admit, give credit.

Where there are fish and fishermen, there are inevitably sea birds. Surely there was no shortage of predatory sea gulls near and on the beach, perhaps waiting for the fishing boats to land their precious cargo. They would dive bomb at any one, any human being if they stand between them and their favourite food.

As soon as we finished the morning routine, we took to a tiny boat with primitive outboard engine that would take ten of us at a time. So it took two trips to deposit all of us on the island. The captain and his mate remained on the boat, as they had visited this paradise island many times.

It seemed every one on the island was aware of our arrival. So nearly the entire population was on the beach to greet and meet us. Welcome was mainly by women and children, as men folk were at sea, in their tiny fishing boats, earning their livelihood.

It was noisy but genuine, heart warming welcome. It was not that common for these isolated islanders to meet people from a big city, which was for most of them as far as the distant lands of Europe and America, if not the moon. Today we may wonder how a distance of just forty to fifty miles could create two different worlds, poles apart, people living in entire different atmosphere, social, financial, ethical and moral. Perhaps there is a complete vacuum today when it comes to moral and ethical standard.

We each were curious about the others, although distributing sweets, balloons and some toys among the children and the old, discarded saris that had long gone out of fashion but in good condition, by our ladies soon broke the ice and made us all popular, a kind of heroes and heroines among these primitive but kind hearted people who showed us what genuine affection, heart warming welcome could be. They were loving, trusting, affectionate and friendly people, although understandably a bit shy and nervous, at least to begin with.

The beach was sandy, going deep inland, slowly merging with the soil that could support only sparse vegetation, as the top soil was coarse and the ground water, on most part was semi salty but there are trees that could grow in any condition, provided there is some sort of water. The nature is more adoptable than we give credit for. Even Artic and Antarctic continent, always covered with ice, with temperature touching -60*°C do support some form of wild life, notably Polar bears, Artic wolves, reindeers and husky dogs who do all the hard work for their human masters! Then we, the humans are expert at exploiting Mother Nature!

The beach was also covered with sea weeds that these islanders collect and turn them into manure and smelt with rotting fish that most of us, with delicate city stomach, could not stand. So we made a hasty retreat to the interior of the island, the part we would like to see and explore most.

The population of the island was some four hundred, fifty couples, the rest being children and old single people who had lost their partners. In such a close knit community, no one would ever feel lonely. It was like living in an extended family, on a kibbutz, on a cooperative farm that was in fashion in communist states at the time, one for all and all for one. How do we miss communal living in the age of IT.? No wonder popularity and demand for retirement homes is so great. It brings quantum improvement in our lives when most needed.

The island was just five miles long and three miles wide at the broadest point, with centre some seven hundred feet above sea level, the highest point in any of the surrounding islands. So one is always within a sprinting distance from the sea. The vast ocean is always visible from any point, from any where on the island. In a way it was difficult to escape from the sea, the cool sea breeze and the whisper of the waves and the whistling pine, not forgetting the noisy sea birds.

These parts of India receive nearly 90% of their annual rainfall between June and August, the height of the monsoon season, which is rapid, raging and furious. Rain comes down in buckets. It rains cats and dogs. So often a big burst can deposit from 10 to 15 inches of rain within a few hours. Such a tiny island may find it difficult to withstand these brutal forces of nature without a well planned and well maintained settlement.

So the tiny settlement was situated as far inland as possible, to avoid the tidal force. The settlement or a tiny village was built like a cross, with the centre having a huge open space where the temple was situated. This was the highest point; completely safe from the worse force of nature, the tidal waves which may penetrate a mile or so inland during worse monsoons but could never reach the temple, which was in a way the last and the only place of refuge for the whole community.

It was a great achievement for such a tiny community to build such a large, spacious and a wonderful temple, fit for a big town. But it was due to the generosity of a local prince and his father Ranaji who were an avid great game fishing enthusiast and naturalist. As these waters were once teaming with sharks, marlin and tunas, not to mention giant parch and Bombay duck, a fish widely eaten in Bombay restaurants even today, the prince used to make the island his base for couple of months a year during fishing season.

After all, this entire tiny island was part of his father, Rana **Mohanrai's** kingdom. Ranaji was a progressive ruler and above all a keen believer in preservation of wild life, a botanist and a naturalist. Perhaps it was the influence of his upbringing and the time spent in England while studying at Sandhurst that made him a conservationist at heart.

But his Youvraj, the Crown Prince loved hunting, especially big game fishing on the Indian Ocean that would take him away from the hustle and bustle of city life, into the wilderness, out of touch with the rest of the world. He enjoyed the solitude that only an open sea, far removed from the shore can provide. It was a paradise in disguise?

Ranaji's generosity enabled this tiny community to build a temple that would serve the need of a population ten times more numerous than Mahuvans, the residence of the Mahuva Island. It was an investment, an exercise in building good relations with the Mahuvan people, his most loyal subjects.

The temple building was divided into two parts, the praying area that could accommodate some one hundred people in comfort. It had the images of most Hindu gods, notably Ganesh, who brings good luck and is considered to be kind, considerate, loving and family oriented. No wonder he is the most widely worship God among Hindus.

Then there were images of Lord Krishna, Lord Rama, Shankar, Ganesh and various Goddesses but the statue of Goddess Ambaji was most prominent, presented to the temple by the Ranaji, as Goddess Ambaji is the patron Devi of most Rajput kings of the bygone era.

Attached to the temple was a vast, spacious community centre. The central hall could easily accommodate a thousand people. Attached to the hall were a kitchen and a couple of small rooms used as a school, where the children were able to complete their primary education, up to the age of twelve. So in a way all the children on the island were able to read and write, a great achievement for such a tiny and isolated community.

There were a couple of large, fully furnished flats to take care of guests who may want to stay the night or even weeks, a legacy of the royal family members who used to spend a considerable time on the island during the fishing season.

The vast compound around the temple was protected by a ten feet high brick wall. It was more of a protection against a tidal wave and to keep destructive goats out than any thing else, as tidal waves could occasionally penetrate up to one mile inland and the island was overrun by goats who provided milk and meat, although most of the islanders were fish eating vegetarians?

The temple garden was the pride and joy of the community. There was a vast and deep lake, holding a considerable volume of water. But the water was semi salty, unfit as a drinking water for humans but goats, camels and most vegetation on the island can survive on such water.

The water from the pond was allowed to flow to a small, shallow cement water trough outside the temple wall where the goats and camels would come to drink. This watering hole was the busiest place on the island, mostly dominated by goats.

There was a deep bore well which supplied the sweet drinking water so essential for human survival. There were also half a dozen big storage tanks that would get filled during the monsoon season and the water used for irrigation, for watering the garden and the fruit orchard.

There were some ten such deep artesian wells scattered across the island, the only source of sweet water for human consumption. But there was no shortage of water as these wells would never dry up, even in worse summer heat. That is why a human settlement was possible here and not on any other surrounding islands.

There were no rivers as such but tiny, fast flowing streams would become alive during monsoon season that may flow for up to four months in a year. But as the main part of the island is made of solid, imporous, sedimentary rocks with many holes and depression, some very deep indeed and broaden by hard work on the part of the residents, these depressions get filled with fresh water during heavy rain and the water so often last until the next monsoon season.

These water holes become tiny oasis for the local wild life, that include various types of birds, purple sunbirds, flowerpeckers, warblers and the common birds like sparrows, pigeons, sky hawks, kingfishers, cliff swallows and the flightless guinea fouls which make a tasty meal, similar to chicken meat.

But the islanders were kind and did not believe in killing any wild life. So they live side by side in perfect harmony, especially as there were no snakes, cats, rabbits, dogs and rats that normally upset the balance. The tall pine trees were littered with artificial nests, placed there during the Ranaji's reign, to encourage the island as a bird sanctuary, helped the wildlife to flourish.

While the island was devoid of big, tropical trees that abound in most part of India, there were plenty of coconut trees along with palm, eucalyptus, whistling pine and special to these islands, Mahuvan pine that grew fast, tall and sturdy, found only on a dozen or so islands in this part of the sea. It was the part of the family of the conifers.

There were plenty of Bawad trees, popularly known as tooth brush trees, as their tender branches were widely used to brush one's teeth before tooth brush became fashionable. It is still used in villages on most part and is so good that users rarely get tooth problems, unlike us, the Westerners who have to go to dentists from childhood.

These trees are so thorny that even camels would not dare to nibble them, thus giving birds a perfect sanctuary. So in a way the island was well forested with plenty of trees, the varieties that suited the island climate and the soil composition but relatively sparsely populated, making it a heaven for wild life. There were tiny pockets which resemble to dense, real forest, a heavenly retreat during the worse heat excesses in summer.

There were also some pippal and neem trees and mangrove swamps and other shrubs, notably Oleander, also known as Pink Rose which produce beautiful red, pink and white flowers with sweet smell but leaves are so poisonous that even goats would avoid them.

These are all of semi desert variety that would grow in harsh, salty soil. But the vast temple garden was full of variety of fruit bearing trees, that included, besides coconut trees, mango, guava, Chania bor (sweet berries) Papaya, pomegranate and similar tropical fruit bearing trees that can survive a dry spell but need fertile soil. As the vast temple compound was covered, up to five feet deep by manure provided by sea weeds, it was a perfect setting for such a mini forest, an orchid of edible fruits.

There was also a flower garden with marigold, Oleander and Champo or Indian Magnolia, Jasmine, Hibiscus and Periwinkle being the popular flower found in most temple compounds.

The islanders successfully used the sea weeds, mixed with goat droppings to produce manure to enrich the soil and grew vegetables like onions, potatoes, peas, runner and broad beans, tomatoes, cassava, aubergine, okra and cucumber to make them self sufficient in food department, although most cereals had to be imported from the mainland, in exchange for dried fish, coconut oil, rope and goat milk products as well as handicrafts and leather goods made from goat skin.

The goat milk which was plentiful was turned into butter, cheese and Indian sweets like penda, a round, sweet solid cheese like sweets made by boiling the milk until it solidifies. It is the most popular sweets, widely used in temples to prepare Prasad or offering to Gods which is then given as alms to the devotees.

The temple was the centre of all activities where the village council, made up of village elders, meet to celebrate marriages, child births, religious festivals like Janmastami, Ram Navmi, birth days of Lord Rama and Krishna, Navratri, Holly and Diwali festival, as well as solemn moments like death and to settle few family differences that may surface from time to time, mainly relating to debt or transfer of land.

Divorce or any sort of crime was unknown on the island. The temple was an oasis of hope, faith and expectancy in an arid and isolated atmosphere, far removed from our so called civilization.

The weekend festival of bhagans, the devotional songs dedicated to Lord Krishna and Lord Rama provided the highlight of the week, so often followed by simple but delicious dinner, not forgetting Prasad of sweet penda, diced coconut cakes and fresh fruits gathered from the fruit orchid in the vast temple ground.

There were some seventy houses, made of mud, bricks and stones, with thatched roofs, using coconut leaves as a standard roofing material with inexhaustible supply, a favourite material for villagers in these parts of India, as coconut trees abound in climate most suitable for these trees.

There was one shop that served all but meagre needs of the people, selling few items of every day usage, such as saris, shirts, dhotis and some clothes, cereals like rice, wheat and millet, candles, lanterns, kerosene and milk and milk products along with locally grown vegetables. But on most part it was a barter trade with minimum use of currency.

The store also provided services such as postal, hair dressing and was the seat of the village medicine man who would prescribe herbal medicine, quite effective on most ailments.

But then villagers were on most part a healthy lot. They had nutritious diet of fish and fresh vegetables along with crisp, unpolluted air blowing from the sea and above all a stress free life unknown in today's world. Stress is the worst health hazard, at par with smoking and excessive drinking.

Although most people lived in the village, there were few isolated settlements scattered around the island, mainly involved in growing vegetables, coconuts, raising goats and turning milk into yogurt, butter and cheese. They also kept hens but mainly for their eggs rather than meat.

Coconuts were dried and squeezed for oil and the roughage provided a good fodder for goats, while the husk was turned into ropes. It was a long process, as the tough husk had to be soaked in water for six months until it become soft and then weaved into thin ropes which were then interwoven into a thick rope as strong as nylon rope but more sturdy and long lasting than any other material. The main mode of transport was bullock carts but there were a dozen camels for more rough terrain.

There was not much to see or do on the island except enjoy natural beauty of different type. Within few hours, using a camel drawn cart, we managed to see, circum navigate the whole island. The south side where we landed had a long and wide sandy beach. It was a dream desert island except that it was not that deserted, a blessing in disguise.

The north side was rugged with a two hundred feet high cliff, a precipice overhanging promontory with a fall down to the foaming sea covered with boulders and dangerous current, an instant death if any one slips or fall down, perhaps a perfect suicide spot for any one tired of life. But it was most unlikely for any one to get tired of life on such a beauty spot?

There was a small lighthouse built some two hundred years ago but not in use any more. There was a primitive but traditional stone wall, in need of repair, around the lighthouse and the cliff, to stop any one going too near to the edge of the cliff which would be extremely dangerous.

There were a couple of old houses nearby, perhaps for the lighthouse keeper but were now empty and in depleted condition. It was as desolate a place as could be imagined, in a way a haunted place where no one would like to spend a night or visit it even in day light on his own. The howling wind was adding spice to this morbid atmosphere!

It was in sharp contrast to the rest of the island where pleasant atmosphere prevailed with laughing children and happy, colourfully dressed women folk and contended men, the adults.

The land here was monopolized by the vast openness, windswept, rugged haunted beauty difficult to put into words. Standing at the edge of the cliff, looking at the vast, never ending sea provided strange, haunting and unforgettable feelings that may remain in one's subconscious mind as long as one may live.

It was such a place on the island of Formentera, off the coast of Ibiza that gave Jules Verne the inspiration to write his most famous book "Twenty thousand league under the sea" a favourite book of most high school kids and collegians as well.

We spend half an hour at this ghostly but unforgettable place, starring at the distant sea, with mind in turmoil. What would be like here after the sun goes down, on a dark, moonless night or in the middle of monsoon when sea goes mad, wind hauling and ready to blow any one off the cliff and into the sea below, was difficult even to imagine, let alone experience?

On our wondering, we visited a couple of tiny settlements with just two to three houses, where we had tea with the locals, in their own homes. They treated us like royalties, refusing to accept money but the children were not averse to sweets and toys. They instantly took to our ladies who would, I am sure make good child minders. Our ladies were all young and not yet mother themselves?

It was the type of hospitality a wood gatherer Shabri provided to Lord Rama. Every one of us was touched and we took to our heart these kind people who treated us like kings, gave us respect that we hardly deserve or perhaps we did, as most of us were kind and considerate people with our hearts filled with love and joy. It was the reflection of the time, the age and the prevailing atmosphere when people would go out of their way to help each other. The milk of human kindness, human benevolence was indeed flowing thick and fast. No one would judge any one and milk of human kindness was flowing fast and thick.

After spending some five hours wondering, we decided to return to the calm and peaceful heaven of the temple with a mini forest of fruit trees and a beautiful flower garden.

We chose a spot near the pond, where there were a couple of beach type open huts with a wooden table and benches. It was a perfect place for picnic, to relax, to soak up the atmosphere and have our long delayed lunch.

Krishna was again quiet today as if lost in his own world, although he was more interested in observing the island, taking photos with his old camera, talking to people, more than any of us.

Then again that was his nature. Perhaps he was missing Mamta, as we were all with our partners but we all tried our best not to make him feel lonely or neglected in any way. Then again it is not the same. No one can take a wife's place in real life.

While we were sitting, relaxing and drinking tea and coffee, Krishna went away in search of some fresh drinking water and some green coconuts that give sweet, cool water, our favourite drink. The temple compound was so vast that it would not be too difficult to get lost among the trees and shrubs, albeit for a short while only.

Suddenly Krishna heard a sweet voice, some one singing a sad song. Although Krishna had never heard the song, the voice was certainly familiar, as if he had heard it many times.

Krishna stopped, stood behind a mango tree and tried to listen to the song which was full of beautiful words, lyrics but sad and the singer was pouring her heart out. Her voice was indeed lovely, in harmony with the song but so often breaking down with emotion.

"Lonely Existence

Alone alone, all alone in this wide wild world
Gone gone, my lovely beautiful child gone
After an association not that long
My early life, my childhood prime
Came into life on this tiny heaven of an island
A jewel in the Crown, in this vast and roaring water expanse
We affectionately call it Indian Ocean paradise
Full of fish and big game hunting
That attracts sports mad, fun loving kings and aristocrats

Who love the sea, sand, sun and having some fun
My little girl, the queen of my heart and every one's favourite
We called her pretty Maya, the affectionate one
Maya the enchanting beauty, the haunting melody
Born an ugly duckling, soon turned into a mermaid
Passage of time, advent of youth, innocence of life
Made her Princess Charming to every one's delight
Loved by all, young and old, friend and foe
Rich and poor, weak and strong
Strolling on the soft sand, dipping the toes in shallow trench
Without a worry, anxiety or a care in the world
Taking in the setting sun's summer warmth
On one early spring's beautiful dawn
Came floating in an young and charming Prince
An angle in disguise, to every one's delight
Laden with gifts of love, affection and kindness
Who won the hearts and minds of the Mahuvans
Call it Kismat, call it destiny, call it what you like
For my innocent Maya, it was love at first sight
They soon got together, never separable
Made their nest, their hideout in the temple compound
They enjoyed each other, many a summer days
It was an innocence friendship, a companionship
Like that of Lord Krishna and Radha
In the Mahuvan forest, a Vrindavan in the making
But their dreams were never meant to last for ever
Perhaps they were only an illusion, creator's cruel joke
The reality soon dawn upon them, in the light of the day
This was an unusual union in many a way
One was a Prince, the other a Pauper, never meant to be together
Their world, their dreams, their goals miles apart
The fun and joy, hope and expectation were all too short lived
Soon the onset of gloom and doom made its mark
Pain too familiar, no escape from reality
One cold, damp and rainy day, a bullet pierced Prince's heart
It was an end of my lovely Maya's dream
Without her Prince Charming, life was not worth charting
It was the beginning of my lonely existence
The end for Maya, when it came, was swift and sad
It was a reunion with her Prince and Mother Nature."

****

When she finished singing, Krishna approached her cautiously, in order not to take her by surprise. When she saw Krishna coming, she stopped the work that of weeding the flower beds, wiped her eyes and got up with difficulty. Krishna rushed in to help her stand on her feet.

Some how her face seemed familiar, as if this was not their first encounter. But the familiarity of the heart did not extend to the brain, not instantly. But how could this be possible, as they were visiting the island for the first time. She was very old, perhaps approaching nineties. Yet there was a spark in her eyes. Her weather beaten and wrinkled face was in a way impressive. Her broad shoulders and snow white hair and her light colour skin must have made her a rare beauty in her young age. She had an aura and self confidence that would be alien to these simple people, isolated, cut off from the rest of the world.

Before any one say any thing, Krishna bent down and touched her feet, in traditional Hindu way, to greet some one who is old enough to be your parents and grand parents.

But this respect is normally reserved for close family members and friends. So Maji (respected old woman) was taken back for a moment. She did not expect such respect from some one residing in a big city.

She spoke in a kind voice, holding back tears that must be due to the sad song she was reciting. "Long live my son. Beta, what can I do for you?"

"Maji, is it possible to get some green coconuts?" Krishna enquired, looking at the coconut trees laden with fruits.

"Beta, there is no one here at the moment. But you can pick coconuts and help yourselves. Pointing at an iron bar firmly planted in cement and a big knife laying nearby, she said, "You can remove the husk and cut the coconut with this stake. There is no need but if you want to pay, then put the money in the donation box which is just outside the temple door. But beta, the water from the well is as sweet. I can bring you a bucket and some earthenware mugs." Maji's voice was cracking up with emotion. Perhaps no one may have showed such a respect to her for a long time, or perhaps Krishna had reminded her of some one she once knew intimately.

"That would be fine. We are sitting over there." Said Krishna, with a kind, sympatric smile, as he left Maji and returned to the picnic hut.

Within ten minutes, Maji came back with a bucket of fresh water and started pouring a mug for every one. When she came to Krishna, he got up and requested Maji to let him do the round.

"Beta, you are our guest. Moreover it is not a task beyond me. I may be old but I am very fit." There was a smile, a twinkle on her face.

But she was taken back when Krishna spoke to her again. "Maji, are you not **Rajba**, the mother of Maya, are you? Please tell me, where is Maya. Is she all right?" Krishna was shaking with emotion, hardly able to control his emotion or tears.

No one could understand what was going on. How could Krishna know Maji? What followed was more like a dialogue from an Indian film rather than a reality.

Although Maji was taken back, this grand woman said in a calm voice, "Beta, how do you know my name, my daughter's name? Have you been here before?"

Now it was Krishna's turn to shed tears. "Maji, don't you recognize me? I am **Deval, Prince Deval.** I have spent many weeks right here, in the flat by the side of the temple." Krishna's voice was cracking with emotion.

"Yes beta, I know you are reincarnation of Prince Deval. You are exactly as I saw you last, not a day older and the same kind, considerate, respectful and obliging person. I felt that when you touched my feet, just as you did on that fateful day, the final farewell, a very long time ago."

Maji hugged Krishna with tears flowing freely from their eyes. But perhaps they were tears of joy, tears of reunion of two lost souls; it was difficult to tell, to separate pain from joy, sadness from elevation of the soul.

Now it was Maji's turn to lose all composure. Krishna let her cry, pour her heart out. After all she had gone through hell. How did she survive for so long was difficult to understand, even to imagine. She was like Bhishma Pitamaha, from the epic tale of Mahabharat who lived to the ripe old age of 190 and died on the battlefield, the arrow that killed him was fired by his favourite great grandson Arjun.

Wiping her tears, Krishna said, "Maji, please don't cry. This is a happy moment. I have found my mother and you got your son. This is a reunion of two lost souls. But please tell me where is Maya?"

"Beta, Maya is no more with me. After your death, she gave up her will to live. She would not eat, sleep or look after herself, take care in any way. She would just sit on the shore and look out at sea, expecting to see your yacht, you coming ashore.

I sat with her as much as I could. She would put her head in my lap and cry like a little girl. Yet there was nothing I could do to lessen her pain, her anguish.

Beta, I would have willing given my life for Maya and you. But it is not in our hand. Our future, our destiny is written up there." She said looking up at the sky and continued.

"How could I consol her, give her hope when there was none. There was no life, no happiness and certainly no future for Maya. Your death ruined so many lives, including that of your father who shot you. He came back to apologize, with tears in his eyes, tears in the eyes of a king!

But it was too late. The damage was already done. The horse had bolted. I am sure he must have gone through hell, suffered as much pain and anguish as me. Anger, hatred, pride and ignorance are a curse on human being. Your father, Ranaji had it all. By the time he learnt humility, that we are all creation of the

Almighty, that we all have souls, feelings, arman and ambition, it was already too late.

One dark, humid and rainy day, Maya took a small boat and sailed into the sea, into the unknown, as far away from here as she could. After a week, we found the boat, stranded on a coral reef, battered by the waves and completely wrecked.

But no one has ever seen Maya again, although some villagers used to say that they sometimes saw her on the beach, either early in the morning or late at night, especially when there was a full moon, dancing, singing, some times calling your name or crying uncontrollably. But she would vanish into thin air if any one tried to go near her. Every one loved her and no one was afraid of her that is of her ghost.

No one believed she was alive or she would harm any one in any way. But she has not been seen on the beach for a long time. Perhaps she has found her prince, her salvation, attained her Mox and she is no longer a wandering spirit in search of her prince charming, her happiness. Her arman must have been fulfilled at last."

While telling us about Maya, Maji was in tears all the time and she collapsed in Krishna's arms as soon as Maji finished her story.

Every one was amazed. Could it be true? Is there a life after death? But then they had a living proof, standing right in front of them. How can they doubt what they saw with their own eyes?

We had our picnic lunch, Maji joining in. But after that we moved back to the beach. Maji took us to the isolated part of the beach, away from the jetty, which was in a way isolated and very beautiful indeed, Maya's favourite place, favourite beach.

While we remained on the beach, we let Krishna and Maji go to her tiny home, to talk and reminisce the past. They had lot of catching up to do and we only had a few hours left, as we had to leave by 5pm.

At ten to five, Krishna and Maji came to the pier. We were ready to leave but Krishna was in two minds. While he was reluctant to leave Maji alone, he could not stay on the island. Mamta must be eagerly waiting for him back in his flat in Bombay.

Krishna tried his best to persuade Maji to accompany him, come with him and let him take care of her. But Maji was reluctant to leave the island. She said, "Beta, I am a very old woman. Perhaps I have a year or two left. I do not believe that I will be happy in a big city like Bombay. Seeing you, spending few hours with you is my best reward since I lost you and Maya. God has at last been kind to me, in my final year of life. But I would like to ask for one favour."

"Maji, you know I will do any thing for you. Just let me know." Krishna said in an emotional voice. He was afraid he may not see Maji again.

"Beta, could you bring Mamta to see me. Some how I feel meeting her will bring back my, our Maya. Perhaps she may have born again, in the body of Mamta. After all you promised to be together for ever."

This really took Krishna by surprise but after what happened today, nothing was impossible.

"Maji, I promise you that I will be back to the island within one month and this time with my wife Mamta, yours and mine Maya will be with me." Some how Krishna was convinced that Mamta was indeed reborn Maya. The departure, the separation was as heart breaking as leaving Ballard's Pier was joy. Krishna took out a small photo of him with Mamta that he always kept in his wallet and gave it to Maji.

As soon as we were on board Jalpari and settled in the vast spacious lounge, with comfortable leather sofas and drinks in abundance, we were eager to hear Krishna's story, in full, without any omission or interruption. Krishna was equally ready to oblige.

Krishna now remembered his previous life as if the events had just happened. Maji's face rekindled his inner memory or whatever one may call remembering one's past life. Most would not even believe in reincarnation. But after what happened today, no one on board will ever doubt that there is indeed life after death.

Krishna was again in jolly mood, happy go lucky person we all know he was and still is. He started jokingly, "Ladies and gentlemen, take your seat. The show is about to start. I don't know what you would make of it but I can assure you that what you are about to hear is a true story, an event that took place on the island a very long time ago.

As we say, truth is often stranger than fiction and the story I am about to tell you is so strange, so unbelievable that even I find it hard to accept. But I can assure you that every word I am about to narrate, speak is absolute truth, nothing but the truth.

In fact it happened before the First World War when the British Empire was at its zenith and Queen Victoria was on the throne. I know you may find it difficult to believe but the proof, the Maji who witnessed the whole scenario is still here, with us and so am I.

In my previous life, I was a prince, the eldest son of Rana Mohanrai, ruler of a small kingdom just south of Bombay. No wonder I am a pauper in this life. After all the lightening does not strike the same place twice nor one may win a big prize in a lottery twice in one's life. But in a way I may have won the lottery twice, as I feel deep down that my Mamta and Maya is the same person, Maya reborn as Mamta.

Ranaji's kingdom was a narrow strip of land along the coast of Maharastra. Although our kingdom was not that large or powerful, it included most of the islands in this part of the sea which were strategically situated. So we had a tiny navy and a luxurious yacht for personal use, as British Raj provided all the security, with their large and powerful navy, the best in the world.

Britannia literally ruled the waves and the sun never set on the British Empire that stretched from Hong Kong in the east to British Guinea in the South America, a distance of well over twenty thousand miles.

All our kings, Ranajis and Maharajas were under the thumb, under the protection of the British Raj, such a tiny nation that ruled our vast nation, the nation that gave the world Lord Rama, Krishna, Emperor Ashok, Chatrapati Shivaji and in recent time Gandhi, Sardar, Tagore and Bose. It seems we the Indians, especially the ruling class, hate each other more than we hate the invaders, the Moguls, the French and the British, the overseas rulers who invaded and occupied this once great and might country, the land of Lord Rama and Krishna, so often with the cooperation and tacit support from the local rulers.

Deval was the eldest son of Ranaji. He was adventurous from the childhood. Although he loved hunting and big game fishing, he would never hunt harmless animals, such as deer, wild pigs, monkeys and foxes that do not harm humans. The only exception was if they raided farms and fields and were a danger to humans, especially young children, then wild life came second to human interest.

Deval, when he returned from England where he had developed a taste for high sea fishing, acquired while going on fishing trips on the Irish Sea, in a yacht belonging to his rich and aristocratic friend.

The Irish Sea was rich, well stocked with tuna, marlin, some twenty species of sharks, some migratory and mackerel. The high sea fishing is indeed a true sport where one has to pitch his strength and skill against a mighty fish, so often weighing ten times the weight of a human being. When Deval returned to Bharat, he started visiting Mahuva Island, using Ranaji's yacht, appropriately named **Rajkumar. (Prince)** At first it was only for taking on fresh water, fruits and vegetables. But later on, when he realized how beautiful the island was and experienced the kindness of the people, he started spending more and more time on the island, trying to convert it into a paradise, by planting trees, enlarging and deepening water holes and digging deep wells that would provide water all year round.

After all it was the favourite place of Ranaji and he had helped the people financially and in every way to build the temple, the flats and landscaped garden, the vast temple compound, the mini forest, as well as creating wildlife heaven for birds and animals. Prince Deval just continued the work his father Ranaji had started but now was too preoccupied with the affairs of the State, his kingdom.

While on the island, Deval met Rajba who had lost her husband when she was only twenty five, with a young child to support. She was employed by the temple authority to look after the flower garden, the orchard and the temple. That gave her some purpose in life and income to support the young child, a beautiful little girl.

Ranaji used to bring his own servants but Deval relied on Rajba and her daughter Maya who was now eighteen. They were requested by the village council to look after the Crown Prince. They cooked, cleaned and did all the work for the prince and his party. Maji was a good cook, especially of sea food which was as fresh as it comes.

As Deval was a kind, considerate and gentle person, he treated Rajba and Maya with respect. Soon Deval and Maya became intimate, spending a lot of time together. It was an odd couple, a beauty and the beast, the beast being in an abstract sense. Maya was a reasonably good looking girl. She was tall, well built with silky skin and attractive hair. At her age, most girls look attractive and desirable, especially in such a romantic atmosphere. Her innocence and school girl type giggly nature and village girl shyness, deceptive innocence only added to her already considerable charm and beauty, not to mention the enormous sex appeal that goes with scanty dressing, especially in a soaring summer's heat.

In the beginning, it was a pure, innocent chat, a simple friendship, a bit of teasing of Maya. But Deval was a friendly person with an attractive personality. He was easy to approach and even easier to talk to.

It was not too long before they realized that they were attracted to each other; there was more than meet the eye in their friendship. The attraction, the desire, the inclination and the yearning was slow, gradual, progressive, unplanned but unstoppable.

At their age and in the romantic surrounding, it was difficult not to fall in love, not to have physical, sexual or somatic attraction, no matter how one may try to fight it off.

For Deval, it would have been simple, straight forward and without any complication to mesmerise Maya with grandeur and false promises, take what he wanted, enjoy the nights in her company and then leave her to her fate. That is what male members of the royal families did, especially when they get involved with girls who were from the so called lower caste, not members of the royal, influential circle.

But Deval was different. He respected every one and all human beings were in a way equal in stature. Perhaps that is what he learnt when he was in England, living with an ordinary English family who treated him with respect but were not over awed by his royal status.

They believed in equality for all human beings, although the British establishment went out of their way to create a class system that differentiated between officers and gentlemen. All high ranking officers in the army and all captains of cricket and rugby teams were, on most part Oxbridge educated gentlemen.

Maji, a widower had only one child Maya. No wonder Maji loved Deval like a son, looked after him and fed him her best dishes, using fresh, temple grown ingredients, the best the island could provide.

In the beginning, Maji was pleased to see Maya and Deval get on so well. She did not realize that such a familiarity, friendship could only end in tears, especially for Maya and Maji.

But then every mother is naïve when it involves the happiness of their children, especially their daughters. So Maji was no exception. Her arman, ambition for her only daughter Maya were paramount in every way and perhaps made her ignore the approaching andhi, the storm.

Fortunately Deval was an exception to the rule. He was not like a bumble bee that would suck nectar from different flower every day. He could easily have trapped Maya, had his fun while he was on the island and then leave her to her fate, move on to pasture fresh.

Deval could not do dirty on Maya or betray the trust Maji had bestowed on him. Maji treated him like a son and the feelings were mutual. In most Rajput palaces, children, princes and princesses were, on most part raised by nannies, so often English nannies. They were even breast fed by Milk Maids, as royal ladies would not risk having sagging breasts that is the part of motherhood, raising children on love and mother's milk.

They even had milk maids to breasts feed the babies, as queens would not like to lose their beauty, have big and sagging breasts that could be the result of breast feeding many children, as in poor families who could only afford mother's milk for their children.

There were neither contraceptive pills nor plastic surgeons to repair, beautify their figures if neglected during pregnancy and while raising children. So mother's love was not always on the card for royal children. Deval had more motherly feelings for Maji than for his own mother **Kuntalba** who was more of a society beauty, a pride possession of Ranaji to show off to his royal guests during grand parties and royal gatherings.

When Deval started staying away from his royal duties, Ranaji was quick to find out the reason. He was not unduly perturbed or worried. But he did seek out Deval and tried to have a father to son, heart to heart talk.

After an early evening dinner, father and son retreated to the smoking room, with a goblet of most expensive Single Scotch whisky and a Havana cigar they both enjoyed occasionally. This was the trademark drink and a smoke for male members of the royal families.

Ranaji started the conversation but Deval was not taken by surprise. He knew Ranaji was eager to have a frank and open talk, discussion with him.

"Beta, it has been brought to my attention that you are spending a lot of your time away from the palace, from your royal duties. I know the island is very beautiful but you have an additional attraction, a girl called Maya. Beta tell me how true, how serious it is?"

"Yes Bapu, (father) you are right. I do spend some time on the island and I do like Maya. She is a wonderful girl, unlike any I have met so far." Deval knew that it would be futile to hide any thing from Ranaji. He had his men; spies would be too strong a word, who kept Ranaji informed about what was going on in his kingdom.

"Beta, when I was of your age, we all had crush on various girls, even on our nannies, teachers and occasionally servant girls. We all know how beautiful Ranak Devi was. She was a labourer on a construction site, yet she became the tool, an instrument in the downfall of one of the most powerful king Gujarat ever had.

This is a learning process. We all make mistakes but wise people learn from their mistakes. In a way it is the prerogative, a privilege, may be a perk of a prince to have the best and the most beautiful girl. But it should not be too obvious. Keep it within the confinement of four walls. You may do what you like in a locked bedroom but it should not become a public knowledge, a topic of gossip." Ranaji tried to pass on his wisdom, his experiences to his naïve son.

"I am aware of royal tradition, how we take advantage of young, innocent virgin girls, use them for our pleasure, our entertainment and discard them like old clothes once our lust, sexual appetite is satisfied. Then we seek fresh challenge; seek pasture new, green and beautiful. We behave like a honey bee who visits different flower every day, in search of best nectar. But neither Maya is that sort of a girl; nor am I interested in cheap, temporary sexual relationship.

Her mother, who looks after me while I am on the island, is like a mother to me. I respect her just like I respect you, respect Rajmata. Moreover I love Maya. I could never treat her like a toy, to play with until a new model comes on the market, nor like a sex object to satisfy my sexual need, desire. I love her and respect her." Deval, as usual was honest to a fault.

The word love, respect and honour rang alarm bells in Ranaji's heart. He was aware that Deval was too honest, too decent, kind and considerate for his own good and the good of his kingdom.

Without losing his cool, Ranaji continued. "Beta, you know that you are not an ordinary person. You are born in a royal family, with a silver spoon in your mouth. You had a privileged upbringing that makes us different from the rest of our subjects. We are not free to do what we like, associate with any Tom, Dick and Harry, fall in love and marry a commoner.

I know this may sound harsh, even patronizing and condescending but that goes with the job, with the territory. After all that is a small price to pay for all the privileges, life of comfort that is but a dream for most. Surely you don't want to give up all these privileges for a girl you met yesterday, the girl you hardly know. The sexual attraction may come and go, like a monsoon rain, like a tide that rise and ebb twice a day, day in, day out." Ranaji said it in a calm but authoritative voice.

Deval had heard this all before. He knew it would serve no purpose to argue with Ranaji but he could not help saying, "Bapu, my love, respect and esteem for Maya is not a sexual attraction. We have not slept together. This is the first time

I have seen a genuine affection, an unconditional love, a relationship not based on my wealth or my background.

Maya will be happy with me even if I was a common labourer, a poor fisherman. I know it will be difficult for you to understand, as our upbringing is such that we are unable to see that there is life outside the palace, the royal circle.

We so often behave like a frog born and brought up in a tiny pond who believes the pond is the beginning and the end of the universe." Deval touched his father's feet to show his respect and left the room before this conversation could develop into a slinging match, a debate that can produce no winner, only losers.

Even when the fishing season was over, Deval kept coming to the island, staying longer. He found inner peace, loved the temple, the mini forest, the pond and above all, the company of Maji and Maya. It was a simple, uncomplicated life, a million miles away from the palace atmosphere, the wheeling and dealing of the royal circle.

He enjoyed fishing, even engaged in a manual labour, doing gardening, mending vegetable patch and cultivating new and exotic vegetables, at least for these people. He introduced green, yellow and red pepper, radish, celery, rhubarb, cherry tomatoes and orange and lemon trees that would grow well in the temple compound. For the first time in his life he was involved in a physical work and to his surprise, he even enjoyed it to no end. After all fruits of hard labour always taste much sweeter than some thing bought from the supermarket shelf?

Deval also did a lot of reading, writing and built up a library of some seven hundred books. Most were in the local Marathi language but there were few books in English, by his favourite authors, Jules Verne, Arthur Conan Doyle, Bronte sisters Charlotte, Emily and Anne, the Irish playwright Oscar Wilde H.G. Wells and many such famous English authors.

They were in their original luxury leather bindings which must have cost him a fortune and are now collectors items, as they are in real good condition, hardly used, only read by Deval.

When Ranaji realised that Deval was still spending every spare minute on the island, ignoring all his advice, their several intimate discussions, Ranaji was forced to withdraw all his privileges, including the use of the royal yacht that was necessary to roam the sea, sail to the Mahuva Island.

Although Ranaji was extremely angry at Deval who had made him a figure of fun in the royal circle, Deval's mother was not unduly disturbed at Deval's changed lifestyle.

She was getting too old for partying, playing the role of a glamorous wife at her age and living a life of deceit, pretence and living in an artificial, make-believe world. She realised that she had not been a caring mother when her children were young and growing. They were more intimate with their English nannies than with their own parents.

This may be a royal tradition but in reality no one can give them real love, a mother's love, care and affection. No wonder, deep in her heart, she was feeling guilty for not playing with them, watch them take first step, not breast feeding them in order to maintain her most vital part in perfect shape, so that Ranaji can show her off at parties and royal gatherings. Even love making with Ranaji was a sedate affair, lacking passion, so as not to spoil her beauty, lean figure and perfect breasts. But then Ranaji could do what he want, make wild and uncontrolled love with a virgin beauty at any time.

When Deval was in the palace, he started taking interest in normal activities, the garden, library, decoration and on few occasions, he even cooked dinner for his mother, shared by all, the young prince and the princess but not Ranaji. By now he had become an expert cook, especially at meat and sea food dishes, learnt from Maji and Maya and his own need when on the island.

It started modestly, making omelette, chapatti and rice. But soon he graduated to more exotic dishes with fish, prawn and mussels, growing his own vegetables and spices like chillies, onion, ginger and garlic. Although every one enjoyed Deval's cooking, no one could dare to invite Ranaji to this feast, as it would be unthinkable for a Crown Prince to get involved in a kitchen, like a hired hand.

With royal yacht out of bound and Ranaji's hostility increasing day by day, Deval decided it was time to move, to make a clean break. With the help of his younger brother, Deval was able to sail the royal yacht for the last time, with all his possession of fishing gears, a couple of guns, books, clothing and every day necessities that he was used to, knowing full well that Ranaji may not allow him to return to the palace, once he knew that he may make the island his permanent home and may get married to Maya, the girl of his dream but perhaps a nightmare for Ranaji.

But it was not a major sacrifice for Deval to shed the royal burden, constraint, coercion and obligation. The real sacrifice would have been to give up his life that he was getting accustomed to on the island, leave Maji and Maya for good. That would have broken his heart, his spirit.

He was sad to leave his mother, now that he was getting to know her and abandoning the young prince and his lovely sister princess Madhumati, a sweet little girl with a heart of gold.

But Deval thought that once the dust had settled down, when Ranaji comes to acknowledge his lifestyle, his arman, his goal in life, then perhaps his mother and other member of the royal family will be able to visit him on the Mahuva island, although he knew that he would never be able to return to the palace with Maya, not as long as Ranaji was in charge. But Deval was willing to take that risk.

Although Deval had moved to the island for good, Ranaji would not leave him alone. It was difficult for him to come to terms that his Youvraj (Crown Prince) had deserted him for a lowly girl, a fisherman's daughter.

Ranaji would send his close aids, his young prince and palace officials to the island to persuade Deval to abandon Maya, his lifestyle on the island and to return to the palace, to his royal duties. Ranaji loved Deval too much to let him go that easily.

Perhaps he could not forget or forgive Deval for breaking his heart, disobeying him, selling him short and above all making him a figure of fun among the royal circle when the story broke out, when Deval's love life became public knowledge. Ranaji's invitations to royal gatherings, high society parties soon dried up. This was a real blow to his pride. How could Maya, a completely insignificant person whom he would not employ even as a servant could snatch his prince from him? Then Ranaji had not met Maya or Maji, spend few hours in their company.

The real victims of Deval's indiscretion, foolishness, folly and lack of judgement were his younger brother and sister. Their chances of getting married in a royal family, especially the one higher in pecking order were practically dashed.

The princess Kamal Devi was indeed a very beautiful girl. Ranaji was hoping to attract the attention of the crown prince of Jaipur, as a suitor for his lovely daughter.

Ranaji had met the prince and introduced him to his daughter and they seemed to get along well, even inviting the Maharaja and his family for a fishing holiday on his yacht. But now all his plans were in ruins, spoiled by none other than his own son. No wonder Ranaji was angry, upset and mad. How dare Deval ruin his life and the lives of all his family members and for what, a two a rupee girl?

One fateful day, Deval found Ranaji and his personal aide Captain Raichand knocking on his door. To avoid the commotion, the inevitable argument in front of Maji and Maya, Deval persuaded Ranaji to go for a walk, to the remote part of the beach where they would not be disturbed.

An hour later, Maya, Maji and most of the islanders heard two gun shots, in rapid succession.

Every one who was near by and heard the shots ran to the beach but it was already too late for Deval. His dead body was lying on the pure, snow white sand and Ranaji, along with his aide were boarding the speed boat to return to the yacht. Within half an hour the yacht disappeared from the horizon, as if it was never there.

No one could believe their eyes. Could Ranaji have shot his own son, his crown prince dead? Perhaps he put family honour, the future of his other children above his love for his eldest son, his Youvraj. Perhaps it was a momentary madness that he did not know what he was doing.

The islanders kept the body for twenty four hours. They all knew that no one would come to collect his body, take him home and give him a family send off. Perhaps Ranaji may not even tell his family members what had happened.

In the end Maji, Maya and the villagers cremated Deval, his mortal remains and scattered his ashes in the temple orchid, the mini forest, and his beloved place where Deval found internal peace, tranquillity, satisfaction and real happiness.

The orchard was the most tranquil part of the island. Once smitten with the carefree island life, it would be difficult to keep away from this heaven. The temple compound was also a heaven for wild life, with squirrels, guinea fowls, small, almost miniature Mahuvian deer and above all some thirty varieties of birds nesting on equally number of different variety of trees that include, beside coconuts; mangos, black plum, pomegranates, guavas, Chania bore (Indian Cherries) neem and thorny bawad trees being the prominent. The human helping hand, in form of artificial nests, the deep pond with fishes and occasional help at feeding when the natural food was in short supply, helped the bird life to flourish. The nesting help were for the small birds like marsh harrier, parakeet, robin, cuckoo, woodpecker and similar varieties, to keep out the big, destructive sea birds like gulls.

Deval was born to be part of such a world rather than be a royal prince and live in an artificial, make belief world where one may have to watch every step one may take, every word one may utter.

A special mango tree was planted to remember Deval. After some sixty years, it was still bearing fruits by the bucketful. Moreover these mangos were the sweetest and one of the best in the region, with plenty of flesh and a tiny stone. (Seed) Unfortunately the stone was so tiny compared to the size of the mango and perhaps infertile that stopped the islanders from producing more trees of this variety. It was, like Deval a one off success which will disappear when this tree stops producing fruits, the end of an era and the last relic of the bygone era.

I have managed to get some fifty mangos. You will be able to sample them with your dinner as well as take some home. Now I am told that the dinner is ready. So refill your glasses and proceed to the dining room, not forgetting your partner?

Krishna was speaking for well over two hours, with only a ten minute break to let them go to the bar and get some bottles of beer and wine.

Practically no one believed in life after death, in reincarnation when they left Ballard Pier. Now practically they did or were at least willing to consider the possibility, give the benefit of the doubt.

By the time the mouth watering, long lasting dinner was over, the Jalpari was approaching the Ballard pier. Krishna was the first to disembark. No one tried to stop him, as he was eager to get back to his wife Mamta after two days of separation or perhaps a reunion after a lifelong separation?

It was well over two hour's journey, from the Central Bombay to Borivali East, where Krishna had his own flat. As it was Sunday and late in the evening, the train was nearly empty. Krishna took an isolated, a corner seat and lost in his own world.

He could not help but wonder that if he is reincarnation of Deval, where is Maya? After all they promised to remain faithful, stay together for ever, in this life and every life, as Maya was a firm believer in life after death, in reincarnation.

Looking at the circumstances that brought Krishna and Mamta together, it was more than likely that Mamta was his beloved Maya, enjoying a married life together that they failed to achieve in their previous life.

Krishna remembered the conversation he had with Maya when he once walked in on her when she had just come out of shower and drying her body in the bedroom of the temple flat, with nothing on.

As they were not yet married, there was no question of them sleeping together, having a sexual relationship that is the norm today, especially in the West. But little bit of romancing, cuddling and occasional kissing was inevitable, inescapable and unpreventable considering the romantic atmosphere and the closeness they enjoyed. In fact if Deval had insisted on sexual relationship, Maya may not have refused, as she knew it was only a question of time before they get married.

Looking at the naked, well formed and beautiful body of Maya, Deval could not help but enter the bedroom and grab her and gave her a long, lingering kiss, without much protest from Maya. It was the first time Deval had seen Maya without clothes. She looked indeed beautiful, with perfect, well developed body which was untouched in more ways than one.

Deval could not let her go for nearly half an hour, kissing, cuddling or just holding her tight, looking at her figure, admiring her innocence and the well formed body.

Deval noticed that Maya had a strange, a rare birthmark high on her right thigh. It was in the form of a Trishul, Lord Shiva's weapon of destruction. It was about three inches high and looked more like a tattoo than a birthmark. It was the most unusual and a rare birthmark, only a handful may have it in the world.

Maya jokingly told Deval that she would bear this birthmark in every life, no matter where and when she may be reborn. If we ever get separated, he should look for this mark, at the same place.

Krishna regretted that he never examined Mamta with such care and attention, as it was the Indian custom to make love in the dark, curtain drawn and light turned off. No one wore that revelling swimsuit either. Very few ladies enter the sea or a swimming pool and most were dressed very conservatively, revelling very little, even when in swimming costume?

It was the age when imagination had to work overtime and modesty ruled the roots. That is why the slightest exhibition of one's private parts, especially the bulging breasts attracted so much attention, curiosity and prying eyes, raises blood pressure.

The circumstances that brought Krishna and Mamta together were some what strange, rather bizarre to say the least. Krishna and Mamta were together in the college but were not that close. Krishna was a year ahead of Mamta but as they had a few common friends, they found themselves together on occasions, especially when going on picnics, participating in sporting events. In fact once they had been mix-doubles partners in badminton. So they knew each other well without being close. Then that was the type of friendship between boys and girls on most part.

After completing his Masters degree in psychology, Krishna stayed on to do his PhD, a minimum requirement for any one who has the aspiration to be a professor in this difficult and demanding field.

It was more of a research, writing thesis and teaching than passing exams. So Krishna only had a couple of lectures to attend to but had to take few classes at the highest level, under the supervision of well established lecturers.

Suddenly from being two college friends, Krishna and Mamta found themselves, albeit on rare occasion, as a student and a professor. But as this was a university with matured, well educated adults, close relationship, even marriages were not a taboo, nor were they frowned upon as long as their interest, their studies and exam results do not clash, their integrity was not questioned.

Mamta was not beautiful in traditional Indian way of thinking, a tall girl with fair skin, long light brown hair and curves in all the right places. But then beauty is in beholder's eyes. So it is difficult to define beauty in a concrete term. Moreover most men like women with big, over bearing breasts, bottoms that go up and down, swing with every step, but only as a mistress, not as a wife?

Although Mamta was tall, at five and a half feet, she had a dark skin and short, jet black hair. But her skin was smooth without any pimple and her short, boyish black hair suited her round, boyish and beautiful face with ever present smile that gave her an aura, ambience of self confidence and self belief that would impress most boys. She was a kind, caring and extremely bright and intelligent person that gave her an instant advantage on most girls.

Her dressing style was also unique, preferring wide trousers and a matching top rather than traditional Indian dress of Saris and Punjabi dress or skirt and blouse that was the standard dress, the trademark of most collegians.

One day, Mamta knocked on Krishna's door. He was surprised when he opened the door and saw Mamta standing there.

"Can I come in?" She said in a casual manner but it was obvious that she was a bit tense.

For a moment Krishna was speechless, tongue tied. No girl had ever visited him at his tiny but comfortably furnished one bedroom flat in the university compound, unless they were in a group.

When Krishna regained his composure which took a while but did not discourage Mamta in any way, Krishna at long last said, "Of course Mamta, you may come in. I was just surprised to see you standing outside my door." Krishna was apologetic.

Soon Mamta and Krishna were having tea with biscuits and Bombay mix, a common offering in a bachelor's flat. After half an hour's of aimless chitchat, Mamta suddenly became serious.

She said in some what shaky voice. "Krishna, what I am about to say will not only come as a surprise but perhaps will shock you as well, but I hope a pleasant surprise. I am sure that once the initial jolt is over, you will be pleased; at least that is what I am expecting from you. Take your time before you give me a reply. I am willing to wait as long as you wish."

Krishna was not only surprised but immensely curious to know what Mamta want from him. It can not be money nor any personal or marking favour, as every one knew his position, his temperament and honesty which was beyond reproach. But he did not have to wait long to know what Mamta wanted from him.

"Krishna, would you marry me? I will make a good wife and will try my best to make you happy, to fulfil all your ambition on social, financial and academic front."

For a moment, Krishna was taken aback. It was a bombshell. He could not believe his ears. "Mamta, could you repeat what you said just now? I am not sure that I understood you." Krishna said in an apologetic voice.

"Krishna, you heard me right the first time but you did not expect to hear what I said. Believe me; I did not expect to say it either. Although it has been in my heart, in my thought but I never thought I would be able to be so blunt, so straight forward, for a shy girl like me." There was twinkle, a mischief in her eyes.

"But now that I have said it once, I do not mind repeating it. Would you marry me, take me as your wife?" Then she mischievously added, "I will not be able to pay you any dowry. But I am sure you do not believe in those old, exploiting and cruel ways, tradition that most of us would like to confine to dustbin." This time Mamta said it slowly, in a calm, cool and pleasant voice so that there is no misunderstanding or any doubt.

Krishna could not help but smile. For a moment he thought Mamta was pulling his leg but soon realized that she was serious. Krishna said in equally definitive voice, "Mamta, I am flattered that such an intelligent and charming girl like you would like to marry me. But I have to ask you why me? I may not be an ideal choice, a real catch? Could I? If you know some thing that I don't, please tell me. Have a long lost relative left me a fortune?" Now it was Krishna's turn to be mischievous, to be a bit naughty and pull Mamta's leg.

"I know you would not take me seriously. But that you find me charming and intelligent is a good start. Well Krishna, I would be completely honest with you. I have to, as I know no one can pull wool over your eyes. Moreover I admire you and owe you the truth.

My father wants me to marry Sheth (Businessman) Ratanlal's son Prasant. I do not know Prasant at all, although I have met him a couple of times. So I can not say any thing good or bad about him except that he has not even passed metric exam, let alone gone to a college. But if he is willing to marry me on the say so of his father, then he can not be a good catch?"

But most important for me is to teach my father a lesson he will not forget in a hurry. He arranged this marriage behind my back, without even consulting me. I am expected to do what I am told, a 23 year old girl with a Masters degree in business administration and financial management.

I understand my father, who is addicted to gambling, owes a considerable amount to Sheth, the money he borrowed on false pretext, to gamble away on horses. Shethji is willing to write off his debt if I marry his son. I know this is not what you would like to hear. But I have to tell you the truth. I can not say this is love at first sight, as we have known each other for a long time. Even if I say that, you are not that naïve to believe me.

But I must admit I have always admired you, the way you have overcome your handicaps and come out on top. One day you will become a professor. I feel we can supplement, compliment each other. The more I think about you, more I feel that we are well suited for each other. Don't you think we will make a good couple?" Mamta knew Krishna's soft point, his weakness.

"I do not want the answer straight away. You may take as much time as you want and let me know your answer when you are ready." Then Mamta mischievously added, "As long as your answer is yes?" Krishna could not help but smile, admiring Mamta, her courage and her vision.

She was not yet finished, she continued, "Krishna we may not be in love but there is chemistry between us. I am sure there is a physical attraction between us, even if we may deny it. After all you are my professor and every girl, every student dream of marrying her professor, especially if he is young, in the same age group and handsome as well. I don't mind admitting to you that I have fancied you since you started taking our classes. You have unique personality that differentiates you from the rest, although I can not say how much you admire me or want me as your wife.

Krishna, sleep over my proposal until you are absolutely sure, one way or another. If you say no, I will not blame you but I will surely be disappointed. No matter what, life has to go on." Suddenly Mamta was philosophical. It was obvious that she had not made any other plans in case Krishna may refuse, turn down her marriage proposal.

"Mamta, I do not mind admitting that I have fancied you for some time as well. But I never thought you will give me the opportunity to say yes or no. Let me sleep over it and I promise you a reply by the weekend. Don't worry, every thing will be fine. You will not have to marry Prasant just to please your dad, to let him out of the deep hole that he has dug for himself." Krishna's heart was already throbbing with excitement and expectation, his blood pressure raised to an unhealthy level!

Once the initial shock was over, the ice was broken; they relaxed, felt at ease and enjoyed each other's company. They had a long, heart to heart talk, confiding in each other as if they had been close friends all their life, even holding hands affectionally from time to time but to no one's surprise.

In fact by the time Mamta left, Krishna was ready to give his reply, to say yes to Mamta but he thought it would be prudent to wait at least twenty four hours. In that way he will get at least another opportunity to meet Mamta, enjoy her company and plan the future together.

The good bye, hasta lavista (see you later) was enough to convince Mamta that she will, in not too distant a future be Mrs. Mamta K. Kotecha, wife of soon to be professor? How could Krishna or any one else in his position could say no to such an offer. There is an Indian saying that when Goddess Laxmi (Goddess of wealth) comes to bless you, there is no time to go and wash your face!

After Mamta left, Krishna could not help thinking how fate has brought them together. How come Mamta chose him? There were many boys in their circle who would be much more of a catch for Mamta than an orphan like Krishna. They came from much richer families than him, as he had lost both his parents by the time he was a teenager. He was brought up by his widowed grandmother.

She also passed away when Krishna was in his final year of the college, reading philosophy, a difficult subject to pass with high grade and mostly a favourite course for girls rather than boys. So Krishna was all alone in the world, without a single blood relative.

As Krishna was a bright student, the college authority gave him a grant, on the recommendation of college Principal, so as to let him finish the course, take his final exam. After graduating, he stayed on to do his masters. This time the grant came from his community educational fund and his weekend job at a local but posh restaurant. Krishna was a good chef, able to cook both meat and vegetable dishes.

So in a way Krishna was a self made person. He was clever, streetwise, capable, a good judge of people and knew how to stand on his own two feet, how to survive in a harsh and unfriendly environment. But he was also a kind, considerate and helpful person, the attributes that comes out of a tragedy, a hard life, a situation where one has to fend for one self, struggle against all odds, face the hardship that the society can throw at you, by a bucketful.

Perhaps that is why Mamta had chosen him; put him on a higher packing order. More Krishna thought, more he pondered, more he realized that this was an opportunity he could not, should not miss. After all, with his background, lack of family support and his financial status, not many dads would be queuing outside his door to offer the hand of their daughter in a marriage. So when opportunity knocks on his door, he should grab it with both hands. This may turn out to be a spring time, a pleasant time in his young but eventful life.

Mamta looked sweeter and sweeter, more charming and beautiful as he thought more about her. Life with her would always be pleasant, sweet, happy and rewarding in every way.

Next day Krishna rang Mamta and arranged to meet on Saturday, go for a meal at a posh restaurant, the restaurant where he was working and then take her to a nearby park. They had a lot to talk, to plan and to arrange, as Mamta would be marrying him against the wishes of his family. So it has to be a registry office marriage, followed by a visit to a temple and in presence of few trusted and loyal friends.

When they sat down in the park, after a romantic meal specially arranged by Krishna's friends at the restaurant, in an isolated place, as far away from the crowd as possible with Mamta looking beautiful and sexy, in a canary yellow Sari, an unusual colour, with sleeveless low cut and bare back blouse that uses a minimum of material and gives a maximum of exposure. She was dressed in a manner that would attract any one's attention, male and female. This was the first time Krishna had seen her in a Sari and how beautiful she looked? This was in sharp contrast to what she normally wear, floppy trousers and tops that would cover her body, most of her curves and female attractions.

Krishna holding Mamta's hand in a gentle and romantic manner, looking straight in her eyes said, "Mamta my answer is yes and yes again. But are you sure this is what you want? You know that once we go ahead, there is no going back. This literally means till death do us part. You know my background and what I can offer you in marriage.

By the way you look so beautiful that I am tempted to grab you, hug you and give you a long, lingering kiss. Why don't you wear Saris more often?" Krishna said it teasingly, but a bit unsure how Mamta would take it. But by now they were at ease with each other, able to tease, have a romantic conversation, and touch one another without feeling embarrassed.

"Krishna or May I call you my Lord Krishna? I know you would love to see me in a Sari, especially in sky blue colour sari, with a matching, sleeveless blouse, in your favourite colour. I knew if you had any doubt, looking at me, you would have to say yes, although I am not wearing your favourite colour. But this is my favourite, my lucky Sari. After all I do look sexy, don't I?" Mamta was as straight forward as Krishna, then added, "I would love a hug and a kiss and much more but not here. I do not want any one to see us in a compromising pose. Technically I am your student and I do not want to jeopardise your future, our future in any way. But behind closed doors, it will be a different ball game. We can do what we please. Can't we?" Mamta was getting naughty by the minute. Krishna thought Mamta was a shy and perhaps a nervous girl, at least when it comes to boys. How wrong he was?

Getting serious Mamta said, "You want to know why I chose you. Well, can you tell me why not? I will be honest and tell you the truth. You are a tall, handsome person. Many girls fancy you but I had the courage to come clean.

Perhaps the events forced my hands. I can not say I would have the courage to propose to you if my father had not arranged my marriage to an illiterate, found a totally unsuitable partner for me.

I know that you have no blood relations and you are a self made person. So you come without a baggage that is what most girls want. Perhaps you may not like what I said, but it is the truth and I am trying to be honest. After all, honesty is the best policy!

I also feel that we are well suited for each other and we will have a happy and wonderful life together. Yes, I am one hundred percent certain, perhaps more certain than you. I am the lucky one and I will give you all the happiness in the world. Only couple of days ago, I told you I am not in love with you but now I can say I do love you with all my heart and I know you feel the same for me. Don't you?" There was a mischievous smile on her face and her heart was beating fast, perhaps not as fast as his?

"Mamta, I am so glad to hear that you love me. Yes, our feelings are mutual and I can say without any reservation that you have stolen my heart. Look at you? Aren't you beautiful, capable of stealing any one's heart? You are naughty but nice, my Turkish delight?" Now it was Krishna's turn to be honest and pay verbal complement, as he could not afford red roses!

Within two months Mamta will be taking her Master's exams and will leave the college. That will end their student teacher relationship, remove any obstruction, any doubt, any suspicion that may harm Krishna's prospect to become a professor, although in reality Krishna was only a student professor and such relationship between two students were normal and totally acceptable to the college authority.

Mamta promised his dad that she will marry Prasant after her exam is over. Until then she would like to be left alone, the proposal, the condition her dad accepted with gratitude and relief.

Krishna and Mamta got married within two weeks of Mamta passing her exams and leaving the college. It was nearly nine months since Mamta knocked on Krishna's door and took Krishna by surprise.

Mamta soon found the job in a bank and Krishna was more involved in teaching, having submitted his thesis. Soon they moved out of the university compound, to a more specious, two bedrooms flat of their own.

Once Mamta's parents came to know Krishna and the fact that he was a much better husband for their only daughter Mamta, than Prasant could ever be, they accepted him and welcomed both in their home. It was a happy ending, mainly due to the courage and foresight of Mamta.

The arrival of the station where Krishna had to disembark; broke his chain of thought. He took a rickshaw, as he was eager to reach home, give a hug to Mamta and see whether she had the birthmark that Maya carried.

As soon as Mamta opened the door, Krishna grabbed her and suffocated her with kisses and a tight embrace. Although by now, they were married for over six months, they had not spent a single night alone, away from each other, Mamta even refusing to stay overnight when visiting her parents. Every night was still a honeymoon night and the physical, sexual attraction was as strong and acute as it was when Krishna saw her in a sexy Sari for the first time, in the nature park when he could not take his eyes of her even for a single minute.

"Krishna, at least ask me how I am before you make love to me? I know how you must have missed me, especially in such a romantic atmosphere, on the boat and on the island. I know how much I missed you!" Mamta was not at all surprised at the intensity of Krishna's affection or what they will do, how they will spend the night. She was ready and excited in expectation.

In reply Krishna lifted Mamta gently and carried her to the bedroom, laid her down on the bed and said, "Now I know why we love each other so much. Why there is such chemistry between us. Please listen to what I have to say with attention.

You may find it difficult to believe it but each and every word I am going to say is the truth, an absolute truth. Mamta listened with attention and when Krishna finished, there was a smile on her face.

She slowly undressed herself, taking off the long skirt she was wearing, revelling her entire lower part of the body. High up on her right thigh, there was the birthmark, a Trishul, the exact copy of the one Maya had. It was of the same size, same place and same design.

Although Mamta could not remember any thing about her previous life, she believed every word, every little incident Krishna told her. As Mamta had recovered fully from her stomach upset, they celebrated this night as their second honeymoon, making love passionately, especially on part of Krishna, as he did not have a sexual relationship with Maya, not until they get married, which did not happened due to the untimely death of Deval.

So it was a special night they celebrated to the full, until they fell a sleep, but not before Mamta expressed her desire to visit Mahuva Island and meet Maji, perhaps her mother in her previous life. Krishna thought and hoped that once Mamta meets Maji, she will remember her past life, just like he did when he first laid his eyes on her. If she could, he will have his Maya and Mamta at the same time. Only time will tell whether Maya and Mamta are one and the same person, as Krishna and Deval are. No matter what, this was a spring time, the happiest time in their lives and they cherished every minute of it.

****

BORN TO SUFFER

My life story is in many ways stranger, more intricate and certainly full of twists and turns than a fiction. Some may say I was born unlucky but I would like to be positive and say the God has given me this opportunity to be strong so that I can overcome all difficulties in life that would make me a strong willed person, capable of not only looking after myself but can be an inspiration to others who may find themselves in similar situations. In a strange way, it is an opportunity to serve my fellow suffers my fellow human beings as best as I could.

Perhaps if I had a choice, I may have opted for a normal life. But then again, it is difficult to imagine, to define what is normal and what is unusual, out of ordinary or untypical in this topsy turvy world.

So I have learned to count my blessings, however few it may sound and go on with my life, as best as I could under these very difficult and trying circumstances. There is a saying that youth, beauty and health never stands still. It is liable to change sooner or later. In my case it changed while I was still in my nappies or perhaps on the day I was born.

As I am so confident, I have decided to give my true name and the names of my family members who are a tower of strength to me. Without their love, their whole hearted support, care and understanding, it would have been almost impossible, not only to achieve my goal but even to survive in my day to day struggle, my day to day life.

When I wrote this piece I was a 21 year old girl, a smart, charming, jovial, confident and beautiful girl with all the hope, arman and expectation that a girl of my age have inbred in them and why not?

No matter where one may be born, the coincident of birth, how rich or poor one may be, how educated or illiterate a person is, our goals in life are the same.

Hope, dreams and expectations have no limit, no boundary, nor any ceiling or constraint. There is no difference between a prince and a pauper when it comes to expectation, achievement in life. On most part, we all would like to be healthy, well educated, reasonably rich so as to have a good living standard, fell in love, get married and have a loving and understanding partner and a lovely family of our own. This is the law of nature, the desire of the heart.

My name is Pooja Shah and I am a university graduate with a first class degree in Business Administration and Financial Management. I hope or rather I am determined to add a couple of more degrees to my CV and that include MBA from one of the famous learning institutions in the West. Now that I have received a bursary, a scholarship to study in Australia, a dream country for me, I know I am capable of conquering the world, going to the moon. My hero is Alexander the Great who conquered half the world by the time he died young, at the age of 32.

When I was at school, geography was one of my favourite subjects. I chose Australia and New Zealand for my studies. Since then I have a dream to visit this country, the continent of Australia.

I am most fascinated by the Great Barrier Reef, off the coast of Queensland. It is one of the natural wonders of the world. I would put it on top of my list if I had an opportunity to visit one of these seven natural wonders of the world.

Others natural wonders are Ngorongoro Crater in Northern Tanzania, right on the border between Kenya and Tanzania, Grand Canyon in Arizona, Niagara Falls, Victoria Falls and sailing the Kerala backwaters, in a converted rice boat which is the main attraction in this state where Western tourists descend, may I say like doves in search of peace and harmony with mother nature.

I know it will not be easy for a young girl, born and brought up in India to adapt to Australian life style. But at least the climate is similar to ours and as I have lived in London for four years, I am some what familiar to Western way of life which will stand me in good stead to start with.

But this is the least of my worries, as I was and still am a born "**JUVENILE DIABETIC.**" Those who are not familiar with this illness, this condition, they may not be able to appreciate fully the every day struggle that I have to undergo in order just to survive.

But I love to fight the odds, the challenges and the obstacles that are thrown at me. If Gandhiji can fight the might of the British Empire, armed with nothing more than determination, truth and burning desire to remove the shackles of political gulami (slavery) and succeed against all odds, then mine is a minor problem, a small inconvenience!

My diabetes was detected when I was two years old, in 1985 and that also on one of the most auspicious day in Hindu calendar, the Dipawali or the festival of lights, the day Lord Rama returned to his capital city of Ayodhia after spending fourteen long years in the forest where he was banished by his step-mother Kaikai.

It is a joyous occasion which is as widely celebrated in India and all over the world where there are Hindus, as is Christmas in the Western world. In a way my life was turned upside down but fortunately I was too young to understand what was happening to me.

Instead my mum and dad had to endure this pain on there own. I am sure Dipawali had never been the same for my parents since that fateful day. But I also hope that looking at me, a mature, beautiful and highly educated girl, a wonderful human being, the Dipawali spirit will re-enter that lives, joy, happiness and fun will overcome the sad memory and enjoy Dipawali as much as any other person. That is one of the reasons I am determined to succeed, make my life a shining example for others who are in the same boat as me.

I was a happy go lucky baby, bubbly and chubby but was entangled by various symptoms like drinking a lot of water, passing urine more frequently than normal, eating a lot for my age and build, crying, feeling tired and sleeping a lot.

Finally I lost consciousness and was rushed to hospital. In fact I was in a diabetic coma. In the 1980s, such cases were indeed very rare, especially in India. The medical team of doctors and nurses had a hard time to find out what was wrong with me, to diagnose my illness.

Numerous tests were carried out and I was put in an ICU (Intensive Care Unit) under twenty four hour observation. The fact that I survived such a trauma is a minor miracle. God gave me a second chance at life and I must grab it and use it to the best of my ability.

After numerous conferences between various professionals, I was finally diagnosed to be diabetic after my blood sugar test which showed the sugar level of more than 600! It is high enough to kill an adult. So how I survived only God knows.

My mum, dad and all my family members were awestruck, aghast and speechless. Obviously they were very upset as they had never heard the word diabetic before.

No one could even imagine what a sacrifice my parents had to make. It is not an easy task to look after a two year old diabetic baby, giving her insulin injections twice a day, forcing her to eat, testing her blood sugar, avoiding hyperglycemias (high sugar) and saving from acute emergency of hypoglycaemia (low sugar)

It is not an easy task, certainly not for some one without any medical knowledge and one person can definitely not cope. My dad had to take a crash course in Juvenile Diabetics and now with years of experience he knows more about this particular form of illness than most specialists in this field.

What my dad needed was a support and understanding from my mum and other members of the family which he readily got. Luckily we were a joint family, a large congregation with three brothers and my grand parents living under the same roof.

This is the time when we need an elderly person, a wise, cool, calm and calculating figurehead who can guide, advice and comfort the younger family members when they are down, depressed or just on the point of giving up, cursing the God for our problems.

We were extremely lucky on that front, as all family members rallied round and even made financial contribution if and when needed. This is our Hindu culture and Indian tradition that has stood us in good stead for thousands of years.

My family, after the first shock, accepted this as a challenge, developed a steely willpower and were ready to do the battle all the way, although they knew that there was an uncertain future and some risk for me.

My mum and dad had a strong heart, optimistic outlook and above all unshakable faith in God. My dad is a strong believer in Lord Krishna and Lord Rama while my mother has a soft corner for every Hindu God and Goddesses.

My mum and dad had to forego every social activity, hobbies and interest. They simply did not have the time or even the inclination except to earn a living and to look after me. This is indeed a very expensive illness in India where there is no National Health? We have to pay for all the drugs and frequent hospital admissions.

My dad who is a highly qualified and an intelligent person made it his life mission to read each and every publication on Juvenile Diabetic, books and journals, to keep an eye on the latest research and development and study in detail every new drug that came on the market.

He even attended camps and conferences especially reserved for medical profession where he outshone many so called experts in their own field. No wonder my dad had to walk out so often when he took me to see a specialist who knew far less than my dad but was unable and unwilling to listen, to come down from his high horse or drop his superior complex. There were some specialists who were willing to listen to him and acknowledge their lack of knowledge, especially about the latest development.

There was no internet at the time to browse and get the latest report on new drugs and the ongoing research. My dad had no time for such ego specialists who may do more harm than good to me.

My mum did most of the practical jobs, including giving me injections. In the beginning I used to cry a lot at the sight of an injection but my mum did not flinch. She did her duty with a smile on her face but tears flowing freely in her heart.

There is some truth and justification in the saying that there is no love like a mother's love. I remember reading a story in one of my school library books about mother's love.

A boy was madly in love with a very beautiful and a charming girl but spoilt rotten. He challenged her to order him to carry out any task and he will do it without a murmur to prove his love and dedication to her.

She asked him to bring his mother's heart in a bag. While he was walking back with her heart in a plastic bag, after killing her, in a dark, unlit street, he stumbled on a pothole in the road.

The heart cried out, "Beta, take care. I hope you are not badly hurt?" This is mother's love that comes without any string attached. It is a pure, unselfish and altruistic love beyond comparison with any other love or sacrifice. It is pure holy water, water from river Ganges or what we call Gangajal.

After few years, when my parents were some what settled in their daily routine of looking after me, the doctors advised my parents to have another child, looking at my delicate health and uncertain future.

They were understandably reluctant, anxious, apprehensive and worried. But after long consultations with doctors, gynaecologists and specialists who assured them that the lightening never strikes the same spot twice, I had a cute little baby sister. We called her Priya Shah.

In the beginning every thing seemed normal. But it was a false hope, a fool's gold, a cruel trick of Vidhata, the Hindu Goddess who writes our future when we are born. There was no pot of gold at the end of the rainbow.

Slowly but surely black clouds gathered on the horizon. In just seven months Priya developed symptoms like me. But this time, my dad had his own doubts and he checked her urine. It was like expecting the unexpected. What he had always feared, in spite of all the assurances from the so called experts. Their fear became a reality.

She had a very high level of sugar and ketone. They took her to the doctor and the cycle of tests, consultations and more tests were repeated and the final result was that, like me she was also a juvenile diabetic. This was incredible, as there was no diabetic history on either side of my family, for three generations.

This was the first and the last time I saw my papa in tears. It broke my mum's heart although I was too young to understand the full extent of the stress this would put our family under. Like before, every one rallied round but ultimately it was the responsibility of my mum and dad.

So now imagine, two girls, a nine month old baby and an eight year old young girl, each need equal amount of attention, importance and care. It was more than a double load of work for my mum and dad.

We took over their whole life. They had to give up each and every outside interest. We became their whole world, centre of their life. We were too young to appreciate the sacrifice they had to make in order to look after us, twenty four hours a day, seven days a week, three hundred and sixty five days a year.

But now that we are both more or less adult, we appreciate their sacrifice and on our part, we try our best to achieve the unachievable, climb the highest mountain, the Mount Everest peak and make them proud of us, of our achievements.

I vaguely remember, initially when I came to know that I am a diabetic, I used to hate it, especially the daily routine of taking injections, the strict diet regime and unable to do routine activities that young girls of my age normally would like to do.

I used to steal chocolate from the lunch boxes of my friends and eat them in a cubical. I felt handicapped, being left out and I envied my friends when they enjoyed themselves and I could not join them.

But slowly and slowly it became a routine, an every day task. When I was in my teens, I went to hospital to visit Raj, a brother of my friend who had leukaemia, a blood disorder, blood cancer.

Although now a days most people are cured of leukaemia or at least live long with regular treatment that include blood transfusion, Raj died within a year of being diagnosed. That made me realized that there are many people who are worse off than me. I should count my blessings, however few, however tiny, however insignificant they may be and get on with my life, make the most of my opportunities.

When I came to terms with my illness, I even laughingly described it as a life long friend who would never desert me, let me down! An unbreakable bond between Pooja and the diabetes was created. Looking after my younger sister and guiding her also gave me a purpose in life. Now I was more determined than ever to climb the highest mountain, sit on the podium and declare bravely to the world that I have arrived! There is no limit, no stopping to my dreams and ambition.

Slowly but surely time went by. Every day was a new day and a sense of achievement for us. Our parents were our best friends as well. Family members always stood by us during our times of sorrow and joy, pain and happiness, ups and downs, tears and laughter.

One good luck came our way when my dad was posted to London in 1991 as an employee of the bank. He was in London for four years where his sister, my aunt Jyoti Gandhi was living since 1972. They have a daughter Nisha who is of the same age as me. So we became the best of friends, besides being cousins. I had a wonderful time in London, an experience that has changed my priorities, given me self belief that most Westerners have.

Naturally people, especially professional people working in the field of medicine were more aware of our condition than in India. Yet no one could believe that we, two sisters had the same condition, suffering from juvenile diabetes, a one in a million chance. It would be easier to win a first price in a national lottery draw then two sisters having such a medical condition.

One consolation prize was that the medical experts in London approved our treatment and our living standard was as good as it could be possible under the circumstances. Therefore no change was necessary.

We received a lot of input from the British Diabetic Association which is a well organized body doing an excellent job in providing the latest information to its members.

We also received the best education and our school, kindergarten, doctors, family members and friends treated us as equals, without fear or favour. In other words we were allowed to live a normal life that was a bit difficult in India. No one paid any attention to our medical condition, at least not in our presence.

In early 1995 we returned to India, to the city of Baroda. Here too, we became members of Diabetic Association of Baroda. (DAB) This membership gave us the boost, an impetus in our lives.

The London education, the experience gave us the confidence to participate fully in the activities of the DAB. We attended meetings, lectures, camps, exhibitions and many other events organized by DAB. It was like a big family of

JDs. The DAB team was like a big friend circle with whom we can mix and enjoy, as most of our fellow participants were also juvenile diabetics.

We were told that "Diabetes" is just a disorder and not a disease. It is a killer but it will be fair to you if you are fair to it and respect it, learn to live within certain constraint, rules and take precautions. Strict diet, medicine and activity management are to be part of our every day routine. In fact it is like a shadow that follows you wherever you go.

Today we two sisters take three insulin injections every day. We do our own blood sugar test and observe a strict diet regime. With modesty, I can say that we both sisters have grown into a beautiful human being, full of charm, love, adoration and expectations similar to yours, the readers of this piece and my fellow sufferers.

We, the two sisters have always taken care of each other. We live each moment to its fullest. We understand the mood swings, the feelings, ups and downs and needs of each other.

We do have occasional pillow fights but as the day go by, our love for each other and our parents increase by leaps and bounds.

One question I and my dad has to face so often is that how and why we get juvenile diabetics as they would like to know more about my illness. To be honest, there is no simple answer, not even an expert in the field could answer this simple question.

It is true to some extent that a diabetes is an inherited disease. But no one in our family had it when we were diagnosed, although now my aunty has a mild form of the disease that she controls with tablets and diet.

Juvenile diabetes is now referred as Type 1 diabetes. In this form of diabetes the beta cells of the pancreas that produce insulin has been damaged or even destroyed due to malfunctioning of the body's immune system.

Type 1 diabetes requires taking insulin injections and using insulin pump. But medicine alone can not help. One has to observe a strict diet regime, take exercise that is to be physically active and taking aspirin, for some, to control cholesterol level and blood pressure that normally goes up in diabetic patients.

There is also a possibility that we may have inherited the diabetic genes. The way science is progressing, it could soon be possible for embryos to be screened and such genes destroyed. But I do not know how the society would react to such a progress that may sound like playing God.

But then people who oppose such an advancement in science are, on most part perfectly healthy people and enjoy the life in full. It sounds familiar to the rich people saying that money is not every thing and one does not need it in order to be happy.

But at the same time they would never give up their wealth under any circumstances. It is easy to advise others, to sit on the high moral ground as long as it does not affect them.

In a way diabetes is an inherited dangerous disease. It can and does affect other vital body organs, such as kidneys, liver and especially eyes. Many even go blind later in life. So any advancement in science that could eliminate this disease is certainly welcome news, a step in the right direction. If we have to lower our ethos, the so called morality code, so what?

Then again, these are my views and others may differ. But I would only respect them if these are the views of my fellow sufferers, not of those who are perfectly healthy and enjoy their lives without a care in the world. Human lives are precious to me. Any scientific progress that improves and prolongs lives is worth the effort.

Going to college has made me a confident person. I am really proud that some one like me, a Juvenile Diabetic has achieved a lot more than an ordinary, normal child. I completed my Business Administration degree course with flying colours. Now I am going to Australia for higher studies, for an MBA course and that also on a bursary. It is a dream comes true, an ultimate goal achieved.

Nineteen years back, around Dipawali time, I was on the death bed. Today, again at Dipawali time, I am flying to Australia, one of the most beautiful country and all credit goes to my mum and dad.

There is no need to say that I have gone through some very difficult time. In fact I have been to hell and back. I was so often depressed, sad and angry. Even going to Australia was a very difficult decision for me.

Although I have lived in London for four years, this is going to be a whole new experience for me. In many ways, it would be a strange country, with different priorities, culture and especially food, as I am a strict vegetarian. But as I passed the medical which I thought I never would do, it was time to take a plunge and leave the rest on God!

Again it was the push from my mum and dad that gave me the confidence to go to Australia, as it was once in a life time opportunity, too good to let it pass me by. Yet the memorable moment was the day when I actually had the final visa in my hands.

It was an unbelievable struggle and constant effort I had to put in for months without the possibility of a positive result. If any thing, I am stubborn, obstinate, headstrong but optimistic as well. These qualities have stood me in good stead in time of difficulties.

So my friends, this is **ME, POOJA MUKESH SHAH.** My journey has just begun. I am determined to succeed on all fronts, no matter what it may take.

I will get my MBA and then I will go for a doctorate, doing PhD. I have never allowed my health to become my handicap, an obstacle. It is a challenge. I could have chosen it to do nothing, wither and perish but that is not me.? **I am Pooja, one in a million!**

I would like my life to be a shinning example to others, especially to other Juvenile Diabetics, as I know from my own personal experience how difficult it is for people like me just to survive, let alone prosper. But I believe that "If there is a will, there is certainly a way."

This idiom, this philosophy has helped me to get through some very difficult times when I was on the verge of giving up and retreat into a shell.

I would like other sufferers to share my experiences and gain confidence. That is the main purpose of writing this piece and giving my true name, my true identity.

In the end,

I bow to **ALLMIGHTY, my parents, my sister and every family member and friend** who have been and will be part of my life, in good time and bad, sharing happy memories and the bad times.

The next chapter in my life, to write about will be when I return from Australia and with a bit of luck in not distant future.

****

LOVE STORY
(Forbidden Love)

In a way this was a sad day for Barry, as he was burying his beloved grandfather, the most influential figure in his life, who had guided him, stood-by him in his hour of need. Then grandparents are always there for their children. Children are their future and the future of the country, the future wealth creator.

In fact those children who are brought up without the shelter, love and company of their grandparents do miss out on real love; affection and so often much fun and games as well.

Barry was a philosophical person. He knew his grandfather had a wonderful life, a long, happy and most satisfying inning and moreover he passed away peacefully in his sleep, at the ripe old age of eighty five, a good age by any standard. So what more one can want, one may desire from our short stay on this planet, where we are but guests, transit passengers, on our way to a better place?

He was leaving behind a loving, caring family, who had all the qualities, good upbringing and business ethics that he would have liked to see, to install in his offspring. He had achieved more than most, his goal in life was over achieved, indeed over subscribed.

Like his father John, Barry was also the only child, the only son. No wonder he was spoilt rotten by his family members, especially by his grandfather but mostly in a nice way. Barry was now a clever, well educated and a mild mannered person who would win any one's heart. He also had a wonderful wife and three lovely children, Eurasian by blood but every inch an American, in appearance as well as in American ethics and full of devotion to their land of birth, their Christian faith and enduring, caring culture.

Barry was much closer to his grandfather than his own father John who was running the family printing business, a well known firm of Prentice Progressive Press.

It was started by Barry's grandfather Arthur; after he came back from the war when jobs were scare, as a specialized printing firm, publishing historical documents, old maps and historical events, as Arthur had a degree in history and had worked for a couple of years in such a printing firm before he was drafted into the navy to fight the naked Japanese aggression in the South Pacific Rim.

Imperial Japan wanted to drive out America, Britain and any European nation from this part of the world that they considered their domain, their backyard, their sphere of influence.

When John entered the family business, he soon realized that, although the business was providing a good living, it had a limited potential. It could even collapse if America was ever hit by a thirties type recession when millions of businesses went to the wall, making people homeless, bagging on the streets and deaths through starvation, a disease America had never experienced since the early days of colonization when the pilgrim ship Mayfair first landed the settlers on the American shores, near Boston and New Jersey, mainly from England and especially from Ireland.

John diversified the business into travel and tourist industry, printing holiday guides, postcards, maps, broachers and such other materials used by the travel trade, travel industry.

The aviation industry, air travel was expanding rapidly, especially with the introduction of jumbo jets which made air travel affordable to the masses, the ordinary people, breaking the stranglehold of the rich and the privileged few.

So John knew that it was only a question of time before people would travel world wide, needing his firm's maps, guides on hotels, beauty spots, historical buildings and related books. He wanted to be the first, the pioneer, to be the part of the revolution in the travel industry.

Today Prentice Progressive Press is a leading publisher of popular romantic novels, space adventure and detective novels; with leading authors and novelists like Agatha Ackerman, Jean Simonson and Prescott brothers Peter and Perry on their client list, a few among many famous authors who were tied with the company on a long term contract which gave the firm financial stability and prestige in the literary world.

Now the firm was successfully run by father and son, John and Barry, with help from the ladies, although Barry's wife Mariposa was a well known professor at the leading university, teaching economics and Spanish.

She had devised the course work and written a few text books in Spanish which were widely used not only in her university but also in many Southern States with considerable Mexican American Population Prentice Progressive Press was a family business, run by the family members with a staff of some fifty people. In this day and age when printing is done by computers, print settings and such specialized skills have long been confined to dust bean.

It is the age of IT skills and computer wizardry that Barry was expert in. So the majority of the staffs were sales person, proof readers, accountants and legal experts who had to go through every page published by the firm; as legal eagles had taken the role of vultures if there was money to be made in litigation. Even chasing ambulances was considered a fair practice, a fair game. Sales persons were employed mainly on commission basis.

During the Second World War, Barry's grandfather Arthur served in the U.S navy, in fact on the ship USS Nevada and was posted to Pearl Harbour in Hawaii, a couple of years after it was so brutally bombed by the Japanese navy, even before the announcement that Japan was entering the Second World War and declaring America as an enemy nation. That fateful day, 7th December 1941 when Japanese navy, in particular their six aircraft carriers, namely Akaga, Hiryu, Zuikan, Shokaku, Soryuz and Kagia with some three hundred planes on board, a new concept in naval and marine warfare at the time, attacked the **Oahu Naval Base** while peace talks were being held in Washington.

The large part of the naval base and several major ships, including USS Utah, Arizona, Western Virginia, and California were sunk or capsized and many more of the twenty capital ships were badly damaged, along with numerous small ships were sunk with a heavy loss of life, to be precise 2395. On the USS Arizona alone, 1177 men died; the highest number of casualties on an American ship during the Second World War.

The eye witnesses told that the bombing on USS Arizona was so intense that it was lifted fifty feet in the air and split into two, sinking within minutes.

The base was totally unprepared when it should have been on the war footing, as it was considered to be impenetrable by sea. The sea lane leading to Oahu harbour where ships were anchored is a narrow lane with twist and turn and only forty feet deep.

Moreover it was protected by elaborate measures that include wire nets, mines and under water fortification that would be difficult to penetrate by the enemy. America under estimated Japanese navy and their resolves, in sailing four thousand miles of the ocean, in complete radio silence before they could unleash such a deadly aerial assault that shook America.

This attack resulted in the demotion of the local commanders Admiral Husband Kummel and Lt-Gen Walter Short who were relieved of their posts. At the time the American public opinion was against entering the war. But this attack totally changed the opinion, the anti war atmosphere, thus enabling President F. D. Roosevelt to take USA into the war riding high on the popular sentiments.

While serving in the navy, Arthur took part in the invasion of Philippines, to liberate that country from the clutches of the short but brutal Japanese rule. His unit was especially involved in the liberation of the small island of **Mindoro,** a strategically place island, just south of Manila, with a clear view of South China Sea, a busy sea route for Japanese navy sailing to Malaya and Singapore, British colonies at the time. It was the supply line Japanese had to keep open if they want to defeat Britain and throw them out of South East Asia and eventually out of India as well, the crown in the British Raj that enabled her to rule the world.

For America, it was vital to take this island and attack Japanese supply line that would wreck their ambition to dominate South East Asia, South Pacific rim and ultimately the world.

The campaign to take this well stocked and fortified island lasted six long months and brutal hand to hand combat with heavy casualties on both sides. American sailors fought guerrilla warfare to attack the Japanese fortification which they could not take by direct military action, a frontal attack, as they were so well protected.

American sailors were helped by the people of the island and the resistance movement who lost so many people; mostly civilians, punished by the Japanese as enemy collaborators and were hanged from every tree on the island, to save bullets and to set an example to the local people.

Arthur owed his life to these kind, caring, God fearing Pilipino people who hid them in their homes, churches and fed them while on the run, in the forest. Many American marines fell in love with the place, with palm fringe beaches, white sand and young, tiny but pretty girls who were as hospitable as their elders and so pleasing to look at. It was some thing like a forbidden fruit, allowed to look at, albeit from a safe distance!

But unlike in Europe, not many American marines got married with these local girls and took them back to America as war brides. Their stay on the island was too short and they were on the move all the time. So they did not have the time to know them better or fall in love.

Moreover the moral standard among these Pilipino girls was completely different from their European counterpart, especially the British. Sex before marriage was a taboo, a forbidden fruit no one would dare to taste. After all Philippines is a staunch Catholic country with a very high moral standard, at least at the time of the Second World War. But now in line with many such nations, the country is ravaged by poverty, declining moral standard, child prostitution and kinky sex predators who would not leave even children alone.

It took some six months and hand to hand combat to drive out, to capture these fanatical Japanese soldiers who would rather die than to surrender to these, pale, uncivilized, over baring American marines who looked more like Sumo wrestlers than disciplined marines, who had no right to be in the South Pacific, a Japanese backyard.

When Arthur was wounded in the jungle, he was nursed back to health in a Pilipino house with three wonderful girls in the family. He spent four weeks before he was evacuated from the island which was by then in American hands. He could never forget the joy and jubilation on the faces of these islanders.

Barry had heard these stories many times in his childhood from his grandfather who was proud of his war wounds and always eager to tell his life experiences as an American marine, perhaps adding a bit here and there that would impress young Barry, the child he loved so much, who was the apple of his eyes!

On return to his native California, he got married to his childhood friend who had kept in touch throughout his time in the Pacific. John, Barry's father was born after five years of marriage.

By now Arthur was well settled just outside Los Angeles and running his own printing business with his wife Kiran, a typical Irish name. John joined the business when he graduated with a master's degree in English. His ambition was to write, to become a journalist and ultimately write a novel, become a famous author like Agatha Christie, James Hilton, Earl Stanley Gardner, Sir Arthur Cannon Doyle, Ian Foster and many more whose books he had read and admired.

But business took over his whole life. He had to put his artistic ambition, his journalistic instinct on hold until he could expand and diversify the business, as more and more of his type of specialist works were taken over by the bigger, well established firms who also wanted to diversify into specialist fields of science, education, history and travel.

John had to put all his energies into the business in order to survive, not to be swallowed by a bigger fish, become a insignificant part of a media mogul. By luck, one of his best friends, a schoolmate was a noted journalist with a national newspaper who introduced him to some well connected literary agents with a big name portfolio.

John's negotiating skill and his apparent sincerity soon made him a popular guest at many parties and book launch functions. He often used to work fifteen hours a day, seven days a week. His hard work paid off handsomely. Within ten years of joining the business, he diversified into travel but above all into popular novels some of which were turned into Hollywood hits, movies and mini series.

His business, the firm's turnover multiplied ten fold. Today Prentice Progressive Press is a major player in the field of publication and their financial future secured. Thanks to all the hard work put in by John, his acute and penetrative insight.

When Barry graduated with a degree in economics and English literature, he joined the Peace Crops, an American organization that sent young men and women fresh out of college to the developing world, to work as an ambassador of peace, brotherhood and comradeship. These young volunteers that include doctors, nurses, teachers, accountants and social workers travel far and wide to spread the message of hope, peace and goodwill. They were like the ambassadors sent out by Emperor Ashok, to spread the words, to part with the wisdom of Lord Buddha, a true son of God, in line with Lord Jesus, Lord Rama, Lord Krishna, Lord Mahavir and Guru Nanak.

Due to Ashok's foresight and the sincerity of his ambassadors of peace, countries like China, Japan, Thailand, Laos, Cambodia, Sri Lanka, Burma, Vietnam and many more are predominantly Buddhist countries and Buddhism is the dominant religion in Asia and the world, with more followers than any other religion.

As Barry had heard so much about Philippines from his grandfather, he naturally chose that country for his first overseas posting, to teach English at a secondary school. He was joined by a couple of his friends from the college who shared his love of travel and admiration for Philippines.

The country is a heaven, a paradise of some seven thousand islands scattered over a vast area of the Pacific Ocean, in the most beautiful location, with lukewarm, shallow, clear blue waters, ideal for swimming and every type of water sport.

Palawan Island with a fast developing tourist industry where Barry was posted, has adopted a sensible and logistic policy for development of the tourist industry, with low rise buildings not right on the beaches but some distance away, thus preserving the beauty of these palm covered beaches for all to enjoy rather than becoming a preserve for the rich and privileged few, the tourist with fat wallet and empty brain.

The land just beyond the sandy beaches was so often turned into a park, covered with palm trees and coconut groves right up to the salty sand, accompanied by a garden full of tropical flowers, Champo or Asian magnolia being the favourite flowering plant, with sweet smell and so often flowers outnumbering the leaves. Other flowers were periwinkle, bougainvillea and pink roses.

The island has numerous attractions that include the Calauit Game Reserve and Wildlife Centre with a collection of local as well as exotic African animals living in a natural surrounding. It has established a programme to breed rare species of birds and mammal, preserve Island's animal life, forest, marine resources, including beautiful corals to rival the corals of the Red Sea, off the coast of Egypt, described by experts as the most beautiful underwater world.

The Pristine beaches of El Nido on the northern most part of the island, with soft, silky sandy beach and coconut palms almost reaching the water, is one of the most visited places on the island.

When Barry first came to Palawan, he was not yet twenty one. He was posted to Puerto Princesa, the capital of this beautiful island of Palawan. This very long and narrow island is one of the most beautiful places in Philippines, with succulent, lukewarm Sulu Sea on the east coast and Palawan and South China Sea on the west, with sea never more than twenty miles away on either side, with rolling hills, tiny mountains with equally romantic names like Cleopatra Needle, Victoria Peak and Mount Mantalingajan, Montana Baja, adding beauty and variety to the island, with pine forest and sub-tropical climate, a place to escape to during the oppressive heat of the summer months which can reach 45° on a really hot day.

The sea around the island, on the eastern side is also littered with numerous small and big islands like Dumaran Island being the largest to provide one of the most exciting sea adventures for the fishing and under sea diving enthusiasts. Fishes like tuna, marlin and shark of every shape and size made Sulu Sea as a heaven on earth for every one residing on the shores of this beautiful island.

Coron Reef is a heaven for snorkel enthusiasts. Numerous Japanese shipwrecks sunk during the Second World War are also found around the cost that include some of their most famous and celebrated ships like aircraft carrier Akaga and destroyer, cruiser, troop transporters, landing crafts and submarines with names like Hiryunu, Kyoto, Kitakushu and Shikoku sunk around these islands, some even in a shallow seas.

These wrecks provide exciting diving places, especially for the Japanese tourists who may have lost their relatives in those ships. This is an added attraction for Japanese tourists who flock to the island for sun, sea and young beautiful Pilipino girls, the ugly and unacceptable face of modern day tourism.

With the decline of religious, cultural and moral values, accompanied by fast rising spending power of the industrialized world, child abuse and underage prostitution is fast gaining popularity.

The capital city of Puerto Princesa is ideally situated on the tip of the Honda Bay and is the tourist centre for the area, with many good hotels serving the needs of the mainly Japanese, South Korean and American tourists but fast gaining popularity with the Europeans and Australians.

The school where Barry and his friend Chris were based was run by an American Christian Association that was eager to spread the words of Jesus along with teaching English and other subjects to the receptive students, as Philippines is already a Catholic country but with a significant and troublesome Muslim minority.

Unfortunately for these parts of the world, the tourism also brings unsavoury characters, the loathsome, detestable men who prey on children. Philippines, along with Thailand and Sri Lanka, are famous for child prostitution. Some of the tourists from the West and Japan specially visit Philippines to satisfy their pervert sexual desire, made popular by American kinky sex videos. This dark and sinister world of sex perverts is beyond imagination for most decent people.

Some six months after Barry was in Puerto Princesa, he celebrated his 21st birthday. His friends gave him a grand party in a five star hotel and more of a joke than any thing else; they booked him a room in a five star hotel, in fact a honeymoon suit while they all returned to their tied accommodation in the school compound.

When Barry entered his luxurious hotel bedroom suit, well after midnight, completely sober despite his friends' effort to get him drunk, he was surprised and a bit angry or perhaps embarrassed as well with his friends when he found a tiny but very beautiful Pilipino girl sitting on the bed.

Barry was about to tell her to leave when she gave him a sweet smile that would melt any one's heart and said in equally sweet voice, "Please sir, don't be angry with me or with your friends. They have arranged a surprise for you. I know you have no idea but I am here to please you in any way I can. If you ask me to leave, then I will be in trouble with my Madam." The women who control such a trade are known as "Madam" in Philippines.

The girl was so pretty, with long light brown hair reaching her bottoms, light blue eyes and fair, milky skin with hardly a trace of Chinese, Japanese features; that of slanting eyes and flat nose and so innocent looking that Barry could not take out his annoyance, his anger on her.

In any case, Barry was not tired or feeling sleepy. He gently lay down beside the girl, fully dressed and asked the girl to keep her skimpy, scanty negligee on as well. He had heard so much about child prostitution, especially about the Japanese tourists who encourage this loathsome trade.

Even Japanese brothels in Tokyo and other major cities are full of underage Pilipino girls, as Japanese society is ultra conservative and Japanese girls; women would not allow their male counterparts to have kinky, peculiar or weird sex with them, made popular by American prone videos. They perform their fantasies, their weird sexual acts on these young girls who are not in a position to say no to these super rich clients.

The girl who introduced herself as Angel, her professional name, was sixteen, the age of consent on the island. But she was so tiny, less than five feet tall, weighing no more than six stone. She hardly looked fourteen. But then in Philippines most girls are tiny and normally look much younger than their real age, especially in the eyes of the Westerners, as their children looked so much older and well built as similar age.

It is due to hot climate, under nourishment and lack of proper medical facilities. Most are even born small, weighing less than five pounds, compared to their western counterparts who all weigh well over six pounds at birth, thus giving them a head start, at least on the health and size front.

Angel assured Barry that she was indeed sixteen, above the age of consent, despite her school girl appearance. But then Barry had no intention of getting involved with Angel sexually. He just wanted to talk, know more about her and the reason why she wanted to sell herself for sex and perhaps hold and cuddle her, as Barry had not enjoyed a female company since he came to the island of Palawan. Some times, necessity, the desire overrides all other considerations.

The school where he was teaching English was a mix sex school with boys and girls up to the age of sixteen. There were many girls in his class who were sixteen but looked even younger than Angel.

No matter how noble one's intention may be but if you put a young healthy man and a beautiful girl together in a bed, it is a recipe for trouble. It would be difficult if not impossible to avoid sex, especially if the girl is willing. Even the God succumbs to the charm, beauty and sensuality of a beautiful female. Our Hindu mythology is full of such tales.

After an hour of talking, cuddling and gently kissing, Angel removed the flimsy, more or less see through negligee, revelling her tiny but perfectly formed breast, long legs and symmetrical body, encouraging Barry to make love to her gently but firmly. She instinctly knew that Barry was not like her Japanese clients and he would not demand kinky sex that Angel abhorred, detest and loathed but was obliged to perform on rare occasion when the punter would not take no for an answer and who may be too strong, too powerful and too rich to be ignored.

Angel may not be able to fight the brutal strength of a big daddy like demanding client who think money can buy every thing and every one. Perhaps money can buy any thing in this fast changing world where material wealth rule over moral values, decency and milk of human kindness.

Barry soon fell for the charm and instigation of Angel. He even let her undress him which she did gently, massaging and kissing Barry to arouse his sexual desire.

Soon Barry started kissing her tiny breasts, her most private parts and after an hour, had a full sex with her. Once the excitement was over, his sexual desire fulfilled, he instantly regretted his action. Barry was a big man, well over six feet tall, weighing twelve stone while Angel was a tiny girl who had to endure the sexual pain that was obvious to Barry.

Barry apologised profoundly to Angel for her pain and that he lost his self control. She was in tears, not with her pain but the gentleness of Barry, as most of her clients enjoyed inflecting pain on her, listening to her sexual moans and groans with pleasure, even taping them occasionally without her knowledge. So it was indeed noble of Barry to worry about her pain, her dilemma.

The suit and Angel were booked until midday, more than ten hours were left, before they had to vacate the room, enough time to have sex several times for those who want their money's worth. But Barry was determined that this act, loss of self control, the pain he had inflected on this tiny pretty girl would not happen again, although he kept making love to her gently, kindly and without causing her any pain, any embarrassment.

They both enjoyed this ritual, especially Angel, as this was the first time some punter had treated her as a human being, taken interest in her and above all treated her gently, felt her pain and refused to inflect more pain on her tiny, fragile body. This was also the first time Angel was having sex with a client out of love and pleasure rather than money. They spent the night in each other's arms, half awake, half asleep.

They had their breakfast in the room at 9am, as they were registered as a married couple enjoying their honeymoon. They did not vacate the room until midday which gave Barry all the time to find out every thing about Angel.

Some how Angel trusted Barry from the moment she laid her eyes on him. She told him every thing, why she became a child prostitute at the age of fourteen, working one or two days a week or rather nights. Her forty year old father had a heart attack and could not tend their tiny plot of paddy field that provided them with subsistence living.

With three little girls to feed, cloth and educate, he succumbed to the temptation of his daughter earning easy money as a child prostitute, mainly for the Japanese and South Korean sex tourists with more money than good morals.

As she was so pretty, clever, educated and accommodating, she commanded high fees, enabling her to work just one or two nights a week, as a high class female company, so often without involving sex but she was not in a position to say no when she earned so much in one night. This income enabled her not only to take care of her family but also to attend the college. She was in her first year of a four year course, doing business studies and financial management.

Barry was really impressed with Angel. He realised how hard working, industrious, gentle, kind, caring and duty bound she was. Angel was doing her duty to her family, with a smile on her face but pain in her heart, knowing full well that she was no more than a high class tart, a child prostitute only fit for kinky sex.

No one would marry her in her ultra conservative Pilipino society. Such secrets soon become public knowledge, so often the family is shunned by the rest of the community. Like any young girl, Angel had arman to be a bride, a wife and a mother and have her own family. That is an inbreed ambition in every woman, poor or rich, educated or illiterate.

While talking to Barry, enjoying the embrace in his vast chest, she could not help telling him how she hated this life, so often with tears running down her pale cheek, wetting Barry's chest. Feeling guilty, Barry often urged Angel to leave if she felt uncomfortable and he would not complain. But he soon realised that Angel was indeed willing and happy to be with him. Soon the feelings turned mutual. Barry was glad he did not ask Angel to leave when he had the chance when he first entered the room.

By the time they had spent a few hours together, knowing each other's history, enjoying each other's company while talking on each and every subject, Barry realized that Angel was not any girl. She was special; some one he could trust and would like to know better. She was the girl who could fill the vacuum, the emptiness and vacuity he was experiencing here, away from his family and friends in California. She could be a very good company in every way.

Before they parted, Barry expressed his desire to see her again, to spend another night in her company. To his delight and surprise, she was more than willing to meet him again. This was a chance encounter which Barry did not want to turn into a brief encounter, a one off encounter.

Their next meeting was after a fortnight, in an apartment rented by the Madam who would be glad to have a permanent client, especially a client her girl liked and wanted to be with. This would provide her with a regular income without hassle.

After spending a few nights and occasional meetings, going on picnic to beautiful beauty spots, Barry realised that he was falling in love with Angel which would be detrimental to his future, his wellbeing back at home. So one day, after spending a gentle love making night together, he told Angel with heavy heart and his voice chocked with emotion that he could not see her any more.

These revelations brought tears in her almond shaped blue eyes, as she had fallen in love with Barry and perhaps subconsciously, unintentionally saw him as a meal ticket, to get out of this heinous, abhorrent and odious life she was forced into by circumstances and family loyalty.

Even Barry has by now realised that Angel had fallen in love with him, head over hills but some how he did not feel right to carry on this relationship which will come to nothing at best and bitterness, recrimination at worse with love turning into hatred. He will only end up hurting Angel more which she neither deserved nor could he justify. This would not be physical pain but pain of the heart, even worse this pain would linger on for a long time, if not for ever.

Angel was too nice a person to fight his decision, try to influence him in any way. So she accepted his decision, respected his wishes but could not help telling him how much she loved him and will miss his company. With a kiss and best wishes for the future they parted company.

But Barry soon realised that Angel was his love, his addiction. She was not only a wonderful girl but could one day become a perfect life partner. Life with her will be a happy one, full of joy, fulfilment and certainly without stress, without fear of divorce that was becoming a disease in the Western society. Moreover it was now a trend to marry some one from the Far East. More and more Americans were coming to Thailand and Philippines to find a life partner, to get married. So why should he feel guilty, give up such a wonderful girl? Barry passionately believed that no one should leave the happiness, the quality of life to chance, it should be a choice. In fact it was his Mantra.

Yes, she was a prostitute but only out of a family tragedy. He could soon stop that and let her live a normal life, let her be a part of the respected society.

After four weeks, he rang Angel and arranged to meet her on the beach, at their favourite place. Barry realised that this unforced separation was ominous for their well-being.

Barry was taken back when he saw her. She had withered like a rose that had been plucked, used and thrown away after a few days. Her face was without a smile and lack of any sort of makeup, yet she looked gentle and beautiful in a sort of way.

Then again beauty is in beholder's eyes. For Barry, Angel will always be beautiful. After a long chat, both acknowledged that they loved each other too much to remain apart, remain separated, ignore their love, their inner most feelings. Barry could see what effect this unforced separation had on Angel. That was the proof of her love for Barry that is if he needed any proof at all.

As Christmas holidays were just two weeks away, they decided to go away on a week long holiday, to a very beautiful place on the island, to Taytay Bay which is littered with hundreds of small islands, most uninhabited, except by wildlife, a perfect heaven for a young couple who were madly in love and would like to go away from the hustle and bustle of a city life. They would like to get lost in each other, make naked love the way Adam and Eve did, away from the preying eyes and ears, without a care in the world.

Before they could go, Barry requested and arranged for Angel to have a full medical check-up, as in her profession, sexually transmitted disease are common but mercifully Aids had not yet become a curse for humanity, infected the mankind and to Angel's relief and delight, she was completely free of any medical problems, any STD of any sort, as she always had a protected sex whenever it was unavoidable.

They hired a boat and sailed around the bay, putting anchor wherever and whenever they fancied, swimming in the warm, clear blue waters, spending nights on the white sandy beach, sleeping under the stars and catching their own lunch and dinner from the sea, drinking sweet coconut water, plucked straight from the tree, as all islands in Philippines are covered with mango, guava, papaya, banana, custard apple and black plum trees and coconut groves growing right up to the edge of the beach. Both Barry and Angel loved these tropical fruits.

Like most Pilipino girls, Angel was a very good cook. It is in their culture to take care of their men, their husbands and take care of their every need, provide every comfort. No wonder divorces are indeed unheard of in Philippines.

By now Angel was a changed girl. She looked so beautiful, so sexy in her bikini, in pale yellow or snow white colour, chosen by Barry. Moreover Barry was pleased to learn that Angel had given up her part time job of pleasing other men. She had taken a job of a waitress in a hotel café where hours were long, working some fifty hours a week. Yet the pay was a pittance, not enough to let her continue her studies.

Although they were alone on the boat and the beach, Barry could not let her go out of his sight, not even for a while. So often he would carry her around like a doll, as she was so light. They were in each other's arms all the time, kissing, cuddling, having gentle sex and having fun as if this was there last week on earth. Their joy knew no bound and Angel was no more a little girl for Barry. She was his equal, his partner and one day, not in distant future, she will hopefully be his wife, his life partner and mother of his children.

It was not as if Barry never had a girl friend. In fact during his Uni days, Barry had many girl friends and was even in a serious relationship with one girl by the name of Rosanna but it did not last long. Perhaps Barry was suspicious, possessive or selfish!

Some how Barry could not resist Angel. She had stolen his heart. He loved every moment he spent with her. She was beautiful beyond his dream, his imagination. He could talk to her on any subject and so often he would come out second best when they had a serious conversation, on the topical subjects. He knew they are destined to be together, come hell or high water, no matter what. Barry's physical superiority was more than matched by Angel's intellectual superiority.

Barry was glad that sex was not the only attraction that attracted and kept them together. It was love, intelligence, respect and the cleverness of Angel, well beyond her teenage years that Barry found so fascinating. Above all he trusted Angel as he had never trusted any one else before in his friend circle.

They even discussed marriage and living in America when Barry had to go back and when Angel had completed her studies. Yes Barry was determined for her to go back to the college, providing the financial help she needed.

By the time their holiday was over, their life was charted, their future plans drawn and ready to be put into action. Each knew what was required, expected from the other and they were determined to do all they could in order to succeed and succeed they must, at any cost and no sacrifice was too much, too large, too demanding. Failure was not the option on card, in their plan.

The week passed in no time at all, as they sailed the Tayta Bay, visiting Batas, Dalang and Dumaran islands, a few among many, mostly uninhabited islands where they had complete freedom to do what they like, no need to wear any cloths, not even swimwear; play Adam and Eve, hide and seek, have picnic, have naked fun and eat the forbidden fruit to their heart's desire. How sweet this forbidden fruit was. It was more of a dream world than a reality. Who cares about reality when in paradise?

When they returned, Barry went to see her parents who were thrilled to meet him, as they had heard so much about him from their daughter. Even they were convinced about Barry's sincerity. They instinctly knew that one day he would marry their beautiful daughter, their princess and give her the life, the happiness she deserves; turn her dreams into reality.

Although Barry was a Peace Crop Volunteer, earning very little money, his wealthy parents and grand parents gave him sufficient allowance to let him live in luxury he was accustomed to at home. After all he was their only child, heir to the throne. So money was not an obstacle.

Angel soon gave up her waiter's job, waiting at tables, under pressure from Barry and rejoined the Uni where she was doing her degree course in Business Administration and Financial Management. She was a brilliant student, always at the top of her class.

Barry gave her a monthly allowance of US $200 which was more that she was earning as a child prostitute. When Barry's friends at the school learnt about this amazing, almost unbelievable love story, they all chip in to enable Barry to rent a flat outside the school compound, to enable him to be with Angel at the week ends.

These were the days when people would go out of their way to help their friends. Money, social status or sheer greed did not rule the roots as they do today. There was humanity, love and brotherhood amongst people, irrespective of their origin, colour of the skin, culture or the religion. It was an innocent world, the world that was still seeking, looking for purpose, trying to come to terms after the brutality of the Second World War that had shaken the foundation of humanity.

With Barry's love, proper living accommodation and nutritious food, Angel soon grew into a beautiful, five feet three inches tall girl with milky complexion. Her tiny, child like breasts, skinny legs and thighs were replaced with full figure, sexy curves and oozing self confidence rare among Pilipino girls, especially when they were in the company of Westerners.

Barry gave her the confidence she was lacking. He was her prince charming, a knight in shining armour who would protect her, be at her side in her hour of need. In return Angel would give her life for Barry. His every command was her wish, her desire and her ambition. It was difficult to determine who was lucky, Barry or Angel to get such a life partner.

By the age of nineteen, through a short cut reserved for brilliant students, Angel had already obtained her BA degree and she was now doing her Masters, along with MBA, in finance, banking, environment and investment, a much recognized American qualification. Not to fall behind, at least in education, Barry joined her in doing MBA which was a great help to Angel, as they can study together and help each other.

After two years Barry went home during school holidays for a short break. He told Arthur, his grandfather all about Angel, how beautiful, intelligent, kind and caring she was, leaving out how he met her and her past when she was a child prostitute.

Angel's past sounded so unreal now that even Barry was not prepared to believe it. Perhaps he wanted to bury this unfortunate episode deep inside his mind, never to be reminded again.

Angel soon reverted to her real name of Mariposa, a beautiful Spanish name which means butterfly that floats gently in the warm air, displaying her beauty. She indeed floats like a butterfly but did not sting like a bee, borrowing the phrase from the vocabulary of Mohamed Ali, the greatest showman on earth during his hay days.

When Barry first came to the island of Palawan, he was puzzled, as practically all the names were Spanish, such as Puerto Princesa, the capital city, San Antonio Bay, Playa Parisia, Playa Doroda, Montana Baja, Parque El Nido and many more but with few exceptions, which were in English. But he soon realised that Philippine was once a Spanish colony and Spanish influence still prevailed on many islands.

Spanish is still widely spoken in most outlying islands, although English has taken over major towns and cities, including the capital Manila. This is due to American influence, as there is a huge marine base near Manila and after all English is the language for business and information technology.

Mariposa, like all her family members was fluent in English as well as Spanish. Her father had made sure that his children speak both the European languages, beside their mother tongue.

Barry showed his grandfather the stunning photographs of Mariposa, in her slim figure, wearing yellow, cream or pure white bikini or one piece swimsuits in dark red and black colours, as well as in colourful dresses. She looked beautiful and stunning in any dress, in any cloths but her real beauty was her kind and caring nature and her love for Barry. Indeed she was a girl in a million.

Barry knew that when the time comes to tell his parents that he would like to marry Mariposa, he will have full support of his grandparents. In a way Arthur felt Barry was carrying out his wishes, living his dream to be part of this wonderful country with kind and caring people. It was Arthur's dream to fall in love with a tiny, beautiful Pilipino girl when he was nursed back to health fighting the Japanese. Now his grandson Barry was fulfilling his dream. No wonder he was happy for Barry and was eager to meet Mariposa and welcome her in their family home.

All together Barry spent four years on the island, in Puerto Princesa. He rented a two bedroom flat overlooking the bay where he stayed for three years, until he returned to America.

Mariposa was very busy in her studies, completing her Masters as well as MBA by the time she was twenty one. Barry also did his MBA but he was no match to Mariposa when it came to passing exams. Mariposa had to stay at the Uni during week days, as she was also taking a few classes while doing her MBA. She would join Barry at his flat at the weekends, eagerly awaited weekends they would spend in each other's arms. Their love was more intense than Romeo and Juliet, Salim and Anarkali, Edward and Mrs. Simpson?

They enjoyed these weekends to the full, as both were young, healthy, in their prime and extremely fond of each other. They watched movies like Saturday Night Fever, Dirty Dancing, Virgin Bride and Prime of Miss Jean Brodie, soft sexy movies that aroused them most and let them make love without restrain or any inhibition throughout week-ends.

This was a perfect arrangement. Barry was over the moon. His happiness knew no bounds. Mariposa was even happier. In just four years, her life has changed so much, turned upside down. Her dark, painful days when she had to go without two square meals a day, sell herself to feed her family were a distant memory, a bad dream, a horror story.

She knew without Barry, this transformation not only in her life but in the whole family would never have happened. Barry was a kind, generous man with a heart of gold.

So often Mariposa would cry while resting her head on Barry's chest, in his tight grip and would say, "Barry, tell me this is not a dream. How am I going to repay your kindness, your generosity, your love for me. You are my hero, my saviour, my reason to live. Please let this dream go on and on, last for ever." She would find it hard to control her emotion, her tears and her happiness.

Barry would say, "Mariposa, you have given me so much happiness. That is my reward. I am looking forward to the day we get married, you become mine and we grow old gracefully together, playing with our grandchildren. This is a two way street. What you have done for me and are going to do for us is my reward. What you saw so you reap." That would put a smile back on Mariposa's face.

While Barry was in Puerto Princesa, Arthur visited him and stayed with Barry, in his flat for a month. He was thrilled to meet Mariposa who was indeed more beautiful than her photos suggested, with a baby face, pale skin and long silky hair that gave her a distinct look, a beauty and made her stand out from other Pilipino girls who all had short hair, like girls in America and Europe.

That was the fashion. Long hairs for girls were considered unfashionable, not keeping up with the time, with the fashion. But both Barry and Mariposa liked her long hair, her unique hair style.

Arthur was also very pleased and impressed with Mariposa's family. Her two sisters, Marina (sea) and Marisa (hen, female bird) have also turned into beautiful young ladies, climbing the educational ladder, following into the footsteps of Mariposa, following in her path. They also knew that without Barry, this success would not have materialized.

More pleasing to Barry was that his best friend Chris, who came to Palawan with Barry, fell in love with Mariposa's sister Marina. He could see how wonderful Mariposa was and the happiness they were having in each other's company. All three sisters were wonderful girls, kind, caring, beautiful, clever and down to earth, although they were all so brilliant at studies.

When Barry and Mariposa got married, they were still relatively young. Barry was twenty five and Mariposa just twenty one. It was a double wedding, as Chris and Marina also got married on the same day, in a joint ceremony. Barry's parents and grandparents came to Palawan for the church ceremony which was followed by a grand reception, a week later in Los Angles.

That was a long time ago, some twelve years ago. Today all three sisters, Mariposa, Marina and Marisa are married to an American and settled in Los Angles, not too far away from each other.

Three sisters joined together to buy a beautiful four bedroom bungalow, right on water's edge, overlooking the bay, for their parents just outside Puerto Princesa. They would visit their parents every second year and stay for a few weeks in this beautiful, luxurious place.

Neither Barry nor Mariposa could forget all the help, love and respect Arthur, his grandfather had bestowed on them, especially to Mariposa who was welcomed in their home with love and affection, a daughter rather than a daughter in law. She never felt she was any one but American.

Barry stayed until the grave was filled, holding Mariposa tight, tears flowing freely from his eyes and heart bleeding as if stabbed. They put down a single white rose on the grave before dragging themselves away, to join the rest of the family who were waiting for them in the church. Arthur was gone but will never be forgotten. His memories will always remain; will occupy one corner of Barry's heart until their time is up, to join him in heaven. An old soldier never dies, only fades away from the memory until it is time to reunite.

****

DIL EAK MANDIR
(My Heart Is My Temple)

The normally unintrusive clock hanging on the wall was ticking slowly but surely. The time and running water, whether in a stream or a mighty river do not stop for any one, nor can it flow backward. It is like an arrow or a bullet, once fired can not be recalled. So one has to be wise and calculating before making a decision that may affect our lives irreversibly.

Time is life's greatest gift, distributed equally to all, without fear or favour. We all have twenty four hours in a day, seven days a week. How wisely we spend, make use of our time, results in laying the foundation of our future. It is in a way reflection of the proverb "What you sow, so you reap." So it is of utmost importance for us to use our time on this earth as wisely and beneficially as possible. After all we are here for a short stay, a transit passenger.

The rhythmetic noise of the clock, like that of a train when travelling a long distance, from one town to another, is normally pleasing to ears or goes unnoticed, especially when one is busy or engrossed in a good book, mind occupied and one may be oblivious to the surroundings.

But such a noise plays on our mind when the mind is in turmoil; the heart is bleeding and filled with emotion.

Kilan was no exception, as the ticking, clicking noise from the wall clock vibrated round his office, small but very well furnished, tastefully decorated office, with a large portrait of Mahatma Gandhi, the father of the Indian nation and Sardar Vallabbhai Patel, the Bismarck of Indian politics and the backbone of the struggle for independence, hanging proudly from the side wall, behind his chair.

Kilan's mind was indeed in turmoil, in agony and in need of divine intervention from above, if at all possible, as Kilan is not in any way a superstitious or even a religious person, a rare distinction in a country like Bharat where every one believes in some thing, some one, some divine power or even a departed soul, an angel. It seems the wheels of the Indian society turns on faith, belief and blessings and why not? It is the squeaky wheel that always gets the grease.

The ceiling fan, although running at a normal speed, was too slow for Kilan's comfort, to dampen the fire of anxiety, anticipation and premonition clogging his heart, his ability to make a sensible, perceptible and above all the right and correct decision that will affect his life for ever, make him a happy or a miserable person. He could not help but wonder whether he was playing with fate?

No wonder Kilan was sweating profoundly; could not decide whether it was the afternoon heat or the inner turmoil, his bleeding heart that was responsible for his physical discomfort and his mental anguish, his rapid heartbeat and raised blood pressure that he has experienced since he first read the letter from **Rishma,** who was once his girl friend, his sweetheart and his world, his sole reason for living, studying and making life a success in this topsy turvy world, with twist and turn, honesty and betrayal where dogs eat dogs, morality has been confined to dustbin and honesty laughed at and generosity abused.

Concentration should be like a laser beam that concentrates all its energy, power and heat at one point, at one target for maximum effect but today Kilan's mind was more like an uncaged monkey, rushing from one thought to another, without purpose, without cohesion and certainly without conviction in his ability to come to a right decision that would make or break him, make his life a heaven on earth or hell.

Kilan got up and raised the speed of the fan, to the highest oscillation but it could neither cool his body, mind or his tortured soul. How can a Sharabi (drunk) quench his thrust with a glass of water, even ice-cold water!

The unleashed fan only blew papers all over the office floor, messing up his files that had taken Kilan hours to sort out. But Kilan is a methodical person, at least when it comes to his office work. He had numbered all the pages in such a way that it would take only a fraction of a time to re-arrange them, that is if he could concentrate on work. But concentrate he must, as he was finalizing Company's cash flow chart, expected rise in profit and reduction in expenditure, in cost, through efficiency and better use of resources rather than a cut in employment, reducing the workforce in the next financial year. His report, his recommendation could result in a hefty bonuses for the staffs and a generous, inflation busting pay rise for all.

Kilan reduced the speed of the fan, gathered the papers that were littering the floor of his 10th floor office with a beautiful view of Marine Drive and the vast expanse of an open sea as far as eyes could see, the most prestigious place to have one's office, given the choice. By any stretch of imagination, first class, eye pleasing, mind soothing environment is an investment, a wise investment rather than an unnecessary expense in this penny pinching cut throat business world where profit precedes every thing else.

Kilan slumbered in his comfortable leather chair, made to order, closed his eyes and began to think, to ponder, to vegetate, to reignite his past, wondering where his life would have taken him, what podium, which mountain he would have climbed, what he would have achieved if his life had proceeded according to his, their plans. Vidhata, the Hindu Goddess who writes, charts every child's future as soon as the child is born, had not been so cruel to him. Kilan had so often wandered if there was any point in his daily struggle to climb the ladder, better his life when there is no one in his life to share it with.

After experiencing half an hour's uneasiness, blank mind and silently sobbing heart, Kilan summoned Manu, the messenger. He gave him Rs100 note and asked him to get a couple of bottles of soft drink and a big Havana cigar, in a metal tube, his favourite after dinner relaxation when he was a smoker.

The peon was a bit curious, as Sahib (boss) had given up smoking a long time ago. But he was in no position to be inquisitive, especially as he had noticed that the boss was not in his normal jovial, cheerful and happy mood when Kilan ignored him when he said good morning sir, early in the morning. So he thought silence is golden, at least for the time being.

Soon Kilan was sipping his favourite soft drink, a combination of lime, lemon and orange, tastefully mixed with soda water, an upmarket drink available in a few selected shops, special outlets.

Half way through the drink, Kilan lighted the cigar, with the lighter presented to him by Rishma, at the airport when she boarded Air India flight to London, sobbing uncontrollably. That was the last time Kilan saw his childhood sweetheart with a face of an angel, a baby face that would sink thousand ships or rather thousand hearts. The baby face Rishma, who had an endearing, puppy like disposition, proved to be a Trojan horse after all. The Cinderella had lost her Prince charming. The spoilt child never grew up!

It was a novelty for the staff, sitting in the vast open space outside Kilan's cabin, looking or rather glancing at him from the corner of their eyes, pretending to be busy, as no one would relish a call and a stern lecture from the boss who was obviously in a foul mood.

It was a long time since Kilan had received a letter from Rishma. It was to give him the good news, more like passing a death sentence on Kilan, that Rishma, his love, his joy and happiness, was getting married to doctor **Naimesh,** a casual acquaintance of Kilan and Rishma when they were at high school, that is until Rishma went to London to study at a prestigious University Hospital in the city of London, where she met Naimesh, renewed the old tie, the casual acquaintance and ended up getting married.

It was a fog of unreality but an inevitable result of the close proximity they experienced while doing night rounds in the hospital wards as junior doctors.

Being a junior doctor is a very demanding job, working some seventy to ninety hours a week, that include on call duty.

They have very little time to socialise outside their own inner circle, consisting of fellow doctors of similar rank and few nurses. It is like a frog's life in a pond that begins and ends in the pond, in the hospital compound with little awareness of what is happening in the outside world, in real life.

So often such closeness leads to a romance and a marriage but not for all the right reasons. It is not the union of two souls in holy matrimony that will keep them united till death do them part. More often than not, it is a union of convenience, some times even due to a mishap, an unwanted, unplanned pregnancy outside marriage that may ruin a promising career. Abortion may not always be an easy option, a way out. This is a complicated world, a private world and in some ways a secretive world. Rishma was in a way a victim of such an environment. She was dragged in, sucked in before she realised, before she had the chance, the opportunity to learn the ins and outs, to be the part of this secretive life. It was, in a way, survival of the fittest, the one who runs fast, gets all the goodies.

Today Rishma was separated from Naimesh, leaving her all alone in a big, bustling city like London where humanity is overflowing but closeness is rare. Many people feel alone and neglected, unless they are in a loving, caring relationship, surrounded by loyal and devoted friends and family members that is the trade mark of our Hindu culture.

Rishma was a bit shy, not at ease with some one she may have just met. She would not make friends easily, quickly or on the spur of the moment, as some do. It takes her a long time to trust a person. But once she trusted a person, as she did Kilan, she would go out of her way to be intimate with that person.

Moreover to qualify as a doctor is a long drawn out struggle, leaving very little time to socialise, mix and make friends. That may be one of the reasons why junior doctors end up falling in love with each other, leading to marriage, perhaps a marriage of convenience.

Although these junior doctors may be in each other's pocket, spending the day and night together, working and socialising side by side, there is hardly any time to know each other intimately, ask the searching questions, to find out whether there is any thing, any interest, any activity they could enjoy together, except their work. They may not even know whether they are truly in love or it is just a sexual attraction brought about by the close proximity in a congested ward.

Today Rishma was separated from Naimesh. She was all alone, like a tall palm towering over the deserted surroundings, where one has to fend and defend for one self, a merciless world where no prisoners are taken, no favours granted.

Now Rishma wanted to rekindle their love, their friendship and start from where they left off when Rishma left for London to enter her dream world, a medical world of wealth and opportunity, trial and tribulation. Virtuous circles are never quiet as self-fulfilling as is commonly supposed to be.

Although Kilan had read Rishma's letter again and again, he took it out from his briefcase for the umpteenth time and began to read once again.

"Priya Kilan

There was a time when I, my pen could not stop writing to you, page after page. But today I am at a loss how to begin, what to write, even how to address you.

Perhaps I feel guilty. I have no right to write to you after the way I behaved, let you down and broke your heart. But I sincerely hope and pray to All Mighty that you will at least read this letter, digest it and think deeply before you condemn me, call me a gold digger, a heart wrecker or any such term that you may feel appropriate to denounce me, find me guilty and banish me for ever from your heart. Perhaps I deserve it and much more.

Going through my correspondence file, I came across your last letter to me. Your words of wisdom which I felt were sincere and came from your heart still vibrates, rings bell in my mind, in my heart. You wrote **"Beauty, health, youth and wealth are never steady, firm or ever lasting. They are liable to change, sooner or later. So if you ever find your self in poor, dire state, alone, abandoned and feel that the world is against you, the way I feel now, please do not hesitate to get in touch with me, approach me, knock on my door. The doors of my house and my heart are and always will be open to you. No one and nothing can ever put a padlock on it. For me love is immortal, ever lasting and only death can part us for ever."**

What a wonderful sentiment, kind thoughts and words of wisdom. I must have been a fool not to understand the real meaning of love, affection and devotion. These kind words gave me the strength and encouragement to write this letter.

I could never have the courage to come and knock on your doors, confront you and ask for your forgiveness if I had not kept your letter. It was as if written by a farista, a saint, people of great wisdom, not by a mere mortal human being like me or Naimesh. Perhaps the logic of despair can be so compelling.

You may not believe me but I have kept an eye, a tab on you, followed your progress or lack of it on the social front at least. I understand your life is like a **"Kora Kagaz"** a blank paper, a half finished novel. So I have, deep down a feeling of hope and expectation that you will forgive me and give me an opportunity to redress my mistake, my foolishness and allow me to spend the rest of my life in your company, to serve you and make you happy.

I may not be Lady Sita but you are surely my Lord Rama. This gesture on my part may or may not redress my mistake, my act of selfishness but I will never know if I do not try. Nothing ventured, nothing gained. I am sure I can bring a quantum improvement in your life. The alternative is almost too heart-rending to contemplate.

I would not blame you if you think that now Naimesh is out of my life, I have turned to you for support, comfort and love. It is but natural that some one, who gets his tongue burnt while drinking tea will look at buttermilk with suspicion, makes sure that it is not hot?

If I do not get a reply from you, I will take it as a just punishment for betraying your love, ruining your life, showing such a poor judgement, not able to separate a diamond, a real gem from the collection of worthless shining stones. My decline, my misfortune is not a matter of chance but a matter of choice, made perhaps in daunting circumstances. I could not differentiate between graffiti and classic literature.

As you may know now, I have never forgotten you completely. I have always taken interest in your progress, even sitting thousands of miles away from you. It was one of the happiest days of my life when I received the good news that you have qualified as a Charted Accountant. How I wished I was by your side to celebrate this achievement.

When I came to London, some what reluctantly, as it was too painful to part company. I was alone in an alien environment, with different values, ever changing climate and unfriendly, unhelpful social environment. It was a rural arcadia which doubles as a training ground for emerging doctors.

It would be impossible for you or any one else to understand my situation, my loneliness, my predicament, unless one is put in such a situation, in such a dilemma and have spent some time on the hospital ward. I was sleeping on a bed of nail every night, the bed I made for my self or rather my ambition got better of me. I so much wanted to return to Bombay where my heart, my love was.

But thinking about my family, my father who had made such a huge financial sacrifice, I was reluctant to let them down, let their sacrifice go to waste. So I stuck to my task, performed my duty like a true daughter and carried on, lost in my studies.

My father was a wise and generous man. He strongly believed that if any one wants to acquire knowledge, broaden one's horizon, they should be encouraged, respected, irrespective of their caste, creed, gender and social or financial standing. These were the ideals of my father that I was trying to uphold. He was one in a million. But it was so often difficult to follow in his foot steps, achieve his standard and upheld his moral values. He was also a deshbhakta, a patriot who used to tell us it is time to stop carping and support national endeavour. We have only one motherland. But we are not all Gandhi, Mandela or Martin Luther King.

If I see a familiar face from my homeland, meet some one I knew back at home, I was over the moon, as if I have found my long lost family member. My joy knew no bounds. But unfortunately many were young punters who will turn up in droves to ride along the wave of popular egoism, to be seen in the company of a high flying young doctor.

This was the time Naimesh entered my life, as he was working, studying in the same hospital as me but was two years ahead of me. Being in London much longer, he knew all the tricks of the trade, how to gain confidence of lonely and innocent girls like me. He had a morality of an unwashed armpit, masked with the over use of cheap deodorant. He was the black sheep of the family.

But at the time, I hailed him as the second coming of a messiah. Radha had found her soul mate Lord Krishna. I thought I have found a thorough breed but it turned out to be plough horse.

Slowly but surely we came closer, started spending more time in each other's company and ultimately moved in together, renting a flat, to get away from the confined space of the hostel. It is the English culture, tradition, almost an obligation to share bed, along with every thing else. The logic of despair, loneliness can be so compelling.

Soon I was no longer the girl you knew and loved so much, to be the love of your life, be your partner in marriage. The line between marriage and cohabitation is blurred and as a result innocent girls like me become the victim, to be sarcastic, you may even say a willing victim but I would say I was a lamb in a lion's den.

Over the time, I changed beyond recognition. I was no more the shy, retreating and sexually naïve girl that you knew, trusted, admired and almost worshipped. Drinking alcohol, even get drunk occasionally, eating non vegetarian food and sleeping with an acquaintance became a norm in life.

This was the atmosphere, the culture, the synonyms and the social etiquette, along with lack of any moral standard that enabled us to behave in a way that is so foreign to us back at home. This is the testimony of the armpit Western culture, especially here in Britain with teenage pregnancies and sexually transmitted disease (STD) highest in the Western world.

The long hours, the deprivation of rest and sleep so often drives young doctors to drugs and drinks, even binge drinking. This may give a temporary relief but leaves a life long headache.

I still remember the incident that brought surprise, the shock, the disbelief and a bit of embarrassment on your face when I kissed you on the lips, a gentle and spur of the moment kiss brought about by the love scenes in the film Sangam that we watched together in the luxurious cinema Maratha Mandir. In the darkness and the surprised state of mind, you unintentionally put your hand, rested it on my breast which I enjoyed but you could not face me and avoided me for few days until I told you, reassured you that what happened was not your fault, nor I feel offended in any way, with a wink and a mischief making smile from a very sexy girl!

The second incident I remember is the swimming pool incident when I joined you in the college pool, wearing a pale yellow bikini showing all my curves which I felt looked really good on me, made me looked so beautiful, so sexy and desirable that you could not take your eyes off me. That was the first time you told me how much you loved me, not once but the umpteenth time until I told you to shut up and hold me tight?

I am sure you do remember these incidents, as these were the happiest days in my life, in our lives. It seems innocent love, how trivial it may be, gives more pleasure than denigrated moral values and bed hopping practice so common in London's high society.

It was now impossible for me to return to Bombay, to you and to pretend every thing is rosy in our love garden, in our dream world. I loved you too much to deceive you, to live a life of lie and a sham.

There is a saying in our culture, that this is the wisdom of a widow who mistreated her husband. Perhaps it applies to me as well.

I could have told you the truth. You may have even forgiven me but could I have your respect knowing how badly, loosely, shamelessly I have behaved? I was not willing to take the risk of losing your respect and admiration for me that had taken a long time to cultivate. I did not want to blur the differences between make-believe world and reality.

I could not have looked into your eyes on our honeymoon night, knowing full well that it was a sham. I thought I was doing you a favour by moving out of your life for good. You will soon forget me and move on, get married and live happily ever after. How wrong I was. There is no happy ending, neither for me nor for you.

In so many ways, life is a funny experience. So often what we may propose, God may dispose. We are the cleverest creation of God, empowered with the capacity to be happy, contended, loyal and genius. But unfortunately we never direct, concentrate our efforts on the right path, a virtuous path that give us permanent peace and attainment. I am the prime example of this foolishness, missed opportunity. We have, I have descended into sickly sentimentality which endorses irresponsibility, fecklessness and the cult of a victim society. Our rich cultural heritage, reading of Gita every night before going to bed, enabled me, gave me strength to get out of the rate race.

I hope I have planted the seeds of everlasting friendship with you and perhaps I may get the benefit of a rich harvest. I would like to be an optimistic and live in hope rather than despair. If we lose hope, faith, self confidence and belief, then life is not worth living. This is what differentiates us from other living creatures, animal life, although I would hesitate to say we are the supreme creation of God!

Naimesh was a Romeo at heart. He could never settle down in a monogamous relationship, consider marriage as a monolith institution. He was like a busy bee, flowing from one flower to another, sucking the nectar until the flower had no more sweetness to offer.

It was not too difficult for Naimesh to find new flower, pastor new, a fresh prey, a new love among young entrants, many from overseas. Then there were nurses, always able and willing, in fact eager to be seen in the company of a doctor. This was a picture of dehumanising behaviour alien to our culture, our religion and our tradition.

It took me some time to realise what type of person Naimesh was, when I caught a mild form of STD. (Sexually Transmitted Disease) I could only have got it from Naimesh which he could not deny, as I had only one sexual partner after marriage.

We both needed treatment. My suspicion proved correct and I realised that there was no way I could change Naimesh, a Romeo, a wondering spirit at heart who would find it impossible to settle down. It opened my eyes, gave me the strength and the reason to be free of him, cut my loses, kick him out of my life and move on.

I have already wasted some of the best years of my life on a low life Romeo with the morals of a Hollywood film star. We were divorced within three years of our marriage. That was some five years ago. There has been no one in my life since then. But then, I am the author of my own misfortune, a victim of value-free sentimental claptrap society that I willingly joined, be part of it. Snobbery stops us from sniping at the rotten to the core society of the rich and the famous. The question of authenticity, frivolity and gravitas remains unanswered.

To-day I can say that in a way I am well settled in my practise, earning a good living as a GP. I have a nice home in a leafy suburb, top of the range car and a good friend circle to mix with, that include politicians, community leaders and members of the medical profession.

We go on holidays, on cruise and socialise at the highest level. Yet I feel my life is empty. There is no one waiting for me when I go home, to a damp, dark and empty house. I wish some one like you is there to greet me, to hug me, that the house is full of people and perhaps children.

I wish I have a partner with whom I can share my success, my joy, my happiness and my sorrow, a shoulder to cry on when I am down, upset and when my heart is filled with sorrow. As you know, in my profession, we see sickness, sorrow and death all the time. But that does not mean we or rather I do not get upset, do not fill the pain, the loss or I am immune to such tragedies. So often death of a patient is like the death of a friend, even a family member. It needs a bunker mentality to remain aloof from the pain and death that surrounds us, a part of our profession.

Recently I met a good friend of yours by chance, at a wedding reception, who told me all about you, your success on the business and financial front that you are a well respected professional person but lack of success on the social and family front, that you are still single, leading a lonely life, rather by choice than by circumstances, lack of good girls interested in you.

I have been thinking about you a lot since the break-up of my marriage but especially during the last few months when I learnt about your lonely life which made me feel even guiltier.

I feel we are both lost souls waiting for each other. But I did not have the courage to contact you, to write to you, to apologise to you and ask for your forgiveness; that is until I read your last letter, more by chance than by design, full of kind words, oozing with wisdom. It gave me the courage to write to you, put my inner most thoughts on paper and ask for your forgiveness.

I am now well settled in my daily but some what lonely routine. But if you still love me, then I am willing to uproot myself, leave London and join you in Bombay.

I can not guarantee you that we can rekindle, reignite our young love, that you will find me as beautiful as you saw me in a swimming pool, wearing a pale yellow bikini that nearly knocked you down or we will live happily ever after. One lesson I have learnt in life is that there is no guarantee in life. So it would be foolish, almost counter productive even to try it. But I can say that I have preserved my looks, my youthfulness and I am still desirable, albeit to the right person, for your eyes? Tell me, can Urvasi, Menka or Radha ever grow old, lose their charm?

After the way Naimesh behaved, I have lost faith in human beings but some how I feel that my trust in you is not misplaced. I will not be beaten, betrayed twice. I am more than willing to try, to give you every ounce of love and affection left in me, in my body that is fermenting for years and is now busting to come out, to explode?

For some reason I feel that we are soul mates, meant for each other, to grow old together gracefully in each other's company, perhaps playing with our grand children.

It may turn out to be a dream, a fool's gold, a mere fantasy that may never turn into a reality. But I am willing to give it a go, take the risk, uproot myself and come to you. I am an optimistic by nature, especially when it comes to you.

So please Kilan, let me know how you feel, let me have your answer when you receive this letter, no matter what it may be. If you reject me, I will take it in my stride, blaming my luck, my lack of judgement in human being, rather than blaming you in any way.

As far as I am concerned, you have not set a foot wrong. It was me who chose a worthless stone when I could have a real diamond. I judged the book by its cover, a man from his clothes, his wardrobe and not his heart. I did not look before I jumped and landed in deep water.

Naimesh was like a Greek who came to me bearing gifts. I did not realise that it was a Trojan horse who came to snatch the beautiful Helen, a girl in a million, created and carved by God in his spare time? Kilan, I am just teasing you, pulling your leg. You know old habit die hard. It is difficult to teach an old dog a new trick. So beware, be warned?

My heart is already beating fast in anticipation of an affirmative reply. I feel as if I am going on my first date. It sounds silly, doesn't it? It is difficult to understand how the mind and the heart work emotionally. There is no guideline or explanation in any medical book.

Take care.
Yours ever loving
Rishma

Kilan could not remember how many times he had read this letter. He appreciated Rishma's sincerity, how well she had understood, analysed, psychoanalysed and summarised his life, his loneliness, lack of purpose, ambition and goal in his life. The letter was emotional, sincere, teasing and even funny, full of past incidents which were as fresh to Kilan as they were to Rishma. Some how, against all expectation, it made a happy, enjoyable reading for Kilan. Perhaps it reflected his views, his inner most desire to be with Rishma.

When Rishma left London, some what reluctantly, promising to be back as soon as she achieved her ambition, fulfil, turn her and her father's dream into reality, Kilan was determined to be worthy of her achievement, her status in society where doctors occupy the highest pedestal.

Kilan worked and studied hard, qualified as a Charted Account, obtained a job with an American company that was trying to penetrate the Indian market. With devotion, dedication and hard work, he soon gained the confidence of the American directors and occupied the position of Financial Controller with some thirty staffs and a budget of $50 million to handle.

Kilan wanted to prove his worth to Rishma that he was worth her trust, her love and a good catch, even for a doctor. He more than succeeded in his endeavour on the financial front. It was not easy. He had to start at the bottom, so often he had to swallow his pride, doing menial jobs well below his status. But he remembered the old saying, the Chinese words of wisdom that one who swallows his pride for a while may be a fool for a while, one who doesn't is a fool for life.

So when Rishma decided to stay in London, make London her home, Kilan was devastated. It seemed the genie was out of the bottle with a vengeance. He feared the worse and he was not wrong. The news of her marriage to Naimesh did not come as a surprise, as her letters had more or less dried up. The tone of her letters, from being a sweetheart, a life partner to a mere friend had changed long before that. Her promise to remain together "Till death do us part" sounded so hollow, empty, worthless words without sincerity.

Kilan searched his heart, thought long and hard but he could not find a single meaningful reason to reject Rishma. His love for her was as intense as ever. Her letter proved to Kilan how sweet, funny, teasing and desirable she was. Even now, after more than a decade, he often dreamt about Rishma, longed for her company, her body, remembered her as a young, beautiful girl in a pale yellow bikini, with long black hair, tall, slim body with mouth watering curves which she soften flaunted openly, some times to tease Kilan but more often to attract his attention, to get noticed, as she loved Kilan so much and wanted to be reminded by Kilan that she was the love of his life.

She felt Kilan was too shy, too much of a gentleman to make any advances, give her a cuddle and a gentle kiss that so often a girl may desire, a reassurance that would make such a difference to a girl, especially when she may be a bit down and in need of TLC, some reassurance if nothing else.

Even when prompted and encouraged by Rishma, Kilan would shyly, almost reluctantly, apologetically give her a hug and hold her tight in his vast arms but never dared to kiss her passionately on her lips, although he knew that Rishma would not object even to a passionate kiss, especially after the cinema incident that resulted in a kiss, a cuddle and Kilan's hand resting on her bosom.

At last Kilan came to a decision, by the time he had drunk a couple of bottle of lemon soda and half smoked his favourite cigar. He admitted, some what reluctantly that Rishma was the only girl for him. Without Rishma beside him, his life would be empty; his dream will always remain a dream rather than turning them into reality.

His ambition will never be fulfilled, materialized or bear fruit. Kilan vaguely remembered the words of King George II, uttered in his abdication speech that without Mrs. Simpson by his side, he will not be able to perform his duties, materialise his dreams. If King George can do it, so can Kilan! After all Kilan did not have a throne and a kingdom to lose and Rishma was certainly more beautiful, clever and charming than Mrs. Simpson!

Yes, some members of his family may not approve or appreciate his dilemma, his decision to get married to a divorcee, especially when Kilan holds such a high position and is admired, seen as a role model in his community.

Kilan could easily marry a beautiful, well educated virgin girl from a respectable, well to do family, equal to his status and his background. But Kilan knew there is no substitute for love. If Kilan had wanted such a girl, he would have got married long time ago. Why should he care what others may think? This is his life, his happiness and his decision. Sink or swim, he has to do it alone.

He remembered the poem, even the words and lines, he read a long time ago, in fact in the college magazine he used to edit. It was written by a young and a charming girl called Ashwaria, who was considered to be a college beauty. In fact she was the only girl Kilan would look at, talk to, had respect for other than Rishma.

"Who Will Share My Loneliness"
When I am alone, all alone and lonely
No one wants to share, to lessen my emptiness
When I am sick, do not feel too well
My body on fire and heart in turmoil
No one wants to nurse me back to health
When I feel let down by my nearest and dearest
No one is there to comfort me, to hold my hand
When I smile, the world smiles with me
When my heart bleeds, I have to weep alone
Who will stand by me in sickness and health
In poverty and wealth, in sorrow and laughter
The sun always shines, but only for a while
So my friend, make the hay while the sun shines
Some come into our lives and leave like a tornado
Others leave a footprint, making all the difference
All that glitter is not gold, all that's white is not milk
So choose a friend, a life partner with a care and diligent
As it will make or break your life, your dream

Make sure there is some one to weep
When you depart, when you die
When you leave me alone in this world
A hostile, uncaring and selfish world
Where there is no place for kind and caring souls.

****

Kilan was sure that Rishma will be that person, especially after her bitter experience with Naimesh. Theirs will be a union until death do them part. He had faith in his decision. At last he felt contended. He scribbled a note on his personal paper, addressed the envelop to Dr. Rishma and gave it to the peon to post it straight away, rather than waiting for the evening post to be dispatched, at the end of the day.

There was a simple message for Rishma in his letter, that he still loves her as much as ever and true to his words expressed in his last letter, the doors of his heart and his home are open to her and always will be. He may not be able to accommodate her in a penthouse, but it will neither be pavement. He would indeed be happy to welcome her back in his life. Hopefully every thing will be rosy in the garden.

So please come back, return to your roots as soon as you can. Kilan was eager to see her in a pale yellow bikini, not faded or too tight, he hoped?

After all life is too short to dwell on the past. Yesterday is history, tomorrow is mystery, only today counts, it is real. So enjoy every minute that God gives you. They have already wasted some of the best years of their lives living apart. All's well that ends well. Hopefully this was a happy ending for both, Kilan and Rishma, beginning of a wonderful journey together to the Promised Land, the land of milk and honey, joy and laughter.

****

ADHURA ARMAN
(Unfulfilled Desire)

The partition, the division, the break-up of a great nation, a subcontinent where people had a common language in Hindi and Urdu, not to mention English, loved the sports of cricket, hockey and wrestling, the pageant and the spicy food and who were as close as peas from the same pod, at least when the religion is kept out of the equation, was always going to be a tricky, risky and dangerous proposition.

But then Britain had always ruled other countries, may they be in Asia, Africa or the rest of the world, on divide and conquer policy, a theory, the technique refined, purified and turned into an art form, pretending to be friends of every one but at the same time poisoning their minds and turning them against each other. But then there was nothing unique in it, as previous conquerors, from Alexander the Great to Moguls used the same old age technique.

My enemy's enemy is my friend, acquiring allies, partners, signing treaties without the slightest intention of honouring them was the trademark of the British rule. Perhaps it was impossible to conquer a nation like Bharat with straight forward battles, fought entirely on the battlefields, in an honourable way. Perhaps the end justified the means, as Britain established the greatest empire in the human history.

India was divided on a two nation theory, Pakistan a homeland for the Indian Muslims while Bharat or whatever is left of India, once a proud and great nation, a homeland for the majority Hindus.

It was a blunder of unimaginable latitude, at least for the people of united India if not for their colonial masters residing some six thousand miles away, on an island nation of Great Britain.

Most Indian leaders with the notable exception of Mohamed Ali Jinha, the father of the newly created nation of Pakistan, carved out of the motherland Bharat, more or less knew that the break-up of Bharat, a country that has remained more or less united, albeit in a difficult, different and most unlikely manner, was a blunder, a stupid mistake that would haunt the people of the subcontinent for a long time, if not for ever, in perpetuity, in eternity.

How right these leaders of pre independent India were, as the independence day of 15th August, 1947 was preceded by the worst massacre, mass murders in the annals of human history, only surpassed by the holocaust with the loss of six million Jewish lives, which took place, was perpetrated over a period of six years, while a well over a million people were slaughtered, butchered, annihilated without mercy, in the name of religion, in less than three months.

Moreover some forty million people were displaced, forced to migrate, driven out of Sindh, Punjab and Bengal, the last two provinces were divided between the two emerging nations.

They had to leave behind every thing they ever owned, with the exception of clothes they may be wearing. Even gold from teeth was extracted without mercy if caught fleeing.

It was the fear of being slaughtered; raped and brutalised that made them flee penniless. Yet so many did not make it to the safety of Bharat, the promised land, the birth place of Lord Rama, Krishna, Buddha, Guru Nanak and of course Gandhi and Jinha who reserved their places in the annals of human history, albeit for different reasons. Gandhi became famous for his saintliness while Jinha for the partition of one of the greatest nation on earth for some ten thousand years.

Not only the people but the ancient land of sages and sanscruti was brutalized beyond imagination. Unfortunately we, the Indians (Hindus) learnt nothing from such a tragic episode. Bharat is heading for another division or even worse, the complete take over by the once minority who will become a majority in less than fifty years.

To-day it was 15th August, the independence day for India. The first Prime Minister of independent India, Pundit Jawaharlal Nehru, an idealist but a naïve politician, was delivering his annual speech from the podium, from the dizzy height of the Red Fort, built by Mogul invaders who were partly responsible for the introduction of, some may say the most intolerant religion that could not coexist with the most liberal, articulate and tolerant religion of Hinduism that has served the country, the nation of Bharat well for more than ten thousand years.

Perhaps the followers and not the religion that may be intolerant. Could it be possible that one may influence the other? How could Islam, a cultured, sophisticated, noble and realistic religion in so many ways could be different from any other religion when it comes to compassion and peaceful coexistence?

No religion preaches mass murders, ethnic cleansing, hatred on the ground of colour, creed, culture or religion. Aren't we the humans responsible for inventing religion, even God in our imagination or is it other way round? Then why countries like Pakistan, Afghanistan and many more are ethnically cleansed? One may even wonder whether we could be better off if we had only one religion or no religion at all.

Today millions of people, by far the vast majority of the Indian population, were celebrating independence, the freedom, the sovereignty gained after a long, hard and so often a bitter struggle that forced the British, who were already struggling to come to terms with their conscience after being forced, dragged into the most brutal Second World War that heaped so much misery on the people of Europe and Asia.

India was the jewel in British Crown, the central point, the pivot of the empire that turned the wheel. Losing India will surely have a domino effect. It will be the end of the greatest conquest, the most amazing and successful empire building in the human history, outstripping even the invincible Roman Empire and the conquest by the unsurpassed military genius and field commander Genghis Khan whose hoards overran most of Asia and Eastern Europe, using mostly primitive weapons and horsemanship, the riding skill.

But Britain was in no position, morally, legally or even militarily to justify the continued occupation of India, having just fought a war to liberate Europe from the clutches of Hitler and his evil theory. If European nations deserve political freedom, democracy and popular government, then why not Bharat who was, in many ways more civilized than Europe?

To make the matter worse, the British people rejected their war hero, Sir Winston Churchill who wanted to continue the occupation of not only India but to maintain and even expand the empire. Surely he was living in a cuckoo land, out of touch with the reality and out of touch with his own people.

He lead his party to a disastrous defeat in the post war election, thus paving the way for the victorious Labour politicians, in particular Sir Clement Atlee to start the process of decolonization, long overdue.

The struggle for independence was so ably, intelligently and cunningly led by a tiny, unobtrusive and in some ways inconspicuous personality who was later declared the personality of the 20th century, ahead of war heroes and fabulously famous people like Sir Winston Churchill, Dame Margaret Thatcher, George Bernard Show, Joseph Stalin, Rabindranath Tagore, the first Asian to receive the Nobel prize for Literature in 1913, who surrendered his Knighthood in 1919, as a protest over Amritsar Massacre, Mao Zedong, a Marxist theoretician who organized the Long March, a leader of war of liberation who founded the present day united China, David Ben-Gurion, the first Prime Minister of the independent state of Israel, President John F. Kennedy, Ho Chi Minh, whose rag tag of a guerrilla army defeated the might of America and many more distinguished personalities of the most troublesome century that saw two world wars, conflict in Korea, Vietnam, Malaya, Kenya and South Africa, to name but a few.

Gandhi's main weapon was peaceful non-cooperation with the British at every level, that included non payment of taxes, boycotting British goods and services, not joining Civil Service, police and even deserting universities that had British ties, British influence.

Britain was at a loss how to handle Gandhi, a mild mannered, affectionate person with a mischievous smile and who would not utter an unkind word for any one, not even the British masters whom he was fighting, so often calling them misguided and lost souls and praying for their salvation.

Gandhi could charm and influence any British politician who would sit on the round table with him and his fellow Congress politicians to talk on any subject pertaining to independence.

Gandhi was supported by a pool of vast talent, politicians of the calibre of Pundit Jawaharlal and Motilal Nehru, Sardar Vallabbhai and Vithalbhai Patel, Lala Lajpat Rai, Netaji Subashchandra Bose, Gopal Krishna Gokhle, Raj Gopalachari, Dr Zakir Hussein, Dr Ambedkar, Krishna Menon, Maulana Azad, Dr Radha Kishan and many more. This was just the tip of the iceberg. In fact the world has never seen the gathering of so many distinguished, illustrious, highly educated and patriotic people in one continent, let alone in one country. This richness, abundance of talent was beyond imagination, beyond realm of reality.

No wonder Gandhiji succeeded beyond his wildest dream, to lead his country not only to independence but to bring Britain, the greatest empire building nation to her knees. His only regret was that Muslims, led by Mohamed Ali Jinha did not trust him as much as the rest of the nation. Even British politicians were awed by his charm offensive.

Gandhi was only ever manhandled by local police, recruited from local Indians and commanded by tin pot British officer who would not get even a manual job back in Britain. But in colonies, they believed they were the supreme race.

Gandhi indeed changed the perception of struggle for independence, from armed struggle to civil disobedience and African leaders like Malimu Julius Nyerere of Tanzania and Dr. Kaunda of Zambia and even Nelson Mandela, the father of the nation of South Africa and the most revered leading personality ever to emerge from Africa salutes Gandhi, his mentor and his idol. He proudly declares that seeds of Ahimsa, the non-violence were planted in Gandhi in South Africa where he went as a young barrister and started his zumbesh against apartheid before moving to his native Gujarat to start his andolan, struggle against British rule.

Yet Gandhi was never awarded Noble Peace Prize, not even posthumously. Yet minor peace activists from Northern Ireland, whose contribution was, at best a drop in the ocean, not known even in their own countries and many such non entities were readily awarded such prizes, thus devaluing the Noble name. In any case most Asian countries regard it as too European orientated and in the olden days, it smacked of racism.

Some of the people who were awarded Noble Peace Prizes were indeed cream of humanity, jewels of mankind, noble souls who grace the earth in recent decades and that include Martin Luther King, Nelson Mandela and Mother Teresa but Gandhi was in a class of his own, the noblest person since Lord Jesus Christ, the saver of mankind walked the earth.

The colonial power was at a loss how to handle Gandhi. He spent a long time in jail, along with other leaders. But prison doors were never locked except to keep the press out. For once, Gandhi would not break the law. He would readily serve the sentence without any protest, imposed by the court, however unjust it may be.

On this auspicious, happy and joyful day, the most important day in the lives of many, hearts were overflowing with happiness. The skies were raining rainbow colours from fireworks let lose from the Fort. The streets of the capital Delhi were overflowing with humanity, to watch one of the best displays of pageantry, the floats, tribal and traditional dances, along with military hardware that would deter the neighbour from encroaching on Bharat's sovereignty, at least in theory but it would never work when it comes to a crunch.

Could it be fate that on this auspicious but fateful day for **Kitan,** he received a letter, painful, unexpected and unbelievable letter he was expecting for the last five years? But it was more in hope, anticipation than reality.

The letter was from his long lost wife **Millie**, an appropriate name which means to find, to discover and for Kitan she was the find of the century. Millie was young, just twenty two years old, beautiful in Sindhi tradition, with long hair and hazel eyes, charming, caring human being who ever graced the earth!

Reading her letter brought back the bitter, sweet but most painful and tragic memories flooding back that no human being has to endure, especially inflected by his own countrymen, his own brothers, sisters, friends and neighbours.

Kitan was the son of a well to do businessman, plying his import export trade in the Eastern Indian city of Karachi. Kitan lost his father he was twenty three, just out of the Uni where he was a brilliant academian, an Ivory Tower full of brilliant ideas, business concepts. But he had a cool, calculating head over his young shoulders for his age.

Besides, he had Millie by his side, a girl of rare talent, immense faith, mesmerising charm and tremendous self belief. Together they weathered the storm of the loss of Sheth (businessman) Ramlal and guided the family out of depression, darkness, doom and gloom to the normality of a joint Hindu family tradition, without letting the business go to wall, as it often happens when the head of the family, the pillar of the financial establishment is suddenly taken away, without warning, without time to adjust, adopt or comes to term with the loss.

But these were troubled times, uncertain period with the break-up of the country imminent. But no one knew which part of Bharat will secede, become Pakistan with the exception of the most obvious provinces of North West Frontier, Baluchistan and East Bengal which were already Muslim dominated areas with Hindus and Sikhs a minority.

Most Indians, especially the Hindus were hoping against all hopes that sanity would prevail, that Jinha would fail in his desire, in his evil intention to divide the motherland, especially when Gandhi offered him the post of Wazir A Alam, the honour to be the first Prime Minister of independent India.

But it came to no avail, as Jinha was hell bent to plunge the knife in the heart of mother Bharat. Perhaps he was doing his duty, giving his followers the motherland they wanted, wished and desired for some time.

Perhaps he was right in his assessment to claim that there would never be peace and harmony, Hindus and Muslims would never be able to live side by side in peace. Perhaps he would have read too much in history when Mogul kings, invaders brutalised Bharat and various Hindu rulers were constantly at war with each other and the Moguls.

But the people who suffered most were docile Hindus, as they were divided, selfish and lacked any pride in their culture, religion and tradition, until the British united India under one Raj. They imposed by force and diplomacy some sort of peace, harmony and sanity on the warring population.

Mohamed Ali Jinha feared that the removal of British influence, British rule and the army may lead to the old bad days of constant conflict between two dominating factions but this time the minority Muslims may come off worse!

The passage of time has proved how wrong both Gandhi and Jinha were? Jinha's beloved Pakistan has not only split up, Bangladesh having seceded but Baluchistan tried to do so at various times, only to be suppressed brutally by the army.

Gandhi's assumption that Hindus and Muslims will live in peace and harmony once British left proved to be a mirage, a fool's gold. India is in a limbo politically with minority enjoying more rites and privileges than the majority Hindus, so often reduced to second class citizens in their own motherland. No wonder Gandhi is not seen as a hero, a liberator by a significant number of Hindu populations in the present day India.

In fact Jinha was a great visionary with big dreams but passage of time has also proved how wrong Jinha was. His dream of turning Pakistan into a secular, modern, democratic, progressive and prosperous nation, a jewel amongst the Islamic nations where every one can live happily side by side could not be further from the truth, with economic stagnation and constant military rule while Indian economy under world's largest democracy is flourishing, attracting worldwide attention, investment and jobs galore. It seems no one, not even God can see the future, predict the outcome.

While Kitan and Millie were struggling to establish some sort of normality, to heal, to mend, to overcome the emotional wounds, the hell broke lose. When the map of the new nation was unveiled, terms of the partition were announced making Karachi the designated capital of Pakistan, the flight started in earnest. No one would pay even a thousand rupee for a property worth a million, knowing well that Hindus will have to leave, leaving behind their properties that they could have for free.

People with foresight and especially those who had no assets, no family ties, no sentimental attachment with the land, nothing to lose were the fortunate ones. They were quick to leave and reach the safety of Bharat before the mayhem started.

While well off, influential and businessmen were caught in two minds, hesitated and caught napping. It is human nature to hope for the best, even under the most difficult circumstances.

No wonder Kitan and his family members were caught napping, in the dilemma of staying or leaving a life of comfort and become penniless refugees in a distant land where they had never set a foot.

When looting, burning, raping and killing started in earnest, the decision of staying or leaving was already taken out of their hands. Indeed it was already too late, as when they left, looked back at their palace like home, above the business premises, it was already being looted, plundered and set on fire.

What broke Ketan's heart, the last straw that broke camel's back was watching their neighbours and long standing friends turning into foes, participating in this carnage with joy and glee.

It seemed humans had turned into wild animals overnight, brutality and barbarism ruled, hearts were filled with hate, anger and vulgarity beyond comprehension. Grand mothers were raped and murdered by children barely in their teens.

Ketan's fifty year old neighbour and grandfather even offered to marry Ketan's beautiful baby sister, just out of her teens, to save her life and to help them on their way, the price they were not prepared to pay to a neighbour and a friend of long standing.

In just one week, Kitan lost every thing. He saw his mother and fourteen year old sister brutally raped before being murdered, in front of their eyes. Yet they were powerless to help, to do anything, even though they were just a sprinting distance from the safety of the new border, the line that divided Punjab, putting Guru Nanak's birth place in Pakistan.

Many Muslims suffered the same fate in the Hindu dominated areas of Punjab. But Gandhi's insistence that Muslims in India should be left alone, treated like brothers and sisters, threatening to fast unto death, saved many Muslim lives. But it cost Gandhi his life at the hands of a fanatic Hindu who had lost every thing in the partition and blamed Gandhi for his loss, his sufferings. Some even sympathised with Nathuram Godsay who murdered Gandhiji in a cool, calm manner.

In the confusion, Kitan was separated from his wife Millie. In his desire to find her, to save her, he ventured into lion's den, trying to reason with the deranged mob that was mad with hate, power and revenge and on drugs.

Mercifully Kitan was beaten senseless and left for dead that saved his life. But was this a blessing in disguise or a curse, life long suffering, a painful life sentence which could be a million times worse than death?

Kitan was found unconscious but alive by a group of Sikh volunteers who were rescuing Hindus and Sikhs who were trapped on the Pakistani side of the border, leading armed volunteers, crossing the border and rescuing as many people as they could find.

When Kitan regained consciousness, he was in a border camp manned by RSS and many Sikh volunteers. He was nurtured back to health and with the passage of time his physical wounds mended but not his soul, his mental anguish. It was scarred for life. Kitan was devastated at the loss of his mother and every member of his family; especially his wife and life partner Millie.

Kitan was hoping against all hopes that Millie will turn up well and alive, living in one of the refugee camps that were scattered on the Indian side of the Punjab border.

But after visiting every refugee camp, listening to heart breaking stories, similar to his own, Kitan had to admit that his beloved Millie, his childhood sweetheart did not make it, cross the border, entered the safety of Bharat. Kitan did not give up hope, believing that she may be held prisoner some where in Pakistan. But deep inside his heart, he knew that they will not be reunited, at least not on this earth. But he was reluctant to give up hope, the only reason that kept him going.

Kitan carefully opened Millie's letter and began to read for the umpteenth time.

"Dear Kitan

After a long and painful soul searching, I have gathered some courage to write this letter, my final farewell note to you, my soul mate, my darling, my sole reason for living. Alias, we had a very short life together but I would not exchange those beautiful days for an entire life of luxury without you.

I am not even sure whether you will ever receive this letter, as I am leaving it with the camp authority. I do not know your address but I do know that you have made it; you are alive and perhaps well, physically if not mentally, as those terrible wounds, scars of watching your mother and baby sister so brutally murdered in front of our eyes, will always stay with us, in our subconscious mind as long as we live.

But I believe the person to whom I am handing this letter, will keep his words, as I know most people here have gone through similar experiences as mine, as ours. They do understand my pain, my misfortune and my desire to contact you, for the first and last time since the partition.

As you know, we got separated right at the end, when the safety of Bharat was just a stone throw away, within our grab. But it was not to be. The luck and even the God deserted us. You were beaten senseless and left for dead while I was abducted.

I was more precious alive than dead. I was a valuable human cargo, a slave that would fetch a good price on the sex market. The marauding gang of thugs and cut throats sold me to a brothel owner in Lahore, not very far from the border.

There were twenty of us, all young and beautiful girls, snatched, separated from their families while fleeing, captured by these gangs and forced to work as prostitute.

The beauty that captivated you, made you fall in love, marry me and put me on a high pedestal turned out to be a curse, my biggest downfall. My long, silky hair, hazel eyes, fair skin we Sindhi girls are blessed with and the full figure captivated the clients, the punters, the sex starved men who could not get enough of us, even the army personals who were away from their families visited us regularly.

Some of them visited us several times a week and we were forced to surrender our bodies to the highest bidders. It was a non stop sex, seven nights a week. It was more than hell. The words can not describe my pain, my humiliation, my shame. It was a death of thousand cuts, repeated every night, a living hell.

I cursed my bad luck. Why did I survive when all around us, all our female family members were dead, brutally murdered. Yet they were the lucky ones. Their pain, their shame and humiliation lasted for few hours only while mine went on night after night until my body could take it no more.

I only came to know that you are alive and safe when I accidentally saw your advert in an old newspaper. That gave me some hope that if I could ever escape this hell, I will have some reason to live, a tiny but bright spot on the horizon. The dark cloud over me could yet have a silver lining after all, perhaps a tiny happy ending!

I knew that I will have to escape soon. Otherwise I will be broken, physically, mentally and emotionally and too ashamed to face you, to have the courage to stand in front of you and say, here I am, your loving, caring wife Millie.

But it was not to be. When we are down on luck, even the God does not want to know us. We were watched like a hawk, always in a secured place, behind closed doors with only one way out. I was at the brothel for three years but I aged some thirty years during that period.

My long, soft, silky, dark brown hair was turning grey, at the age of twenty five. My once full and shapely figure was akin to an old lady. My once shapely breasts were sagging as if I have raised, breast fed a dozen children.

My face was dry and wrinkled and body all puffed up, due to drugs we were forced to take to enable us to work all night, every night. I never thought sex could be so unpleasant, such a torture, a living hell.

So often we were forced to have kinky, unnatural sex, a five and a half feet tall girl, weighing no more than eight stone brutalized by huge men, weighing twice our weight. If we do not cooperate, then the demand, the kinkiness got even worse. Punters had no shame. We were the target of what they always wanted to try, have sex in any and every way but could not dare to ask their wives, they performed such acts, experimented on us. Even your imagination would not match the reality.

Our pain, pleas and tears had no effect on them. I tried to commit suicide many times but even God conspired against us. It seems those who are down and out of luck are abandoned by all, including the God that is if there is a God for us to plead to.

My small relief came when I became pregnant. But that lasted no more than two months in total. Within two weeks of the birth of my little girl, I was forced back to work.

I realized afterwards that so often we were allowed to become pregnant deliberately, as some punters preferred what they called Milk Maid. We learnt in history that in ancient Egypt, the Pharaohs raised their male children, the princes on breast milk until they were practically in their teens, as no one can poison breast milk when drunk straight from the breast. So often these princes, who were practically adults, were having sex and being fed at the same time?

But I never knew that a six feet tall man in his prime would have similar taste, come back night after night to suck us dry. This obscene brutality completely ruined my health within a year but made a fortune for my owner.

When I was no longer attractive, could not draw the punters, I was sold to a client who was a regular and had seen me at my best. He was one of the first one to have me, seen me when I was really beautiful and sexy in true sense. He was old enough to be my father. But he treated me gently.

In a way, he was kind, considerate and gentle, that is if any one visiting such a place can be called a gentleman? He so often booked me for the whole night, even a week and that gave me relief, time to recuperate and relax, as I had to deal with one client only. Every one called him Chacha or the uncle.

In a way the time I spent with the uncle were tolerable times. In a strange way I may have even fallen in love with him. So when he bought me, I thought it would be the end of my nightmare, the end of my hell. In a way it was, at least for a short time.

He had a wife and an ailing mother who needed constant care and attention. So I was bought as a personal carer for his mother, to look after her, bathe clean and feed her and give her medication on time. Moreover he was willing to shelter not only me but my little girl as well whom we called Masuma, the innocent one.

In any case my body was too brutalized, sagging and lose to attract any one physically. It was a blessing in disguise.

After a year or so Chacha realized that I was too ill to be of any help to any one, that I was suffering from various sexually transmitted diseases. It was also the onset of tuberculoses, the most dreaded disease that easily spreads to others living in close proximity, in the same house.

T.B. was, on most part incurable and the treatment would cost an arm and a leg. Only super rich can afford the treatment, the drugs, the rich food and the dry climate needed to get better.

There was no way Chacha could keep me in the house, risking the health of every one. The best Chacha could do, the only way he could help us was to take me to the border which was just on the horizon and let me cross into India where I could take shelter in a refugee camp. He did this as much for me as for my lovely girl Masuma. He knew that he could be the father of this lovely little girl, an angel and it broke his heart to let us go, especially little Masuma whom he loved so much and treated her like his own, with love and kindness. But he was helpless and had to put his family first.

This is how I ended up in the Sahara (shelter) Refugee Camp, where my daughter was taken into care, as I was in no condition to look after her.

At last I am free but does it mean any thing except that now I am free to end my miserable life, unbelievable sufferings beyond imagination, some thing I wanted to do the day we were separated, the day I was sold into prostitution, the day I ceased to exist as a human being, became a chattel to be bought and sold at the whip of the owner.

In any case I am given just six months to live. So why not to bring this hell this sufferings to an early end? I have enough morphine to go to sleep and never wake up. This is not suicide. It is an escape, reunion with Mother Nature.

My one and only request to you, my darling, my God, my reason for taking birth on this earth, is that if you ever loved me, want to remember me, want to see my living image, then please visit Sheth Mafatlal Ashram where Masuma is living, registered under the name of Meera Kitan Irani.

You may not be her father but I am certainly her mother. She is and always be a living image of me. I will be watching her, keeping an eye on her from above there, on my little angel.

She is the only ray of light to come out of this hell. It would give me a great pleasure, release me from the burden of failing Masuma if she is adopted, brought up as a normal child in a respectable family environment that every child need and deserve.

She is an innocent victim of human inhumanity created by religion, politicians and the greed. It is now time for me to go, to say my final farewell, to leave this world, to meet your mum, your baby sister and my parents. Goodbye, Alvida, sayonara until we meet in heaven!

Yours most unfortunate **Millie.**

This was the first time Kitan was able to read the letter in full. Several times, he tried but broke down half way through. Now he realized that he was the lucky one, even his mother and sister who were brutally raped and murdered were more fortunate than his wife Millie. Words could not describe her pain, her anguish and her humiliation, the hell she was in for such a long time.

In a way Kitan was relieved that her Millie, his childhood sweetheart was dead, in heaven, with all his and her family members, that is if there is God, heaven or hell up there! He had lost his faith, his belief a long time ago and reading Millie's letter made him realize how right he is.

These were the times when even the most devoted were tested to the limit, their faith, their belief put on ice, if not thrown down the gutter with the bath water.

But Millie's letter gave Kitan one purpose in his empty, shattered, and purposeless life. He was determined to find Meera and brought her up as his own daughter, to fulfil the last wish, the dying request of his beloved Millie, whom he could not protect, cherish, pamper in real life.

Meera will give him a purpose, aim in life, a ray of sunshine, a light at the end of the tunnel. He would not rest until he has find Meera and brought her home where she belonged.

****

Epilogue: Today was a happy day for Kitan. At last he saw a ray of hope at the end of a dark, long and depressing tunnel. He brought home Meera, his little Millie, after a six months struggle with the arrogant Camp Officials who demanded all sorts of certificates? But his persistence prevailed and Meera was handed over to him.

Moreover he met some of his old friends and business acquaintances while searching for Meera who had moved to Bombay, formed an association, a kind of cooperative society to help each other. They promised to set up Kitan in business and he was just packing his bags to move to Bombay. It seems at last his life was moving in the right direction, towards a distant cloud with a silver lining. Perhaps with the passage of time, the wounds would heal and he may be able to re-establish his business, as Sindhis are united community with shrewd business acumen, ever ready to help each other.

****